hugo & rose

hugo & rose

BRIDGET FOLEY

st. martin's press ✖ new york

HUGO & ROSE. Copyright © 2015 by Bridget Foley. All rights reserved. Printed in the United States of America. For information, address St. Martin's Press, 175 Fifth Avenue, New York, N.Y. 10010.

www.stmartins.com

Grateful acknowledgment is made for permission to reproduce from the following:

"Downtown." Words and music by Tony Hatch. Copyright © 1964, 1965 Welbeck Music Ltd. Copyright renewed. All rights in the United States and Canada controlled and administered by Songs of Universal, Inc. All rights reserved. Used by permission. Reprinted by permission of Hal Leonard Corporation.

"You Belong to Me." Words and music by Pee Wee King, Redd Stewart, and Chilton Price. Copyright © 1952 (renewed) Ridgeway Music Company, Inc. All rights reserved. Used by permission. Reprinted by permission of Hal Leonard Corporation.

Designed by Anna Gorovoy

The Library of Congress Cataloging-in-Publication Data is available upon request.

ISBN 978-1-250-05579-8 (hardcover)
ISBN 978-1-4668-5954-8 (e-book)

St. Martin's Press books may be purchased for educational, business, or promotional use. For information on bulk purchases, please contact the Macmillan Corporate and Premium Sales Department at 1-800-221-7945, extension 5442, or write to specialmarkets@macmillan.com.

First Edition: May 2015

10 9 8 7 6 5 4 3 2 1

For my Giddy girl

one

Were you to ask her boys, they would tell you that for Rose, there had always been Hugo.

This was not strictly true. He had come to her first when she was six. Before that was a desert stretch of forgotten dreams and nightmares, populated with the common anxieties of childhood: monsters made of discarded laundry; princes and dresses and tiny pink ponies; mean, dirty neighbor children.

Before Hugo came, Rose dreamed like any other girl child, small damp fists curled, heart-shaped face placid, the calm rise and fall of small lungs under a tangle of blankets.

Of course, she looked the same while she slept after he came to her . . . but her dreams were very different.

Rose could recall only one of the dreams that came before

Hugo: a nightmare. Lost in a department store, she'd searched for her mother inside an enormous rack of clothes. As she'd pressed her face farther and farther into the slick polyesters, the clothes began to smother her, closing in until she couldn't move. Terror and loss overwhelmed her and she woke racked with sobs.

Sobs that brought (*oh my sweet, oh my darling*) her mother. Reunited and reassured, little Rose was able to return to sleep.

Rose thought she must have been about four when she'd had this dream. She remembered faint images of the nightmare, but these were slippery and unsure. She wasn't certain if she was truly remembering the dream or if she was picturing the story she must have recounted to her mother that night in the darkness.

This was unlike her adventures with Hugo in every way. These she could recount as easily as she could list the things she had accomplished since breakfast.

Rose knew this was out of the ordinary.

In college, when their excitement for each other was still new and "above the clothes," and Josh's nightly stubble was still exfoliating patches of cherry on Rose's face, the man who would be her husband told her about a particularly raunchy dream she'd featured in.

"I've never had a sex dream," said Rose.

"I don't think that's possible," said Josh, his hand tracing the denim seams on her leg.

But it was, and that early, early morning was the first time Rose told anyone about the boy in her dreams.

Stretched close to Josh on his twin bed, their heads on a single pillow, atop a twist of sheets in sore need of a wash, Rose began to describe the world she'd inhabited since she was a little girl. A place she'd gone to every night that was more familiar to her than her parents' home.

She described an island ringed by a beach of pink sand.

"Not Bermuda pink, more like flamingo pink. *Pink* pink."

"Like Pepto?"

"Do you want to hear this or not?"

Josh laughed, filled with the smell of her. Her breath warm on his face. "Of course I do."

The sky there was almost always covered in clouds, but when the sun broke through, shafts of light would strike the beach, changing the sand. The grains would begin to sparkle.

"When they do that, if you hit them right . . . Run at them just right, they throw you into the air."

"Like flying?"

"More like bouncing, really, really high. It's fun."

"Hmm."

"This feels weird."

Rose sat up. She was still dressed, miracle of miracles, but somehow she felt that Josh had hidden her clothes. Tucked them into a dark corner of his dorm room.

She shouldn't have said anything. Shouldn't have betrayed her secret. Or Hugo.

"I'm sorry. . . ."

Rose was quiet in the dark. She stared down at the silhouette of his cheek on the pillow and fought the panic that she'd blown it.

Shit, she'd blown it.

But after a moment Rose felt his wide, warm palm come to rest on the small of her neck. Its gentle gravity *inviting* her toward his chest . . . but not insisting that she go there.

"Please. I want to hear . . . I want to know everything about you."

Rose decided then that maybe she didn't need to tell him all of it . . . maybe she could just stop at the beach.

But somehow that night, after she succumbed to the pull of Josh's body, she told him everything. Unveiled the secrets of her dreams, of the life she had lived with Hugo. In the dark, Rose painted a landscape of her hidden childhood: the warm waters of the Green Lagoon, the fields of saw grass tall as corn, the Blanket Pavilion and its hundred rooms fluttering in the breeze. The Bucks. Blindhead. The Natters. Spider Chasm. The Plank Orb. Castle City.

And Hugo.

Beautiful. Brave. Heroic Hugo.

Josh listened to Rose carefully . . . more carefully than he had listened to any lecture, any seminar. He *wanted* her to quiz him: for her to know how well he attended to her dreams. Because he already knew he loved her . . . though he wouldn't tell her for months yet.

This night was, in its way, more intimate than the night they first made love, three months later. Or the night of their wedding.

On the night Isaac was born, after the doctors and nurses had cleared away, leaving Josh and Rose alone to admire this new tiny being they had made—only then did they experience the same unfolding, the naked shift into the new, that they had the night that Rose told Josh about Hugo.

After Isaac came Adam, born the first year of Josh's residency. There was then a short duration of years, hemming, hawing, and negotiations, before the arrival of Penelope made their family complete. While Josh was busy with the work of becoming a surgeon, Rose settled into the business of motherhood. Diapers and cracker crumbs littered Rose's waking life in those early years.

When Josh found a placement in the dry reaches of Colorado—a nice-sized hospital, he said, enough population to give him a steady stream of bodies to practice upon—Rose moved house with an efficiency of lists. School districts were researched. A mortgage was calculated. Without too much drama they found a nice home in a nice neighborhood in a nice suburb.

Rose had pictures hanging before they went to sleep that first night.

"It feels more like home that way," she said, curling into the crooked "S" of Josh's body.

Rose and Josh quietly slipped into the pause between youth and middle age—the moment when all the questions that plague the young have been answered: "Who will I marry? What will my children be like? How many will I have? What will I be when I grow up?" They reached an age when one realizes that all these questions have been answered and now the only thing is to watch one's life unfurl. There were still questions, of course, but these questions were by their nature less exciting than the ones that came before: "Will we get sick before they grow up? Will we be able to afford to keep the house? What if that *terrible something* happens? That nameless *something* that waits for those unlucky masses?"

Rose, for example, was saddened by the fact that someday, inevitably, either she or Josh would have to experience the death of the other. She hoped she would go first—though it seemed unfair to wish the pain of loss on Joshua.

It was, however, the unavoidable cost of having someone so dear that the idea of living after they're gone seems impossible.

And so Rose and Josh watched their life unfurl. The boys grew from sweet, sticky toddlers into wild-legged children, their shouts and protests the music of the house. Penny toddled after, happy to simply be acknowledged.

Josh put in the early work of a career surgeon. His hours were long and odd, leaving and returning while the house was still abed. The lessons he now learned were more terminal, in the meat of the human body.

This left Rose alone with the routine of motherhood. Children up. Bodies dressed. Breakfast made. Book bags packed. Every day a list to be checked off.

She was a good mother. Loved by her boys, who also knew enough to fear a certain pitch her voice could take when they played too rough.

Perhaps because it didn't seem to matter otherwise, or perhaps because this is just the way of things, Rose settled into the sweatpants years. The close attention she paid to the dressing and care of three little bodies left little room for her to attend to the dressing and care of her own. Her body bloomed, thighs no longer the straight, taut lines Josh had traced that night so long ago. More often than she would have liked to admit, the shirt she went to sleep in was the one in which she had woken up: though since Josh was rarely around, there was no one to witness Rose's resignation to piggishness.

She could not remember precisely when she began telling the boys about Hugo.

The beaches of her dreams were populated with tiny white crabs, their shells and legs constructed of the delicate tines of feathers. When they were young, she and Hugo would place these creatures on each other's necks, to see which of them could tolerate their ticklish skittering the longest.

"Tickle Crab" was a favorite bath-time game for the boys when they were very small. Rose would lean over the edge of the tub, her belly soft and round with Penny, snatching at their slick, brown bodies. The "Tickle Crab" would grind them into giggling submission, until she would relent, pulling away.

Adam would kiss his tiny wrinkled fingertips against each other.

The sign for *"more, again."* And then a gentle swipe across his chest, *"please."*

Of course, little boy, littler boy.

As they grew, the boys learned to ask Rose about her dreams. The simple, straightforward adventure of their mother's nightly visits with Hugo appealed to their testosterone-fueled little-boy fantasies. Isaac and Adam would reenact Hugo and Rose's never-ending quest to find a way into the glowing spires of Castle City. They would beg her to pull the chairs and unfold the sheets to make a "Pavilion" for them. They recruited Josh—when he was around—to play the part of a giant Spider (*Bigger, meaner, Daddy!*), whom they would kill and then resurrect, but only so they could kill him again.

It was through the boys that Hugo came to occupy Rose's household and not just her dreams. They argued over who would get to be him, never implicitly stating that whoever was *not* him was by default their mother and therefore a *girl*. Hugo was Han Solo and Anakin Skywalker and Batman all rolled into one—a personal superhero they didn't have to share with anyone but each other.

They plotted maps of the island, drew pictures of the places in Rose's dreams. They quizzed her and appealed to her authority to settle debates.

"Is the Plank Orb like a submarine?"

"Yes, but it's much smaller and made of wood."

"Why is it so small?"

"Well, it only ever has to hold the two of us."

"Why is it called the Plank Orb?"

"I don't know . . . that's just what we call it."

Even the loneliness of Hugo's island, which, but for the mystery of Castle City, was populated only by Hugo and their mother, played into their innate desires for self-reliance.

The boys also sensed, in their young way, the distance between their mother and Hugo's companion. Though ostensibly they were the same person, they couldn't quite reconcile the sharp taskmaster who cut their hot dogs lengthwise before placing them in the bun with the heroine in their mother's tales.

As she had grown older, and rounder, Rose, too, had recognized the divergence between her waking and sleeping selves. The mirror would daily force her to recognize that her current state—the stripes of stretch marks, pulled sad nipples, creases of crow's-feet and brows—was as good as it was going to get. Yet on the island, she was still as beautiful as she had ever been, probably more so.

On the island she was Rose the Spider Slayer. Rose the Fearless, who danced from treetop to treetop and rode the backs of charging Bucks. She was the trickster who led Blindhead into knots around the trunks of trees. The mouse-quiet thief of the Natters nest.

But in her home or in her car, she was simply Rose.

Saggy Rose in the pajamas with the fraying cuffs. Rose at the stoplight, breathing the stale, dust-speckled air of her minivan. Rose in the butcher section of the grocery store, comparing the price of pork chops and London broil. Rose at the bus stop, among the other mothers, acrid coffee cooling in her mug, watching her boys push their way to their seats.

Rose knew she was no one special.

That is, unless she was to recognize in herself that certain specialness, of which it has become the fashion to recognize about everyone. The modern impulse to hand out trophies to every player in the game, regardless of their score. In that way, Rose supposed she was special, which is to say that all people are special and therefore none of them are.

The truth is that Rose knew she was special to only a few people: the small ones she cared for, the old ones who had raised her, and the tall one who slept next to her in her bed.

To everyone else she was just another someone.

And if in her dreams she was a *somebody* . . . well, that was just the way of things.

Of what consequence are the dreams of housewives? she would think whenever she caught herself daydreaming of Hugo and the island. The odd phrase would interject itself, with its strange archaic cadence. *Of what consequence* . . . Like a canker sore in the mouth of her mind, her brain would tongue at it, sending a shock of pain into her fantasy life. *Of what consequence* . . . A mental tic. A strange old song stuck in her head.

What did any of it matter?

In traffic, Rose would find herself studying the slack faces of other drivers at stoplights: trios of landscapers in the cabs of trucks; blown-out blondes in face-swallowing sunglasses, with their sullen teenagers texting shotgun; aging men in expensive cars; pretty girls without the armor of their smiles; bumper-riding boys, fists full of energy drinks.

To Rose, they were dreamers all.

She imagined them following their paths through their own days, leading them to their own beds. Each of them surrendering consciousness.

A nation of unconscious protagonists.

Rose supposed that there was spread among these ordinary people the ordinary proportion of cowardice and bravery. They all had their own share of the small victories and defeats of ordinary lives.

But when they dreamed? Rose wondered. Were they masters of the universe or garden slugs? Victims, heroes, or villains in the absentminded movies of their own minds?

Rose would shrug off the thought. What did it matter? The victories and disappointments of ordinary people's dreams would have slipped into the haze before they poured their first cup of coffee.

Of what consequence . . .

But since Rose's dreams did not disappear upon waking, since her adventures with Hugo had something of the substance of genuine memories, she did struggle with the question as to which Rose was the "true" Rose.

Oh, she knew reality from fantasy.

But when she found herself bullied by a persistent PTA mommy, or frustrated with the boys' constant need for a referee, or fed up with Penny's nighttime wakings . . . it was easier to believe that the brave, strong, calm Rose of the island was her true self.

And that this woman leading this drab, disappointing life was . . . something else. Not *not* her, exactly. But not *really* her.

And what exactly do I have to be disappointed with? Rose would ask herself as she loaded dishes or folded laundry. She had three beautiful, healthy, intelligent children. She had the love and devotion of a man who was not only well employed and attractive, but looked as though he were going to go to his grave with a full head of hair. She got to be home with her children while they were still young enough to want her. She had a nice home filled with nice things. She was healthy, still young.

Well, if not young, then youngish.

This was the life she had said she wanted.

So what if Josh wasn't home enough? Or if Penny was taking forever to potty train? Or if Isaac's teacher said he wasn't paying attention in school? She knew these things wouldn't last forever. Penny would be able to wipe herself by the time she went to college. Isaac would (*God willing*) get a teacher next year who didn't bore him to tears. And Josh would someday be able to make someone lower on the totem pole take the worst shifts at the hospital.

Rose tried to imagine different lives, ones in which she didn't marry Josh or have the children. Career paths. Lifestyle choices. These alternative lives seemed wrong. Empty. Sad.

She knew she had made the right choice. Chosen the best life possible.

And yet her disappointment did not abate.

two

For her sixth birthday, Rose received a bicycle. A late-spring snowstorm had forced her party inside, and so the bicycle, which was meant to be presented to her under the mild May sun, was instead placed with a bow on the cement-floored confines of the family garage.

It was a beautiful thing. A light brown frame with a dance of pale pink daisies across its crossbar and pale cream banana seat. Pink and white streamers trailed from its plastic grips. An after-market basket had been attached to its handlebars, daisies on this as well, naturally.

"For your Barbies," said Rose's mother.

It was she who had spent the early morning crouched in the garage in her robe, weaving streamers through the bicycle's spokes.

Rose's father had picked up the bicycle with a box of training wheels the evening before. These extra wheels had not yet been affixed to the bike, as had been the plan. This was due to the fact that Rose's mother had spent the prior evening spinning her own wheels about the changes to little Rosie's party required by the next day's forecast—which led to Rose's father spending the evening reassuring her that it would all be fine.

Rose stood shivering in her cotton party dress in the garage. "Thanks, Mommy. Thanks, Daddy."

The weather remained chill that year all the way through the middle of June. At Field Day, in the last week of school, Rose's classmates all clutched at their sweatshirts and pulled their ankle socks against the cold wind before running races against one another. School might have been ending, but it didn't feel like summer yet.

The bicycle was moved to the side to make way for Rose's father's car. The training wheels remained in their box, set out of the way on a high shelf in the pantry by Rose's mother.

The bicycle wasn't forgotten, but just as one doesn't think about sleds and snow shovels at the beach, nothing about the season sparked feelings of "bicycle-ness."

And six-year-old Rose . . . though very pleased with the bicycle when she had seen it, had not thought about it again since she had returned from the cold garage to the warm, squealing girls of her party. She had gotten plenty of lovely, indoor toys that day: toys she already *knew* how to play with.

In fact, the only person who thought of Rosie's bicycle at all was her father, for whom its location in the garage was creating an obstacle to exiting his vehicle. As he would contort his body around it, squeezing past the driver's-side door, he would think about how much the bike had cost him and how his wife had insisted that Rosie must have it.

But, kids, he'd say to himself with a sigh. *What are you going to do?* And head inside.

Summer arrived overnight two weeks after school had ended. The coldish spring was burned away by a hot July sun, arrived early, too impatient to wait for the end of June. All around the neighborhood, mothers dragged sprinklers onto their front lawns, told the kids to entertain themselves, and returned to the cooler dim of their homes.

Rosie spent her days shuttling between her neighbors' houses. Jennifer had the best dollhouse. Brittney's mom bought name-brand Popsicles. Kara's parents let her watch MTV.

For these trips Rose used her own two feet, shod in a pair of aqua jelly sandals. And though the shoes left her with delicate, oddly placed blisters, she still never thought about the bicycle she had been given for her birthday or that she could travel much more comfortably upon it. She didn't know how to use it, and no one had yet undertaken to teach her.

Besides, the jellies made her feel like a princess.

It wasn't until a hot Saturday after the Fourth of July that Rose's father finally hauled the bicycle out of the garage. He had spent the morning weeding and drinking beer. Rose, who had at first insisted upon her fitness to help him with the task (the weeding, not the drinking), had quickly given up and instead lolled on the grass, complaining of boredom.

"Go find your mother," suggested her father, who thought that if he was to be made to work on his day off, at the very least he could be spared the whining.

"She's not here," whined Rose.

"Where is she?"

"I don't know."

Rose's mother was in fact out doing chores, something she'd informed both Rose and her father of before leaving. But both had not thought the information worth remembering, and so it was to both of them as if Rose's mother had disappeared from their living room without so much as a by-your-leave.

"Well," he said, turning from the flower bed, "whatcha want to do?"

"I dunno."

"TV?"

"Nothing's on."

"Go see Jenny?"

"On vacation."

Rose's father studied his daughter. Suddenly, his mind was full of the bicycle he'd had to move out of the way to get to the gardening tools that morning. He took a swig of beer.

"Come on, let's go."

Rose was not so sure about this.

She straddled the crossbar and looked up at her dad. Unable to find the box of training wheels after ten minutes of searching, he had decided that Rose didn't really need them anyway.

"Why bother putting them on when you're just going to ask me to take them off in a week?"

He had tried to cajole Rose into mounting the bike without them. And when that didn't work he had bullied her. Insisted he thought she was a "big girl." Maybe he was wrong.

Rose knew when she was being accused of being a baby. She had socked Pete Koernig last week when he had suggested that she still wet the bed.

Rose had gotten onto the bike. But now, perched on the edge

of the seat, her toes skimming the ground, she thought maybe she *was* a bit of a baby. Maybe it was *better* to be a baby. Safer.

"We'll take it slow, okay, honey? You just keep your feet moving."

Rose's father gripped the back of her seat and her handlebar. With a sharp inhale, Rosie pulled her feet up, located the pedals, and pushed.

Pushed.

Pushed.

They were moving. Rose laughed. So did her father.

"See! You don't need those silly wheels!"

He led her in a steady, straight line past the neighbors' houses.

"We're going to turn now."

Gently, he pulled an angle into the handlebars. Rose's breath caught—sure gravity would kick in now—but instead they just executed a wide loop, before straightening out.

Rose's confidence grew as they looped around and around in front of their house.

Her father, sensing this, began to loosen his hold on the bike. First they did a circuit with his hand barely gripping the seat. Then they executed another, this time his fingertips only lightly guiding the bars. Pretty soon, she was doing it all by herself, though he kept pace with the bicycle.

"Don't let go, Daddy."

But he already had. Rose's hair was streaming in her self-made wind, her tongue between her lips in concentration.

Rose's father held back and watched her go. Still unaware that she was doing it on her own.

She was about to make the turn when he shouted, "That's my big girl, Rosie!"

Rose, surprised by the distance of her father's voice, turned toward it and let go of the handlebars. The wheel jerked to the side, suddenly perpendicular to the bike, forcing the whole contraption into a complete and sudden stop.

From where he stood, Rose's father watched as her small body pitched up and over the handlebars. A little rag doll landing headfirst, *crunch*, on the asphalt.

She was not scared. At least, not at first. And she wasn't in pain. She was simply on the ground, whereas a moment before she had been in the air. And before that? Where had she been before that? Rose couldn't remember.

Somewhere, beyond the expanse of pebbles and tar of the road, she sensed movement. Feet running toward her.

And then there was the hot, bare sky and her father.

Rose anchored on his face. Her father's unshaven face. It was stricken. Terrified. He was shouting something, looking at her, but she couldn't tell what it was he was saying.

It was then that she became scared.

Her father's fear infected her. It welled up through her tiny body, invading her chest, her limbs, her neck. Fear poured out of her, bubbling over, spilling out of her ears, running out of her eyes.

Rose drowned in her father's terror, sinking further and further away from him until she couldn't see him at all.

I t's about time you got here."

The beach smelled of caramel. And so did the little boy.

Rose was confused. "Where is here?"

"I dunno. Here. Here is here . . . I guess. Here is where I've been waiting for you."

Rose sat up, the pink sand shifting under her bottom.

"Here," wherever it was, was beautiful. A short expanse of beach emptied out into a gulf of clear, warm water. In the shallows, Rose could see the flashing of piscine bodies as schools of fish shifted and flocked in the current. A gentle kiss of a breeze carried the scent of salt and lilac across the water. Mounds of sea grass clutched at the sand, before yielding to a sun-speckled forest.

They were in a tent of some kind. White sheet walls, sloping up to big top peaks. Like the blanket forts she made for herself on rainy days . . . but so much bigger. Grander. Like the circus, almost, but lighter, prettier. A pavilion.

"Want a snack?"

The boy offered her a seashell. A small cowrie. Like the ones on the necklace she had brought home after her trip to Hawaii with Mom and Dad.

Something about that thought bothered her. What was it? Rose pulled her legs in and shook her head.

The boy shrugged and popped the shell into his mouth. Cracked it with his teeth.

"Are you crazy? Don't do that."

"Why not? They taste like candy."

He offered Rose another, this time the slightly larger fan of a bivalve shell. His teeth crunched down again.

Rose took it. She let her tongue flick across its surface, bracing herself for its saline grit.

Instead a sweet warmth rolled over her. The warmth of Sunday breakfast. Butter and maple and flannel pajamas.

"It's good, right?"

The boy turned onto his belly, digging into the sand for more seashells.

At age six, Rose didn't really make a habit of looking at boys.

To her, they all seemed to be loud, dirty things with a proclivity toward hitting—not worth as much study as, say, the Toys "R" Us circular or the back of the Cap'n Crunch box.

But this boy was different, as much as this place was different, and Rose took a moment to really look at him.

He wore a black vest over a white shirt and a loose pair of pants that ended below his knees. He looked a bit like a pirate, Rose decided, or more likely a stowaway on a pirate's ship. A plucky cabin boy like in that Swiss Family movie.

He had brown eyes. Rose had never noticed the color of anyone's eyes before save her mother's and her own. Rose decided that she liked his brown eyes. They were the color of chocolate.

His hair was curly and too long, as he kept having to brush it out of his face. It was that color that is neither blond nor brown but somewhere in between.

His smile started on one side and crept its crooked way across his teeth, before activating the dimple on the other side of his face.

He was a big kid. About the size of the second graders at her school. The size of kids who can read chapter books and tie their own shoes.

And as Rose had already noticed, he smelled of caramel.

"I'm Hugo. What's your name?"

three

Hugo had been waiting for her for "like a million years." Or so he said. And while he'd been waiting he had done a little bit of exploring, though never straying too far from the beach.

"Come on, there's something I want to show you."

He grabbed her hand and pulled Rose up to the crest of a sandy ridge.

"That is Castle City."

From the horizon rose a mass of shining spires of all different shapes. Some were rounded and some were pointed. Others had jagged bits that stabbed at the sky. There were hundreds of them all collected together behind a single unbroken wall.

Around it all hung a yellow halo of sorts, giving the place the look of a city in a snow globe.

"That's where we have to go. Because that's where everyone is."

"Everyone?"

"Everyone. In the whole wide world."

"Even my daddy?"

"Especially your daddy."

Rose looked at this boy. This Hugo. He seemed to know what he was talking about.

"Is he in trouble?" Rose almost remembered something . . . felt it tickling at the back of her brain. Her father's face, worried about something.

"Yes. Kinda. Maybe. They need us to rescue them."

"Oh. . . . From what?"

Hugo shrugged. "I dunno. Something bad. There's gotta be some reason why they're all in there and we're the only ones out here."

"Huh."

Rosie sat on the edge of the ridge and considered the city. Considered everyone she loved being inside, and herself and this boy being the only people outside.

She was not used to being the person doing the rescuing. In neighborhood games, she always elected to be the princess in the tower. She had never considered being the knight. She had never considered herself a hero.

"Hugo . . ." She tested the feel of his name. "Aren't you . . . aren't you a little scared?"

He scoffed. "Nah. What for?"

And he smiled at her in such a way that she could not help smiling back.

Since everyone in the whole wide world was in the Castle City, there was nothing for it but for them to go there.

She and Hugo had filled their pockets with seashells and set out in the tall saw grass that lay in the direction of the city.

"How long do you think it will take us to get there?"

"Dunno. It doesn't look too far. All morning?"

"Is it morning?"

"Feels like it, doesn't it?"

Rose noticed that the towering blades of grass were in fact shiny with dew and that they seemed to be that particular shade of green one sees only in the early hours of the day.

"Yeah. I guess," she said, wanting to agree with this older, smarter boy.

They walked in silence for a bit. The blades clattered against one another as they pushed them out of their path.

"You wanna sing a song?"

"A song?"

"Sure, sometimes I do that. When I'm walking. You know any?"

Rose knew lots of songs, but she was afraid Hugo might laugh at the ones she knew by heart. "If I Knew You Were Coming" and "How Much Is That Doggy in the Window" seemed too babyish to sing on an adventure.

She shrugged.

"You know this one?" His voice rose in a sweet trill across the grass: "When you're alone and life is making you lonely, You can always go . . ."

"*Downtown!*" Rose loved this song. Knew it from her time at the roller rink.

Hugo smiled at her, excited she was catching on. "When you've got worries, all the noise and the hurry, Seems to help, I know . . ."

"*Downtown!*" they shouted together.

Hugo had a better hold on the lyrics than Rose, but she

filled in the gaps with "dedums" and soon they were racing their way to the end.

And you may find somebody kind to help and understand you
Someone who is just like you and needs a gentle hand to
Guide them along
So maybe I'll see you there
We can forget all our troubles, forget all our cares
So go downtown
Things'll be great when you're downtown
Don't wait a minute more, downtown
Everything's waiting for you, downtown

Hugo finished by grabbing Rose around the waist and swinging her in an open patch in the grass. Her bare feet swung out from beneath her and she clung to his chest, smiling up into his tucked chin.

He tumbled sideways, and they both fell to the ground. Curled into fits of giggles. Rose rolled to her side and watched as he sat up. Brushing off his hands.

"You're funny, Hugo."

"So are you, Rosie."

Hugo spent the morning teaching her songs as they walked. "The Crocodile Rock." "I Was Made to Love Her." "The Love You Save May Be Your Own."

Rose absorbed the lyrics and the melodies as they kept pushing forward. She almost forgot what it was they were meant to be doing . . . the learning of songs seemed to be reason enough to be walking through the grass. Simply spending time with Hugo.

But then the saw grass ended.

They reached a clearing, which finally afforded them a view

of the horizon. Castle City remained stubbornly the same size in the distance, yet they had been walking for hours.

Hugo was quiet. Disappointed.

"We need to get there. We need to rescue them."

Rose nodded. Serious in that way that only a child can be. Seriously serious.

"Maybe we're doing it wrong. Maybe we need to try to get there a different way."

The different ways they tried led them through the landscape of the island, which they discovered was an island because they spent a great long while walking on the sand and ended up in precisely the location they had left.

It was just after that journey that they found the Plank Orb bobbing awkwardly in a rocky cove.

"What is that . . . thing?" asked Rose, not sure what to call it. "Some kind of boat?"

Hugo waded out to it, careless of his pants getting wet.

The "thing" rocked gently in the waves. It was clearly made out of wood, the kind of blockish two-by-fours one's father picked up at the hardware store for home projects.

But somehow these lengths had been curled around an open space, creating a kind of wooden bubble that rose and fell with the water. The whole thing was weathered and gray, splintery like an old fence.

Hugo caught the edge of something on its top. Pulled it toward him.

"There's a way in!"

Rose watched from the shore as he hefted himself up onto the contraption and disappeared into a door at its peak.

She decidedly did not want to climb onto that thing. She decidedly did not want to follow Hugo into that darkness. Or get her skirt wet. Or any of it at all, thank you very much.

He poked his head out. "Come on, Rosie!"

Rose crossed her arms. Determined to stay.

And yet, she took a step into the water. And then another. And another. All carrying her toward the strange wood bubble and Hugo.

He held out a hand to haul her up its side and helped her down into the cavity below.

It was dark and close. The sound of water straining against wood filled the space with its thumps and groans. There were windows, round shuttered portholes covered in chipped white paint. Through these Rose could see the crystalline waters of the cove, the distant movement of fish.

"Did you see this?"

Hugo held up a length of wet chain that threaded between two small holes in the floor.

"What's it for?"

He smiled and slammed the door above them shut, plunging them into a warm, wet dim. He crouched to the floor and yanked the chain.

The Orb lurched and dropped under the water—pulled like a bead on a string.

Rose put her hand to the window, her mouth making a perfect small "o" as the marine world swept past them at a clip. Candy-colored reefs populated with small creatures drew close before they were pulled away.

"Where are we going?"

Hugo shrugged. "Dunno. But I feel like . . . like it's going to be somewhere important."

"I feel that way, too."

They pressed closer to the window. The sunlight cut a dancing path through the water beyond the Orb. Large bodies of whales rolled in the deep distance.

Rose thought about how she had not wanted to get into the Orb at all; how if she had stayed on that shore as she had wanted to, she never would have seen any of this. She was grateful to whatever impulse it was, shame or fear of being left behind or some other, more powerful force that had pushed her into the water.

"I like it here," whispered Rose.

"Me too."

I t took them an hour to get her to stop crying when she finally awoke.

Her father sat vigil next to her tiny body for the five days it took for her to emerge. He had traced the events of that afternoon over and over again during that time, listening to the beeps and blips of the monitors. He tried to decide which mistake was the one that led him here, to this hospital room, talking to doctors who told him nothing.

Maybe it was the third beer. Or the fourth. Not putting on the training wheels. Pushing her to get on the bike. Letting go. Which decision had caused her little body to leap over those handlebars and meet the pavement at that particularly horrible angle? Which decision had he made that had caused his daughter to lose her tether to the conscious world?

All of them. None of them. What did it matter, when there was nothing he could do that would make Rosie wake up?

He sat there for five days, thinking the same thoughts, arriving at the same nonconclusions.

And so he was there when Rose awoke and almost immediately began to wail.

The moment Rose's father saw her eyes, he knew it would all be okay. Thanks be to God, they were open and lucid and clear. She was upset, but in her eyes he could tell she was undamaged and blessedly awake.

He climbed onto the bed and wrapped his arms around her. Consoling. Crying warm tears himself.

"It's okay, sweetie. You're okay, sweetie. It's okay."

He thought, of course, that she was frightened by waking in a tangle of tubes and IVs. The bright sterility of the hospital room. The sticky leads that monitored her half existence for the past week.

But little Rose wasn't frightened, she was mourning.

She cried because it wasn't real. She cried because Hugo didn't exist. She cried because now that she was awake, she thought he was lost to her.

Little Rose did not know while she slept in that hospital bed that she was dreaming. This was in part because she did not remember losing consciousness in her father's panicked arms, but it was mostly because nothing about the island felt like a dream.

She knew that usually a dream slips around one's consciousness, like the sand shifting away under your feet as the tide pulls itself into the ocean.

But the island to which Rose had been brought had felt as solid as clay beneath boots.

And so she cried. She grieved that whole day in that hospital. She quivered and sobbed as the doctors put her through a battery of tests, drawing blood and taking X-rays. The smiling nurses and happy doctors annoyed her. Her laughing mother and exuberant father were so antithetical to the deep sadness that sat inside her little body. They did not seem like they could possibly understand.

Her mother cooed and tried to settle her the way she did with all Rose's nightmares. *There, there, baby. It will be all right.* Rose cringed and clutched at her mother's chest, waiting for Hugo to disappear from her mind. Waiting for him and his wonderful island to fade like the dream that he was.

That night, tired out from the tests and the visitors, the doctors finally felt sure they could let Rosie sleep. They no longer worried that if she slept she would not wake again. Rose's mother let her sip water from a plastic straw and turned out the lights in her hospital room. Rose closed her eyes and rolled into a fetal curl.

She fell asleep.

And there he was again.

Hugo. Waiting for her that night on the shores of his island. Ready to try again to get to Castle City. To fight the island's monsters. To bound down the rainbow trail.

And so he would be every night for the next thirty years.

As Rose grew, so did Hugo. He matured from a beautiful boy into a beautiful man. They kept to their purpose. Reach Castle City. Rescue the people there.

And for thirty years, the city eluded them.

four

Rose was flying through the air when Adam woke her up.

She and Hugo had climbed out of the Orb just as the clouds had started to shift and break, the light bleeding through their seams.

"Rosie, look!"

Hugo pointed upward as the first shaft broke through. The stream of light cut through the air, striking the sand of the beach.

Hugo laughed and hauled himself over the lip of the door. He tumbled into the shallows, salt water splashing his face.

More shafts of light burst through the cover, setting an illuminated path down the stretch of shore. Under each pool of light the sand began to iridesce, set alight with a special kind of magic.

Hugo pulled himself upright, his pants and shirt clinging wet.

Rose slid down the side of the Orb, more careful than Hugo but still quickly, her skirt lifting with the water as her feet reached the silt.

Hugo was already running.

"Race you!"

Rose laughed and gave chase.

These "rainbow" paths, stepping-stones of light down the beach, didn't last long.

"Stay with me, Rosie!"

Hugo drew closer to the nearest pool of illuminated sand, his bare feet shod in slippers of wet grit. Rose was just behind him, the wind pressing the wet warmth of her skirt to her thighs, her breath heavy with effort and anticipation.

Hugo leaped from the darker surrounds into the pool of sparkling sand—

"Momma!"

A voice from the other world beckoned.

Rose rubbed her face, eyes adjusting to the dark. On the nightstand the monitor light jumped with Adam's cries.

"Momma! Mommy!"

Rose sighed, prying her body from the bed. Hands lightly touching the wall. Finding her way in the dark.

Adam was sitting up in the night-light glow of his room. A nightmare.

"Hey, little boy. Momma's here."

Rose knelt by his bed. Pushed the fringe of bangs from his face. Wiped the hot tear from his cheek.

"See? Everything's okay. Just a bad dream."

Adam's little body shuddered, but he calmed, alert to the safety of his room, the comfort of his mother.

"Water?" he whispered, and Rose handed him the cup from his bedside. She watched his small hands wrap around its plastic sides. Watched him take a sip. Silently he handed it back, wiggling down into the covers.

Rose gave him a sleepy smile. "Do you want me to give you ideas for some good dreams?"

"You always tell me the same things: puppies, kitties, ice cream."

"And baseball." This deeper voice came from the other half of the room. Isaac, in his bed, awake now to his mother and brother. Soon to be eight to Adam's six.

Rose sighed. "I need some new material, huh?"

They nodded. Rose buried her head in Addy's covers. Tired. "Give me a break, guys. It's the middle of the night."

Rose made it a habit never to ask the boys about their nightmares. On the rare occasions that Josh would go to them in the night, she would cringe when she heard him ask them what they had been dreaming about. What was the point? Why give the dark dreams any more hold on their consciousness? Instead she would give them new things to dream about. Happy thoughts.

But at the moment, she was having a tough time thinking of anything other than the rote list she always supplied them with. A minute ago she had been with Hugo . . . she searched her half-dormant brain for ideas.

"Can you tell us what you were dreaming when you woke up? Was Hugo there?"

"Shut up, stupid! Hugo's always there!"

True, thought Rose, but still, "Isaac, that's a bad word. You owe me fifty cents."

Adam was excited now, curling his knees under his blankets. "Did you guys get to Castle City?"

"They can't get to Castle City, 'cause it's got an invisible shield around it."

"Hugo can figure out how to get past an invisible shield."

"No, he can't."

"Yes, he can."

"No, he can't."

"Stop."

The boys looked at her. Alert as a spring afternoon. Expectant.

She sighed.

"We were on the beach."

"The pink beach?"

"Were the Spiders there?"

The boys talked over each other, their questions a tumble of syllables. Rose smiled. "Yes. No."

"Adam's afraid of the Spiders."

Rose crept a playful hand toward Isaac's bed. "So am I. They could gobble you up! Yum! Yum!" Isaac giggled as she found his belly, burying tickles in his soft flesh.

Adam was not going to let her get off topic, though. "But you said—"

"No Spiders this time."

"Did the sun come out?"

Rose nodded. Her mind filled with the memory. "And it lit a path all the way down the beach.

"And Hugo was so excited. And he ran.

"And I ran after him. And then when he reached where the sun was shining he jumped . . ."

For a moment Rose was in two places. The dark close of the boys' room and the open reaches of the shore. She remembered Hugo's feet meeting the illuminated sand, then his body rising, back arched, joyous, open to the sky.

"And he flew high, high, high into the sky." Adam knew this dream by heart.

"And then so did I."

Rose felt her own feet impact the sand. Felt her breath escape her as her body was thrown into the air. Above, Hugo reached his hand back toward her, his face in shadow. She reached up to take it.

"And then what?"

Suddenly, Rose was only on the floor of the boys' room. The smell of salt replaced by the yeasty sweetness of her children.

"And then I heard a little boy who needed me."

She kissed them each on her way out. "Good night, little boy. Good night, littler boy."

Josh was sitting on the bed pulling on his clothes when she got back to their room. Rose groaned and fell onto the rumpled covers.

"Is it four already?"

"Quarter till."

The sound of the boys' whispers crackled over the monitor. Talking about Hugo.

"You know, they really are too old for that thing."

"I like knowing I'll hear them if they need me."

The boys giggled in their room. Conspiratorial.

"I have to admit, I'm a little jealous of Hugo."

Rose pulled at the duvet pinned under her husband's rump. "You should be. He doesn't work twenty-four-hour shifts. No mortgage. No student loans."

She managed to free the blanket, pulling it up over her shoulder. Josh leaned over her, a wolfish smile curling his mouth. "You know, I've got fifteen minutes."

Rose turned her face to the pillow. "Seriously? I don't remember when I showered last."

"I think you smell amazing."

She felt his hands brush the dough of her hips. He shifted the blanket, letting in a rush of cold air. Pulling at her shirt, planting kisses on her shoulder, her neck. Hungry.

"Josh, please. I just want to go to sleep."

He paused, chin resting on her arm. Looked up at his wife. Her face was quiet, eyes shut. Already on her way out.

"Right."

He sat up. If he left now, he could look over that new study before rounds.

"Love you, Rose."

Penny had taken to pooping behind the couch. Every morning after breakfast, Penny would climb down from her booster seat and pretend to play with some toys, all the while checking out her favored corner of the family room: a little blind spot of privacy behind the arm of the sectional and the wall.

"Do you need to poop, Penny?" Rose would ask.

Penny would shake her head.

"You look like you need to poop."

"No poop," she insisted.

"Are you sure you wouldn't like to try?"

Penny shook her head again.

They had this conversation every morning for weeks. And every morning for weeks, Penny would wait until Rose was distracted, attending to some need of Adam's or Isaac's, before ducking behind the couch.

Rose was getting tired of rinsing out "big girl" panties.

But since the books all insisted that backsliding into diapers would prolong the problem, Rose persisted. She told the boys to warn her if they saw Penny heading over there (they never did) and blocked Penny's access with a large empty box (Penny just pooped next to it).

Finally Rose began moving the potty seat to the kitchen in the morning and making Penny sit on it for ten minutes after breakfast.

This was something the books also advised against, but once again, Rose had had it with washing shit off of the smug, smiling faces of Rapunzel and Belle.

And so Penny and the family became accustomed to her chubby body hunched on a little toilet in the middle of their routine morning chaos. From this vantage, Pen would watch her big brothers searching for lost shoes and swinging on their backpacks. Adam and Isaac would play "Hugo" in the five minutes before the bus came, wielding their foam swords over her head. Penny could see her mother assembling their lunches, asking about permission slips, and scraping uneaten breakfasts into the trash.

It was so much nicer than being banished to the cold loneliness of the powder room, left alone to "make a b.m.," as Mommy would say. Not wanting to miss anything was why she had started pooping in the family room in the first place.

Rose, for her part, worried what people would think if they knew she was sanctioning defecation not five feet from her breakfast table. A stronger mother, she thought, would be able to *make* her two-and-a-half-year-old use the bathroom. A better woman wouldn't have to drive her boys to school twice a week because they missed the bus so regularly. She wouldn't have to cobble together lunch because they were out of bread (again), knowing the boys would come home (again) complaining about their almond-butter-and-jelly *burritos*.

But these were the scenes of her life. Playing over and over again. The same morning, the same night. The same conversations.

"Puppies, kitties, ice cream."

"You *do* need to poop."

"Please, not tonight, dear."

The dialogue changing a little each time, slight variations in the timing, but so small as to be indistinguishable from the last time it played. If last night she put Josh off sex by saying that she hadn't showered, next time it would be that she was tired. If today she had to push Adam to clear the table, tomorrow it would be Isaac.

Perhaps it was this repetition that made it so that Rose could not get this other "better self" out of her mind. Like an actress whose poor performance was slowing down the movie, she just needed to be recast to make the whole thing work.

Recast with someone who wouldn't prefer sleep to sex with her husband. Someone who didn't yell to get her kids to listen. Someone as chipper as those women in the magazines, so orgasmically happy to be mothers, milling their own organic baby food and running catering businesses on the side.

She hated those women.

Rose even felt bad about feeling bad.

If she was depressed, she didn't have any right to her depression. This was just life, how it is. Over time these repetitions would amount to larger changes; eventually the children would get the knack of the current "issue" and then struggle beneath a new challenge. Eventually when she heard that low sound in Josh's throat, she wouldn't cringe at the thought of him touching her disappointing flesh.

Though she worried that instead the day would arrive when he stopped making that sound altogether.

That would be so much worse.

Rose had started seeing a therapist about two months after Penny had been born.

Josh had been able to take a week off work, her mother had visited to help with the boys, but in the end it was left to her to find a way to fit a newborn into the rhythm of her life.

Penny was a good baby. The pink-and-cream girl Rose had craved. She smiled early, nursed well, slept often.

Adam and Isaac transitioned well to her presence, whispering during naps, kissing her head while she ate in Rose's lap.

But Rose, having fought so hard to convince Josh of the need for this third baby, this hard-won girl, plummeted into the blue. She was living her life but felt as if she were watching it from a distance—its colors faded, its flavors stale.

Sleep was her escape. Sleep and Hugo.

The island was vivid as ever. Even more so compared with the washed-out world her reality had become.

She would drop the boys off at day care and rush home to sleep in her queen-sized bed, Penny snoozing by her side.

She resented every time the baby pulled her out of the dream. Every dirty diaper, every little wail for attention.

One night Josh discovered Rose sobbing uncontrollably during a feeding.

"I can't do this," she cried. "It's too much." Josh looked at the little person sucking hungrily at Rose. There was something frightening and hollow about his wife's eyes in that moment. The edge of a void.

He took Penny from Rose's arms and sent her to bed.

That night he made a few phone calls, got a few recommendations.

The next day Rose met Naomi.

It was Josh who asked Rose to call Naomi by her name. It bothered him when Rose referred to her as her therapist. "Shrink" bothered him even more.

And as for referring to Naomi as her "doctor" . . . well, everybody knows psychiatrists aren't *real* doctors.

At least, not the way *he* was a real doctor.

But Naomi had been selected specifically for her "doctorness." Josh had picked a psychiatrist so that she could quickly and *chemically* fix his broken wife. No waiting for a referral. A prescription to get Rose going, talk therapy to keep her moving.

But Rose had resisted the offered drugs.

She was nursing, she said. She worried about what might pass to the baby. How it could affect her still-wrinkling brain.

But she was glad to go to the appointments. The appointments meant she could justify a babysitter. The appointments meant she could buy two hours of freedom from her never-ending obligation to her family.

And so, Rose talked herself better.

Marginally better, but better. Better enough to activate a dormant love for her newborn daughter. Better enough to be able to smile when the occasion called for it. Better enough to get by. Better enough for Josh.

Still, as she listened to herself talk, it drove her mad how cliché her life was. The things that she struggled with were nothing compared with the *real* problems other people had.

"What are 'real' problems?" Naomi would ask.

"You know what I mean."

"But what comes to mind? I'm sure you're thinking of something when you say that."

Images flew through Rose's mind. Foreclosure signs. A man with a sign by the highway. The hungry African children in those late-night commercials. She shook her head. Even her ideas of real problems were cliché.

"There's a woman at the boys' school. Another mom. She just got implants."

Naomi laughed. "Okay . . ."

"I mean, her boobs are huge. So fake. And there're always just *out* there. Like she wants you to look."

"That's possible."

"It's just she got them to save her marriage. But then she made a joke about the fact that if her husband left her, at least her new boobs were one thing he couldn't get fifty percent of."

"She said that?"

"That's the thing—I don't even know this woman. I've just seen her in the parking lot. It was another mother who told me she said that stuff. . . . People are talking about her, making jokes about her marriage. Thinking about her sex life. It's possible none of this is true, I wouldn't know."

"So this woman, she's who you think of when you think of someone with real problems?"

Rose shrugged. "They seem more real than my problems."

Rose also told Naomi about Hugo and the island.

Naomi was intrigued. She encouraged Rose to talk more about them. Her adventures with Hugo, the same tales that enraptured the boys, seemed stale and immature in Naomi's clean, dark office.

And she sensed that Naomi didn't believe her. Naomi would call the dreams "fantasies" and ask Rose what she thought they meant.

"I don't think they mean anything. They're just dreams."

Which is what Rose said but was in truth not what she believed. Her time with Hugo *meant* a great deal, but it didn't *represent* anything. It just . . . was.

Besides, she was happy with her dreams.

It was her life she didn't like.

five

Rose hated soccer.

The boys had been dutifully enrolled in a mini-league when Isaac turned four. Rose, as always, had done her research, questioning other mothers about which association was best—as if "best" could be used to describe anything that involved a passel of preschoolers clumping around a ball and aiming kicks at one another's shins.

But of course the other mothers had a great deal to say about which league was best. Some leagues were noncompete, all games ending in a tie—while others sidelined the less athletically talented children, refusing to guarantee time on the field. One association's head coach was said to hit on the players' mothers,

while another's was suspected to be gay, not that there was anything wrong with that, but, *you know* . . .

Rose didn't know. But she also didn't find out.

She ended up picking the most popular league, which ranged
somewhere near the middle on the competitive scale, and at
which, so far, she had witnessed no sex occur, heterosexual or
otherwise.

Rose began shuttling the boys to practice in the afternoons
and to games on the weekends. As they grew older, entire weekends would revolve around their game schedule since it often happened that if Isaac's game was on Saturday, then Adam's would
be on Sunday, and vice versa.

During games, Rose would watch the boys from the sidelines,
trying to look interested. Clapping when Isaac made an assist,
shouting when Adam blocked a kick.

But, dear Lord, was it boring.

So fucking boring!

And the other parents didn't seem to think so at all. She felt it
was all she could do to smile, and they were screaming at their
kids. High-fiving when they scored. So invested in the game, as if
there were something actually at stake other than cultivating the
competitive spirit in a bunch of five-year-olds.

What was wrong with them?

Or better yet, what was wrong with her that she wasn't feeling "it"?

Instead she *hated* the parents who bounced and clapped from
the sidelines. And once she connected a child player on the field
to his or her screaming, wailing counterpart on the sidelines,
she found things to hate about the child as well.

Sydney, whose mother questioned every decision the referee
made, ate her boogers while waiting for the game to resume.

Cooper, the goalie, had a ratty face. He looked like a smaller version of his father, who clearly viewed his son's position on the team as equivalent to an NFL draft pick.

Jaden-with-an-E tripped smaller kids.

Jaydon-with-an-O didn't share the ball.

Emma wasn't going to be very pretty when she got older. She didn't look as if she were going to be very bright either.

Rose would cycle through these judgments, finally turning her eye on her own children.

She would see them the way she imagined others saw them.

Isaac's pretty mouth would sneer when another player stole the ball from him. She could tell when his wheels were turning. His eyes would get that nasty narrow look and Rose knew by the direction in which he stared during the breaks which player he was going to target with an "accidental" blow to the shin. More than once, it was a member of his own team.

Adam was careless, daydreaming. Other players often had to shout at him to get him to pay attention to the game. More than once he had lost the team goals because he wasn't attending to the action on the field.

She could tell by the way the other parents would glance over at her when this happened—Adam was a loser.

Rose hated herself so much.

Hated herself for thinking horrible things about children. Hated herself for seeing anything ugly in her own. Hated herself for not being able to truly care whether it was the "Bobcats" or the "Pirates" that won the game, because all she wanted to do was get away from the noise and damp grass and screaming parents, go home, and take a nap.

———

Hemsford Fields was over an hour's drive away.

Though there had been no indication of that on the schedule, which had simply listed it as "Quarter Finals Tournament, Hemsford Fields."

Under which someone had typed, "Snack Captain—Isaac A."

Rose had been fortunate that she had overheard some players' mothers complaining about the distance, how much it was going to cost them to get there. "The price of gas nowadays, minivans aren't cheap." Singsong voice: "But what're you gonna do?"

Rose did the sad calculus of the soccer mom.

Adam's first game was at eight thirty, but Isaac's started at eight. Check-in was at seven thirty for all players. An hour's drive with an extra fifteen minutes for buffer. And she had to make the snack. Load the kids in the car. Josh was working, so he couldn't help. . . .

Josh was always working. . . .

Maybe the boys could sleep in their uniforms.

Maybe she could shower before she went to bed.

Maybe tomorrow wouldn't be miserable.

The boys loved the idea of sleeping in their uniforms, though Rose had drawn the line at shin guards. Too sweaty.

Isaac watched her face as she was tucking the covers in around his body.

"Mom, I want a bike for my birthday."

It wasn't a request. It wasn't really a demand either. It was a simple statement of fact, the kind made by children whose parents make sure Santa Claus brings them *everything* on their list. His tone was the tone of a boy who simply expected to say what he wanted . . . and get it.

"I'll talk to Dad about it," Rose said, though she already

knew the content of the conversation she would be having with Josh.

There was no way Isaac was getting a bike.

Do kids even bicycle anymore? thought Rose as she swept up for the night. The dishwasher hummed quietly, belching a chemic-lemon fragrance. *I mean, aren't they all stuck inside on the Internet? Playing video games so child molesters can't snatch them from their backyards? Isn't that why they keep saying every other kid has type two diabetes?*

No. Isaac couldn't have a bike.

He couldn't have a bike because to Rose bicycles were so caught up in her mind with "near death" and "brain injury" that the idea of gifting her son one was akin to giving him a death trap.

The bicycle her parents had given her was gone the day she had returned from the hospital. Rose's parents, grateful that she had been returned to them, had gotten rid of it. A totem of their misfortune.

So Rose had quietly passed out of childhood without ever learning how to ride one, a deficit that seemed to matter less and less the older she got.

Isaac couldn't have a bike because his mother didn't know how to ride one. He couldn't have a bike because she was convinced a bike would take him away from her, carrying his body away from consciousness.

Rose knew this was irrational.

Maybe a few more years. . . . He still seemed so small.

She hated to disappoint him, but there was nothing for it. Isaac was going to *have* to want something else. They had time. His birthday wasn't for weeks. This happened a lot: Isaac and Adam would decide that they needed something desperately, begging for it for days, until some *new* thing caught their attention and they began to insist they couldn't live without *that*.

Oh, God, *Adam*. She hadn't even thought of him.

If Isaac got a bike, Adam would want one. He would *insist* on one, and sibling parity was not something either of them let drop. If Adam got a lolly, Isaac squawked until he had one, too. It was just how they were.

Rose supposed that was her fault. She had made them that way. When they were young they were so close together that it was just easier to bring two of everything; if one asked for juice, she'd fetch a second for the other. If one got a Tonka, she put a second in the other's hand.

For a moment, Rose fought with the image of both the boys' bodies lying on the pavement, their heads sporting identical cracks, leaking identical trails of blood and brain.

No. There was no way Isaac could have a bike.

Josh shouted when he came in, "Guys! I'm home!"

Rose ran heel-toe to the foyer, arms waving. "Are you crazy!" she hissed.

"But, it's nine thirty."

"Exactly."

Rose receded to the kitchen. Josh followed, his eyes trailing up the stairs toward his sleeping progeny.

"I thought you let them stay up on Fridays."

"Tournament tomorrow. Hemsford."

Josh made a face. "That's a hike."

"I have to get them up at six. It's not going to be pretty."

Josh quirked his mouth. A day in the sunshine watching his boys, talking to other dads. Seeing families be people and not next of kin. Sounded pretty great. "I wish I could go with you."

Rose pursed her lips. Thought, *Me too*.

But she didn't say it.

She didn't need to. There were a lot of things Josh and Rose didn't say to each other now. There was no reason. They both already knew the stifled complaints. He was never home. She was never interested. He was lonely. She was resentful.

Why talk about things they didn't have the energy to change? Someday it would, but not now. Right now it was better just to accept that the best their marriage could do was keep its head above the swells. Tread water and wait for the waves to carry it closer to shore.

Rose changed the subject. "Just in case Isaac tries to divide and conquer, he asked for a bicycle for his birthday. . . . It's not . . ." She trailed off, correcting, "Just don't get suckered into promising anything."

"He's gonna be eight, Rosie."

"If he gets one, Adam will start and I don't—"

"I see injuries all day and I think you're making more of this—"

Rose closed her eyes to him. Buried her face in her hands.

Her husband stopped talking. Stared at his wife. It was quiet for a moment as they both gauged the things they didn't want to say.

The dishwasher shifted cycles, grinding out a new pitch.

Finally, through her fingers, Rose's voice emerged. "Can we just . . . can we just . . . put a pin in this? All I want is for my day to end."

Josh nodded. It was a pass. A near miss of a disagreement. "Yep. Sure. Got it."

Ten minutes later, Josh was deep into the DVR's cache of *SportsCenter* and Rose was on her way to the island. They did not forget to kiss each other good night.

Their lives would have been simpler had Josh and Rose stopped loving each other. Or if their love had faded into the background, like so many other relationships—a remnant of the past, the reason for the present.

But Josh and Rose loved each other with a depth and breadth that surpassed the love they had before their children were born. To an outsider, witness to the facts of their marriage—the lack of sex, the disagreements, the absenteeism—this might not be obvious, but their love evidenced in the smaller truths that built the facts.

On most nights, almost without fail, after the kids were tucked into bed, Rose would catch Josh scrolling through his cell phone, scanning their retirement portfolio. It was a ritual that seemed to soothe him, so it never bothered Rose. It wasn't an act of greed, an obsessive concern over the accumulation of money.

Rose knew that, for Josh, it was an act of romance.

It was not numbers he saw in those expanding and contracting accounts, but a life lived with her. In them he saw the boys grown into men, Penny blooming into a younger version of his wife. The house they would one day be able to live in, the vacations they would one day be able to take. He saw Rose happy. He saw Rose relaxed, because there was finally enough of what they did not have now—money and time together.

Rose understood the numbers and columns were an affirmation to Josh that now was not all there would ever be. He would be reassured, as he pushed through long and difficult shifts, that there was a reason for all of it. Someday things would be different.

Josh's love for her shone through in his words and actions. It was there in his smile, when she'd catch him looking at her across the dinner table. It was in his eyes as they made love—his eyes, always open, always full of love and hope. His eyes, always on hers.

And it was this certitude, this intensity of his love, that worried her. It was the root of her avoidance, that even the slightest physical contact could lead to the intimacy he craved. Rose often worried he'd interpret her distance as a loss of affection. But the truth was far more complicated.

New lovers become old lovers. Their ways become practiced. In time they come to *see* less of each other, their minds wandering while their bodies couple.

But Josh had never stopped *seeing* Rose. He made love to her in the same way he had when their love was fresh—more practiced than he was then, an expert now in her body, but still the entire world eclipsed by *her*. Looking at her. Smelling her. Being with her.

Rose never wondered if he was thinking of someone else while they had sex . . . his eyes were wide and clear and hungry. There was no escaping them.

But Rose was terrified of being seen.

Josh had barely changed, but she had dissolved into a frumpy housewife, overweight, overtired. Sexless where she had once been sexy.

Each time they made love she thought surely this time he would finally realize she wasn't worthy of his worship. Surely, this time, he would realize he could find someone more beautiful to give his soul to.

Rose ached at the thought. She could not lose Josh.

But she also knew that she risked his loss by not letting him make love to her. So she parsed out sex to her husband, rationing it like a finite resource.

———

If they had stopped loving each other, they would have settled into a comfortable acceptance of their lives. If they had stopped loving each other, Josh's mind would have wandered while they fucked and Rose would have felt shielded from losing him. If they had stopped loving each other, Josh wouldn't have been so driven to protect their future together and he would have been able to be home more.

If they had stopped loving each other, it would have been easier.

R ose and Hugo spent her dream retrieving the Blanket Pavilion from the Natters nest. They had been resting inside when an avian shadow had suddenly painted itself on the ceiling of the tent. There was a screech and suddenly they were naked to the pearly sky of the island, watching the larger of the two Natters fly into the distance, white sheets trailing in his claws. Hugo and Rose had traveled to the reaches to get it back, climbing the bird-poop-stained peak to their nest. Both giant seabirds were there, beaks poking the fabric of the tent into the bed of their home.

"Why have they never laid any eggs?" whispered Rose, hiding beneath the lip of the nest.

"Because we never let them finish it." Hugo winked and leaped into the bird's line of sight. "Hey, you, overgrown seagulls!"

The birds startled, their huge gray-tipped wings whipping the air. The female drew back her throat and released a shattering cackle, while the male snapped his beak at Hugo. He turned and began running down the side of the mountain.

Rose waited, holding her breath. For a while it seemed that

only the male was going to follow him. The female had hung back, chattering and beating at the air.

The male pursued Hugo on foot, his razor-sharp beak pecking at the ground behind him. Hugo turned toward the bird and slipped on a patch of scree. His feet flew out from beneath him and suddenly he was sliding down the side of the mountain on an avalanche of gravel.

The male cried and launched himself into the air. In the nest, the female finally gave up holding back and took off, the air of her wings buffeting Rose's body.

Rose pulled herself up and made quick work of pulling the cloth of the Pavilion out of the branches and fallen trees that made up the nest. At the base of the mountain, she could make out Hugo rolling into a run and disappearing into the thick forest. The Natters pecked into the treetops after that, beating their wings and calling in frustration.

When they reunited on the beach, Hugo looked no worse for his tumble down the mountain. They spent a purple twilight eating seashells in the rebuilt Pavilion, their bodies cradled in radiating sand. Rose was content. She ran her hands down the smooth muscles of her arms, the gentle slope of her belly, her hair a glossy tumble on the sand.

"Are you happy, Rose?" Hugo asked, his eyes closed.

"Always."

The rattle of the alarm pulled her into her bed.

Five A.M.

Five-God-damn-A.M.

Fuck soccer, she thought.

But still Rose dressed. Padded downstairs. Evidence of Josh's evening lay around the house. An empty bag of chips on the coffee table. Crumbs on the countertop. An unrinsed plate by the sink.

Rose sighed and took care of it. She took care of everything.

That wasn't really true, she knew . . . but still she let herself think it while she sliced the oranges for Isaac's team's snack. She let the thought marinate while she loaded the bottles of water and sports drinks into the cooler, pouring the ice around their necks. She let thoughts of her own put-upon-ness wash over her while she hefted the coolers into the back of the minivan and packed a bag of snacks and sunscreen, toys to distract Penny, and changes of clothes for all.

Pen did not wake when Rose lifted her out of her crib. She cooed into her mother's neck and stayed asleep while Rose snapped her into her car seat, wrapping a blanket over her against the cold of the morning.

The boys she woke up. They stumbled sleepily down the stairs and out to the garage, climbing into their boosters and buckling themselves in. They were asleep again before Rose even started the car.

Rose checked her reflection in the rearview. Smoothed the frizz of her hair. She should have taken the time to shower last night. Should have gotten up earlier.

She exhaled.

Too late now, she thought. Already behind, and only at the start of her day.

Adam woke with the sun in his eyes.

The sunlight poured through the windshield, flaring on the streaky glass, bouncing around the car. He closed his eyes against it, and it left dark bluish trails on the backs of his eyelids.

He squinted, putting his hand up. Zackie snored next to him, his mouth open, a line of drool shiny on his chin.

Zackie'd probably make fun of him if he saw Adam drooling. Call him "drool baby" or something.

In the front of the car, Mom was quiet. One of her hands was on the flap thingy that folded down from the ceiling. She was leaning toward it, trying to keep the sun out of her eyes.

"Mom?"

Her hand jerked away from the wheel for a second and she gasped. Surprised.

"Sorry."

Mom shook her head. "No. Kiddo. I'm sorry. I . . . I thought you were asleep."

"I woke up."

Mom smiled back at him in her "kid watching" mirror, her face all bulbous and round on its surface.

Adam rubbed his shoulder under his strap. Rocked a butt cheek to the side. He hated his booster.

Once when he and Isaac had been out with Daddy, they had bought a new barbecue to surprise Mom, but when it was time to go home there wasn't enough room for it in the back. Zackie and Addy had ended up waiting outside the van while Dad pulled out the seat with Zackie's booster on it to make room for the box.

And then Zackie got to ride home in the front seat, even though it was *very bad* and *unsafe* and all those other things they said. Adam had asked why he couldn't be up front and Dad had said it was because Isaac was older, which was unfair because Isaac was only eighteen months older, which wasn't much at all.

And then he said they shouldn't tell Mom because it would spoil her present.

So he didn't. Even though he wanted to.

Still, though . . .

"Can I come sit up with you?"

Mom was quiet for a second. Maybe there was a chance.

"Sorry, Addy. Not tall enough yet. It's not safe."

Adam shrank a little bit. *Isaac hadn't been tall enough. Isaac still wasn't tall enough. But he had got to.*

The car seemed to be quieter now, after there had been talking, than it had been before he had spoken. And something about Mom had changed since she found out he was awake. Like knowing had shut a door somewhere inside her.

"Mom?"

"Adam?" Mom used her "serious" voice. The kind she used when she was teasing them in a good way.

"Can you tell me what you dreamed about Hugo last night?"

"Why do you always ask me to tell you about Hugo?"

Adam liked to hear about Hugo. He liked to think about what had happened on the island. He had lots of reasons why he always asked about it . . . but he decided to tell her the best reason. He knew the right word for it, too. *A compliment.* He was going to give Mommy a compliment.

"Because you look pretty when you talk about him."

Mom didn't say anything after that at all. She just got all the way quiet, like someone had locked the closed door inside her.

Rose had to search for parking among the vans and wagons— the practical family movers with their decals of stick-figure relations, stickers for karate, and a dozen varieties of awareness ribbons.

The boys strained to look out the windows, searching for familiar faces. Teammates. School friends. At the registration tents, Rose spotted the mom-with-the-implants. *What was her name?* She wondered if she was divorced yet. Rose felt bad for her.

———

Later, after she had found a parking space, the boys whined, chattering as she smeared their skin with sunscreen next to the parked car.

"You got it in my eyes."

"Well then, Isaac, you're a big kid, you can put it on yourself next time."

Rose hated putting SPF on the kids as much as they hated having it put on. It brought out the worst in all of them, making the kids wiggly and impatient while turning Rose grouchy and snappish.

Adam was shivering. "It's cold."

"I warmed it up in my hands."

"You didn't even say sorry!"

Rose looked at Isaac. "What?"

"You got it in my eyes! You didn't even say sorry."

Isaac was scowling at her, his mouth hard. Next to him, Adam clutched his arms, gooseflesh rising in the wind.

"Say you're sorry, Mom!"

Rose broke. Pissed at Isaac, hating that look on his face. She was angry. Angry that she had to be responsible for such a thankless task. Angry that he had the audacity to be angry with her. Angry that she even had to be on this shitty field, in this shitty wind, in this shitty town.

"I'm sorry, Zackie! Okay? I'm sorry!"

"Hi there!"

Rose turned to the bright voice behind her.

It was what's-her-name. Mom-with-the-implants.

"Rose, right?"

Rose stood, wiping her hands on her jeans. "Sorry. We were having a moment."

The other woman smiled. She put a sympathetic hand next to her cleavage. "No, no, I get it! Totally get it. I just . . . Isaac is on Simon's team and I thought . . . maybe you could use a hand."

She gestured over to the curb, where a good-looking blond boy was bouncing a ball on his knee. This must be Simon. Rose noticed the way he was aware of people watching him execute the trick. Exhibitionism ran in the family.

Her name flooded back to Rose. Kaitlin, her name was Kaitlin.

"Thank you. That would be great. That would be amazing. . . . Zackie?"

Isaac scowled at her. But he shouldered his bag, marching his way toward the curb. He was upset with her now, but hopefully by the time the game was over . . .

"Thank you, Kaitlin. Seriously. Thank you."

Kaitlin glanced at Adam, who had pulled his legs up under his shirt and was balancing on the running board. Penny was beginning to pull at the straps of her car seat. "Don't worry. My husband 'works' on Saturdays, too. It's hard enough with one, I can't imagine with three."

Rose recognized the look on Kaitlin's face.

It was pity.

T houghts crowded Rose's mind as she watched Adam's team play.

She *feels sorry for* me. . . . *She knew my name even though we've never spoken. . . . She knew about Josh, the kids . . .*

Rose laughed, but it wasn't funny.

People were *talking* about her. Just as they had been talking about Kaitlin and her boobs and her struggling marriage, they had been talking about Rose and her absent husband. Of course they had.

People thought she was pathetic. Barely keeping it going. And she hadn't given them any evidence to the contrary.

Clouds were stacking against the mountain range. From this distance, Rose could see them piling against themselves. The wind was picking up.

They put the tournament on hold. Officials had run around pausing games still in play. Lightning had been spotted. Everyone was to head elsewhere and await word.

Rose was still collecting their things when the rain started down, pelting the stragglers running toward their cars. Rose struggled to keep a grip on the cooler, its plastic grips awkward in her hands. She was soaked by the time she reached the van. The boys watched her as she opened the back, their faces stoic.

Adam hadn't had any problem leaving. He'd barely played, spending most of the game sitting on the sidelines.

But Isaac had been doing well. He had scored a goal ("You missed it, Mom") and didn't like being interrupted.

Rose tried to keep it positive as she climbed inside. She forced cheer into her voice. "They haven't canceled it yet. Maybe it will clear up."

Isaac frowned. "It won't."

Rose sighed and looked at her son.

Zackie. Little boy. Child of my body.

Sometimes I wish you weren't so like me.

Adam blew a cloud onto the window. Drew a happy face in its mist.

"I'm hungry."

There was a line of cars backing out of the McDonald's drive-through; it wrapped around the building and curled onto the street. Through its windows Rose could see it was a madhouse of displaced soccer players, their damp heat fogging the plate glass.

Penny was wailing in the back. Rolling her head from side to side. Tired of being in the car. Rose knew how she felt.

"We could go inside." This from Isaac.

"We're not going inside."

"We never go inside."

Rose drove past the line of cars, searching. Hemsford was a small town, not much more than a pit stop off the highway on the way to better places. A few motels. A few more gas stations. On her way in, Rose had spotted a small Christian publishing factory. But other than that and the soccer fields, a two-minute drive gave you the entire tour of the small strip of its main drag. After that you had to turn around and head back.

Why would anyone live here?

Just before the turn, Rose spotted it.

"The Orange Tastee," read the faded street sign. Next to the words was a cartoon of a manically grinning Orange with arms and legs. It wore an orange blossom as a hat and winked at the cars below.

For a second she thought it was shuttered, a relic of the town's better days; but the lights inside were on and the paint on the windows declaring, "Soft Serve 99¢!" was fresh.

And its drive-through was empty.

Rose turned into its parking lot and the boys erupted into complaint.

"What is this place!"

"I want McDonald's. I want a Happy Meal!"

"Change of plans, guys." As long as this place didn't serve rat-poop tacos, they were getting lunch here.

"Do they have Happy Meals?" Adam was whining, worried.

"I don't know. Maybe. We'll find out."

Penny's wailing changed pitch, picking up on the tension. Isaac crossed his arms. "You promised us Happy Meals. This place doesn't have Happy Meals."

Fuck fucking Happy Meals! thought Rose. *With their cheap pieces of landfill fodder and pink slime burgers. I wish I'd never taken you to McDonald's, so I wouldn't have to hear about it all the time. So I wouldn't give in to your whining. So I wouldn't use it to give me five minutes of peace once a week.*

But aloud she said, "Maybe they have something *like* a Happy Meal."

Isaac dug in. "They don't. Only McDonald's has Happy Meals."

"I want french fries. Do they have french fries?"

"You promised, Mom! You promised!"

Penny's wails were high-pitched, piercing, cutting around the interior.

And then suddenly Rose was screaming.

"Quiet! Please! Just shut the hell up!"

Instant silence. The children stared at her. Stunned.

Rose rubbed her forehead.

"Are you okay?" crackled a deep voice.

No, thought Rose. *I am not okay. Nothing about me is okay.*

"Ma'am?"

Rose looked around for the source of the deep voice. Outside her window sat a fiberglass version of the winking Orange, its grinning teeth replaced with the battered grille of a speaker.

Rose looked at it for a moment. Trying to find her voice. Trying to find her sanity.

"Uh . . . Kid's meals?"

"We got 'em."

Rose took a breath. In the back, the kids were still silent. Frightened of their mother.

She managed, "Three, please."

Rose pulled forward. Clutching the wheel. Knuckles white.

You do not cry in front of the kids. You do not cry in front of the kids.

But she *was* crying. She wiped at the hot welling in the corners of her eyes. Fighting it. Trying to calm the stress.

"Nine fifty, please."

Rose looked over. At the pickup window a pair of hands held out three small bags.

Rose riffled through her purse, finding calm in this simple interaction. She could regain her hold of the situation. Reassure the kids. Maybe they were all just hungry. Some food would fix it. Some food would make it all go away. She handed over a twenty and took the bags, distributing them back.

"Make sure Penny only eats one fry at a time, okay, Isaac?"

Zackie nodded, stuffing fries into his mouth. Rose took a breath. It would get better.

"Your change."

"Thanks." Rose reached out to the pile of bills from the hands, looking up at the cashier holding them—

It was Hugo.

six

Of course it couldn't be Hugo.

Rose stared up at the cashier, mouth open. It couldn't be. But it was.

There above her, in the window of this crappy fast-food restaurant, was the face of the man she had been dreaming about since she was six years old. It was a face she had seen grin down at her as they flew upward into the clouds. A face she had known as a boy and watched grow into a man.

It was him.

Older. Heavier. With glasses. But definitely *him*.

He turned back to the register, never really looking at her. Even from behind, the angle of his neck, the way his earlobe met his jaw . . .

Hugo.

Rose's heart slammed against the walls of her chest. She wasn't breathing.

Honk! A car was waiting behind them. Impatient for its turn.

Rose pulled forward, a small sip of oxygen finally making its way into her lungs. She paused in the parking lot, her foot on the brake.

Hugo.

That was Hugo.

It couldn't be, but it was.

Hugo in the building behind me. Hugo in a paper cap. Hugo in real life.

Hugo.

Hugo.

Hugo.

The van was filled with the smell of fried potatoes and salt. The children ate quietly, listening to the rain hit the roof of the van, a tin tap-tapping the only sound. Rose's mind raced.

Years before, when she was pregnant with Isaac, Rose had seen her aunt Barbara walking away from her in the international foods aisle of the grocery store.

What's she doing here? Rose had thought, delighted at the unexpected chance to catch up.

She had gotten as far as shouting "Bar—" when she remembered that Barb was dead. That she had been dead nine years, since an aneurysm had quietly plucked her from life. That Rose had helped her cousin pick the jewelry Barb's corpse would wear for the viewing. That she had let the flowers from the church wilt in the heat of her car during the gathering afterward at her uncle's home, and when she returned to it that night, it had smelled overwhelmingly of lilies, stale water, and floral foam.

The woman at the other end of the aisle stopped and turned toward the stilted sound Rose had made. Rose's eyes met hers for a moment, and the details that had made her "Barb" melted away in the contradictions. The high-waisted jeans over the flat landscape of her butt, the dry ginger cast of her hair, the slight hitch in her gait: The "Barb-ness" of her was still there, but it was subsumed by the "not-Barb-ness." The angle of her eyes. The gray cast of her skin. The slackness of her face.

The woman had looked away quickly and Rose had shuddered, pretending to study the rack of lasagna noodles while she composed herself.

Later, when she told Josh about the encounter, he had said that that sort of thing happened because the brain was a "pattern recognition machine," but it was a lazy one. Rose's brain had taken a shortcut, its best guess given the stimuli it was given (*ass, hair, walk*), and sent a ghost down the aisle of the Piggly Wiggly.

When Rose had said it was "spooky anyway," Josh had grinned and said the human brain was the spookiest thing he could imagine. "It's all dark corridors and creaky staircases," he had said in a mock dark voice before launching himself onto her with a kiss.

Sitting in the parking lot of the Orange Tastee, Rose tried to use the memory of Josh's voice to slow the heart racing beneath her seat belt.

To a brain, a person is nothing more than a pattern. A collection of stimuli . . . What had Josh called it? *A neural pathway.*

That's what had happened.

Rose racked her mind for the details that would melt him away. The "un-ness" that had dissolved Barb that day in the grocery store.

They did not come.

Maybe if I just got another look at him . . .

But she shook that thought off as soon as it arrived. Barb at least had been real. She had once been a living, breathing human with children and a wicked tennis serve.

But Hugo?

Hugo was never real. Rose was not asleep and on the beaches of her dreamland. She was conscious and sitting in her car in a shitty small town in eastern Colorado.

The tournament was canceled. Isaac's coach sent a mass text, which Rose received just as the kids were finishing up their meal.

Isaac took the news better than expected. The unfinished game defaulted in his team's favor, meaning that the winning goal had been his.

Rose drove them home on the rain-slick highway, stopping halfway at a gas station for a potty break. The boys begged to buy candy from metal display shelves, a wish that Rose uncharacteristically granted, handing each a dollar.

She put a mix of children's music into the player for the rest of the ride. The boys sang along to the songs about planets and paleontologists, listing the colors of the rainbow. They ate their candy bars and looked for Volkswagen Beetles on the highway. Penny fell asleep. They were happy.

Rose's mind raced. Filled with Hugo.

J osh had Sunday off. Though he'd wanted to take the kids to the park, maybe convince Penny to try the slide, the rain spoiled his plans.

Instead he had made pancakes. He had had to ask Rose

every step of the way where the necessary tools were ("Whisk?"
"Top drawer." "Griddle?" "Lower cabinet"), but he had managed
to make a family meal without poisoning them all.

Even Rose, who could get testy about the mess Josh would
make in the kitchen, didn't seem to mind as much as usual. She
sat at the table, staring out at the rain hitting their backyard,
while he took requests from the kids: A kitty for Pen. A Mickey
for Adam. A spider for Isaac.

After breakfast, everyone stayed in their pajamas. Though
neither Rose nor Josh said it, there was an implicit agreement
that today would be a "do-nothing day." Josh lay on the floor with
the boys, playing a third to their adventures; policing Penny,
making sure none of their Legos ended up in her mouth.

He was enamored with them. Fascinated. When did Penny
start stringing so many words together? When did Isaac's legs
get so long? When did Adam start looking so much like a tiny,
male version of Rose?

Josh looked at his wife, holding a cup of coffee, her feet
tucked up on the couch. Her eyes were distant, lost in thought.
He loved looking at her when she didn't know he was looking.
There was a tension that appeared around her mouth when she
knew she was being observed.

God, she is lovely.

Josh wanted to take her upstairs right now. Slip his hands up
the soft cotton of her T-shirt. Pull at the waistband of *his* pajama
bottoms, the ones she was wearing and had claimed for her own.

Josh saw none of the ugliness Rose saw in herself. She was to
him the perfect Rose. His Rose. His beautiful, single, blooming
Rose.

He got up from the floor and kissed her. Soft and sweet.
Chaste enough for the kids to see.

When he pulled away, she smiled at him. Distracted still, but appreciative of the gesture. He sat next to her, breathing in the smell of coffee and the tangy scent of her neck. "What are you thinking about?"

Rose's eyes sharpened. Finally with him, instead of the somewhere else she had been in the reaches of her mind.

"Nothing . . . I'm not thinking of anything." She chirped, "Should I make more coffee?"

Over the next week, Rose's mind boiled with the man from the drive-through. She made detailed lists of the things about him that were not Hugo: the cheap plastic glasses, the soft cup of a double chin, the thin peaks of hair on his forehead. In her dreams Hugo's eyes were perfect, able to see the herds of Bucks moving through the saw grass at a distance. And his jaw was firm. And his hair was full, shiny as it picked up in the breeze. The man in the window was nothing like Hugo.

But still . . .

His eyes had the same chocolate hue. His smile the same crooked shape. The plane of his nose the same angle.

The man looked like Hugo in disguise. Hiding the real him beneath a poly-blend shirt and the fledgling inner tube of male middle age.

Rose felt the way she had felt at her high school reunion, witnessing the decline of the beauty of youth. The faded jocks and wrinkled princesses. This man was as alike to Hugo as all those people were to their youthful counterparts. And like those strangely familiar grown-ups, this man looked like the Hugo she knew, but *worn*. Hugo without the gleam of the man in her dreams.

Rose tried to put him out of her mind. Concentrated on the immediate tasks of her life. Doing the laundry. Cleaning the car. Dropping the kids off at school.

But the man from the drive-through bubbled to the surface

even during these menial tasks. He was everywhere. He was a french fry crushed into the upholstery of Penny's car seat. He was the grass stain on the seat of Adam's soccer shorts. He was the head of the PTA, peeling an orange for her youngest, inquiring whether Rose would be attending Mommy's Margarita Night.

Rose had watched the woman's fingernails slide under the skin of the orange, pulling the fruit from the pith. *It wasn't possible. But still . . .*

"Rose? Will you be there?" The woman had had to pull her away from her thoughts of fast-food restaurants and imaginary men.

"Yes. Maybe. I—I'll try," Rose stammered, trying to cover.

Her dreams during this time did not change at all. There was nothing different about the island. Nothing different about the business she and Hugo conducted. Castle City remained a distant goal, the island remained a paradise.

No, that wasn't entirely true. There *was* something different. Rose noticed it in the moments of calm, when she'd watch Hugo as he beamed his confident grin at the distant horizon, studying the shape of his jaw, the trace of his hairline, comparing him with the Hugo she'd seen in her waking hours. The Man Who Was Not Hugo.

On those occasions, when Rose would turn to him to steal a look, she'd catch him glancing away furtively. As if he'd been studying her, too. And wondering the same things.

But upon waking, instead of lolling in the remembered glow of her time with Hugo, or resenting the fact that she had to wake up at all, Rose would lie in bed, her thoughts immediately traveling to a truck stop town sixty miles away, an inconsequential food stand, and the man who could be starting his shift there.

———

Naomi had a theory.

Rose had debated telling her about the apparition. She was worried it would make her seem crazy in a "not good" way. Movie crazy. Institution crazy.

That was why she had not told Josh. She didn't want to see the look on his face that would confirm her worst fears. That she'd come unhinged. That her mind had broken. That she was a disappointment yet again.

But somehow with Naomi, it came out.

The events of the day: the boys, the rain, the man in the window. The words spilled from her almost against her will. She felt more like a storyteller than a witness. *Was that how things had happened? Had it happened?*

When she finished Naomi was quiet for a moment. Rose could tell she was selecting her words.

"You said you started dreaming about Hugo when you had a bicycle accident. When you were six?"

Rose was surprised by this tack. "Yes."

"And Isaac, who'd been giving you trouble that morning, he wants a bike for his birthday."

Rose shook her head. She wasn't sure where Naomi was going, but she was certain it was the wrong direction. "That's not. It's not . . . I did *see* him."

Naomi was cautious. Gentle. "I'm just suggesting that dreams . . . That this man in the window . . . maybe in the heat of the moment, you were so upset with the boys, so out of control of your emotions, maybe your mind felt like you *needed* Hugo, so this man . . . coalesced with your image of him."

Rose was silent for a moment. This idea that her brain was tricking her. It was what Josh would have said. Dark corridors and spooky houses.

Of course that's what it must be. It sounded right.

But it didn't *feel* that way.

Still, Rose knew what she needed to say.

"Maybe."

Naomi looked at her a moment. "Rose, you *know* it wasn't really him."

"Yes. Of course."

That afternoon Adam got off the bus wielding a piece of paper. He waved it as he ran toward Rose.

"I drew a picture of Hugo!" he yelled, excited, breathless.

Rose held the page. "Who's this?" She pointed to the smaller figure, with a red crayon "U" of a smile standing next to Adam's vested rendition of Hugo.

"That's me. That's what I'll look like when I meet him in real life."

Rose held her breath. *In Real Life.*

"Hugo's imaginary, honey. You can't *actually* meet him."

"I know, but . . . it would be cool, though. Right, Mom?"

Right. Maybe. Or maybe it would mean you'd gone crazy. Rose wasn't sure what to say.

Isaac saved her. "Cool picture, Addy!" His eyes were quick, sliding over the details of the page. "I want to make one . . . Mom, can we draw before dinner?"

"Sure."

Later Rose put all three of the children in the bath at once. They were getting too big for it, of course, but they hadn't yet started complaining. The boys would bracket Penny's small girth in the tub, Isaac curling his long legs up and Adam sitting Indian style, his back to the faucet. There was always some drama when Penny's inevitable curiosity led her to grab at their penises, but even here the boys were accommodating.

"No, Pen-pen. That's a private area," they would tell her, gently pushing her small hand away.

Rose noticed that the boys were less likely to complain when she rinsed the soap out of their hair during these group baths. Since Penny would let Rose pour water on her head without a fuss, the boys were braver than when they were alone. They didn't want to be shown up by the baby.

Rose put on makeup while they splashed in the bath. Mommy's Margarita Night. A fund-raiser raising *funds* for . . . *what?* Rose didn't know, but she *had* gotten the e-mails and the phone calls and the flyers in the boys' backpacks. It was "Not to Be Missed!" and "Very Important! Full Parent Participation a Goal!!"

Rose didn't even like margaritas.

But she was going. Josh said it would be good for her to get out. He could get home early. . . .

Rose checked the clock. He was *already* fifteen minutes late.

She had showered. Put on a pair of pants with an actual zipper rather than a drawstring or elastic. They didn't look great, but . . . *at least I got the button to close.*

Rose sifted through the aged makeup in her bag. She couldn't even remember buying most of this stuff. She found an eyeliner that wasn't crumbling and put it to her lid.

The image of Kaitlin-with-the-boobs at the soccer fields flew into her mind. The way her perfectly mascara'd eyes had softened with pity for Rose and her poor neglected kids.

Fuck her and her fucking face. Rose flared with anger.

But before she was even done with that thought—before she could even feel bad for that *uncharitable,* mean thought—there he was again. Rising to the top of her mind.

The man in the window.

Hugo.

She had seen *Hugo* just hours after Kaitlin and her puppy dog sympathy and the new knowledge that Rose herself was the subject of "Mommy Gossip."

Rose corrected. *No, not Hugo. You didn't see Hugo. You just saw a man.*

"Mom?"

"Yes, honey."

She turned. All three of her children were sporting soapy Mohawks. They giggled at their conspiracy, grinning wildly.

"Very handsome."

"Not Penny. Penny's pretty."

"Of course, Adam. Penny is my pretty little punk rock girl."

From downstairs came the bang of the front door hitting the jamb. The distinct jangle of Josh's keys, the zip of his vinyl bag against his pants. "Sorry! Sorry! I'm home!" he shouted, accompanied by the crunch as he set his bag down. The thump of steps on the stairs.

"Patient transfer went a little long. I didn't forget I was babysitting."

Rose grimaced. "It's not called babysitting when it's your kids, it's called—"

"Parenting. I know."

Rose gave him a sad smile. She kissed the kids on their soapy foreheads. Three nosefuls of bubbles.

As she stepped into the hallway, Josh followed her. Alone for a moment.

"Hey."

Rose stopped, looking back at him.

His face was concerned. "I really am sorry."

She nodded, pulling up her chin. "I know. I'm just . . . late."

———

Rose watched them from the dark interior of her car. Packs of mothers making their way into the restaurant. All in their "going out" clothes, their hair freshly done. They smiled and laughed as they walked from the parking lot to the door. Happy to have an evening away from the kids. Happy to have an excuse to drink on a school night. What did they call Chardonnay? Housewife heroin.

She noticed many of them had carpooled, emptying out of minivans like clown cars filled with middle-aged women of privilege.

No one had asked Rose to carpool. They had pestered her, yes. Insisted she come . . .

But no one had asked her to share a ride.

Dear God, she didn't want to do this.

She didn't want to be the woman these mothers thought she was. She didn't want to spend a night trying to think of the next thing to say. *She didn't want to be who she was when she was who she was.*

And then there he was again. Filling her mind.

The man in the window.

Hugo.

Not Hugo.

Rose started the car and pulled out of the parking lot, her mind finally quiet; still not ready to acknowledge what she was about to do.

It took her fifty minutes to get to Hemsford, though Rose didn't know it. She hadn't looked at the speedometer or the clock the entire way, driving instinctually in the dark, weaving around the red taillights of the other cars.

It seemed to Rose that one moment she had been accelerating onto the street away from the gathering pack of mommies and the next she was pulling up to the curb outside the Orange Tastee. It was frightening to realize she'd driven all that way, barely conscious of her actions, her thoughts otherwise occupied.

Of course her husband would tell her this was due to yet another miraculous trick of the mind. The prefrontal cortex handing the drudgery of the steering and braking off to its subordinates, farther down the chain of command . . . so she could put her mind on more important things.

Like the man from the window's face.

Rose peered through the plate glass of the restaurant. Inside, two teenagers, a boy and a girl, were leaning against the counter, talking to each other. The yellow Formica tables of the dining area were all empty, reflecting the green-light stutter of the fluorescents above.

What the hell was she doing here?

Idiot. Rose leaned her forehead against the curve of the steering wheel.

The boy hefted his bulk onto the counter. Making himself more comfortable. He was talking with his hands. Universal gestures favored by teenage boys for use while bullshitting.

Whatever he was saying, he was lying. Rose could tell by his posture, by the way he didn't move his shoulders.

But the girl was fooled. She shifted position, too, stepping a little bit closer to him. Taking the paper hat off of her head, running her fingers through her hair. Laughing.

Rose exhaled. *This is so stupid.*

A banging sounded from behind the building. A slam clatter. Plastic against metal.

Rose lifted her eyes to it. And there he was.

Hugo.

"No," she said. Aloud.

Not *Hugo* but still . . . *Him.*

The Man Who Was *Not* Hugo.

He was behind the restaurant. Pushing bags of trash into a Dumpster.

Rose stopped breathing.

He wore a blue windbreaker over his uniform.

He had very little of Hugo's beauty. None of his swagger.

And yet the way he moved his body—it was the same.

He jumped with Hugo's knees, threw garbage bags with Hugo's wrists. The muscles of his back, straining to push the lid of the Dumpster over the top—they were Hugo's trapezius, Hugo's latissimus dorsi, Hugo's iliac crest—but moving with a weariness Rose had never ascribed to him at all.

The man did indeed have very little of Hugo's grace . . . but there was something. A ghost of some kind. Like the remnants of a drink left on the sides of a glass.

Rose watched as he swung closed the gate of the fence surrounding the Dumpster. He locked its chain with a key on his ring and walked to a tired blue car in the parking lot, then swung himself inside. Rose watched his silhouette pull the shoulder belt. The running lights of the car flared to life.

She followed him to a small matchbox house in a neighborhood north of the soccer fields. The homes here suffered a little from the stink of eau de white trash, weeds peppering the sidewalks, ratty garbage bins in front of the houses.

The Man Who Was Not Hugo pulled into the driveway of a house nearly identical to the rest. It was, Rose noticed, a little better kept than the others. Its grass was freshly cut, its garden hose in a neat coil by the front step.

Rose parked just down the street, killing her lights as he got out of his car.

She squinted, leaning forward toward her windshield. Trying

to make out as much as possible in the sodium glare of the street lamp.

Her phone rang, startling her. Josh.

It could be an emergency.

But the Man Who Was Not Hugo was suddenly on the steps of his house. If she took the call, she could miss something. Some clue. She let it go to voice mail.

A cat ran out of the darkness, leaping onto the stoop. A white-and-orange tabby. The kind Penny called "sun kitties." The Man Who Was Not Hugo knelt to greet it, stroking under its chin.

He unlocked the door and let himself and the cat inside. Behind the shaded windows, Rose saw the lights of the house switch on. A flickering blue indicating he had turned on the television.

The phone rang again. She picked up.

Josh wanted to know where the sheets were. Adam had wet the bed. He'd let him have too much milk before bedtime. When would she be home?

seven

They were on the beach when they heard the rumbling. A growing thunder from beyond the saw grass. Rose's eyes tripped over the waves of green, searching for the source.

"That can't be good."

She turned to Hugo and he flashed her a grin. Tall gorgeous tan toothy Hugo. *Rose's* Hugo.

The rumbling grew louder. Closer.

"We should get moving."

He shrugged, smile still on his lips.

The tops of the most distant grass began to bend and shift, cutting a wide swath toward them. The thunder broke into its distinct components, the sound of a thousand hooves beating the ground.

"Oh God." Rose began to run just as the antlers of the first Bucks burst from the grass.

A stampede.

Hugo was closer to the edge of the shore. His feet bit into the sand, seeking traction as he sprinted farther up the beach, the shifting grit slowing his pace.

But despite this, he was in less danger than Rose, who had been on firmer ground but yards closer to the point where the Bucks had emerged from the grass.

The animals were panicking. Their eyes wide, revealing the recessed whites. They were gnashing their teeth at one another, lips curled, exposing ruminant incisors.

But more dangerous were the antlers. There were no females in the island's herds, no gentle does, only thousands of horned males. Their antlers grew to enormous proportions, points sharpened against the trees in the forest or in combat against one another.

Rose's bare feet carried her closer to the loose soil that banked the saw grass; she could move faster here than she could closer to Hugo on the open reaches of the shore. Behind her she could hear the clattering of antlers striking one another. The Bucks were running close, preferring the safety of the stampeding herd to the less treacherous exposure of solitude.

The Spider leaped out of the saw grass, landing on the beach, its diamond-shaped metatarsals sending a spray of pink sand into the air. It was a large one, even by the standards of the island, its thorax hovering ten feet above the ground.

"Rose!" Hugo was still moving, making the best of his head start, but his neck was turned toward the monster behind the oncoming horde. He needed her to know of the real danger.

She knew.

The Bucks were gaining on her, their panic rising now the hunter was in the open.

Rose angled closer to the blades of grass, reaching out toward them. Every step that didn't push her farther away from the Bucks and their clamoring hooves and their clattering racks was a risk. But she needed a weapon.

The first two plants slid from her grasp. She was moving too fast to catch hold. But she was able to wrap her palm around the third, using the momentum from her body to pull it from the ground.

In her hand the blade transformed, growing a handle to fit her grip, pulling into itself, its sides sharpening. A sword. As strong as steel, but still as green as the plant it had come from.

She had what she needed, but they were running out of space. Up ahead the saw grass gave way to a rocky outcropping . . . the herd was going to get pushed onto the beach.

It was then that they overtook her.

She was lucky she wasn't speared in those first moments. The lead Bucks were less close together than their brothers farther back. Rose pulled as close as she could to the body of the nearest animal, her free hand trying to catch hold of the lowest prong of its antlers. Maybe if she could swing onto its back . . .

Behind her and yet somehow *above* came an inhuman scream. The Spider had plucked one of the animals from the rear of the herd, seizing it with its enormous palpae. Rose turned her head in time to see the Buck's spine crunch between the monster's dark mandibles. The Buck screamed again before folding in half and slipping farther into the Spider's maw.

The herd turned onto the beach. Rose tried to keep apace, but she had two legs to their four. Ahead of her the end of a Buck's antler caught the eye of a second, blinding it. The creature tumbled, its front legs folding.

Rose leaped over its body just in time to miss the second animal that collided with it.

Where was Hugo?

The sword felt sweaty, slippery in her hand. Her thighs burned. She could barely breathe.

Where was he?

Movement to her right. A dark shape. Brown hair studded with sand. Striking from above.

Rose veered left and the Spider's palpae seized the Buck next to her, yanking it from the ground. She looked up; its hooves tread air, still running, going nowhere but into the beast's mouth. A spray of blood hit the back of her neck as the Spider consumed its latest morsel.

Where the hell was Hugo?

A stream of sunlight bored a hole through the clouds. It threaded through the air, making its way to the surface of the island. The thread grew, prying the clouds from the sun, until the whole of the far end of the beach was alight with a magic shimmer.

There he was. Standing in the shadow, watching the edge of the newly glowing sand. His face was calm. Waiting.

Behind him the line of sunlight raced forward, moving toward Hugo and the galloping herd.

He turned as beams struck the sand just inches from his feet and began running toward Rose. The vanguard of a pure line of light.

The Spider was now among them, keeping pace above the charging Bucks. Rose looked up. Its abdomen loomed above her, its pelt sticky with gore and sand. A metatarsus pierced through the air, punching the ground next to Rose. Large hairs jutted from the shell of its mottled leg.

Rose hacked at it with the blade, piercing its carapace. There was a wet snap as the sword cracked into its exoskeleton, a brittle break into the meat of its leg.

The Spider reared up with a shriek, its lower abdomen dropping, knocking the bodies of the Bucks in its path forward. The deer, wild-eyed, broke through its legs, scattering onto the beach.

Rose pulled on the blade. It was wedged in the ugly shell of its leg. She wrapped both hands around it—

Something whisker soft brushed the underside of her arms.

And then suddenly she was in the air, sword in her hand, pulled out like a splinter—and she the tweezers. The hairs of the Spider's pedipalps jutted through the soft cotton of her blouse, a secure hold about her waist.

The beast was still shrieking, a river of blue-green blood gushing from the rent in its leg. It shook Rose, whipping her about—

—giving her a view of Hugo, running toward them. A blinding edge of light in his wake.

And then the beams hit the area beneath his feet . . . and he was flying. Forward motion launching him from the glowing sand directly into the Spider's thorax, driving it backward. Rose was thrown from its grip, the sword flying from her sweat-drenched palm.

Hugo clung to the beast's carapace, his hands catching hold of its piebald layer of hair. The creature shrieked as he braced himself on the edges of its joints. Out of reach and climbing.

Rose hit the sand solid on her back, all the air in her lungs rushing out at once. She gasped, stunned by the impact.

"Rose! The sword!"

Hugo had crested the Spider's back and was clinging as it whipped around wildly, trying to throw him off.

Rose rolled to her knees. She felt like she could barely see. Still, she had been holding the sword only a minute ago. Where had it gone?

The Spider's shrieking rocketed up an octave as Hugo saddled himself on the bony ridge above its eye.

A glint under the sand. A few feet away. Rose crawled to it, frantic, her hands sweeping . . .

A pair of bright cartoon eyes winked up at her beneath the pink silt.

Rose felt her brows crease.

It was the Orange Tastee. The sun-faded fiberglass speaker from the drive-through. She brushed at the sand, pink particles escaping into the battered grille of its mouth. *What is this doing here?*

"Rose! There."

She looked up. The Spider was thrashing, its legs unable to reach the pest on its back. Its motion had carried them farther down the shoreline. Hugo was pointing away from Rose. Her eyes followed the line of his hand.

The sword gleamed bare in a mound of coral sand. Like Excalibur, only waiting to be pulled.

Rose raced toward it, the mystery of the Orange forgotten. She wrapped her hand around its handle and winged it, throwing it end over end toward Hugo.

He caught it in the air and drove it two-handed into the beast's flat black eye. The Spider collapsed to the ground, a pulsing hemorrhage of oily blood spilling down its body.

Atop its corpse, Hugo laughed and brushed his hair out of his eyes. He smiled down at Rose on the sand.

His car had not been at the Orange Tastee when she arrived, an hour and fifteen minutes after kissing the boys good-bye and watching them find their seats on the school bus.

Maybe it was his day off.

She searched for his house by instinct, lefts and rights by feel, not remembering the dark path she had followed him on that night. Though the town was small, daylight revealed a sad sameness to the dwellings of its citizens. Each street was identical in its shabbiness. She drove through its tired little neighborhoods, turning onto streets labeled "Oak" and "Sycamore" that showed no growth of either of those noble species. Her heart raced, convinced she would never find the place where the Man Who Was Not Hugo lived.

It was the coil of garden hose that finally let her know she had found it. Its neatness, a tidy stack, unique in this ugly, fallow place. And then she saw his car in the driveway, two cement strips separated by a patch of dying grass.

Rose noticed that the Man Who Was Not Hugo's license plate read 349SXY. She presumed it wasn't intentional and was instead one of those accidental DMV abbreviations people were sometimes saddled with: 47GYN0, L3BTW7, 57ROTF.

She parked opposite. A few houses down. Close enough to see . . . not close enough to draw notice.

He exited about fifteen minutes later, wearing the same blue jacket she had seen on him before. On his head was a battered Broncos cap, its cloth-over-plastic bill frayed on the edge. Rose could almost see him as good-looking. The kind of attraction that increased as you got to know someone. He was older, paler, and at least ten to twenty pounds overweight, but certainly not repulsive in any way.

At least no more repulsive than she was in comparison with the woman *she* was in her dreams.

I guess we have that in common, Rose thought . . . and then she shook off the ridiculousness of her supposing this actually was *Hugo*.

He bounded down the stairs and into the car without looking up, without looking over, without noticing the minivan parked across the street or the watching woman behind its wheel.

The Walmart she followed him to was three towns away.

The Man Who Was Not Hugo found a parking space and locked his car just as Nemo was reunited with Marlin. Synchronicity.

From the back of the car, Penny's voice said, "Mama? We go in now?"

Rose turned to her daughter. Penny grinned at her from the car seat. She kicked her legs, little feet ending in the scalloped white sandals she had insisted on wearing that morning.

Through the windshield, Rose could see the Man Who Was Not Hugo pull a cart from the row and head toward the automatic doors.

"Yes. We go in now, honey."

Rose knew this wasn't healthy. She knew people had a name for this behavior. She knew that following *anyone,* much less a complete stranger, was generally the first part of those real-crime television shows that ran constantly on the higher reaches of her cable box . . . and that after the commercial break the story always took a turn for the worse.

But she assured herself that she wasn't doing anything *that* wrong.

She was just *looking.*

And Penny had been perfectly happy to watch videos in the car. As far as she was concerned, today was no different from any other day she ran around town doing chores with Mama.

Rose figured it wasn't even a complete ruse, as long as she got a few things here. If they happened to pass something the family needed, she would just drop it in her cart.

Besides, they would look less suspicious that way.

Rose shook her head. *People who are just shopping at Walmart don't worry that their empty carts look suspicious.*

But it did not stop her from circling the store until she caught sight of the faded orange of his hat. Perusing the shelves in the automotive aisle.

Rose paused by a display of paper goods. Rolls of Bounty paper towels. Walmart was rolling back the price to $8.99 for thirteen. Rose took note that this was a good deal even as she cheated her body behind the display so she could see him.

The Man Who Was Not Hugo was crouching by the motor oils. He had pulled two from the shelves and was comparing them, reading their backs. Judging the various weights. The advantages one brought over the other for a few dollars more.

Rose studied him.

The subtle arc of the beds of his fingernails. The way his dark hair curled under the plastic joining of the cap. The way the bone of his wrist met and twisted beneath the meat of his hand.

Rose could almost see those hands as she had last night. Plucking a shining green blade out of the sky, driving it down into the brain of a monster. Strong hands.

It was impossible. Everything about this man was impossible. How could this stranger look so like the man who lived in her mind?

"Mama!"

He looked up, his attention drawn by Penny's shout.

Rose quick-stepped behind the display, her heart racing.

"Mama. We look at toys now?"

Rose shook her head and fled. Trying to catch her breath as she pushed Penny and the empty cart toward the front of the store and escape.

Rose's surveillance of the Man Who Was Not Hugo went on for weeks.

It became routine. Put boys on bus, pack snacks for Penny, drive to Hemsford, follow *him*.

She became an expert in the pattern of his life. That he did his errands during the week told her that his days off were Tuesdays and Thursdays—from which Rose extrapolated that he must work on weekends. His visits to the Laundromat told her that he didn't own a washer or a dryer. Rose would watch him as he sat outside reading, waiting for his clothes to finish; he favored cheap science fiction, the kind with aliens and large-breasted women on the covers. He ate lunch out a few times at a local pizza joint, ordering the salad. Through the windows Rose had noticed the way he stabbed at the iceberg shreds, dousing them in ranch dressing.

That's exactly how Hugo would eat salad, she thought. *I mean, if I ever saw him eat salad.*

The nearest grocery store was twenty miles away, a trip he dutifully took once a week. He always stopped at one of the larger towns' chain restaurants before heading to the store. Olive Garden. Chili's. Applebee's. Rose's heart sank whenever he pulled into one of these places . . . she knew she had no chance of watching him from the windows, their darkened interiors protecting him from her scrutiny.

After the close call in the Walmart, Rose never again followed him inside the places where he ran his errands. She knew she could very easily slip inside one of these restaurants, just another customer. Order the kid's meal for Penny. Watch *him* from the darkness of an upholstered booth.

But if she did, he might see *her.*

The thought of this terrified Rose.

Rose didn't know what she thought would happen if the Man Who Was Not Hugo saw her. . . . Something . . . something not *bad,* but also not *good.*

The idea of it made her stomach feel hard. He couldn't see her. Shouldn't see her.

So she stayed outside the restaurants and the Laundromat. Hidden in the safety of her minivan.

In all this time she saw him take only one phone call. He had stepped outside the Orange Tastee, cell to his ear. Paced back and forth in the shadow of the restaurant's eaves. As he talked, he squinted at the bright cars passing on the street. And for a brief moment, his eyes had passed over her car, parked on the opposite side.

For an instant Rose felt as though he had seen her. Caught.

Adrenaline flooded her body, causing her muscles to tense, her breath to quicken, pupils to dilate, the delicate hair on her skin to lift at the root.

But he looked away quickly, seeing only the reflection of the street on her windshield. Rose knew she was safe.

But her body still roiled with the aftereffects of the flight impulse. It took minutes for her heart to steady. The hairs on the back of her neck and beneath her panties shifted, settling back to their unalerted positions.

His phone call was short. Eight minutes, Rose noted, before he headed back inside.

The Man Who Was Not Hugo led a life of quiet routine. He seemed happy enough, though Rose had seen an existence that looked lonely. *Probably single,* she thought. There was little evidence of anyone in his life.

But Rose supposed she could be missing things: things that happened on the weekend, when she could not get away to watch; things that happened in the evenings, when she was required at home.

It was during these times that she thought of him most, extracting meaning from the details she had observed. She made dinner and tended to the kids and Josh with the same parts of her mind that had driven her to Hemsford in the first place. She ran on automatic, all the while allowing her higher functions to fill with the life of the Man Who Was Not Hugo.

Penny, compliant baby, happy girl, was witness to all of this— though "witness" is a hard word to use for the way a two-year-old observes the world.

The little girl settled easily into Rose's new routine, soothed with the electronic crack of Disney's oeuvre playing on repeat over the minivan's entertainment system. She napped in her car seat. Ate lunch in her car seat. Lived in her car seat.

After a spectacularly messy accident, Rose had started to bring Penny's potty seat on these trips. This she would set up in the aisle of the car, where Pen would sit, straining her neck to keep her eyes on the still running movie.

Rose would empty the leavings in a gas station on the way back home. All the driving was certainly having an effect on how many times she needed to fill up during the week. Thankfully, Josh never looked too closely at the credit card bill.

So Rose limited Penny's fluids. Less in meant less out.

When the car was finally too much and her little girl started whining and pulling at her seat belt straps, and even Elsa and Anna couldn't convince her to settle, Rose would drive to the flat, grassy park on the edge of town. There she would watch Penny romp through the playground for an hour, hanging from the swings, digging in the sand. And when time was up, Penny would easily climb back into her seat, ready for another "wideo," as she would say it. Rose would then drive back to the Orange Tastee, hoping to get one last look before heading back in time to meet the boys as they disembarked from the bus.

Penny's mother knew none of this was good for her. Penny had a full life back home, filled with music class and pre-preschool, swimming lessons and enrichment. Penny had playdates, scheduled weeks in advance.

She deserved better than this, Rose knew.

But Penny's willingness to go along with whatever Mommy said made it easy for Rose to think that this "thing" she was doing wasn't all that bad. Pen wasn't unhappy. For her, all these videos were like a vacation.

And there was the added benefit that she couldn't yet tell anyone what Mommy was doing all day.

Rose canceled three appointments before Naomi called to ask if she was terminating therapy.

"Oh no," Rose had said. "No. I think that would . . . I think that would be a bad idea." At the moment she said this she had been on the highway, driving back from Hemsford.

When Naomi finally had her, guilted into the gloom of her office, Rose confessed only to following the Man Who Was Not Hugo *once*.

She told her the tale of Walmart.

Naomi's reaction made her glad she had not let on to the deeper truth. Her therapist's body shifted as she spoke, alerting to the danger in Rose's words.

"This was just one time?"

"Uh-hm." Rose was afraid a full "yes" might reveal the lie.

But leaking this smaller truth allowed Rose to finally give voice to the thoughts that had occupied her for the past weeks.

"I feel like . . . like, he's hijacked my brain. It's becoming a problem. I'm always thinking about him. Obsessing."

Naomi was quiet.

"I know he's not Hugo." Said Rose firmly, "I do."

Naomi relaxed a little in her chair. The danger had passed, her patient had a grip on reality. "Okay. Let's try another tack. Let's *indulge* this fantasy that this is the man of your dreams."

"In," Rose responded.

"Pardon?"

"He is the man *in* my dreams. Not *of*."

Naomi pursed her lips at the distinction. Moved on. "What would happen if you introduced yourself?"

A granite hardness landed in Rose's stomach.

"Rose, you're asking me for the quickest way to detach yourself from this fixation. This man *isn't* Hugo. Hugo doesn't exist. But some part of you—the part that is obsessing over him—isn't quite convinced. The quickest way for you to convince that part of yourself that this man isn't who you think he is is to introduce yourself to him."

Introduce yourself? Rose couldn't really wrap her brain around the idea. One introduces oneself to people at weddings, to insurance salesmen, to neighbors. One doesn't just walk up to strangers and hold out one's hand. "Hi, my name is Rose and I've been stalking you for weeks."

And this man *was* a stranger. Though she knew details about him, the schedule of his life, he was no more to her than any other person in the world. *She didn't even know his name.* He was just some *guy*, who through some trick of the genetic lottery looked an awful lot like someone she had made up in her mind.

"If I do this . . . then what? What happens?"

"You will confirm that he is just a man. That he is not Hugo. You will be able to detach from these obsessive thoughts and go back to your normal life."

And my normal thoughts, thought Rose.

She had been so occupied with this man, the project of following him, that it had been weeks since she had thought about what a disappointment she was. What a failure she was. What a waste of sad flesh she was.

It had been nice, obsessing about someone else instead of her own failings.

A holiday from herself.

But still, it had to stop.

Rose just wasn't sure that letting *him* see her was the way. It felt perilous—though what the danger was, she had no idea.

Her stomach was still hard as stone when she drove away from Naomi's office.

Isaac was giving the hard sales pitch as Rose got them ready for school. Talking a mile a minute: "Ben Winters said if I had a bike, then this summer we could ride on the trails by the river. And Teddy Kosar said *he* got a bike when he was five. And Ben said he got his when he was *three*, but I don't believe him."

"I don't believe him either." Adam was trying to be helpful.

Oh, Lord, thought Rose. *Again with the bikes.*

Isaac was refusing to act as he had in the past. Until now he had never settled for long on what toy he most desired; the constantly shifting landscape of greed made Christmas shopping difficult and birthday shopping a nightmare. At Christmastime Rose combated this proclivity by making the boys write letters to Santa in the first week of December. That way when they (inevitably) changed their minds about what they wanted, she could remind them they had written to Santa about their old heart's desire and that he wasn't likely to be able to read their minds.

That said, this did not keep Rose from going shopping on Christmas Eve, attempting to put whatever newer better cooler thing they craved into Santa's sack. But at least if she failed, she had managed to curb their expectations and avoid a little bit of Christmas-morning disappointment.

Usually this far out from "B-day" Isaac would have changed his mind five or six times already, leaping from the latest gaming system to whatever new piece of masculine crap Nerf was selling and back again.

But, to Rose's chagrin, the bike was sticking.

Rose had left toy catalogs on the kitchen table in hopes of something new catching Zackie's eye. Instead of fast-forwarding through the ads flanking the boys' favorite shows on the DVR as she usually did, she had let them play, steeping the boys in their bright commercial flogging.

But still the bike stuck . . . though Zackie had a few fresh ideas for what he'd like from his grandparents.

Finally Rose just told him to pick something else.

"But why?" he'd asked.

She had shown him the scar buried in her hair. She had told him the story of that day when Papa had shown her how to ride a bicycle.

"Bicycles are dangerous, sweetie. And I don't know what I would do if anything ever happened to you. I just want you to wait a couple more years."

"How much longer?"

"Maybe when you're ten."

Isaac had closed his mouth at this. Looked away. But he was quiet.

Rose knew better than to think it was over.

Instead of accepting his mother's proscription, Zackie began collecting evidence in *his* favor, hence the polling of his friends for the age at which they had gotten their bikes.

And he had, naturally, recruited Adam in this endeavor, which was even worse, as Adam discovered that most of his friends, too, already had bikes and knew how to ride them.

"Dad said the reason you got hurt is because when you were kids people didn't wear helmets . . . and I would always always always wear my helmet."

Rose wanted to murder her husband. *When had he said this? He knew how she felt about it. So much for a united front.*

"Did Daddy also tell you that I didn't wake up for five days and that Baba and Papa thought I might never wake up?"

Adam's little mouth opened. "Like Sleeping Beauty?"

Rose shook her head. "Not fun like Sleeping Beauty."

Isaac furrowed his brow. Rose could tell he was already thinking of his next plan of attack.

Josh was repentant.

"Sorry, honey. I didn't think it would be a thing. He just asked after you showed him your scar."

Rose had had Josh paged. He had called immediately, thinking that something had happened to one of the children, and was relieved to find that it was just this quirk of Rose's. He relaxed. Even though he could hear the edge of frustration in her voice, it was nice to hear it during the day. She sounded clearer than she had in recent weeks, closer.

Rose sighed. "I'm sorry. This is my fault."

This had happened because she hadn't been paying attention. She had been too busy thinking about that *man* to attend to her kids.

"Oh, before I forget, the preschool called me. They must have our numbers mixed up."

Rose felt her heart stop. Penny hadn't been to school in weeks.

"They left a message asking if Pen was okay. They said she hasn't been in in a while?"

"That's weird." Rose felt the lie come easily. "Must be another Penny in one of the other classes. I'll call and let them know they have the wrong one."

"You're such a good mom, Rose."

Rose was quiet. *She was a horrible mother. She was the worst mother. She was a negligent liar of a mother.*

"I love you so much."

"You too."

Rose hung up. She had to fix this. She had to get rid of these thoughts that had pulled her away from her family.

Her stomach seized again.

eight

She called the neighborhood woman. Mrs. Delvecchio, the widow with the lovely garden and the house that smelled of stale potpourri. *Could she take Penny for a few hours?*

Of course, dear.

Rose had dropped her off with a stuffed diaper bag and a promise to be back soon. The ancient television in the Widow Delvecchio's den was already running network cartoons when she left. Rose shrugged it off.

"No worse than she's gotten in the car with me these past few weeks."

She was getting started later than she'd like. Talking with Josh and waiting for Mrs. D to call back had eaten away her morning. She'd be rushing to get back on time.

But what she had planned wouldn't take too long.

Just a quick encounter, a brief eye contact, and she'd be healed. She'd be home in time to have ants on a log waiting for the boys when they got back from school. Their mother returned to them, as good as she ever was.

Whatever that was worth.

Rose had decided she couldn't do what Naomi had suggested. She couldn't *introduce* herself.

But there was a simple way to get close to him. To look him in the eye and *see*.

Today was his shift. All she had to be able to do was order lunch.

Traffic was heavier this late in the day. Clogged with trucks from Denver's distribution centers sent out to the exotic reaches of Nebraska, Kansas, and beyond. It took Rose longer than usual to reach the battered exit sign, to turn onto the loop of the ramp and head into town.

Two large touring buses dominated the parking lot of the Orange Tastee, their bifold doors open. Teenagers teemed out of them, filtering from the buses to the restaurant. Rose parked the van and watched them through the windshield.

She could tell they weren't American teenagers. The boys' pants were just a little too high and the girls' shirts were just a little too loose. European, probably, possibly German, their faces characterized by wide, round cheekbones. A few of the boys wore highlights in their spiked hair, shyly touching the hardened tips as they smiled at the girls.

This was good, Rose reasoned. She could just slip in among them.

Still, her heart thumped. *No. No. No. No.*

It was two thirty.

If she was going to do it, she had to do it now. The boys got home just after four.

Rose sat for another five minutes before she finally was able to force herself out of the car.

Inside, the restaurant was packed. Every table was filled with exuberant Aryan teenagers, happy to be off the bus, filling the air with the scent of foreign pheromones. These *überkinder* flitted from one table to the next, chattering in their hard language, their cadences a strange music in this place.

Rose stood in line behind a passel of them. *What were they doing here? What lame tour of America had included this stop?*

Though she had stared at its interior for weeks, Rose had never been inside the Orange Tastee. She hadn't tasted its food. Even that first time she had ordered only for the kids.

It smelled of oranges and burning meat, the char of the grill carrying over the sickly sweet smell that comes from too much fruit. The scent called to her mind the bees and flies that hover over trash at summer barbecues.

The small staff was clearly overwhelmed with the demands of the customers, ordering hot dogs and Pepsis in careful, Teutonic-accented English.

The teen girl Rose had seen that first night was at a register ("Could you say that again, I don't understand you"), struggling to handle the influx of cash and sending the orders to the cooks in the back.

Rose saw no sign of the boy who had been with her on that first night. The Bullshitter was absent.

For an oddly hopeful moment, Rose thought maybe the Man Who Was Not Hugo would not be there either. Maybe she had gotten the days wrong. Maybe he was sick. Maybe she wouldn't have to do this.

But then he stepped out from the back, shooing the girl away from the register. Sending her into the recesses of the store-room to fetch more cups.

Rose couldn't breathe.

Everything will be okay.

Rose repeated the mantra that got her through takeoffs and landings.

Everything will be okay. Everything will be okay. This is perfectly safe.

Rose looked at the glass doors of the exit to her right. She could leave.

"Ma'am, may I take your order?"

Rose looked up at *him*. His eyes were on the register. Waiting.

This was as close as she'd ever been. She could see the spot on his cheek where he'd missed with his razor this morning. The frayed edges of his fingernails.

She swallowed. "Uh . . . a Tastee Dog . . . and fries."

His fingers danced over the keys.

"Would you like a drink with—"

He looked up and Rose saw it happen.

His bland smile faltered as his eyes met her searching face. Pupils widening. His breath stopped.

"—that."

He stared at Rose, the pink draining from his cheeks. Rose heard a sound bubble from her lips.

"You . . ."

He pulled his eyes back to the register, his head shaking slightly, flicking her away. Shaking her off. Swatting at that impossible thing that just transpired, sending it away.

Recognition.

"You know me."

Rose heard a voice say it, and he flinched. It took a moment for her to recognize the voice as hers. *Her* voice speaking words from *her* mouth, far away, beneath the rushing sound in her ears.

He turned away from her, his hands shaking as he pulled a tray from beneath the counter. He pulled a dog and a cone of fries from the stainless shelf.

He turned back, head down. Avoiding her eyes.

"Will that be cash or charge?"

Maybe she had imagined it. Rose started to doubt what she had seen just seconds ago. Her brain felt as if it were falling, reaching for a thought to hold on to, something to make sense of the "thisness" of this moment. But the thoughts were coming too quickly to form; there were no words for this sensation, no precedent for this moment.

She handed him her credit card.

He took it without looking up. Again he shook his head. Pinched at the spot where his eyes met his nose.

"I'm sorry, did you say you wanted a drink?"

He waited for her to answer. Rose could barely make sense of the syllables he had said. Finally, reluctant, he looked up at her.

And she *knew.*

"I thought I was . . . but . . . you *know me.*"

The Man Who Was Not Hugo . . . Who Could *Not* Be Hugo . . . shook his head, a violent jerk. He was trembling. Sweating suddenly and profusely, a small, clear smatter of dew appearing under the lip of his paper cap. He was breathing in sharp sips, gasping, a panic attack setting in.

And in the center of this storm his eyes anchored on her. Locked. Hooked on her. He was lost in seeing her. He was lost in looking at Rose. In the impossibility of *her.*

The stone in Rose's stomach lurched upward into her lungs. *Recognition.*

He turned suddenly, almost a spasm, knocking her tray to the floor. The fries and the dog hit the tile, rolling toward the kitchen.

"Hugo, are you all right?"

It came out of her mouth naturally. *His name.* Surely his name. Indisputably his name. She said it as she had said it a thousand thousand times on the island, making sure he was safe, making sure he was there.

Hugo.

His eyes went *wide* at those two small syllables. He stepped back, distancing himself from her, tripping over his feet. Suddenly he was falling backward into the prep station, tumbling to the floor, and everyone was staring at him. The employees, the Germans . . . and *Rose.*

He gasped, "Air. I need air!"

He stumbled to his feet, his arms forward, flailing. He pushed past the counter, his hands slapping the glass of the door. Pushing. And then he was outside.

And then, as she had done a thousand thousand times before, Rose followed him.

She followed him onto the cold, clear shimmer of the pavement. The stark Colorado light reflected off the parked cars, sharpening the shadows on his back as he ran from her.

"Hugo! Hugo, please stop!"

He stopped and turned to her. His face was angry. Furious.

"Nobody calls me Hugo anymore."

Rose stopped. Ten feet from him . . . trying to make sense of what he'd just said. *Anymore. Which meant . . .*

He shifted, his palms curling into themselves. Gone was the

gasping man at the counter, and here was a rattlesnake. A coiled threat.

"Look, this isn't funny. I'm sure whoever got you to do this thought maybe you could pass . . . and you're very close, but . . ."

"But what?" Rose heard herself speak. Words lost in the wind. She sounded like a child. Tiny.

"No offense, you sort of look like her, but not really. You're like her older, fatter sister."

Rose felt his words real as a slap. Full-handed sting.

And finally all the feelings and thoughts that had been flying past her as she had stood in that line, too fast to be fixed on, finally settled on a firm desire.

Violence.

Rose wanted to hurt him. To make him feel the way she felt. To fly across the space between them and bury her thumbs into his eye sockets. To pound his face into nothingness until he looked nothing like the man she dreamed of every night, until he was just some fat, ugly stranger with a bad job who lived in a shit town.

But instead she started screaming, "Do you think you look exactly like you do in my dreams? In child molester glasses? Or a polyester shirt? Working in an Orange Julius rip-off?" Rose felt the tears coming, racing toward her eyes, the hot flush on her neck, the ache at the back of her tongue.

She would not let him see that. She would not give him that.

"Goddamn it!" And then she was moving toward her van. Reeling toward it.

Escape.

"Wait!" she heard in the distance.

She wrapped her hand around the door, pulling. It jammed,

the lock stuck between positions. Rose cursed, begged, pleaded, yanking on it. *Please get me away. Let me out of this.* The insurgent tears reached her eyes.

"What do you mean?"

He was walking toward her, his eyes softer now. "What do you mean, 'in my dreams'?"

The lock gave, the door releasing. Blessed escape. Rose threw herself inside, jamming the keys into the ignition. He was almost next to her.

The stone inside her had reversed course and was pulling her under . . . down . . . down.

Rose crumpled behind the wheel, burying her face in her hands. *Idiot. You pathetic idiot. You thought this would make things better, you thought this would make it so life could go back to normal. But this is so much worse.*

He knocked on the glass, his face concerned. He said something, but his voice was muffled.

Rose couldn't look at him. She shook her head as she started the car. "I was wrong. This is wrong. I don't even know what I'm doing here." She didn't know who she was saying it for, for him or herself.

The wheels squealed as she pulled away.

Adam and Isaac were waiting on the front porch when she finally got home. They had shed their backpacks, dumping them onto the stairs. They sat on the threshold of the locked door, pressing closer together than usual for warmth. It was colder here, closer to the mountains, than it had been out on the plains.

Isaac had stood up as he saw Rose's minivan turn onto the street. His arms were crossed.

"Mom, where were you?" he said as soon as Rose opened the door.

Adam was right behind him, his words falling just behind. "It was so cold. And we were waiting and waiting."

Little Boy and Littler Boy. Angry and sad.

So like their mommy.

"I'm so sorry, guys. I'm so, so sorry."

Rose wondered if any of the neighborhood moms had seen them out there, cold and neglected on the front stoop. Evidence of their mother's unfitness. Her delinquency.

Her relief that they were okay was short-lived, replaced by an uglier relief that no one had caught her; that only her children knew what a bad mother she was and not the world. Rose felt the hot flush of shame roll over the hangover of the tears she had cried on her commute.

A fender bender had backed up traffic for miles on the highway. She had marinated in the jam of cars, beating at the steering wheel, cursing herself. Because she could not explain why she was where she was, she could not call anyone to make sure her boys were okay. Instead she had sobbed and prayed for the cars to start moving.

Once she passed the site of the accident (broken glass, crumpled engine, a parked ambulance), she had floored it, leaning forward behind the wheel as if that would bring her home faster.

She opened the door for the boys to put their backpacks inside. "Who wants to walk with me over to Mrs. D's to get Penny?"

The boys looked at her, wary. She knew it was going to take something big to get them to forgive this transgression, this trespass.

"And after we pick her up I think we should bake cookies. But I'm just not sure what kind."

"Chocolate chip." They had a consensus.

R ose set about her penance.
  She would be a better mother. She would be an attentive wife. Neither children nor husband would ever know about the craziness of the past few weeks. They would simply gather the benefit of Rose's atoning for her sins of negligence.

Rose scheduled playdates for Penny, willingly suffering the mother's chatter about vaccine scares and the latest craze in "mommy shaming" so that Pen could play with some other toddler's toys. Rose took her to the children's museum for a special treat, read extra books at nap time, let her eat a few more cookies.

The boys she took bowling after school as a surprise, watching them hoot and holler as each other's balls pinged off the bumpers. She took them out for pizza after soccer practice, to the pool for open swim.

She initiated sex with Josh, something she had not done since she had been willfully trying to get pregnant with Penny. Josh sensed that Rose's heart was not in these couplings, her smile a little forced, her moans a little too enthusiastic. But the change was good, the sex was nice, and he did not want to question its source too deeply.

During these sessions, whenever his hands brushed the stubbly whiskers of her unshaved armpits, or when they gripped the dimpling cushion of her thighs, Rose felt the same repulsion for herself she had felt before. But she felt now that she must suffer that ugly feeling, that she deserved it, because she was in truth a horrible, ugly person inside and out.

But her family must never know.

Rose's dreams of Hugo did not change from their usual course at all during this time.

The appearance of the Orange Tastee under the sand had been the only deviation from the norm, even during the weeks of Rose's stalking of the Man Who Was Not Hugo. Otherwise they had gone about their typical adventures: battling the island's monsters, riding around in the Orb, trying to find new ways to get closer to the city.

Same old, same old.

Regarding the events that had taken place inside the Orange Tastee in Hemsford: the way the man had reacted to seeing her, her chasing him into the parking lot, the horrible sneer on his face . . . To Rose, these things felt more like dreams than her dreams did. Like a nightmare, in which someone you love turns into a monster who hates and hunts you.

Looking back, she was mystified that she had ever thought this man looked like Hugo. Hugo's face couldn't twist in such ugly ways. Hugo could never have barked such unkind things.

What had he said?

Rose couldn't remember. Quite. When she tried to think about the Man Who Was Not Hugo shouting at her in the parking lot, it came to her only as muffled rage. Shouts in another language.

What had really happened there? It was so confusing, the sequence of events, the emotions, his sneering, ugly face. Thinking about it made her unsettled, as if she had witnessed some horrible accident but could not later assemble the facts of it.

By the time she lied to Naomi about what transpired, Rose had almost convinced herself that her lie had to be a version of the truth.

"So after you ordered from him . . ."

"Nothing happened. He just . . . gave me my fries. I ate them and then I drove home."

"And your fixation? The obsessive thoughts?"

"I don't think it'll be a problem anymore."

The teachers at Penny's pre-preschool program had looked at Rose quizzically when she dropped her off for the first time in weeks. Rose could tell by the way they paused when they greeted her that they expected her to fill them in on where her daughter had been. They felt they deserved an explanation.

Nosy bitches, thought Rose.

But she had smiled back. Lied to them, saying Penny had had a persistent cough and she was just playing it safe—didn't want to expose the other kiddies.

Penny had settled right back in, running to the cornmeal table to play parallel to the Emmas and Coopers of her class.

Rose had driven home resenting how little freedom this "best of the best" preschool actually bought her. Barely two hours, less if she included drive time. Enough time to go grocery shopping, unload everything at home, and head back. Enough time to do a load of laundry, but not enough to dry it. Enough time to maybe consider going to the gym (ha!), but not enough to shower.

But all Rose wanted was to be alone.

She just wanted to sit in her quiet house and listen to the sound of the refrigerator humming . . . which was as near to the sound of nothing as she could imagine.

Her penance was exhausting her.

It felt as though she were building a defense for a trial, a list of evidence as to her fitness as a mother. *You see, Your Honor, the defendant could not possibly be a bad mom, as she took her children to Chuck E. Cheese's, and as you know, that is something only a very good parent would do.*

But she was witness, defense, prosecution, and judge to herself—and no matter what character evidence she gave, she always knew the truth.

She knew that she resented every second at that Chuck E. Cheese's. That she hated the flashing lights and the plinging ringing of those Plexiglas games with their crummy toys. She knew that she thought the man in the threadbare rat suit was creepy, a likely child molester, and she didn't want him near their table. She knew she thought the pizza was shitty, the soda was watered down, and the ice likely to bear listeria. She knew she hated how greedy being there had made Adam and Isaac, running through their tokens in minutes and coming back to the table, their germy hands open, asking for more.

She knew she was a shitty mom.

She was even shitty for wanting to be alone for just an hour.

Shouldn't she miss her boys when they were at school? Shouldn't she mourn not being with her baby Penny, even as she recognized that her daughter was doing the important work of learning how to socialize with others? Shouldn't she cherish every moment with them instead of wondering how she was going to make it through the hours between when they got home from school and she turned off their lights at bedtime?

She might be good at faking it, but even if everyone else didn't see it, she knew she was a fraud.

What had he called her?

Ugly. Old. Fat.

Rose shook off the image of that sneer. Trying to dismiss the flush of shame that accompanied it. *Never happened. Couldn't have happened.*

The mail truck was pulling away as she rolled into the garage. Rose checked to make sure none of her neighbors were walking to their boxes before heading to hers. She didn't want to get caught in a "friendly" conversation and lose any of her precious minutes of solitude.

She closed the garage behind her and carried the pile of mail to the kitchen. The house was a sacred tomb of silence. No one pulling toys from their rightful places. No one unmaking made beds. No one screaming, screeching, hitting, whining, tattling, asking for attention, asking for food, or love or sex or anything— for one blessed hour, the house was hers.

She might even be able to poop in peace, an act her children so far seemed determined to prevent.

Rose decided she was going to take a catalog to the powder room with her. And she was going to leave the door open as she did her business, the ultimate declaration of solitude, the open-air bowel movement.

At the bottom of the stack of mail, under the pile of bills and catalogs, there was a manila envelope.

Rose had assumed it was for Josh. They usually were: medical journals, conference invitations, or glossy studies done by pharmaceutical companies touting why there was a real need for their particular brand of drug.

But this was addressed to Rose, with her name written in neat block letters.

Rose took a knife from the drawer and sliced it open.

A small hard flat *something* slid out and plinked against the floor, resting against the toe kick of the cabinet.

Her credit card.

Rose looked at it. Confused.

She had noticed the card was missing. But she had assumed that she had tucked it into some obscure fold of her pocketbook while she was in a rush. And since every time she had opened her purse subsequent to that time she had also been in a rush (paying for mini-golf, and ice cream, and pizza), she had given her purse a cursory look and then simply grabbed another card. Each time this happened she told herself that when she got home she would empty her purse and find the errant piece of plastic, but until this moment she had forgotten.

She had not once thought she had lost it.

Rose knew she was very good about such things. She didn't lose credit cards.

But then she realized when she last had held it.

Holding it out. Watching a trembling hand take hold of it, battered edges circumscribing the edges of familiar nail beds.

Rose felt her breath grow shallow.

She pulled the contents from the sleeve of the envelope.

It was a comic book of sorts. Clearly homemade. Pen and ink, no color. Bound with a spiral. But the image on the cover was sophisticated, professional—

And of *Rose.*

She gasped.

There she was on the page, inky lines tracing the curves of her knees, the ripples of her skirt, the firm edges of her breasts as she knelt in the sand. In her hand was a grass sword, her neck extended, her defiant chin turned toward the hulk of the enormous Spider as it reared up over her.

Above the image, the Spider's palpae jutting just in front of it, hung the title:

The Adventures of Hugo & Rose.

Her heart was thumping. Pounding.

She felt the paper bloom with damp, sudden sweat, under her thumbs.

She opened it. Flipped through the pages rapidly, each page revealing more and more: her dreams on paper.

It was all there. A thin black line drawing of the corona of Castle City, its spiky towers and shining windows pricked out in ink. The whorls of the wood of the Orb, the shutters of the porthole, the knots in the boards that kept them separated from the marine world outside. The singing trees tattooed against the dark water of the Green Lagoon. Small diamond shapes hovering over the beach where it was lit by the sun, attempting to capture the effervescence of the phenomenon.

But *she* was the real revelation.

On the pages, Rose saw herself for the first time in the way she *felt* when she was on the island. She was a superhero. Her arms strong and thin. Her waist small, her bottom round, the muscles underneath it powerful: made for leaping and fighting and climbing. Her hair whipped around the boxes of the strip, almost in constant movement.

And Hugo looked like Hugo. Beautiful Hugo. Brave Hugo. Flying through the air, launching himself fearlessly at the beast. His words in bubbles, beckoning her to the next step in their adventure.

At some point Rose had sunk to the floor as she flipped through the book, because she was leaning against the drawers when she reached the final page.

The final image was a picture of Rose, close up on her face as she lay on the sand that made the floor of the Blanket Pavilion.

She smiled up from the page, a private, satisfied smile. The picture was intimate, and immediately Rose remembered that exact moment from the dream, the missing part of the scene, the image that the artist had *not* drawn . . .

It was Hugo, lying across from her, smiling that same smile back at her.

At the bottom of this page sat the only blotch of color in the book. A fluorescent-green Post-it note; on it someone had written, in the same neat block script as the envelope, "PLEASE MEET ME."

Beneath that, there was a phone number.

nine

She did not call right away.

She had lost sense of time while she read and reread the pages, scanning them for details. Each time she looked she saw some new thing, the delicate feathers of the Tickle Crabs on the corner of a page or the distant shadow of a herd of Bucks in the grass, all confirming the impossible.

An eyewitness account of her dreams.

She was late to pick up Penny, and soon after they got home, the boys arrived, filling the house with their loud, masculine energy.

It did not feel right to call with the children around.

If she called at all.

Rose hid the book in her bedside drawer, under the lube and

the cough drops. The kids knew that was for Mommy's private things and thus forbidden, and Josh never went looking for anything without asking first.

She visited it several times that afternoon, making excuses to get away from the kids, opening the drawer to catch a quick peek of this drawing or that . . . just to make sure she wasn't imagining it.

He was real.

Hugo.

The book was unsigned, but that was the only explanation. A crazy, irrational explanation, but the only one that made sense.

He had drawn it.

All these years, she had thought Hugo was just some manifestation of herself. That he was an alter ego, a useful tool of her psyche—built to cope with the trauma of the bicycle accident and then sticking around as she grew up, to mitigate the other minor traumas of adulthood.

But he was *real.*

And he had been there for all of it.

When Rose looked at the pictures, she felt the brush of a familiar feeling. She felt *seen,* the way Josh saw her when he made love to her.

But instead of the shame that accompanied her lovemaking with Josh, her response was something else. . . .

A giddy syrup of a feeling. Warm and oozy, spreading through her limbs and chest.

Someone knows the real me, she'd think as she thumbed through the pictures. *Someone really knows me.*

She waited until the kids were asleep, their monitors silent, to call the number. Josh had texted he'd be home late. Rose cleaned the kitchen, made a cup of tea that she forgot to drink, and sat down at the kitchen table—staring at the Post-it and her cell phone.

She dialed the number into the screen, her thumb paused above the dial button.

What would she say? What would he say? Maybe she shouldn't do this.

Yes, she should definitely wait.

Rose debated for some time in that chair in her kitchen. She studied the phone number on the screen, searching it for clues, looking for an answer in its numbers.

Finally she decided to wait. She could always call tomorrow.

But still she sat. Staring.

In the end, her thumb betrayed her, twitching slightly from her nerves and brushing the screen.

It set in motion the chain reaction of connections, impulses of electrical information sent beaming from her cell to space and back again, finally to a receiver in some place unknown to her, to some random number assigned to some random person, reorganizing in that distant speaker the zeros and ones of digital information into the distinct sound of Rose's breath heavy in the receiver.

It went to voice mail.

"Hi, this is David. I'm not available right now, so please leave a message and I will get back to you as soon as I can."

It was his voice. *Hugo's voice,* picked out of her mind and playing for her here in her kitchen.

But *David?*

The beep sounded and Rose realized she had spent a few seconds simply breathing into the phone.

She hung up.

It was all too much. She needed to calm down. To think about this. About what this meant.

It meant something impossible.

She was considering throwing away the Post-it note when her phone chimed with a text.

Rose?

Rose felt her lungs halt. She felt faint.

Another chime:

This is Hugo.

Rose felt her head shake. *No. No. No. No.* But beneath that, the syrupy, oozy feeling began to rise, drowning out the chorus of the impossibility of it all.

Another chime:

Please, is this Rose?

Rose tapped out three letters.

Yes.

They decided to meet in the food court of an outlet mall that lay off the highway about half the distance from both of their houses.

When *he* had suggested it, Rose wondered how he knew where she lived. And then she remembered the envelope, the blocky handwriting, and the credit card that had led him to her like Cinderella's slipper.

They met on Tuesday. His day off, Rose knew, and a day on which she could get Mrs. D to watch Penny.

Rose showered. Did her makeup while the boys got dressed. The children stared at her funny, so odd to see Mommy in anything other than sweats this early in the day.

"Why are you doing that?" asked Isaac, waving a noncommittal hand at Rose lining the edges of her lips.

"Because I want to look nice."

"Why?"

"Because I have some errands to do."

"You don't look nice when you do errands usually."

Rose fixed him with a glare. "Isaac, go clear your cereal bowl."

He crossed his arms. "I already did."

Rose raised her eyebrows. "I'll be down to check in thirty seconds . . . one . . . two . . . three . . ."

Isaac bolted, rushing to make a truth of his lie.

She drove directly to the mall from Mrs. Delvecchio's, arriving an hour earlier than they had planned. She had been here a few times before. Josh's mother was a deal hound and often tried to bond with Rose on her visits by dragging her away for a girls' shopping excursion. Rose dreaded these outings, following Josh's mother in and out of the factory stores, trying to look interested in last season's sweaters, with their stretched-out necks and dinge of gray from being tried on so often.

She wandered the halls for a while, past the big-draw stores and the struggling local vendors. There were more empty storefronts than she remembered from her last visit. Signs hung on empty windows: "Over 10,000 sq feet of ideal retail space."

Even half-occupied, the place drew shoppers. People wandered the corridors, singly or in pairs, dressed in unseasonable shorts and socks with sandals. They filtered into stores with evening gowns in their windows, causing Rose to wonder if perhaps they really *were* shopping for the dresses. Had these unattractive, lumpy midday shoppers been invited to balls and state dinners? Was that what had driven them out to this place on a Tuesday morning, desperately in search of something sexy but tasteful? With sequins?

Or were they here for some other reason? Did looking at expensive dresses (even at clearance prices) make these people feel something they couldn't get in another way?

Rose ducked into the ladies' room.

She peed, staring at the walls of the bathroom stall.

Washing her hands, she studied herself under the stuttering fluorescents.

Even with makeup and a shower, she was a closer relative to the shoppers with their fanny packs and paunches than she was to the woman who had been drawn in that comic book.

Rose sighed. There was nothing more she could do. She could not have plastic surgery, lose fifty pounds, and age ten years backward in the next ten minutes.

She dried her hands and went to the food court.

The cafeteria was a world tour of crappy fast food. Sbarro. Panda Express. Yoshinoya. Taco Bell.

The designers of the place had incorporated this theme into their décor, and on the walls someone had affixed three-foot cartoons of children from around the world in their native dress. The drawings bordered on racist, with slanty-eyed Chinese children in coolie hats and brown-skinned Mexican kids in sombreros. It was like "Small World," but without the ninety-dollar admission price, the smell of chlorine, or the whiff of corporate shame.

Rose sat in the middle of the dining room, her eyes searching for him.

Hugo.

But he wasn't there yet. Rose's eyes swept the growing clumps of shoppers. It was still early.

"I thought it was a prank."

Rose swiveled and there he was.

He wore the same blue windbreaker she had seen on him before. But he had taken more care with his hair. It was still dampish, showing the lines where the comb had dragged through.

He took a step closer to her.

"There was this guy. A kid. One of the employees. He broke

into my office at work and I caught him looking at my comics. Like the one I sent you."

Rose didn't understand.

"I thought he sent you to get back at me. Because I fired him." They stared at each other for a moment.

"But it's not a prank, is it?"

Rose shook her head. His face was absorbing hers, lapping up the details where the fact of this Rose overlapped with the woman in his dreams. She did the same . . . such a strange moment.

Rose felt the syrupy, goopy feeling again.

She laughed.

It burst out of her, nervous, excited, girlish. She slapped her hand over her mouth trying to keep it in, but—

"This is soo weird," she said.

Hugo smiled back at her . . . the way he always did—that slow creep of a smile, moving from one corner of his mouth to the other, until it filled his face.

They grinned at each other a moment . . . then they both laughed.

"It's you," said Rose.

"It's *you*," said Hugo.

They sat talking through the lunch rush. The tables surrounding them cycled through diners, scarfing their meals wrapped in paper as quickly as possible in order to get back to their shopping.

At one point Hugo asked Rose if she was hungry, and she remembered the first time he had asked her such a thing—a little boy on the beach, holding out a seashell that tasted like candy.

Rose watched from the table as Hugo stood in line at the Taco Bell. For a moment she felt the way she had during those weeks when she was following him, his back turned to her.

Then he felt her gaze on him and turned, smiling at her from across the dining room.

It made Rose feel light and nervous. Perched on the edge of a laugh.

There was something familiar about the way Hugo smiled back at her from a distance. Something about the manner of it . . . Rose realized—

It made her think of Josh. The way her husband sought her eyes across the room at a party or on the other side of the airport security line. It was that reassuring look that said, *I am with you.*

Josh.

What would he think of this?

Rose shook off the thought. She didn't want to spoil this feeling. Just for this moment, she wanted to be *just* happy. With no other feelings in between.

Hugo returned to the table, his hand wielding a tray of franken-Mexi-food. Rose watched him as he tore open five sugar packets and poured them into his Styrofoam cup of coffee.

"You like it sweet."

Hugo looked at her, quizzical. "Yeah?"

She shrugged. "It's just . . . I *know* you. You've been with me as long as I can remember. But stuff like that—"

"My coffee?"

"I don't know little things. Like how you take your coffee. Or big things, like . . . are you married?"

He took a sip and shook his head. "Divorced. A while ago. You?"

Rose pictured her family, bunched together and dressed up, like the portraits she had had taken last Thanksgiving.

"Married. Three kids. Two boys and a girl."

Goodness, she thought. *"Married. Three kids."* Is that all that *my life boils down to?*

But Hugo smiled. "I have a daughter. She lives in Florida with her mother."

Rose was quiet a moment. There was more there, obviously, a distant child, a divorce. There must be pain, shame, loss, there beneath that sentence.

But she had no right to it. She had no right to pry into the disappointments of his life . . . she had just met this man who sat across from her.

She switched the subject. "You said no one calls you Hugo anymore."

His face colored. Embarrassed, he looked away. "I . . . changed it. After high school. I go by David, now."

"But not in the dreams."

"There are a lot of things about me that are different in our dreams." He put his hand behind his ear and waggled his glasses at her. He jiggled the softness of his potbelly, grinning.

Rose giggled.

"But you're still *you . . . Here.*"

He shrugged. "I guess. How much is anyone really themselves in their dreams? The real me is fat and losing my hair and managing a fast-food restaurant. But when I'm asleep . . ."

He trailed off, but Rose knew what he was thinking about. On the island they were heroes. On the island they were beautiful and strong and young.

"Do you ever dream of anything else?" Rose had almost whispered it.

Hugo shook his head. Quiet.

"What do you think it means?"

"I don't know."

He walked her to her car. Squinting in the sunlight, they said one of those strange formal good-byes one gives to people one may or may not ever see again.

Because at that point they were still unsure.

Even having discovered the miracle of their dreams, they both knew that there was no logical juncture in their waking lives for a relationship. Rose was a married mom with a mini-van. Hugo was . . .

Well, Hugo was *David* in his waking life. And as David he had his own proportion of responsibilities and obligations . . . even if they were less formal than Rose's.

There was a moment, though, at the end of their good-bye, when to an outsider it would have been clear that they would see each other again, even if to them it was not. They had said their finals and Hugo was heading away. Rose watched him for a moment before searching through her purse for her keys.

His hug caught her by surprise.

He had turned and rushed back to her, wrapping his arms around her, trapping her purse between their bellies. It was the first time they had actually touched. The first time they had confirmed the fleshy truth of the other.

"I'm so glad," he whispered in Rose's ear. "I'm so glad you're real."

Her chin lifted above the warmth of his shoulder. She caught the faint smell of caramel.

Rose was on time to pick up Penny at Mrs. D's. There was an open bag of M&M's on the table, evidence that certain dietary indiscretions had taken place. Penny's breath was dark with chocolaty sweetness when she kissed Rose on her arrival, her tongue stained with streaks of blue and red. But Rose was too content to say anything to the Widow Delvecchio about the dangers of childhood obesity and using food as rewards. Instead she smiled as she handed over the neat pile of bills to the old woman. "Wave good-bye, Penny. Say thank you."

The buzzy, happy feeling had followed Rose all the way home from the mall.

When the boys got home, she took everybody to the park for some air. She even treated herself to a drive-through latte on the way there, and she sat on a bench and watched Adam and Isaac chase each other over the play structures, sipping it, thinking of Hugo and all those packets of sugar.

Isaac came bursting out of a tunnel, his eyes looking for her. "Mom! Adam's doing it wrong!"

Adam emerged behind him, his face guilty.

His brother ran up to her, breathless. "He wants Hugo to rescue you from a witch, but I told him that there wasn't ever anybody else on the island—not even a witch, so we can't do that!"

Adam was watching his mother. Rose shrugged. "You guys can do what you like . . . if Adam wants there to be a witch, then pretend there's a witch."

Adam grinned. Isaac insisted, "But that's not the *way*. That's not right!"

Rose took his wrist gently, smiled at him. "Zackie, it's only a story. You guys can do whatever you want to it."

He scowled at her. She leaned close to his ear. "Do this for five minutes, okay? Be a big boy for me."

He rolled his eyes. "Oh-kaaay." He and Adam ran back into the structure. "But you have to be the witch, okay, Addy?"

Josh was home early enough to have dinner with the kids. Rose chopped vegetables and sprinkled flour onto the countertop, supervising the children as they made pizzas.

Whatever shift Josh had sensed in Rose had clearly bloomed now. She was playful with the children, taking pretend chomps at the toppings in their fingers. They would snatch them from her, giggling, then offer them again.

He wondered if maybe she had started taking antidepressants without telling him . . . it wasn't unprecedented for Rose to keep something like that private. She often kept things that she was "handling" from him, not wanting to worry him.

She was so strong, his Rose.

The boys begged for Daddy to put them to bed, and he obliged, rushing through the books they requested, eager to get back to his wife.

He emerged from their room, wondering if there was a bottle of wine somewhere in the house that they could take to the bedroom, but Rose was not downstairs.

He heard her voice, quietly singing on Penny's monitor.

"See the pyramids along the Nile, Watch the sunrise from a tropic isle, Just remember, darling, all the while . . ."

Penny's garbled voice joined her mother's: "*You belong to me . . .*" Though as Pen sang it, it sounded like "You be-wong to me."

His sweet, sweet Rose.

She smiled when she saw him standing by the monitors in the kitchen.

"She's having trouble settling. Too much fun before bedtime."

"You're amazing." He pulled her into a kiss.

Rose let his kiss wash over her. He could tell she wasn't thinking about the dishes as he did it or the chores that needed to be done. She was just there, with him, leaning into his body.

When they pulled apart, she gave him a sleepy smile.

"Today was a good day" was all she said.

They were in the Plank Orb.

Pale filtered sunlight streamed in through the portholes, setting a watery glow in the small cabin. The air was humid, warm, and close. The wood of the vessel moaned and creaked, under pressure.

Rose's hands were on the length of chain. She was pulling it toward her, threading the bead of the Orb.

"Do you know where we're going?"

She looked up at Hugo. He leaned against the wall, his arms casual on his knees. He was relaxed. Restful.

Rose gave the chain one last yank. "No. But I know we're almost there."

She sat back opposite him. This was what they always did in the Orb, sat across from each other and talked, passed the time while they waited to get wherever they were going.

"Something's different."

He was right. Something *was* different. "I feel it, too."

Rose noticed a particular whorl in the wood behind Hugo's head. A distinctive eye made by the pattern of the grain.

It had been in the comic book Hugo had drawn.

Had he remembered the details of their dreams that specifically? So well that he could duplicate the very configuration of the whorls of the wood in his drawing?

Or were their dreaming minds creating that distinct pattern there because they had seen it drawn in the comic book?

Rose didn't remember noticing it before.

But then again, she didn't remember *not* noticing it.

It was this strange overlay of awareness that Rose had never had before. *Hugo was real. . . .* And though he was sitting right across from her right now, bobbing along under the water, he was also *somewhere else. Asleep.*

He laughed. "I keep picturing you in your pajamas."

"Me too!"

"Well, at least I'm not wearing them." He nodded at her.

Rose looked down. She was indeed *wearing pajamas.* Whereas she usually wore a skirt and blouse while she was on the island, she was now in an oddly frilly nightgown. It was a light blue color, sleeveless, with a ruffled bib and buttons on its chest. It had that slick acetate sheen to it . . . the kind she remembered from the sleepwear of her childhood.

"Trust me, I do *not* have a nightgown like this."

Hugo looked at it a little closer. "I think my mom did."

Rose raised her eyebrows at him. *Really?*

Hugo rolled his eyes and shrugged as the bottom of the Orb thumped up against the sandy floor of the *somewhere they were going.* There was a shush-shushing as it dragged to a stop.

"Wanna see where we are?"

Rose crouched under the porthole, turning its brass wheel.

She opened it into the emerald world of the Lagoon.

The Orb had banked against a shallow spot in the calm cerulean pool. Fiddleheads blanketed the shore with their soft spray of leaves. Overhead, the branches of the trees meshed into a lacy canopy, with clumps of gray-green moss hanging from them. The roots of these trees were massive, defining the edges of the pool with their twisting reach.

In a few hours, Rose knew there would be fireflies here, hovering over the ground, lighting up over the water. When they did that, the Lagoon felt like a field of dizzy shifting stars.

Rose lowered herself down the side of the Orb. The water was warm, lapping at her ankles as Hugo emerged.

Rose looked back at him. "Did I tell you that Adam asked me if the Lagoon looked like Dagobah?"

"Where Yoda lives?" Hugo hefted himself over the lip of the porthole.

"I told him it was prettier. Greener."

Rose waded to the shore and sat on one of the roots. The reflection of the trees in the water rippled as Hugo jumped down.

"You've never talked about your family before . . . here, I mean."

"I've also never worn your mom's pajamas before and yet . . . here we are." Rose smiled at him.

But he was right.

That was what had changed. This was the first time that either of them had acknowledged that there was a world beyond the island. A world with sons and mothers and the films of George Lucas.

It was a strange feeling.

A wind raced across the water. The trees shivered.

Hugo and Rose spotted it at the same time.

Deep in the wood, obscured by branches, stood the dark figure of a *man*. Watching them.

Rose gasped, uncertain for a moment that she was seeing what she was seeing. It must be a Buck, away from the herd. Or the clumping of shadows in the forest, tricking her eyes.

But then the figure turned and Rose's eyes confirmed it. Without a doubt it was a man, no mistaking it now that she could make out his arms and legs . . . legs that were running, carrying him away from Hugo and Rose. Fleeing.

"We can't lose him!" Hugo was already moving, his arms wrapping around the trunk of the closest tree. His feet found their purchase and he was climbing, impossibly fast, up into the canopy.

Rose pulled her feet under her, toes landing on the rough skin of the tree root. If Hugo was going to travel the trees, she would keep to the ground . . . closer to the figure. She leaped from the root, her front leg landing on the next span, some six feet away.

Above her the branches bent down with the weight of Hugo upon them . . . he alighted on the edge of the topmost limbs before throwing himself toward the next tree.

Rose bounded from root to root, leaping over the hollows between the trees, her hair streaming behind her. Ahead the figure swerved, trying to lose them.

A cracking sounded from above.

"I can't see him!"

"Go left!" Rose was closing the distance between this dark man and herself. Growing closer as the trees began to thin out . . . the width between their roots growing longer.

Rose's mind was racing with the implications. *Someone else! Someone else on the island! Where had he come from? Why was he running? Was he leading them to somewhere? Or something? Had he been there all along as well, only to just discover them now?*

In between the trees, Rose could see that the swamp was soon to give way to a familiar rise of grassy hills. Beyond those hills lay Castle City.

A sharp pain suddenly pierced her foot, and then she was falling, tumbling into the space between the tree roots. She put her hands out to brace the impact, gravity driving her down toward the loam.

The blow knocked the wind out of her. Rose pulled her head from the ground, her palms covered in forest debris. She blinked her eyes.

She wasn't alone.

In the corner of her vision she sensed movement. It was close. Not five feet away. In the pit *with* her.

Rose threw herself back against the tree root, ready to defend herself.

Across the hollow, *she* did the same thing.

A *mirror*.

Rose's reflection stared back at her from an antique gilt frame that leaned against a stack of old dining room chairs, their seats upholstered in threadbare silk. A battered steamer trunk sat next to them, its surface gray with dust, the leather of its straps deteriorated with age.

Rose saw herself and leaned forward to get a closer look. *What a strange place to store furniture. Who put it here?*

"Rosie! . . . Rosie!" Hugo's voice was excited, not too distant.

Rose turned from the strange jumble and climbed the tree root. "Did you get him?" She moved quickly to the forest's edge.

She sighted Hugo standing at the crest of the hill. He was alone.

"He's not important! Rosie, look!" He pointed at the horizon.

Rose followed the line of his hand. In the distance Castle City loomed large. Closer than she had ever seen it before.

And its shield was gone.

ten

Rose woke herself and Josh with her shouting.

"We could get in!" she had said, her body sitting up, thrusting her mind from that world to this one.

"Honey? Are you okay?"

Rose turned to the dim form of her husband, eyes adjusting.

A moment ago she had been on a hill, looking out on Castle City, it shining towers freed of their halo. Closer to their goal than they had ever been before.

And now she was here in the dark with Josh.

"Yes. Sorry. Go back to sleep."

Rose stepped out of their bedroom into the hall. The house was dark, a night-light glow bleeding into the hallways from the children's open doors. Rose made her way down the stairs without turning on the lights, her hand trailing against the wall for balance.

She had tried to go back to sleep, but her mind was too full of the dream.

What did it mean?

There was someone else on the island. Another person.

Rose couldn't help wondering if the figure that they had seen wasn't yet another dreamer. Someone like her and Hugo, some sleeping mind that had happened upon their playground.

Or maybe whoever it was had escaped from Castle City.

Rose felt her heart race at the memory of it. Without the halo of the shield blocking their view of the towers, you could make out their details. The unique features of their architecture, cupolas and spires, gargoyles, rounded windows. Their colors were clearer than ever before, reflective blues and greens and yellows.

And just before she woke up, in the windows she had seen movement. Proof of life.

Rose felt a chill under her robe.

She poured herself a glass of milk, the refrigerator spilling light onto the wood floor. She closed the door, feeling the cool sweetness reach her belly.

It was two o'clock. If she didn't get back to sleep soon, tomorrow was going to be a disaster. She'd be short with the kids, resentful of Josh. She'd drink too much coffee to keep herself going and then have that afternoon crankiness that always followed too much caffeine and too little sleep.

She felt a smile creep onto her lips. *They could get in.*

A buzzing sounded somewhere in the kitchen. Rose found the edge of the counter, feeling her way to her phone plugged into the wall.

A text from Hugo:
I need to show you something.

M rs. D couldn't take Penny. She said she was feeling poorly and would be going to the doctor's that afternoon.

As Rose hung up, she had the uncharitable thought that Mrs. D was lying. That she was just making excuses because she didn't like Penny or didn't approve of the way she had behaved during her last visit.

Well, thought Rose, *if you give a toddler chocolate, she's going to act like a holy terror.*

But still there was the issue of how she was going to see Hugo.

She wanted to talk to him about the dream, to see the *something* he had promised, but with Penny to watch . . .

Rose looked at her sweet girl. Pen had run after Adam and Isaac as they left for the bus.

"Kiss! Kiss!" she had screamed, her pajama'd feet getting wet from the grass, the damp sneaking up onto her legs.

Rose ran after her, but not before Adam doubled back, leaning down to let Pen plant an openmouthed smack on his lips. Isaac watched from the sidewalk, eyes rolling, arms crossed.

"Kiss, Zackie!" she cried.

Isaac looked at Rose. *Do I have to?*

Rose shrugged, a benign smile. *Do it for me.*

Zackie came over, kneeling for his sister's ministrations. "Eww, she slobbered all over me."

But even though he made a big deal of wiping his face, Rose could tell as he climbed onto the bus that he was a good boy, a big boy, who loved his brother and sister. And his mother, too . . . though sometimes he did not let on.

Little Boy. Littler Boy. Littlest Girl.

Rose had dressed Penny while she waited for Mrs. D to return her call. Penny was beginning to give her opinion on the clothes Rose chose for her. The boys had never cared one shirt from the other. Finally Rose gave up and just let Penny choose. She tugged on the tights and skirt, figuring they would be Mrs. Delvecchio's problem during potty time today.

Then came the call. She couldn't do it.

But Rose wanted to talk to Hugo. To see his face as they talked about this new aspect of the dream.

Penny sat on the floor, quietly pulling books from the shelf and looking through them. She ran her finger along the words and babbled, pretending to read.

Maybe it wouldn't be so bad . . . maybe she could bring her.

"We get out now?" Penny was astonished when Rose opened the door.

Of course she's surprised, thought Rose. *Every time we've been here before we've sat in the car for ages.*

But Hugo didn't know that.

Hugo had texted Rose the address of his home. Rose had felt a flush of shame at this. At Hugo's ignorance. At her omission of the fact that she had been following him for weeks before she revealed herself. That she already knew where he lived, where he shopped, what he did with his days off.

But what did it matter now?

Now that they had found each other and could just tell each other the details of their lives—no reason to confess to her earlier sins.

Rose held Penny on her hip as she made her way up the cracked concrete walkway. So strange to be walking on something she had studied for so long, like stepping through a bubble while keeping its structure intact.

She rang the doorbell. Pen wiggled to be let down, her attention captured by a line of ants that marched from a crack in the stair.

Hugo's lips were spread in a broad smile when he opened the door . . . but it faltered upon seeing Rose with a toddler around her waist.

"Oh."

"I hope it's okay. I couldn't get a babysitter." Rose pushed her way past him into the house. Maybe if she rushed through this moment—Hugo's disappointment that they wouldn't be alone—it would have less impact. It would be a glancing blow to their time together rather than a fatal setback. A flesh wound.

Rose corrected herself. Corrected her thinking.

Penny was a fact of her life. She had children. A life outside of her dreams.

Hugo would just have to deal with it.

Rose swung the diaper bag onto the worn coffee-colored wall-to-wall, taking in the inside of Hugo's home.

In all her time watching him, she had never seen more than the shallow angle he revealed as he came out the door. Hugo was private, his shades permanently drawn. When she knew he was inside, she would imagine him moving about in the hidden world behind the shades. She wondered what the furniture looked like, the walls, the tile in the bathroom.

She had gotten it right.

It was clearly the home of a bachelor. Swiss coffee walls. Dusty baseboards. The couch was angled onto the TV, situated so that one could sprawl on it alone, legs extended, and surf the channels.

The few pictures on the wall were stock prints, the kind that came with a frame, and all of them had the haphazard look of art hung as an afterthought. Rose recognized one of them, a cool-color still life with a jug, berried branches angling out from it. It had hung opposite the toilet in the powder room of her parents' home for years and was thus subject to more reflective study than any of their "good" art in the more public areas of the house.

"I had that same picture in my house growing up."

Hugo beamed, forgetting Penny for a moment. "You did?"

He was clearly pleased with the concurrence. It was strange for Rose seeing it here, but also somehow comforting. A connection they had beyond the dreams, like having the same blood type or loving the same flavor of ice cream.

Rose's mother had declared the print "dated" and banished it to the attic. She wondered if she could get her to send it.

Penny wriggled.

"Will your cat be all right if I put Penny down?"

Rose cringed. Inside for only ten seconds and she'd already made a mistake.

How would I know he had a cat?

Idiot. Liar. Fake.

But it was already out there. She turned to Hugo, ready to see the questions in his eyes.

But his eyes were locked back on Penny, straddled on Rose's hip. Distracted.

"Uh . . . she's out . . . so . . ."

Penny looked at Rose. "No kitty?"

"No kitty, honey." Rose set her daughter down and began pulling the toys she'd packed out of the diaper bag. Best to move on to the next subject, keep things moving. Ignore the toddler in the room.

"I actually woke myself up. That's how excited I was. Every

night for decades that thing has been there, covering the city . . ."
Rose felt Penny's small hand creep up the back of her shirt, the
air hitting the exposed skin above her waistband. The unsexy
elastic of her stretched-out panties.

Ugh.

She pivoted, angling her exposed back away from sight. Keeping up the same frantic pace of conversation. "And then . . . it's
gone. . . . I honestly couldn't believe it. And I would have waited
until I could get someone to watch Penny. But I wanted to see
you. . . ."

Rose looked up at him. His eyes were still on Pen, watching
her pick up the toy cell phone Rose had tossed onto the floor.

"Hugo, we could finally get to the city. . . . Hugo?"

It took him a moment to tear his eyes from her daughter, to
swing them to Rose. "Uh. Sorry. Yes. We could."

And then his eyes were back on Penny as she squatted, awkward, next to Rose, reaching her rounded hands into the recesses
of the diaper bag.

This was a mistake, thought Rose. *You should go. Take the child
and get back in the car. Come back another time, when you're free,
unfettered . . .*

But it was impractical. Too far a drive. She was already here.
"What did you want to show me?"

Hugo's eyes snapped back to life, suddenly present. "Uh . . ."

He glanced back toward the hallway . . . almost as if he expected someone to step out. He was holding his breath. Deciding.

Penny grabbed his pant leg and Rose caught his visceral
flinch at the touch.

"No kitty?" Pen wanted to be sure.

Rose swept her up. Carrying her away from Hugo and his
discomfort. Setting her on the couch. "No, honey. No kitty."
She handed her a pile of books. "Here, you read."

Rose perched on the edge of the sofa next to her. Placing her body between Hugo and the girl. She wouldn't let Penny touch him again. She didn't want to see him cringe again at her daughter's touch. Didn't want to explore what such a reaction could mean.

"I'm sorry."

Hugo shook his head. "No, I . . ."

"Why don't you show me, while she's occupied?"

Hugo hesitated. He glanced back at the hallway. This was not quite what he had planned. But then:

"Stay here."

The albums he brought out were large. Leather bound. Their spines were rounded and wide, four inches at least, enough to accommodate the hundreds of pages inside.

Hugo had handed her the topmost of the first stack, before leaving to get a second pile. "Here, this has the oldest ones."

Rose opened it.

On the first page, carefully wedged between two sets of photo corners, was a child's drawing. A picture of a beach, ocean, sun, clouds. Two smiling stick figures sat upon it, a triangle and two lines flanking the head of one of them, signifying its female gender.

It could have been one of the drawings Adam taped so faithfully to the wall above his bed.

But in the lower right-hand corner, in a careful black crayon scrawl, it read:

"Hugo."

"Oh, my goodness," Rose heard herself say.

She turned the page. Another. Another. The book was filled cover to cover with drawings, scenes from their dreams as children.

Rose heard a thump as Hugo set down another stack of port-folios.

"I put them in the books a few years ago. There were a lot and most of them weren't dated. . . . I did what I could."

Rose looked up at him. His mouth was closed. Waiting.

"This is every picture you ever drew of us?"

He shook his head. "Just the ones I kept."

Rose gasped. "I remember this!"

On the page, a crude drawing of Rose as a child dangled from a vine strung between two cliffs. Above her, the meaty legs of a giant Spider reached down from the cliff's edge.

"I was at sleepaway camp when I had this dream! I woke every-one up when I started screaming in my sleep . . . they didn't leave me alone about it all week."

Hugo leaned against the wall, grabbing his wrist. "I drew that one a lot. You'll see, I wanted to make sure I got it right."

Rose flipped a few pages, and indeed there they were. Mul-tiple studies of the same scenario, all in a childish hand: from below, above, elevations that removed the second cliff.

"Wow."

Rose reached the last page and closed the portfolio. She grabbed the next one. The work in this one was older, more mature, the crayons giving way to colored pencils. A few pages in she found a self-portrait of Hugo.

"Oh, my God! You used to look like this!"

It was Hugo at about twelve, his face just starting to lose its roundness. His eyes large and chocolate. Lips coral. Hair curled above his eyebrows.

"I don't know if I ever actually looked like that."

Rose looked up at him. "You did. You were beautiful."

He smiled at the compliment. Shy.

Rose turned back to the portfolios. Engrossed. The drawings matured, Hugo's birth as an artist. Line drawings became sketches, bringing dimension to the paper. Soon the planes of her own face began to emerge, the bridge of her nose, the curve of her smile. They were very definitely *Rose,* so like her that they could have been copied out of her parents' photo albums.

Rose sighed. *Once there was a time when what I looked like in my dreams and what I looked like in real life weren't so far apart.*

But she didn't say it. She didn't need to.

She kept turning pages. The pencil sketches gave way to watercolors, and here it became clear that young Hugo had found his medium. The colors washed across the bumpy paper, pulling together the pink and green hues that saturated their dreamworld. Each page was a memory, something from her past. A hand buried in sand. A still life with a Tickle Crab. The blue cast of the Blanket Pavilion in the sun, set against the blowing saw grass.

"It's like watching myself grow up."

"Well, we grew up together."

Rose looked up at him. "We did, didn't we?"

He smiled at her and Rose felt that syrupy feeling rise. This man knew her, had always known her.

It was such a lovely sweetness. To feel *known.*

Rose kept flipping. Hugo brought a chair in from somewhere, so he could watch her go through the albums.

Penny had found her way back to the diaper bag and was entertaining herself by pulling out its contents: bags of snacks, wipes, changes of clothes. Every once in a while there was a bleep or a blorp from one of her toys or books, but Rose ignored it . . . awash in the sea of memories Hugo had drawn.

Rose paused, unfolding a charcoal sketch that had been folded to fit in the album. It was another self-portrait. Hugo facing off with Blindhead, a grass sword in one hand, the other braced against the lip of one of its jagged glass mouths.

"These are incredible, Hugo."

"I just drew what happened."

Rose turned the page. "Now, I know this never happened."

Hugo leaned forward in his chair to see the contents of the drawing. He blushed.

Unfolded on Rose's lap was a pencil sketch of her at about age sixteen. She was lying on bent grass, her eyes staring directly at the viewer . . . and she was nude.

Hugo cleared his throat. "I was a teenager."

Rose laughed. "I wish I had an actual picture of myself from when I looked like this."

The portrait was beautiful. Tendrils of her hair brushing the skin just above her nipple. Her hand casual on her hip, fingers touching the slope of her belly.

Had she ever been this sexy? This assured or relaxed? Rose didn't think so . . . not even in her dreams with Hugo was such a thing possible.

She could only look this way in the fantasies of a teenage boy. Not even in her own dreams.

Hugo got up from his chair. Uncomfortable. Rose sighed and turned the pages to a series of unpopulated watercolor landscapes. The Lagoon. Spider Chasm. Castle City.

"I wish I could show these to my boys. I try to tell them what it looks like . . . but I never get it quite right. . . ."

"What did they think of the comic I sent you?"

It took a moment for Rose's mind to jump from her thought to his. The comic?

The book he had sent her. The pen-and-ink drawings she revisited daily, locked behind the bathroom door, hidden from the boys in her bedside drawer. If she wanted so much to share with them, she could have shown them that.

Rose stammered, "I—"

"You haven't shown it to them." She could see the disappointment in his face. He deflated a little. Grown shorter.

"I thought about it. I thought about showing it to Josh."

"Josh." His voice was flat.

"My husband. He's been hearing about you since college."

"But . . ."

Suddenly Rose was very aware of Penny. She had pried one of the bags open and was munching loudly on snap-pea crisps.

Hugo was waiting.

"I can't figure out a way that it doesn't seem crazy. It's one thing when it's just us . . . but other people . . . what it sounds like . . ."

Rose watched Hugo closely. She didn't want to hurt him.

Finally he shook his head. "I haven't told anyone either."

Rose let out her held breath. "So you understand."

"Yeah, yeah, of course." His voice was pitched high as he said this, waving his wrists and sitting back in his chair.

She gauged him for a moment. Unsure.

On the floor, Penny rocked a small baby doll, her torso twisting with the motion as she sang, mouth full of fried snacks, a lullaby about silver planes and pyramids, photographs and souvenirs. Her high-pitched voice ended each refrain with her favorite line: "You bewong to me. . . ."

Rose giggled. Why was she so nervous?

"Sorry. It's her lullaby."

Hugo lifted his eyes. "I like it."

He was quiet for a moment, then, "I wish I could meet

them. . . . I know you can't tell them. But they're part of you. . . . I know it's stupid."

Suddenly Rose was jumping on, her thoughts and her words tumbling over one another. "No! You should meet them! [*What?*] I want you to! [*You do?*] I can't tell them. [*Never. No. No.*] But you should come to Isaac's birthday party. [*No. No. No.*]"

"Really?" Hugo's eyes grew wide at this idea. Softer.

"Yes! [*No.*] I want you to meet them. [*No.*] Really I do. [*Liar.*]"

But then Hugo was smiling . . . really grinning. Like a child who has been given the toy he most desires.

And all he wanted was just a glimpse of her life. Just a fraction of what she had taken from him for all those weeks without asking, following him. But *he* politely had requested it and she had volunteered it. Rather than what she had done—stealing information about him. Stalking him.

She had just gone through pages and pages of documents proving that she had grown up with this man. That she knew him.

Why the hesitation to let him in? Why should *her* life, *her* privacy, be a higher value than his?

On the drive home, Rose's mind was filled with thoughts of the particulars of Isaac's party: where she would order the cake, whether or not they would get balloons, and how she would explain Hugo's presence there.

J osh called on his way home from work. He had picked up chicken from that place the boys loved, couldn't wait to have dinner with everybody.

Rose sighed. The children were already at the table, bites already taken from their mac and cheese, nibbles in their carrot sticks. Their schedule never changed, but Josh could never quite hold it in his head. Dinner at six, bath at six thirty, stories at seven, lights out at eight.

But still, dinner with Daddy was a rare treat.

Rose cleared away the dishes (*they could eat this tomorrow*) and sent the boys to run their bath. She read picture books on the couch while they waited, Adam's and Penny's damp pajama'd bodies under her arms, their tiny tummies growling. Isaac rolled on the floor in front of them all, pretending to be too big for baby stories.

Josh came in with a grin, wielding the oily bag of chicken high in the air. The children ran to greet him, grabbing at his legs. The hunter returns triumphant.

Rose tried not to chide the boys for wiping their greasy hands on their clean pajamas. She left Josh with them to put Penny to bed; her sweet girl had started to nod off in her booster.

When she came down she saw all three of them laughing together at the table. Josh was blowing bubbles into Adam's milk with his straw . . . the boys were doubled over with giggles.

Little Boy. Littler Boy. Biggest little Boy.

Rose spoiled their fun, sent them to bed. It was already late. She'd be up in a minute to make sure they'd brushed their teeth.

"And make sure you do a good job! I'll know if you just used mouthwash!"

Josh shot her a grin. "Can you really tell?" he whispered.

Rose shrugged. "Not by their teeth. But their faces always give them away."

"When I was a kid I always used to wet the toothbrush."

"Don't tell Isaac." She smiled.

Josh helped Rose clear the dishes from the second dinner of the evening. She ran the faucet, loading the dishwasher.

"They posted the new residents today."

"Yeah?"

"Our department is getting two more than we did last year."

"Oh, gosh. I'm sorry, honey."

But Josh didn't look displeased at all. "No, it's good news. It means less scut work. More hands."

"More competition. More people coming up from behind."

He shook his head. "More time at home."

"That is good news."

Josh fixed Rose with a look. "I miss you."

Rose rolled her eyes and kept loading the dishwasher. "I'm right here."

He grabbed her shoulders . . . ceasing her motion. "I *miss* you."

He had that hungry look. That *seeing* look. The one that made Rose so uncomfortable in bed.

She tried to make him laugh. "The last time you said that I got pregnant."

"I mean it. I'm tired of only seeing you when I stumble in at midnight. I want a date. I want grown-up drinks and cloth napkins. I want to know what's going on with you."

Rose shook her head, her mind full of the earlier events of the day. Of Hugo and his albums.

"Nothing's going on with me."

He seized her, swinging her into a hug and spinning her around. "Then I want to hear about nothing."

eleven

It was decided that Isaac would be getting a large Lego set for his birthday.

This, of course, meant *Rose* decided what Isaac would be getting and informed Josh of the expense of said gift.

"One hundred and twenty dollars!"

"Plus tax," added Rose.

This was a common refrain for the two of them. Josh had no idea of the actual cost of many of the items in their household. This was not because of any willful dissembling on Rose's part, but more because it had been quite some time since Josh had been in charge of any purchases save for the lunch he bought for himself in the hospital cafeteria.

"It's just a bunch of plastic blocks! It's not even assembled!"

"Josh, the whole point is assembling them yourself."

"Still, it's ridiculous."

Among the other things Josh found ridiculous: the cost of karate lessons, the price of new couches, and the hourly rate of babysitters.

"Look, I finally got him to say he might want something other than a bike. I don't want to push it."

Josh sighed. *The bike again. A boy should have a bike. He had a bike when he was Isaac's age. Hell, he had one when he was Adam's age.*

"Sure, honey." He kissed his wife on the forehead. "If you think it's worth it."

"I do." She smiled at him, knowing the price of Zackie's gift was but a fraction of the total it would run them to celebrate their oldest's birthday. The bounce house rental, the cake, the snacks, the party favors and decorations . . . it would cost them just under four hundred dollars.

But most of the expenses would be hidden. A higher grocery bill. An expensive trip to Target.

Sometimes it seemed to Rose that Josh thought she made the substance of their lives appear out of thin air and that her ability to do so had nothing to do with the line items on their bank statement every month.

B ut Josh and Rose had plenty of money.

Each month Josh earned enough to pay their mortgage, their loans, the property taxes, insurance, utility bills, and credit card balance. They had enough so that Rose could stay home for the children, a luxury they felt, but a necessary one to ensure the proper care of their progeny. Though this was a choice they had made together, there was a certain resignation that both felt upon opening the envelope containing the balance due on Rose's school loans. It was, it seemed, a very high principle to be paying for an education that was currently being used for dramatic readings of *Pat the Bunny*.

Josh even made enough to sock away for their retirement, those investments he tracked religiously while thinking of how lovely Rose would look with streaks of silver in her hair.

No, Josh and Rose had *plenty* of money.

Odd word that, though . . . *plenty*.

Because while they certainly had enough, neither Josh nor Rose felt the *plentifulness* of their financial lives.

The world seemed to them fraught with economic disaster. A local surgeon Josh did not know was sued for malpractice and lost his house. One of the mothers in Penny's preschool had pulled her son from the program for a less expensive (and less prestigious) one across town.

And then there was the ever-growing list of must-dos:

Isaac looked like he would be needing braces. Adam's penchant for art needed to be encouraged with classes. Penny was starting to show an interest in ponies. Family vacations were needed to build happy memories and sibling bonds. Toys and birthday parties were to be acquired and planned so that none of the children felt any less worthy than their peers who had had the same.

And then there was college, of course. Three college educations would not be cheap.

So even though they had *enough* of it, Josh and Rose worried constantly about money.

Every night while Rose tripped about the island, Josh lay next to her, his mind filled with fantasies of insufficiency.

Most of these he could not have relayed, forgotten as they were upon waking from his too-short spans of sleep. But they were played out for him nonetheless. Josh dreamed of letting others down, of forgetting essential articles or information. In one dream a surgery went on forever, organs changing as he repaired them, until finally he was staring at a body cavity that resembled nothing human.

And though these may seem to be nightmares, they were in fact something of a mental exorcism for Josh. His dreams repurposed the stress and strain that during his waking hours had the name of "never enough" and played them out in ways that made sense to his dreaming mind. He awoke with only fleeting images and feelings about his dreams, but his mind had done some of the work of lessening the impact of the "never enough."

Rose, whose dreams were forever concerned with the attainment of Castle City and the drama of the island, did not experience this same exorcism. The feeling of "never enough" was never relieved. Her nights were already too full solving the puzzle that she and Hugo had been working on since she was a little girl.

So when Rose woke from the island to the real world, the feeling of "never enough" loomed just as large for her in the morning as it had in the night.

The air in the saw grass was muggy. Something about the closeness of the blades trapped the moisture from the ground, keeping it from escaping into the outer atmosphere.

Rose's arms ached, the handles of the woven buckets digging into her palms.

She was, admittedly, a little grumpy with Hugo.

From all vantages it continued to appear as though Castle City were still unshielded. Rose had witnessed the Natters fly through it, their dirty white bodies gliding between the towers.

But despite the fact that the birds seemed to be able to enter the city, Rose and Hugo were frustrated in their attempts to get to it.

It loomed larger, looked closer . . . but it remained unreachable.

They had first tried to get at it by way of the Lagoon . . . where they had spotted the change. But when they returned to the hill, just outside the forest, they discovered that several Spider burrows had been dug into the hillside.

This, like the disappearance of Castle City's shield, was something new.

"What are they doing here?" Rose had whispered to Hugo as they hunkered down in the shadows of the trees. Inside their fresh dirt lairs, she could see the Spiders' dark, hairy limbs at rest.

Hugo shrugged. But they both knew they wouldn't be getting to the city this way.

They had tried the Orb, but the string of its destinations seemed to have shortened. It would carry them from the Rock Cove to the Lagoon and back again, but the areas to which it had reliably delivered them before—the headwaters, the swamp, the ruins—all of these seemed to have been permanently closed.

The new proximity of the Spiders to the Lagoon ultimately rendered the Orb useless. Soon after they discovered the Orb now had only two destinations, they realized that something about the mechanics of its travel was calling the Spiders into the Lagoon when it arrived.

No sooner would they open the porthole than they would hear the crashing of a Spider making its way to the Lagoon. On one occasion the Spider had already been waiting there and Rose had barely had enough time to close the door before it leaped onto the Orb, rocking it in the water. Rose had half worried it would cling to the vessel and follow them back to the cove. But they had arrived safely and the Spider had remained behind.

With the Orb out of commission, Hugo suggested that they try to reach the city on foot. He reasoned that since some of the Spiders had taken up residence outside the Lagoon, it might be possible that their numbers were fewer in the Spider Chasm, where they had traditionally been found.

Just beyond Spider Chasm, the land gave way to the rocky hills that eventually curled around the Lagoon's forest. If they could get over the canyon, they could follow the ridge of the hills and get at the city from that angle.

But even with fewer Spiders, the Chasm was still a dangerous place. Climbing its sides took hours, and it was never a good idea to allow oneself to be trapped between two stone walls.

So Hugo decided that they would leap over the Chasm . . . they just needed sand from the beach and sunlight.

Which was why Rose was carrying grass buckets full of pink sand through the muggy saw grass and quietly resenting Hugo.

She watched him walk ahead of her, pushing the grass away with his elbow, his own set of pails in his hands. He hadn't so much consulted her about this idea as *told* her this was what they would be doing next.

And there was something else . . . he'd gotten quieter since they had discovered the shared nature of their dreams. More private now that each knew the reality of the other.

Whereas before he would have been singing or telling

jokes as they made their way through the saw grass, now he was silent.

Rose could hear him breathing hard. She felt a drop of sweat join another on her forehead and make a break down the side of her neck.

"Do you think it's weird?" Rose's voice sounded strange in the heated quiet.

"Huh?" Hugo didn't look back at her.

"Do you think it's weird that this is the first time the island has changed?"

Hugo stopped, setting his buckets down. "What do you mean? Things have changed before now. When I first met you here, we were kids. You're not a kid now."

He gave a playful leer and winked.

"You know what I mean!"

Hugo nodded, wiping his brow. He looked up at the clouds covering the sky. "I do, Rosie. . . . Just, can we talk as we walk? I want to be ready when the sun breaks."

"I'm not the one who put down my buckets." Rose glared at him.

He sighed and picked up the load again. "I'd say your attitude is something that's changed."

Rose realized he was right. He may have gotten quieter, but she had become increasingly frustrated with the state of the island. She couldn't help feeling that they should be at that (*goddamn*) city by now.

This *was* a change. They had been trying to get to Castle City for years. For decades they had spent their nights finding new ways to try to get there, the same obstacles always thrown in their way. And until recently she had been comfortable with the never-ending pursuit.

Why was she so impatient with it now?

Hugo suddenly stopped up ahead of her, his body obscured by the stalks of grass.

"Wh—"

Something about his posture stopped the word before it was fully formed. From behind, Rose could make out the baskets in his hands quivering.

And then she saw it, waiting silent beyond the weave of grass. A gloss of scales stretched taut over an eyeless skull the size of her living room sofa.

Blindhead. Only one of its skulls was visible, the tight skin blushing with an unnatural glow, pulsing ugly hues of red, green, and blue—a pattern Hugo and Rose had come to know and fear. It meant prey was near.

And it meant that Blindhead was hungry.

Hugo was only steps from the mouth. Its wire-thin tongue flickered out, back and forth. Searching. Sensing.

Neither Hugo nor Rose moved.

Rose forced herself to breathe shallowly. Her eyes strained in their sockets, scanning the surrounding grass. *Where were the others?*

Slowly, Hugo bent his knees, lowering the sand toward the ground. The baskets sagged as they touched down, bulging as he pulled his fingers from their handles. Only a foot from Hugo's lowered face, the monster's tongue continued its ceaseless waving.

Still crouched, Hugo angled his hand toward the nearest stalk of grass. His fingers wrapped around the blade with slow deliberation; he'd need a sword if they were going to get out of this.

He pulled.

The blade's roots tore free from the soil, lifting the basket and setting loose a soft swish of pink sand.

At the sound, all three of Blindhead's sightless skulls flew up from the grass. Their single body rose up beneath them, a redwood-thick cylinder of scaled muscle twisting into a coiled tower thirty feet high. The heads hovered over Hugo, tongues rattling against jagged teeth. Poised to strike.

Hugo stood frozen beneath the massive serpent, his hand still on the saw grass. Its heads would be on him in seconds.

On instinct Rose began shouting. "Hugo! Chasm! Sand!"

The heads snapped in her direction as she turned and started to run. Rose ran *at* the stalks, pushing them into one another, hoping to make as much noise as possible.

The beast took the bait, whipping its bulk away from Hugo. Straight toward Rose in a twisting spiral, the heads competing for first place.

One of her baskets caught on a stalk of the saw grass, wrenching Rose's arm and dumping its contents onto the ground. Rose turned . . . the creature was gaining quickly.

Usually they encountered Blindhead in the forest, where it was no work at all for Rose and Hugo to tangle it up in a mass of trees. But like the Spider and the Plank Orb, Blindhead wasn't operating by its usual rules. Out here in the saw grass there was no way to trap it. No obstructions. Nothing to hide behind.

Rose hoped Hugo understood what she had shouted.

Still running, she threw the empty basket out over the grass. It made an arc in the sky before landing and rolling over the tops of the blades. Beneath it the stalks began to clatter. One of the monster's heads turned toward the sound for a second . . . slowing a bit. But the other two heads continued forward, the new sound less enticing than the steady beat of Rose's feet against the ground.

Rose chucked the other basket. Heavier, this one dropped a trail of sand in its wake, a quiet *shoosh* that made even less noise than the last.

Shit. Shit. Rose's only option now was to keep running.

The sun broke overhead, beating down a clear heat. Behind Rose the swishing of Blindhead's body against the grass and the rattling of its tongues against teeth drew nearer. Rose's lungs burned with effort.

A *thunk* landed to her left. Then another. And another.

Rose looked up in time to see a large rock fly over her head and land among the saw grass. The sound drew the attention of two of the heads. It stopped moving forward, now confused as to which sound to follow.

Hugo.

Rose turned away from the descent of the stones, now trying to soften her steps. She wove between the blades of grass, holding her breath. The grass began to thin out as the soil beneath her feet became more and more rocky. She was close to the edge of the chasm.

Maybe she had a chance . . .

She looked around. Blindhead's central skull was still fixated on her, pulling against its brothers. It released a glassy hiss in her direction.

And then Rose stumbled, her arms flailing outward, knocking the stalks nearest her. The blades knocked against one another. Too loud.

All three heads turned toward her. The confusion was gone. The monster began to move again.

Rose dropped, hunkering down onto the balls of her feet.

She tucked her mouth into her knees . . . *Don't breathe, don't move. Not a sound.*

The swish of Blindhead's movement paused. But it was close.

Rose could make out the edge of the chasm through the thinning stalks. Her eyes swept the ground. *It has to be there. Please, please be there.*

A small pool of iridescent sand . . . right on the edge. Sparkling in the full, clear sunlight. Rose almost cried into her knees.

Above her, a volley of small rocks swooped through the air. Rose took off toward the sand as the rocks hit the ground in a loud patter. *Thump, thump, thump.* The snake's heads braided themselves in confusion, their necks pulling in different directions. A chorus of angry hissing followed Rose as her feet hit the sand and her body launched itself into the air above the canyon.

She landed badly, her feet impacting the hard dirt of the other side. She fell forward a few steps before collapsing to her knees. Rose stayed there a moment, panting.

"That's . . . easier . . . to do . . . on the beach."

She looked up. Hugo was right next to her, smiling. "Thanks for the help."

"Ditto."

Rose rolled over. Flopping onto the ground. Breath slowing.

Hugo walked to the edge of the chasm. On the other side, Blindhead slithered along the edge, its heads flailing. Searching for a way over. Hugo's laughter echoed over the canyon, and all three of the snake's heads hissed as the sound reached its ears. It turned and disappeared into the grass.

Rose sat up and took in the sight of Hugo watching the creature disappear. Everything about him was so lovely. The lines of his calves disappearing into the frayed cuff of his pants. The spread of his back, angled beneath the soft white linen of his shirt, the way it moved as he put his hand up over his brow.

Her rescuer.

He was so beautiful here.

And, of course, so was she.

But in real life . . .

Rose frowned, not wanting to think about it.

Hugo turned, seeing her dour face. "Stop it, Grumpy."

"Stop what?"

"You know what."

Rose sighed. "Doesn't it ever feel to you like we've just been watching the same bad monster movie from the fifties over and over again, only we never reach the end? I mean, it's run from the giant monster. Defeat the giant monster. Try to get to the city."

"We're getting closer."

"You always say that."

"It's always true."

Rose fixed him with a look. *Come on.*

"Rose, things are finally happening! We met each other in real life! We saw someone on the island, the shield is gone. Things are changing, new things are happening. Even just now . . . even that was new. I'm telling you we're going to get to the city."

"But *why* are we trying to get to there?!"

Hugo shrugged and sat next to her. "Because . . . I don't know. Because it's important. Because everyone's there."

"But why are they there? Why have we been doing the same thing, over and over again for years? I just want to know why. Why do we do what we do? Why this? Why us?"

He smiled, gentle. "Because you're my Rosie. And I'm your Hugo."

"That's not the reason."

"It's my reason."

Rose turned to look at him. His face was inches from hers. He was looking at her, taking in every detail of her face.

And then he leaned in to kiss her.

The skin of his lips was soft and warm, pressed gently against her mouth. His eyes closed, naked to the sensation. Rose breathed in the salted caramel scent of him.

And surrendered to it.

The kiss haunted Rose.

It *was* something new.

But unlike the shield on Castle City, the shifting location of the Spiders, or even seeing another human on the island . . . the kiss had provoked something Rose had never experienced in a dream.

Lust.

Rose shook her head to think of it . . . but that's what it was. *Lust.*

That blooming warm sensation five inches below her navel. The ache in her breasts, the spread of heat across the back of her neck.

Of course she had felt it before. With Josh and earlier boyfriends, that sudden urge to jump on top of them. To put her mouth on them, anywhere, everywhere. To consume them.

But, Rose would be the first to admit, it had been a while.

Goodness, it had been a long, long time.

The night they conceived Adam. Soaked in tequila. Isaac

with her parents for the weekend, so they could attend a friend's wedding.

Rose had pushed Josh onto the hotel room bed, yanking on his trousers, hiking up the hem of her cocktail dress. They should have just undressed, their clothes were a mess by the time they got back to the reception, but Rose could not have waited. She wanted the feeling of Josh inside her, his mouth on her nipple, his eyes full of her.

That was what she had felt when Hugo kissed her.

The beginning of that dangerous, wonderful feeling of *need*.

That *was* something new.

But it was just a kiss.

twelve

I t took Rose days to get ready for the party.

We should have just booked a place, she thought, dusting the baseboards. *Then I wouldn't have to clean.*

In addition to the shopping and the wrapping, the calling of mothers of those children with allergies, the tracking down of those who had not yet RSVP'd, the assembling of gift bags and the ordering of cakes, there was the *cleaning*.

When Rose complained of this task to Josh, he rolled his eyes.

"The house looks fine."

And indeed, to him, it did. Rose kept a neat house, but it was not in her eyes *clean . . .* or at least not *clean enough to be seen.*

While Josh thought of Isaac's party as a gathering of boys, Isaac's friends from school and soccer, Rose saw it as an invitation to judgment by the larger counterparts who would accompany them.

Namely their mothers.

Mothers whose eyes would look past the balloons and the streamers and see the dark spots on the carpet, the dust behind the television, and the crumbs by the toe kicks. Mothers who would notice the weeds on the beds next to the house and the cobwebs on the stucco.

So she dusted. And mopped. And weeded. She power-washed the garage door. Took a broom to the sides of the house.

She even deep-cleaned the rooms no one would have any business visiting. The bedrooms got a thorough going-over, because even though the party would be held downstairs and in the backyard, one never knew.

But still there were things she could do nothing about. The stubborn stain on the couch. The dry patch in the backyard.

Isaac had invited Simon from his soccer team, which meant that his mother would be coming. *What's-her-name, with the boobs and the judgy look.*

Rose hated the thought that *she* would be here, seeing the inside of her house. Feeling sorry for her when she saw the dry patch (*Oh, poor Rose, can't afford new sod*) or the stain (*Well, of course it's stained; Rose can barely keep up*).

But . . . *Kaitlin, that was her name* . . . was just one of the invading horde. Rose felt vulnerable to all of them.

But Zackie invited who Zackie wanted. And he was a popular boy.

So Rose cleaned and hoped they would be able to put the bounce house over the dry patch. She bought a pair of throw pillows to hide the stain.

There was, of course, another person Rose thought of while she cleaned.

Hugo.

He would be coming, too. She thought of how he would see the details of her life: the family portraits on the wall, the granite countertops, the row of little hooks holding the children's jackets and backpacks.

This, too, was uncomfortable, in its way. But a less formed feeling than being seen by Isaac's friends' parents. It made her unsettled to think of *him* here among her things, in the same room with her children and Josh . . . but those uncomfortable feelings were mired in the warm syrup of her other emotions.

Several times she caught herself thinking of the kiss . . . but each time she shook it off. No time for such nonsense with a party to plan.

Josh disappeared the morning of the event. Rose had been planning on his being there to sign for the deliveries and supervise the inflating of the bounce house. But when she called for him to answer the doorbell, he didn't reply and she had had to do it herself, which put her behind schedule on getting the fruit cut for the trays.

As the deliverymen were backing away, Josh pulled into the drive, his face apologetic. "Sorry, sorry, that took longer than I thought it would."

Rose was tense. She didn't even want to know where he had been, she just wanted him to "keep the kids out of my hair."

Josh kissed her forehead and headed inside, eager to be with the children, happy. "You're such a good mom."

Somehow everything got done. Rose was tying balloons to the door when the first car pulled up. She smiled and waved at the mother behind the wheel. "Hi, guys! We're so glad you're here!"

Adam was very interested in the cake.

He had seen it yesterday when they got home from school. A long white box on the counter, smelling of sugar and vanilla.

Mom had let them look at it as she moved things around in the fridge to make room.

"It says, 'Happy Birthday, Isaac,'" said Zackie, but Adam didn't need him to read it to him. He could read it very well himself, thank you very much.

It had Spider-Man and Darth Vader and Pokémon on it. Isaac had insisted that he wanted a cake with all three, even though Mom had said it might be a little confusing. Zackie said he didn't care. Adam remembered that Isaac had told him Pokémon wasn't cool anymore . . . but he guessed his brother had changed his mind about that.

Adam told his mom that he wanted a picture of Hugo on his birthday cake.

She had given him a funny look for a moment and then ruffled his hair. "You don't know what Hugo looks like, honey."

"Yeah, I do," he'd insisted. "He looks like Han Solo and Indiana Jones."

Mom had laughed. "Harrison Ford?"

Adam had no idea who that was, but he'd nodded anyway. Whoever *Harry's Son Ford* was, he must look like Hugo.

Mom had pulled the cake out again this morning, carefully taking it from the box and setting it on the end of the counter, next to a pile of small paper plates and plastic forks.

"No touching, Addy," she'd reminded him.

It was hard. It smelled so good, even better now that it was warming up. But Adam was a good boy and he listened to

Mommy. He visited the cake several times before the party started, resting his nose on the countertop, studying the spray of the sugar paint on its surface, the pattern of tiny waves made by the piping on the edge.

Dad had let all three of them jump around in the bouncy before everybody got there. Isaac and Adam had wrestled, throwing themselves at each other, landing and rolling around the quilt of inflated vinyl. Penny had laughed at them, throwing her tiny body on top of their pile.

But as soon as his friends had arrived, Zackie wanted no more to do with him. He ran off with the bigger boys he saw at school and told Adam to play with Penny. "We don't want to play with babies," he said when Addy tried to keep up with them.

The pile of presents on the little table Mom had set up grew larger and larger. Adam wondered if Zackie would share. Probably not.

Dad was busy watching Penny and talking to the other parents. Mom was busy picking up plates and cleaning up, her mouth a thin line in her face.

So Adam went back to visit the cake.

But somebody was already there, looking at it.

A man in a blue jacket. Shorter than Dad. A little fatter, too.

Adam labeled him a "daddy," as he did with all men of a certain age.

"Don't touch it," he warned the man.

The man looked over at Adam. Surprised.

"Not even to taste the frosting." Adam wanted to be sure the man knew the rules.

"I won't," he said, and smiled. But the man was looking at the cake again. Maybe the man thought *he* didn't have to obey the rules. Grown-ups sometimes thought they didn't have to. "You can't even do it if you think they won't know. 'Cause my brother will know."

Adam nodded at Isaac in the backyard. His brother had put on a paper crown and was leading his friends back into the bounce house.

"You're Adam?"

The man knew his name. Adam furrowed his eyebrows at him. Suddenly he realized that even though this man was a "daddy" he was also a "stranger." He'd been talking to a stranger. A stranger who knew his name.

The stranger pulled something from his pocket.

"I brought something for you . . . I didn't wrap it, 'cause it's not your birthday."

He held out a small, shiny compass. The red arrow wobbled in its center, trying to find north.

Suddenly Adam was not so wary. "Cool!" he said, snatching it from the man's hand. He couldn't wait to show it to Isaac. At least now he'd have something he wouldn't have to share. Something Zackie might be willing to trade for access to his new toys for a little while.

He bolted for the door.

"Adam!" he heard his father. "What do you tell the nice man?"

"Thanks!" he said, barely turning back to answer. He needed to find Zackie.

Josh had watched Adam's interaction from a distance—appreciating the calm, direct way his youngest son addressed the man by the cake.

Goodness, Adam was different from Isaac. Isaac would have ignored the man or run away. But Addy had had a whole con-

versation with him, forgetting his manners only when he had
been given a gift.

"Thanks for that, by the way," Josh said, walking toward the
man after Adam disappeared into the backyard. "It can be tough
to see your big brother get all the presents. I'm Josh. Isaac's dad."

The man took his hand, shook it. "David."

Josh loved meeting other fathers. It made him feel he was
meeting a fellow brother in the fraternity of parenthood. He
looked out on the backyard, trying to find the smaller version of
the man next to him. "Which one's yours?"

"Uh—"

"You're here!" Rose was at the door, both hands full of dirty
paper plates. Her eyes were a little too bright, smile a little too
wide. She was tense, he could tell; Rose hated parties.

"Honey, you know David?"

Josh saw a brief *something* pass between David and his wife.
A pulse of some kind.

And then Rose was talking, quickly. "We went to elementary
school together. I ran into him in the grocery store. He just
moved here and doesn't know anybody." She set the plates down
and stood next to Josh, wrapping an arm around his waist.

An old flame, he mused. *Worried I'll be jealous. I'll have to
tease her about it later.* He squeezed her shoulders, playful. "Well,
he knows you!"

David hadn't said anything yet. Just goggled at the two of
them. He must be one of those socially awkward types.

"I thought it might be nice for him to meet some people. So
I invited him to the party."

His wife, adopter of strays. "David, you should come to dinner. Can we do that, Rosie?"

Rose nodded. "Of course we can."

Josh gave David a broad smile. "It's a date, then."

———

Rose had stayed with Josh and Hugo as long as possible. She was worried that Josh would start quizzing Hugo before she had caught him up on the lies she needed him to tell.

But she needn't have worried. The sound of Adam and Isaac fighting in the bounce house had rung out over the party, and both she and Josh had excused themselves quickly from Hugo's side. They had found the boys on top of each other, their little foreheads sweaty. Adam was trying to pry a small round something out of Isaac's hand.

"Give it back to me! It's mine!" he cried, clawing at his brother.

Rose could tell by the look on Isaac's face as he twisted from him that Adam was telling the truth. Whatever it was in his hand, Zackie's face had that mean, greedy cast it got when he was up to no good.

Rose hated birthdays.

"You take care of this," she said to Josh. She didn't want to yell at Isaac on his birthday. Didn't want to be convinced she was raising a bully.

He wouldn't always be a bully, she knew.

It was just . . . sometimes it was hard to remember that.

Josh had it all sorted by the time everybody gathered around for cake. Adam was still sniffling, sitting next to his brother, taking shuddering sips of air, but the tears had stopped and Isaac looked as if there had been no altercation at all. He beamed over the cake (*such a handsome boy*) and counted the candles, confirming that there was one to grow on.

Rose noticed Simon's towhead at the far end of the table, but she had not seen evidence of Kaitlin or the "mammary twins." There was a collection of fathers whom Rose had not met hovering in a group, just behind the children's table, their noses pressed down into their BlackBerrys. Simon's absentee/divorce-considering dad must be among that number, not working this Saturday.

And there behind them was Hugo. Looking out of place in his blue windbreaker among the polo shirts and North Face pullovers.

Rose smiled at him.

He smiled back.

Josh lit the candles, blocking the breeze with his hand. Isaac got them all out with one blow.

A while later, Rose sat next to Hugo. Alone at the picnic table, the breeze lifting the tablecloth. Above them the sun filtered through the cottonwood tree, setting a lacy shadow to dance over them.

If she closed her eyes, she could have been dreaming.

She had brought him a slice of cake, carrying a plate for herself. They sat in silence while they ate, watching the kids in the bouncy, hopped up on sugar now, their parents letting them burn off as much energy as possible before they had to drag them home.

"You have a beautiful family."

Rose quirked her mouth. "Thank you."

"Josh is a doctor?"

"Trauma surgeon." Rose cringed a little at this automatic answer, hearing Josh's influence in it. His insistence on the distinction between a *doctor* and a *surgeon.*

"Wow."

Rose shrugged. "He works hard."

So much was buried in that statement. *He's never home. He's pompous sometimes. We miss him. I miss him. He's proud. I'm proud.*

Hugo was quiet for a moment. Watching the children.

"Do you . . . think it could have been us?"

She pursed her lips. "What do you mean?" she said . . . though she knew.

"Do you think, if we had met earlier . . . that maybe . . ."

"Maybe."

There was a beat, and Rose knew that they were both thinking of their kiss.

Hugo was the first to speak. "But we didn't . . . meet."

"No."

"He's very lucky. Josh."

Rose didn't say anything. She never believed anyone would be lucky to have *her* . . . even when Josh said it himself she never thought he meant it. Not really.

Suddenly Hugo stood, brushing the crumbs from his pants. "I have to go," he said, and started walking toward the house.

Rose called after him, quietly enough so that only he would hear, "See you tonight."

He turned back to her. He nodded to show he understood. "See you tonight."

Zackie was an "asshole."

Adam felt the rightness of this illicit word he had overheard from one of the fathers. The way the word fit over his brother.

Asshole. Asshole. Asshole.

Of course, he didn't say it out loud. Adam was a good boy and he knew it was a bad word.

But if he kept it in his head, just said it to himself, no one would know. You could think about bad things, but as long as you didn't do them or say them, you didn't get in trouble.

Asshole. Asshole. Asshole.

Zackie called him a baby in front of his friends. Zackie told

him he wasn't allowed in the bouncy. Zackie took the cool compass that the man had given him and tried to keep it.

Asshole. Asshole. Asshole.

Dad had given it back to him. But not before Zackie had
made Adam cry, in front of all the bigger boys.

Asshole.

Tomorrow Isaac would want to play Hugo again. He would
want to talk while they fell asleep. He would pretend that none
of this had happened, that he had been nice to Addy. That he
loved Addy.

Asshole.

After everybody ate the cake (*which didn't taste as good as it
had smelled*), Adam had gone inside. He was tired of being ignored by the bigger boys. He wanted them all to go home. He
wanted the bouncy to pop and for it to fall on all of Zackie's
friends and then they would cry and throw up on Zackie and
then the party would be over.

'Cause when Zackie's friends were gone, Zackie would go
back to pretending that he liked Addy best of all, and Adam
liked that more. Even if he knew Zackie was just pretending.
He didn't mind.

The house was almost empty. Everybody was in the back.
All the grown-ups were standing around talking with their
drinks.

Adam pulled out the bin and carried it to the small table Mom
told them to use for their Legos. Mom had made them put away
the map they had constructed of Hugo's island. She had said they
could put it together again when the party was over. When Isaac's
birthday was over.

Adam laid the flats on the table. Some of the structures had
remained fixed in place when they had put it away. Small green

plastic fronds jutted up around the cut-paper Lagoon they had pasted to the board. A few mounds of brown blocks, showing the hills around the island. Gray to show the Rock Cove. One of the boards was marked up with a forking of Magic Marker where the swamp met the beach.

Mom had been mad when she'd seen that, but it didn't come off when she'd tried to scrub it.

In the bin were the labels he and Isaac had written with the names of the places and then cut carefully with their safety scissors. Adam piled these neatly on the edge of the table, next to the plastic spider rings he and Isaac collected at Halloween. Mom said their legs were too spindly to be like they *really* were, but it was the best they could do.

Outside, the big boys were racing around the yard. Yelling, happy.

Assholes. Adam tried out the plural form. It felt good.

He pulled the mess of tissue paper and toothpicks that was meant to be the Blanket Pavilion out of the bin. Isaac had made it, with Adam supervising. It had looked pretty good at first, but now it was kinda wadded up, crushed by the Legos in the box. Adam set this on the beach of flat pink and white pieces.

A vague pressure tugged under his belly and he felt a little bit of wetness spread on the fabric of his underpants. A warning drop, Mommy called it.

Adam ran to the bathroom. He did not want to wet his pants in front of the big boys.

Rose watched Hugo disappear into the darkness of the house. He was sad, she knew.

But why had he said it? Why hadn't he just kept it inside the way she had?

She thought of his face when he'd asked her if it could have been them. How sad it had looked when he wondered what would have happened if they had met *before*.

Before Josh. Before Isaac and Adam and Penny. Before the facts that made up her life had been locked into place.

Oh, Hugo.

She had wondered it, too, of course. Was that why they dreamed of each other? Were they somehow supposed to end up together?

But only since the kiss.

The kiss had sparked the questions . . .

Until the kiss, she had just been excited by the reality of Hugo. Fascinated by the fact that someone else shared the mystery of their dream.

She hadn't for a moment wondered about the *maybe* of it all.

Until the kiss.

But the answer was a resounding *No.*

It had to be.

How was she supposed to consider a life without her children? That they were the product of some cosmic mistake.

And Josh . . . oh goodness, Josh.

She loved him.

He was a good man. A smart man. A good father.

And he loved her well . . . better than she loved him.

From Josh sprang everything: her children, her life, her being.

But then why Hugo? Why this rising sticky *lusty* feeling?

Why had the universe conspired to send her dreams of the same person every night of her life and then present him to her *now*, when there was nothing to be done about it? When her life was already locked into place. Her husband chosen. Children born. Investment plans selected.

How inconvenient it all was. To meet the man from her dreams *now*.

It made Rose grumpy.

Hugo shouldn't have said it aloud. He should have kept it in. His disappointment in seeing the fixedness of her life. He should have seen what she saw: the catastrophe inherent in the impulse.

Rose heard a distant cheer. The backyard had emptied while she'd been thinking, the straggling parents walking casually to the side yard.

Another excited whoop of children's voices carried over the corner of the house. What was going on over there?

Rose stood and made her way across the yard.

Turning the corner, she could see that the children had clumped around a central point. Rose made her way through their parents, benevolent smilers at the group's edge.

And then she heard it.

The distinct trill-ring of a bicycle bell.

In the center of the group stood Isaac, his head wrapped in the shiny maroon of a helmet, his feet on either side of the bicycle's frame.

"Oh, my God, Dad! This is so cool!" He was looking up at Josh.

That bastard.

Adam washed his hands, even though he was pretty sure he hadn't gotten any pee or poop on them. He used the paper towels Mom had put in the bathroom for the party, instead of using the good towels or his pants. He turned off the light and opened the door.

There was a man kneeling by his Legos. Playing with them.

Adam pulled back into the dark of the bathroom, suddenly shy.

Adam recognized him as the daddy/stranger who had been

thinking about touching the cake. The one who had given him the compass. Adam could feel it there now, in his pocket.

The man was leaning over his little table, putting things on it.

Adam watched him pinch up the little pile of labels. The man smiled as he read them . . . then he placed them, one by one, on different parts of the table.

Something caught his eye in the bin. He turned away for a moment and Adam could see him pluck two tiny objects from the pile. The man paused, looking at whatever it was in his hand. Then suddenly he turned back to the map, lifting the crumpled wad of the Blanket Pavilion and placing the objects under it.

A cheering sound carried in from outside.

Assholes, thought Adam.

But the man turned toward the voices, like he was remembering something. He stood quickly. Adam was surprised when he didn't go out back; instead the man thumped his way to the front door. Adam heard his footsteps get fainter and then the sound of the front door closing.

When he was gone Adam left the safe darkness of the bathroom, rushing to his Lego table.

The daddy/stranger had put everything in the right place. . . .

Well, almost. He'd put a few Spiders just outside of the Lagoon, when everybody knew they all belonged in the Chasm— unless they were hunting.

But the man had put all the labels right where they belonged. "Rock Cove." "Swampland." "Green Lagoon."

Adam lifted the Blanket Pavilion.

Under it the man had set two mini-figures. A dashing man and blushing woman. He had set them on their sides under the tissue. Facing each other.

Adam set the Pavilion back on top of the figures, his mind turning.

Josh already had Isaac out on the street while their guests were leaving. Zackie was skidding along, feet pushing against the ground, waving good-bye to his friends with Josh at his side. Rose's husband was helpful as ever, making sure everyone had their goodie bags, shaking the fathers' hands, hugging the mothers, remembering everyone's names.

Rose wanted to murder him.

She got them inside with the promise that they'd open presents as soon as they'd picked up. Isaac came swiftly, dumping the bike midway up the drive. She glared at Josh, hands on hips, as he made his way toward her. He picked up the bike to pull it into the garage, and before she could even say anything he said, "I know. I know . . . but, *later*. Okay?"

Screw him. And screw later.

But Rose waited. She wrote the names on a legal pad while Isaac opened presents. He'd be doing the thank-yous tonight. Josh held Adam on his lap while Isaac opened presents. Assured him he'd get his turn on his birthday.

There was a brief moment of tension when Isaac caught Rose pulling the large rectangular box she'd wrapped from the bottom of the pile.

"What are you doing with that?" he asked.

"I need to take this back," Rose said with a quick glance at Josh.

"But—"

"No *buts*, honey. You got some really great presents." She smiled at him, trying to soften the blow. Isaac pouted.

Josh moved to intercede (*Come on, honey, just let him have it*), but she cut him off with a look. *Don't say anything.*

Rose put the wrapped Lego box in her closet, hoping she would be able to find the receipt without too much trouble. She hit the lights, trying to keep her temper about the whole thing in check.

How much had he spent on that bike, anyway? Certainly more than the hundred dollars she had spent on the Lego set . . . but only after she'd called all over town and searched the Internet to find the best price.

So, no, Isaac was not getting to keep the Legos, no matter that it was his birthday. No matter that he had already seen the present. No matter that he had heard the rattle of the blocks inside and already knew what was beneath the paper.

Because Isaac's dad had gotten him a bike. A bike would have to be enough.

Rose stopped for a moment in their room. She sat on the edge of the bed.

She was a petty person.

Why was she punishing Isaac for something Josh had done?

But still, they couldn't afford to spend so much.

How much was that bike, anyway?

Maybe she wouldn't return the Legos. Maybe she would just tuck it into the attic. Save it for Christmas. Give it to Isaac then.

The monitor on her bedside lit up with a little cry. Penny was up from her nap. Rose went to get her and brought her back down to join the boys.

Why *did* Josh buy that bike? What drove him when he woke up the morning of Isaac's birthday party to look up listings of local bike stores, despite the fact that he knew he would suffer the wrath of his wife?

He didn't rightly know.

And when he slipped out of the house without telling her, gone to run his fingers over the soft leather of saddle seats, to smell the off gas of those still prickly new tires? What was he thinking?

He had seen Rose secure the wrapping paper to the expensive kit of Legos the night before. He had smiled at her and nodded when she had said, "He'll like this, won't he?"

But somehow when he looked at the box later, he could only imagine the disappointment in Zackie's face. The "not-bike-ness" of the present.

It's just that things in his life had been feeling so *right*. The pieces all perfectly aligned. Like a family portrait drawn by Adam, two big happy faces, three smaller happy faces.

And that wrapped present Rose had shown him . . .

It was *not right*.

He thought of how grown-up Isaac looked the night he brought home chicken for dinner. His voice was deeper than Josh remembered it being the week before. Not changing yet, but carrying more gravity than it had previously. He would be a teenager before Josh knew it.

A teenager should know how to ride a bike.

It was ridiculous that the boys didn't already know. A product of an overcautious mother and a dad who worked too much.

This particular thought was tripping its way along his dendrites when he saw the bike he wanted for Isaac. The bike he could picture his son on.

It was gorgeous. Shiny red and chrome. The tread of its tires was a pattern of flames licking at their whitewalled centers. Its seat was two-tone leather, even more flames stitched here, probably by hand.

A proper boy's bike.

Josh barely noticed the four-hundred-dollar sum that the

clerk rang up. His mind was too full of thoughts of what Isaac would look like on his beautiful new bike. How grateful he would be.

Josh felt giddy with the knowledge of what was in his trunk all through the party. Knowing that no matter what, the look on Zackie's face would be worth it.

And it was. Isaac loved it. Josh could tell this was a moment he would remember for the rest of his life.

And Rose?

Well, sometimes people needed a little push. He remembered in medical school some of his teachers had encouraged them to . . . well, if not to *bully,* then to *lean on* reluctant patients. They *were* the doctors, after all; they knew best.

She was going to let the boys have bikes sooner or later . . . so why not *now,* when Isaac so dearly wanted it? When he could get it in front of all of his friends and enjoy it on his birthday?

Josh was certain she would come around. There was nothing else for it.

thirteen

J osh knew that Rose would be sore about the purchase of the
bicycle. He also knew that the way in which he presented
it—as Isaac's birthday present, in front of a crowd of people,
and at a time during which she would have difficulty pulling
him away to yell at him—would all work to his advantage.

By the time the children were asleep and Josh and Rose could
talk about his purchase, alone in their bedroom, Rose was still
angry with her husband. But the damage had been done, and
because she loved him and did not *want* a fight, she was ready to
concede the loss.

There was also the fact that Rose had had the opportunity
to actually see her son on a bicycle as he waved good-bye to his

friends. On an actual bicycle, Isaac had looked quite different
from how he had ever looked in her mind. Rose realized now
that in all her imaginings of Isaac and Adam spread out bleeding on the pavement, the bikes that lay next to them were always
twins to the one she had gotten as a child. In her fantasies the boys'
heads were never in helmets, and they were always unconscious—
this was quite a difference from the happy, helmeted boy that
Isaac had been that afternoon.

So perhaps it wasn't all that bad.

Still, she was sore with Josh for going against her. When he
defended his actions by saying that "they were going to give him
one eventually," Rose did manage to see the truth in his words.

But there was something about the way he said it that pushed
at Rose. Had Josh been able to seem even a little bit sheepish
about the purchase, about his circumventing her authority, Rose
could have forgiven him easily. She wanted to forgive him.

But Josh could not bring himself to pretend that he felt bad
about his action. He felt that he was right to have gone around
his wife . . . that she had *needed* him to push her.

So Josh sought neither permission nor forgiveness.

And to not seek forgiveness was, to Rose, unforgivable.

"Rose, can you just recognize for a moment that your feelings on this are just a little bit irrational?"

Josh could not look at his wife and see that an apology would
cost him nothing and gain him peace . . . but an accusation of
irrationality would only be greeted with sarcasm.

"Nice, Josh. Nice." Rose felt the desire to forgive her husband slip from her grasp.

"I just want you to acknowledge that what happened to you
was a fluke. Every kid who climbs on a bicycle doesn't end up in
the ER."

With that statement, Josh planted an image of Isaac in a hospital bed into his wife's mind.

Rose bloomed with a fresher, newer anger. Forgiveness was now out of reach. Her husband had not thought of any of the practical realities of Isaac's bike ownership. "I can't ride a bike, Josh. I have to watch Penny and Adam. You teach him to ride and he's going to want to ride. What am I supposed to do when he's tired of riding to the end of the block and back again?"

"Tell him I'll take him out."

"You're *never* here!"

And there it was. The old resentment. The unstated truth of their lives. Josh was there now, but he wouldn't be later. He wouldn't be there most of the time, no matter what he said.

That was the reality of their life.

But Rose had broken the rules by saying it. Josh was quiet. Rose sat on the edge of the bed, head in her hands.

"I just . . . want to go to sleep."

Josh was angry now. Didn't she see that he was trying? Didn't she know how hard he was working, to give her what she wanted? Didn't she know that he *knew* he was never there, that he hated it, and that was why he got Isaac the bicycle?

For a moment, through his anger, Josh saw Rose as she saw herself. Ugly, fat, and aging, hunched over on the edge of the bed. He wanted to wound her, to make her feel the way she'd made *him* feel.

"Sure. Go to sleep, Rose. Go see your dream man, who's always there for you and who does everything you want."

Josh decided he would go downstairs and pour himself a Scotch. Maybe watch *SportsCenter* for once. Try to forget about this.

Feeling petty, he turned off the lights on his way out of the room, pitching Rose into the dark. Rose felt her way to the edge of the blankets and climbed under them. She hadn't yet brushed her teeth or washed her face, but somehow, at that moment, sleep seemed so much more important.

H ugo spotted a cave halfway up the cliff of Rock Cove. Rose had never noticed it before, though they'd been coming to the cove for decades. Had it always been there? Or was it part of this new "shifting" island?

"I think it's always been there," said Hugo, hands on his hips, "I just think we've always come here for the Orb and never really looked at the cliff."

He suggested they explore it and started to climb the rock face before Rose really had a chance to respond.

"What if there's something in there?" she called up after him.

"Then we'll kill it." He didn't look down at her. "We always do."

Rose followed him up, her bare feet clinging to the rock. Hugo was right: they always did kill the "something." What an odd question for her to ask.

Why was she afraid? She was never afraid on the island.

But she was.

Rose looked up at Hugo, mildly irritated that he hadn't consulted her before starting to climb.

Goddamn it. That was new, too. Irritation. Grumpiness. Anger. Fear.

Lust.

These feelings from her other life were bleeding into the dream. She never used to feel anything but strong and beautiful here.

Hugo was waiting for her at the cave mouth. Excited. "It goes really far back! This could be the way to Castle City!"

Rose felt herself roll her eyes.

"Rose, are you okay?" Hugo was staring at her, his face concerned.

Was she okay? Rose didn't know. It was just that when Hugo had said "Castle City" she had felt . . . what was it . . . Tired? Bored? Not quite. But it was a familiar feeling.

Suddenly she was thinking about how she felt when the boys roped her into their playacting. How she was always just humoring them . . . thinking about how long she would have to do it before she could get out of it and get to the stuff that she really wanted to do.

But that couldn't be it.

"I'm fine," she said, smiling. "Let's go."

The cave did go quite far back. Though at the cliff face it was large enough to stand, as they moved farther in, the cave ceiling dropped and soon they were crawling, feeling their way through the darkness. Each time Rose thought they had reached the end, Hugo managed to find a passageway into another cavern. They continued crawling, though Rose could tell by the drop in temperature and the way their whispers echoed that the caverns they moved through were vast. She had no idea how Hugo was finding his way forward, but he never hesitated.

"Hugo," she whispered, her voice sharp.

"Mm-hmm."

"What happens if there isn't a way out? What happens if we get lost in here?"

The sound of his knees against the ground stopped. He had stopped moving.

"Well, I guess we'll just wander until we wake up."

He was right, of course. That's what always happened. They

searched for the way to Castle City. They didn't get there. And
then they woke up, lived their real lives, and the next night, they
went to sleep and did it all over again.

Rose felt the heel of her hand slip and dig into the sharp
edge of a stone. A hot gush of fluid broke out over her palm.

"I found something," Hugo said, and there was light.

Rose turned her head away, the sudden brightness a pain to
her eyes. She shielded them, and in the light she could see the
blood on her hand, red trails staining her life and love lines.

"It's the ruins." Hugo's voice was disappointed.

Rose crawled forward and squinted into the brightness.
Hugo was already fully out of the cavern, standing scout on the
parched earth that blanketed the place. Trying to get their
bearings.

Rose cradled her injured hand to her chest and pulled herself
through the hole. She could see the crumbling clay brick Hugo
had pushed aside to reveal the passage.

She climbed to her feet, her eyes adjusting.

Over the rolling peaks of the hills, Rose could just make out
the tips of a few of Castle City's towers. The flats went on for a
mile or so in the other direction before ending in the flat blue
line of the sea.

"Damn it!"

Hugo picked up a clod of dried earth from the ground and
threw it against one of the crumbling mud towers. It shattered
and fell to the earth, leaving a cloud of brown dust hanging in
the air.

Rose watched as he pitched another clod at the tower. Then
another and another. Hugo's face was twisted in a way she had
never seen . . . at least not on the island.

"Fuck!"

He threw another shard. But this time it was the tower that

cracked, a fracture radiating out from the site of impact. Hugo's eyes widened as the top half of the tower slipped and began to fall toward him.

Hugo just managed to get out of the way as the whole thing came crashing to the ground, breaking into large chunks of dried dirt. The air was stained reddish brown, clouds of particulates loosed into the ether.

He emerged from the cloud, dusty, coughing. "That was unexpected."

Rose couldn't help it. She started to laugh.

And then he did, too.

"I am in a bad mood." He grimaced.

"Me too."

They sat, facing away from the city. Toward the flat and the sea.

"You said fuck." Rose giggled.

"I did?" Hugo was surprised.

She nodded, girlish. "I don't think I've ever heard you swear before."

"Well, I do all the time . . . In the real world."

Rose took a breath. In the real world. She thought of her real world as she had left it. With Josh so angry at her and Isaac on his bicycle.

Bicycle.

"Do you remember when we met?"

"You came to my work." He smiled at her.

Rose shook her head. "No. When we met here."

Hugo nodded.

"I was in a bicycle accident. I was learning and I fell and hit my head. I was in a coma for almost a week . . . but I wasn't . . . I was here with you." Rose looked at Hugo. His face was serious. "Until I saw you in that drive-through window, I thought you were something my mind created to keep me from dying from fear."

"Rosie, your hand." Hugo took her wrist and turned it so he could see the wound. The blood had dried, but new stuff was still welling up from the gash. Slower than before, but still there.

Rose ignored the new feeling Hugo's touch brought up in her. She needed to say this before she forgot. "Hugo, I was so sad when I woke up in the hospital. I cried. My parents thought it was because I was frightened . . . but it was because I thought I'd lost you."

"But then the next time you went to sleep . . ."

"There you were."

"Always."

Rose fought the impulse to lean into Hugo. To push her mouth against his. She made herself look away.

There in the distant shimmer of the flats, Rose saw a *something*. Several *somethings*, lumpy and irregular.

She squinted.

It was the stack of old dining room chairs. She remembered them from when they had been chasing the figure through the forest around the Lagoon. What were they doing here?

And the black shape next to it . . . it must be the old battered trunk. Two brown somethings sat on it . . . boxes?

Rose stood up, pulling her hand from Hugo's grasp. She walked closer to the mirage. There was a scrawl on the boxes, something written there.

"X-mas Decor."

And on the other, it read: "Mom's Photos."

Rose turned to Hugo. "What happened to you before we met?"

But he wasn't looking at her. Or the somethings. His eyes were fixed on the blue line of the sea in the distance. . . .

Or the not-so-distance.

Rose's eyes widened. The water had formed a wall and it was racing toward them at an incredible rate. It was huge, gray. Filling the horizon as far as she could see.

Rose looked back at Hugo. He was terrified.

S he woke up just as the water came crashing down over them.

Her body was wet.

It took her a moment to realize that it was sweat causing her clothes to stick to her body . . . the water of the looming dream sea had not drenched her in this world.

She rolled over.

Josh's side of the bed was empty.

R ose would have liked to talk to Naomi about all of this—about the fight with Josh and the new feelings of her dreams, about the strangeness of having Hugo meet her family.

But she couldn't because she had stopped seeing her.

When Rose lied to Naomi about what occurred in the parking lot of the Orange Tastee in Hemsford, she had halfway convinced herself that what she told her therapist must be the truth. When she said that she "ate lunch and went home," it was still possible for a part of Rose to believe it.

But there was no such possibility of self-delusion when Rose met with Hugo in the food court of the outlet mall.

Yet when Rose met with Naomi that week, setting her purse on the coffee table in the dark confines of her office, Rose decided that she would say nothing of her encounter with the man who lived in her dreams.

There were many reasons for this, the first being that she would have had to admit to the lie, and Rose, like most people, did not enjoy being thought a liar . . . even when it was the truth.

The other reason Rose did not mention her encounter was that she was not crazy.

And she knew that the belief that you have been sharing your dreams with a stranger for most of your life, and that you have now met him in your waking life, is an insane belief.

And just as Rose did not want Naomi to think she was a liar, she also did not want her to think that she was a loony.

Which, one supposes, can be a bit of a handicap when one is seeking help within the mental health community—that is, people trained to recognize madness.

So Rose told Naomi of the events in only one half of her life. She complained of her struggles with the boys, her concerns about Isaac, her frustrations with the life she was leading—but she never let on to the wonder of her discovery of Hugo. This made her hours with Naomi exhausting, as she had to make sure nothing she said revealed her true mental state to her doctor.

This is, of course, something that mental health providers are used to experiencing from their patients.

Naomi knew that she was getting only half of Rose . . . but she never suspected the truth. She thought perhaps Rose had begun drinking heavily or engaging in some form of self-abuse that she wasn't yet ready to discuss. Like many therapists, Naomi decided that Rose would soon enough get around to talking about whatever it was she was not saying.

But soon enough never happened.

Naomi went on a ten-day vacation (Barbados), a happenstance that interfered with two of Rose's appointments. When she told Rose this at the end of a session during which Rose had had to rack her brain to come up with non-Hugo-related material, Rose had told her she wasn't sure what her schedule would be and to call her when she got back.

Naomi had a lovely time on the island (though she did get a sunburn), and when she returned she left a message on Rose's voice mail. "When would you like to come in?"

Rose never called her back.

She justified this by saying that she was simply too busy, that there was just too much going on for her to take the time to go *talk* about herself.

She also told herself that it was too expensive, and even though the insurance paid for most of it, there was still the babysitting she had to get for Penny. That managed to add up.

So Rose erased Naomi's voice mails without listening to them and tried to ignore the twinge of guilt she felt when she did it.

There were times when she missed Naomi, when she would have liked to have someone to talk to about her life. But she couldn't fathom catching her therapist up on the events regarding Hugo. It would take forever, and doing so would reveal all the lies she had been telling.

And Rose had to admit she was a little afraid that Naomi might become alarmed at the current state of Rose's mental affairs and she might call Josh.

———

R ose did not see Josh again until the next evening.

They kissed and pretended that nothing had happened. No one mentioned the bicycle. No one complained about Josh's hours.

No one apologized for anything . . . to have done so would have been to recognize an infraction had occurred.

Josh told Rose gossip he had heard about the hospital administrators. Rose caught Josh up on the various school events he would likely miss. She would tape them for him, though they both knew he would never watch the tapes.

Josh told her he had a free evening this week if she wanted to have David over.

"Who?"

"David. Brown hair. Little pudgy. The guy you went to school with."

Hugo.

"Oh. Right."

"I thought we should have him over here. The kids are always a pain at restaurants."

Rose reeled. She had never thought he would actually follow through on having Hugo over. People said they should get dinner all the time. It was just something people say, without ever actually meaning to do it.

"Does he have any family?"

"A daughter . . . but she doesn't live here. It would . . . it would just be him."

"He's a little weird don't you think? I mean, nice, but you know . . ."

"What?"

"Nothing . . . he seemed . . . lonely. But I guess if he's just moved here . . . I dunno, was he always like that?"

No.

"I don't remember. Maybe. It was a long time ago." Rose shrugged as she felt the lie slip over her shoulders.

"Well, text him and see if that night will work for him. I can't imagine he has too much going on yet."

Rose nodded. She knew already. Even if he was busy, if she asked, Hugo would come.

H ugo brought cupcakes, the grocery store kind with tacky plastic knickknacks buried in room-temperature icing. Isaac and Adam squealed when they saw these in their visitor's hands.

"Can we have those instead of what you made, Mom?"

"Yeah. Please, Mom? Please?"

Rose had made a beautiful nut cake, grinding the flour in the food processor for almost half an hour, microplaning orange peel into the glaze. The completed loaf was cooling in the pantry, making the room smell like a bakery in Paris, but to her boys it was no competition for the lure of Crisco frosting and football-shaped rings.

"Sure, guys."

The boys cheered and ran back into the kitchen. Hugo looked sheepish. "Sorry, I guess I should have asked. . . ."

"It's okay."

"I just thought . . . Someone told me when you go to someone's house, you bring something."

"It's fine." Rose smiled at him and he smiled back. He was nervous. "Coat?"

He turned and she helped him take off his windbreaker, her hand grasping the worn collar against his neck. She felt the

warmth of his shoulders through his shirt on the backs of her
fingers.

This was so strange. Why were they doing this?

She felt Hugo's eyes on her as she turned to put the coat on
one of the hooks that held the boys' jackets. Its blue nylon enveloped the bright yellow of Adam's parka, like a hug, hiding it
away.

"I'm just going to put some music on!" Josh called in from
the kitchen. Suddenly jazz blurted out of the speakers in the ceiling, and farther in the house came the sound of Isaac and Adam
groaning in unison. Hugo furrowed his brows at Rose. She giggled, but before she could say anything, they heard Josh's voice
again. "Come on, guys, it's not that bad." But the music shifted
to an apparently less offensive mix of forties standards.

Rose took a deep breath and grimaced at Hugo.

Not Hugo. David.

She would need to remember to call him David.

Josh made a big deal of presenting his herbed haricots verts.
It was one of the few things he knew how to make, and he had
texted Rose twice to make sure she got the ingredients for him.
It was sweet, she supposed, but for a man who regularly saved
people's lives on the operating table, Rose thought he made a
bit too much out of his ability to steam green beans.

Rose had given Hugo/David a beer as soon as he had come
into the kitchen. One of Josh's microbrews. He had taken a sip
right away, but his mouth had puckered almost instantly. She
offered him something else, but he had refused, insisting that
he liked what she had given him.

By the time they sat down to dinner, the bottle was sweaty
with condensation, still full to the neck.

Adam whispered secrets into Isaac's ear, both staring at Hugo, as Rose carried the rosemary pork loin to the table. "Stop it, boys. Be polite."

Adam snapped his hands back from Zackie's ear and sat on them. Whatever they were up to, Rose just didn't want it going on at the dinner table.

Josh slipped Penny into her booster. She had a bib on over her pink-striped pajamas. Penny smiled at Hugo, pointing at him with her fork. "No kitty?" she asked.

Hugo looked at Rose, stricken. She answered for him. "No, honey. Mr. David does not have a kitty."

Josh smiled at their guest. "She asks everyone that."

Nervous, Hugo took another sip of his beer and immediately grimaced at the taste. He coughed a little, covering his mouth. Everyone was staring at him. "I . . . uh . . . I want to thank you for having me over. It's been a while since I had anything that could be called a family dinner."

Hugo looked at the table while he said this, his eyes resting on nothing in particular.

"Rose said you had a daughter."

Hugo shot a quick glance at Rose, then to Josh. "I do. I don't get to see her much. She lives in Florida. With her mother."

Josh provided a "That's too bad," but his condolences were overlapped by Isaac, whose ears perked up at the mention of the Sunshine State.

"Where Disney World is?"

"No, lower. Fort Lauderdale."

For Isaac, who imagined Florida as a penis-shaped puzzle piece with a pair of mouse ears in the center, "Fort Lauderdale" had no meaning at all. He supposed this man's daughter must live with the alligators, since that was the only other knowledge he had of the place.

"You must miss her," said Rose.

"They've lived there for a while." Hugo's voice was ambivalent.

Josh caught Rose's eye and she could tell he was thinking, *What kind of guy doesn't miss his child?*

But Rose felt herself instinctively push against the thought. This was her Hugo, after all. Yes, she had heard it, too, the flatness in his voice, but there must be a good reason for it. A story she didn't yet know and was too polite to ask for. But it couldn't mean that he didn't actually care about his daughter. Or that he hadn't seen her in a long time. She knew Hugo, after all, and he just wasn't that kind of person.

She was half-lost in this thought when she heard Josh ask if David's parents still lived in Cow Town.

"Cow Town?"

Rose nearly choked. "That's what—" She hit her chest. "That's what—" She hit it again. Josh and Hugo watched her as she took a sip of water and croaked out, "Excuse me . . . That's what Josh calls *our* hometown."

Rose hoped desperately that Hugo would understand her, that he would hear the emphasis in the *our*.

But Josh was grinning, getting ready for the setup. "I call it that because—"

"More cows live there than people." Rose joined him in the familiar singsong. It had been a joke he had made when he had first visited her parents, driving past the cattle yards on the outskirts of the county. It wasn't really funny then, and it wasn't now, but it had become a "bit"—something Rose groaned her way through and Josh enjoyed doing. Ultimately it became cute. Rose and Josh thought about it as one of their "couple things."

But Hugo didn't laugh, though he did get the joke.

"Oh . . . No . . . my parents died when I was eight."

Rose's mouth dropped. How did she not know?

"Isaac is eight," said Adam, helpfully.

"Adam, hush." Josh looked grim.

Rose's hands were on her mouth. "I'm so sorry."

Hugo shrugged. "It's okay. It was a long time ago."

There was a long, awkward pause while Josh's and Rose's brains searched for something appropriate to say regarding the loss of one's parents a very long time ago. Hugo's revelation had sent all sorts of chemical washes lapping through the meat of their gray matter: grief, fear, lack of comfort, curiosity, shame.

Josh's mind quickly surveyed the situation and rang the Klaxon known as "subject change." It lit up to this sudden alert in a similar way when he was a Little League hitter, taking in the information of an oncoming baseball and sending the impulse to step into it and hit the ball in another direction.

"Well . . ." He said, "Adam and Isaac, did you know that Mr. David went to school with your mom when she was a little girl?"

Josh's boys were appropriately astonished. Josh relaxed as the ball of the conversation sailed back on course.

"You did?"

Isaac got to the heart quickly. "Did she ever get in trouble?"

Rose stepped in before Hugo had to think of a lie. "No. I never got in trouble. I was perfectly perfect. All the time."

Isaac looked from his mother to the man who could confirm her statement. "Was she?"

"I thought she was."

Rose smiled at him and he blushed. A shy smile back.

Josh saw it pass between them again. The same brief pulse he'd seen at the party. The same *something*, but it seemed here more intimate than it had then. More *immediate*.

"He knows about Hugo!"

Suddenly all three adults were staring at Adam.

"What?" said Josh.

Isaac answered, "Adam broke the map we made of Hugo's island—"

"Did not!" insisted his brother, but Zackie continued.

"—and he put it back together all by himself. He knew where everything went." Zackie's hand was pointing at their dinner guest.

Adam was nodding furiously. "I saw him do it."

Rose felt her stomach clench.

Hugo was nodding. "Uh, it wasn't broken."

"See." Adam stuck his tongue out at Isaac.

"It was at the party and I saw . . . I just put some of the pieces where they belonged, that's all."

"You know about Rose's dream friend?" Josh's face was still as he said this.

"Uh . . . well . . . I know Rose . . . so . . ."

Rose felt the rock in her stomach condense, compressing into itself. She wasn't breathing. *Please let this stop. Please.* But Adam was talking again—

"He knew where to put all the labels and he even knew to put the Spiders in the Chasm, but not on the beaches."

"Well . . ." Hugo's face was lit up. "Sometimes the Spiders are on the beaches. But they don't live there."

Isaac got excited. "Like when the deer stampeded onto the beach because the Spider was chasing them and Mom got caught in the middle of them."

"And then Hugo slayed the Spider!"

Hugo was grinning. "Well, your mom helped."

"You remember that from when you were a kid?"

Josh's voice was dark. Hugo turned to him, the joy on his face melting.

"Well. Uh . . . yeah." Hugo lied, "She talked about her dreams a lot."

fourteen

"Who is he?"

The children were in bed. Their guest was gone. The dishes lay stacked by the sink. . . . But the table still bore the crumbs and paper from the cheap cupcakes the boys had consumed, their appetites intact, unaware of the chill that had settled upon their parents.

Rose had brought out the nut cake for the adults, but the slices still lay uneaten on Rose's good china. Three plates in the sink.

"Who is he?"

Josh said it quietly, sitting at the table, not looking at her. His fingertips made a line of the orphaned yellow crumbs.

Rose leaned against the edge of the counter, gripping the rim for support.

"Nobody. Just a guy."

Josh inhaled through his nose. His index finger pulled another crumb into line. "He's three years older than you. I asked him."

She was quiet, watching her husband pull the bits together on the tabletop. The line on the table grew.

"So . . . I know you didn't go to school together."

Rose nodded. She knew he knew. She felt a folding within herself. A desire for a small, dark space.

"Are you fucking him?"

The word was like an arrow. *Fuck.* Pointed and fricative. Thrumming on its target.

But this, too, Josh said calmly. The surgeon getting all the pertinent details, sizing up the damage that had been done. Figuring out the extent of the trauma.

Rose shook her head. "No."

"Who is he?"

"Nobody."

"You didn't look at him like he was nobody." Josh divided a crumb with his fingernail, pressing it into two pieces, stretching the line.

Rose felt as if her entire self were sinking, pulled down into the stony gravity in her center. Josh was still not looking at her.

"You won't believe me."

She heard someone say it . . . *herself* say it . . . but she was still sinking and the sound of her voice, so small and distant, was far, far above her.

Josh had collected all of the crumbs. A line dotted across the table.

His finger paused in the center . . . then pushed the crumb

there forward an inch. He started speaking, still quiet, but as he spoke he pushed the line forward, punctuating his words with each crumb.

"I won't believe [*push*] that this person [*push*] who came into my house [*push*] and knew intimate [*push*] details [*push*] about my wife's [*push*] fantasy [*push*] world is nobody [*push*]. I won't believe [*push*] that you lied [*push*] to me about how you knew him [*push*] and sat [*push*] him across from my children [*push*], to eat food [*push*] I paid for [*push*], out of the goodness of your heart."

His hand swept over the line, scattering the bits of cake across the table.

Finally he looked at her.

"Who the hell is he, Rose?"

Josh watched as she dug through her nightstand. As she pulled a pile of the children's drawings from the drawer, placing on top of it a fistful of hair ties and ChapSticks. Change. Some errant Lego pieces. The lube.

Finally she pulled out the sleeve of a manila envelope. Its edges were worn, and there were darker patches where it had been handled, the trace oils from his wife's hands. Her name was written on it in neat block letters. Their address.

Rose swallowed as she handed it to him.

She looked as though she were going to say something, her jaw loosening its hinge, but then she shook her head.

Josh pulled the contents from the sleeve and sat on the bed to read.

Rose waited, leaning against the door frame, her breath shallow until he reached the final page and closed the comic.

Josh closed his eyes, hand resting on the cover illustration. Beneath it the Spider's legs splayed out in hairy ink.

"I don't ever want you to see him again."

Rose blinked, not understanding.

How could Josh not see the evidence of a miracle in his hands? Her dreams on paper? The impossibility proved of its existence?

"But . . . It's the truth. He's—"

"Rose"—Josh cut her off—"What you're suggesting . . . it's not possible."

"But, it's all there." Rose took a step into the room. "You *read it*. The pictures."

Josh shook his head. The pages in his hands were not a marvel; they were simply a more advanced version of the drawings his sons sometimes did. A retelling of his wife's dreams, but not by any stretch of the imagination *proof* that the man who had been at dinner had somehow been sharing dreams with Rose for almost three decades.

"Maybe he found a diary you wrote. Or heard a story you told. Maybe he's a scam artist, and he does this sort of thing all the time."

How could he not understand? This wasn't something that could be faked. . . .

"But my dreams—"

Suddenly Josh was standing. Angry. "He is *not Hugo*! The man in your dreams does not exist!"

"Then who ate your beans tonight?"

Josh's head rocked violently. Words pelted out of his mouth. "A huckster. A con man. Somebody who wants something from you and went to these ridiculous lengths to get it." He seized the comic book and tossed it onto the ground.

Rose went to scoop it up. "He is not a con man."

Josh's chest was heaving. His neck flushed, teeth bared. "I have to believe he's a con man, Rose." He paused, swallowed rage, and continued, "Because the alternative is me putting you in an institution because you've lost your mind."

"I'm not crazy."

"Then what does Naomi have to say about all this?"

Rose pictured the empty couch in her therapist's office, but she said nothing. Josh could tell by the look on her face. Beneath the rage, he felt the beginnings of more frightening emotions, pain, fear, loss. His wife was threatened or she was a threat . . . either way, anger was the more comfortable option. He leaned into it.

"You didn't tell her . . . because you knew if you did, she would know you'd fractured your reality. You didn't tell her because you know this is insanity."

It was decided that Rose was never to see David again.

Which is to say that Josh decided Rose would never see David again.

Josh was very careful when he said this, never once referring to the man as Hugo.

Of course, this decision came naturally to Dr. Josh, whose mind was filled with the case studies he'd read in medical school about twin psychosis and hallucinations caused by brain lesions. This belief of Rose's must be the symptom of some malady. He was angry with Naomi for missing it, but what could you expect from a *psychiatrist*? He would call some more people. Schedule some tests. Get a view to the inside of his wife's head.

But in the meantime, this *thing* between his wife and this man needed to stop.

He had made her cry. His beautiful Rose. He hated to do it.

But he could tell that she needed it. That she still *believed*, despite the fact that she also knew it was impossible that this man had been dreaming with her.

So he used the children against her. He used her love for them to get her to give up the delusion. Told her what happens to mothers who lose their minds, where they end up, how much their children miss them, how badly they suffer.

And Rose cried.

But she agreed. She nodded her head through her tears, and Josh held her. Rocked her. Rubbed her arms. She was a little girl in his embrace, asking for forgiveness. He gave it to her with a kiss on her forehead. They would get through this.

So when she said she needed to call *him* to tell him it was over, Josh nodded. That would be best.

Rose took her cell phone into the children's bathroom to call him. She wanted someplace dark and private. She had thought about going out to the garage, calling him from behind the wheel of her minivan—but she knew that would make Josh wonder. Wonder what she was saying. Wonder if she was leaving.

So she left the lights off in the bathroom. Sat against the vanity cabinet with her feet braced against the cool porcelain of the tub. In the dim she could make out the faint lines of the children's tub toys: Isaac's submarine, Adam's water whistle, Penny's mermaid.

Rose felt the rising hiccup of a sob. The half catch of her breath. She didn't want to do this.

But Josh . . .

The phone rang twice before Hugo picked up. Her throat ached and suddenly the tears were there again. At the fore. She couldn't say anything.

"Rose?"

A small sound. A tiny squeak of a sound.

"Rosie, are you crying?"

"Hugo . . . ," she managed, and then sniffled. A hot, wet sound in his ear. "I . . . I told him. I showed him . . ."

On the other end of the phone, Rose could hear his silence. The sound of his lips parting. Her throat felt like it was going to break.

"He didn't believe you," he said finally.

"He told me I could call you one more time and tell you that I can't see you anymore."

"What? Why?" His voice sounded like Isaac's. Like a hurt child.

She was hurting him. This was all her fault. It was she who *saw him*, who *followed him*, who *pursued him*. She who confronted him at work, who let him know she was a real person.

"I don't think we were ever supposed to meet." This she said quietly, brushing a tear away with the heel of her palm.

"Rose—"

She cut him off. "I think . . . I think we were just supposed to be in each other's dreams. I don't think this was ever supposed to happen."

"But it *did happen*."

"He said . . . he said mothers need to be in touch with reality for their children . . . and . . . I think the same thing."

"What we have *is* real."

Rose shook her head. It was, but it couldn't be. She couldn't let it. There was too much to lose. That's what Josh had done. He'd just reminded her of what she'd forgotten.

"It'll just go back to how it used to be."

"Rose, no . . ."

"We'll see each other every night. And maybe . . . maybe we can forget this ever happened."

She hung up the phone and folded in on herself, letting the waves of tears wash over her.

Rose's hand was on the wall of Castle City.

It took her a moment to realize this. Her field of vision was filled with dark green stones, smooth and cool under her palm. She turned and saw behind her the golden field of wildflowers that she had seen a thousand times from a different vantage.

It was then that she knew for certain.

Rose stepped back, angling her neck up. A few steps from the wall and the first tower appeared, nosing its way up from behind the stone.

Rose laughed.

All these years. All those attempts. Searching the invisible fence for the weak spot. Looking for a way in.

And here she was . . . by no effort of her own, the island had simply brought her here.

"Hugo!" she shouted, looking for him. There was no way she could have come here alone. He must be around here somewhere.

She bounded farther out into the field, the grasses tickling at her ankles. "Hugo!"

She turned to look up again at the city. To make certain of the fixedness of it. The towers grew from behind the wall, tall, rounded spires ascribing the full gamut of a single hue: forest green, leaf green, spring green, grass green, emerald, jade, olive, lime, chartreuse.

Rose cocked her head. For the first time she noticed something familiar about the city.

"It looks like Oz."

Why had she never noticed that before?

Movement by the wall pulled her attention.

Hugo. His back to her, running. Retreating around a corner.

Rose gave chase, her feet chewing up the distance between them. She rounded the bend and caught sight of him. He stood under the arch of an enormous portico, his hands loose at his sides, staring at the bases of the towers. Pausing on the cusp of the city.

The way in.

"Hugo!"

He turned from the city to look at her. But his face was slack, his eyes absent their usual glow.

Rose took a step back. It was wrong. Everything about this was wrong.

"Mom! Mommy! Momma!" She heard a cry from the other world.

R ose opened her eyes to the scaling light of the monitor.

"Mom!" It was Adam. A nightmare.

She pulled herself from the bed. Hand against the wall to steady herself.

What had that been about? They had gotten to the city. About to go in. There should have been joy, but instead there was that look on Hugo's face, so empty.

She was in the hallway by the time she remembered the evening, her conversation with Josh, her phone call with Hugo— the dream had swept it away, but now it was back, the grief from earlier, like a hangover, her waking body remembered.

But life must go on. Children must be tended to. No matter how much pain their mothers are in.

Rose entered the blue glow of the boys' room. Adam's little

body was turned from the door, still crying, curled under the covers. She gave a quick glance to Isaac, still asleep in his bed, and knelt by Adam's side.

"It's okay, honey. Just a bad dream."

Adam twisted and clung to her, her shoulder cradled to his chin. He was calming, the cries slowing down. Rose closed her eyes and just let herself feel the wonderful weight of her little boy, the rise and fall of his chest under her arms. The soft down of his hair against her neck.

This was what Josh had meant. She could not lose this.

He shifted against her. Rose stroked his back.

"Do you want me to give you some new dreams?"

There was a muted *shoosh*ing sound. Like sugar poured into a bowl. Rose felt a soft slither trickle its way down her back.

"Adam?"

Rose pulled her son away from her body. A trail of pink sand landed on her shoulder and the floor.

It was pouring from Adam's open mouth. Torrents of coral sand flooding from his little body, pooling on the sheets of his bed, his mouth a rictus of horrible surprise. His eyes huge with panic.

"Adam!" Rose tried to catch the sand with her hands. To stop it from coming up, but his body was spasming, calling up more silt.

An animal snort sounded behind her.

Rose turned.

A Buck stood in the bedroom. Its antlers were lowered, its eyes glowing red . . .

Ready to charge.

Rose awoke with a shout on the floor of the bathroom. She had fallen asleep, face pressed to the tile.

Her hand ached, sweaty and stiff. Curled around the flat rectangle of her cell.

Hugo had called fifty-nine times.

fifteen

Penny was going to try to poop by the couch, Rose was sure of it.

"Pen! Potty!"

"No need poop, Mama!" She put her chubby fists on her hips.

"Yes, poop."

"No. Poop."

Rose's head hurt. Her eyes hurt. Her stomach was sore from coughing out sobs. She felt hung over . . . though that sensation at least was the result of something that had been fun. Instead there was a flat, cold feeling inside of her.

Hugo.

Not now, she thought. *No time to think of it now. Put it away, Rose.*

The boys were making a racket. They had devoured the toaster waffles she had caved to, and with extra time to burn, they were careening around the kitchen, waving swords at each other. Zackie was playing aggressively, his foam saber too near his brother's eyes for Rose's comfort. But Addy was loving it, grinning in the warm shower of his brother's full attention.

His face was so different from the way it had been last night, a yaw of panic. A stream of sand pouring from his throat. But he was fine this morning. As though nothing had happened.

Because nothing had. Rose forced the word on herself. *Nightmare.*

Was that what they were like for the children? All these years she had been comforting them, trivializing their dreams . . . she had never known how horrible they could be.

Penny started crying. Someone had knocked her over.

"That's it! Backyard!" Rose pointed to the door. The boys' faces were suddenly pictures of innocence. "You have twenty minutes before the bus gets here."

They stood stock-still on the carpet, staring at their mother. Penny rolled to her feet, rubbing her head.

"Out."

The boys walked slowly to the door, giving Rose ample time to change her mind. She didn't.

Zackie turned to look at her once he passed the threshold. "But it's cold outside."

"It's not cold."

"It's colder than in the house."

Rose needed them out of her hair. Just a few minutes of peace. They would be fine. "Move around. It'll keep you warm."

Zackie crossed his arms. Her little adult. "Mom."

He sounded like Josh. That flat, reasoned tone. It pissed her off.

"Adam. Chase your brother."

Addy grinned. He roared and charged Isaac. Isaac took off, jumping from the steps to the patio and landing in the grass.

Rose closed the door, muffling the sound of the boys' yells. She put her forehead against the cool glass. In twenty minutes they would be out of here and she could . . . what? Sleep? Think? Cry?

"Momma?"

Penny was tugging on her sweatpants.

"Yes, honey?"

"Need to go poop."

Rose looked at her little girl. This was a milestone. "Then let's get you on the potty."

Rose helped Pen pull down her panties. She watched her lower her little bottom onto the potty seat situated in the middle of their kitchen floor. The two of them sat across from each other a moment, Penny's eyes searching her mother's for approval. Rose managed a thin smile. "Good girl, honey."

Outside the boys were yelling, their play more raucous in the outdoors.

Rose's head hurt.

"You want Momma to get you a book, honey?"

Penny nodded.

"I'll be right back."

Rose made her way up the stairs. Maybe she'd call Mrs. D to take Penny for a few hours. . . . She could figure out some way to distract herself. To make herself feel better.

They had gotten to Castle City last night.

The thought sent a thrill through her body. The thing they

had been waiting for for years. The place they had been trying to reach, they had gotten there.

But then there had been the nightmare. And before that, the phone call. Josh's anger. His threat.

Rose couldn't live without her children.

And though she didn't believe she was crazy (*I'm not; I can't be*), she also knew how it looked to her husband. How it would look to the world. If they knew what she believed.

Hugo.

Her chest ached remembering the silence on the other end of the phone. What he'd said.

What we have is real.

But not as real as my family, Rose told herself. She reached Penny's room and knelt to pull books from the bottom of the bookshelf. *Good Night, Gorilla. But Not the Hippopotamus.* Penny's favorites. The ones she would pretend to read aloud.

A corner of paper protruded from under the throw rug. Rose tugged it out.

One of Adam's drawings.

Hugo and Rose at Castle City.

We were there. We got there.

Rose wanted to call her friend. She wanted to apologize for hurting him. She wanted to say she was sorry she ever saw him. Sorry she ever brought him out of her dreams and into her life.

But she couldn't.

She crumpled the paper up and put it in the waste bin by the door.

Penny was singing as Rose made her way back down the stairs.

"Just remember when a dream appears, You belong to me. . . ."

She handed the books to Pen. Something was wrong. She couldn't hear the boys. Or see them through the window.

"Did Adam and Isaac come back inside?"

Penny shook her head.

Rose walked to the door. Adam and Isaac were hunched on the porch steps.

With Hugo.

He was bent over them, his back to Rose. The boys' eyes were round, their mouths open to whatever tale he must have been spooling for them. Their heads were close together, conspiratorial—breath making small clouds in their midst.

Rose opened the door. "Time to come inside, guys."

Isaac turned to her, the spell broken. "But—"

"The bus will be here soon. You need to get your backpacks."

The boys hesitated. Hugo was staring at her, his mouth closed. The skin under his eyes was dark and baggy.

He made her heart hurt . . . but this . . . him appearing in her backyard . . . It wasn't okay.

Rose took a step onto the porch. "March, boys."

Isaac and Adam tumbled into motion. Launching themselves at the sound of Rose's command.

Rose didn't take her eyes off Hugo. But she waited until she heard the door shut behind her.

"You—"

"I needed to see you."

"I told you." Rose's throat felt as if it were being pulled. As if it might tear.

"But we almost . . . Please, Rose. Just . . . just one more time."

His face looked like it did in her dreams. Like it had when he was a boy and he had told her how long he had been waiting for her. A sweet, open pleading.

She had known him her whole life.

She owed him more.

Rose felt herself nodding. "Let me . . . let me take care of them." She jerked her head back toward the boys and Penny inside.

"Thank you."

"I'll meet you at your house . . . just . . . go."

W hen Rose was about nine years old, her mother had campaigned to get her father to join the local country club. Dinnertime talk and drives home from church were peppered with casual talk about how it "would be good for business" and "healthy for Rosie."

Rose's mother had tempted her with visions of snack bars and tennis courts, hoping to recruit her to the cause. Rose had remained ambivalent, namely because there had also been mention of a swim team with early practices that would "get her out of the house for the day."

Rose's father had remained stoic through all of it. Noncommittal. Nodding without ever agreeing to anything. Whenever Rose's mother pushed him, he had shrugged and said, "I don't know. I'm of two minds about it."

Two minds. Rose pictured her father holding two jars with brains in them. The man with two brains, like that Steve Martin movie she had seen a few minutes of before her mother had caught her and turned off the TV.

They did not end up joining the country club, but the image had stuck with Rose as she grew. The ridiculous picture of two brains in jars held by a single person would flash into her mind as she grew: deciding whether or not she was going to lose her virginity to her high school boyfriend, or whether to go to the college that offered her the highest scholarship or the one with the better reputation. It had even briefly visited her when she held the pregnancy test that had announced the coming of Adam, years before any other baby had been planned.

I don't know. I'm of two minds.

It came to her again as she waved Hugo away from her back door. A static image of brains in vitro.

Because if Rose knew anything, she knew her brains were at war.

They had, in fact, been fighting since the moment she spotted Hugo in the drive-through window. Her brain for weeks had been the site of bickering. But her confession to Josh and his subsequent "line drawing" was the bombing of Pearl Harbor. An incitement to full-out combat.

Josh had only made clear something she had been telling herself for weeks: that Hugo was a threat to everything she held dear. That whether or not there was any truth to her dreams, she should not hope to have a relationship with this strange unmarried man. That it was unsafe. That it was unseemly.

But then there was her "other mind." Source of the deep, rising syrupy feeling that came with Hugo's kiss. The whisperer of "what if." The curious wonderer who reminded Rose that she had known Hugo all her life. Who needled her to find out *Why him? Why you? Why now? Why?*

Rose hated that mind. Hated herself. Wished for the conviction of Josh, always so sure.

But then there was the look on Hugo's face. This was all her fault. She owed it to him, this promise. This final good-bye.

Rose's minds warred as she prepared to go see Hugo for the last time. One driving her to shave her legs and put on a skirt, but the other urging her to skip the makeup. One making her tell the Widow Delvecchio when dropping off Penny that she would only be a few hours, the other keeping her from naming a specific time at which she would be back. One who told her even as she exited the highway into Hemsford that she could turn around, go home, never see him again.

And the other who shrugged and said, *Why not? You've already come all this way.*

It was this mind that pushed her out of her parked car and onto Hugo's front porch.

H ugo's house was a mess.

Though, to be truthful, "mess" was a kind word for it. Mess implies a kind of homey clutter. Papers that need to be filed. Shoes that need to be put away. Beds that need to be made.

But as Rose sat on his couch, perched uncomfortably on the edge, the disorder around her had none of the casual, "get around to it" feel of a "mess." Clothes were everywhere. A shirt draped over the couch. Pants caught under the front door. Used plates and glasses stacked in the sink. She resisted the urge to start picking up. Jesus, what the hell had happened here?

She had.

She was the reason Hugo's life was falling apart. Rose felt this with a deep certainty.

Hugo had answered the door quickly, swinging it open before she had even landed the first knock. He had smiled, relieved she had come. As she stepped inside, Rose noticed his skin looked different from the way it had earlier in the morning light of her backyard.

It looked gray.

He offered her a glass of water. Rose nodded, saying nothing as she took in the systematic decay that was his living room. He motioned for her to sit on the one clear surface in the center of the couch.

So she sat and she looked and she listened: The sound of the faucet squeaking on. The ringing clank-clank of water pressure knocking plates in the sink against one another. The change in the sound as he moved something under the stream. Then the rising ring of a cup filling.

He returned, pained smile, his fist clamped around a still damp mug. "Sorry. I had to clean a glass."

Rose nodded. She still hadn't said anything. She didn't think she would be able to. She felt . . . *flayed*. Raw. As though she'd been stripped of her skin and everything she was experiencing was right on the exposure of her nerves.

"Rose?" He still held out the cup.

She took it and he sat on the couch, his weight displacing the air in the cushions for a moment and lifting her. Rocking her.

Rose felt a word bubble up. "Hugo—"

"They fired me."

She didn't understand. His smile was gone. He was staring at the mug in her hands, his eyebrows furrowed.

"At work. They fired me."

Rose's brain finally computed the information Hugo had given her. She had been expecting something else, so it had taken a moment to get it. *Hugo had lost his job.* Her brain had no idea how to handle what it had been anticipating, but *this, this loss of employment* . . . this had precedent, appropriate responses. It was almost a relief to know for a moment what to do. *Comfort. Sympathy.*

"Oh, Hugo . . . I'm so sorry."

He swallowed. Shook his head. "It . . . it's not a big deal. I just wanted you to know." He took a shallow breath and shifted. Rose felt his movement through the cushion. His gravity changing her position. He inhaled sharply. "It's just sometimes I feel like *this part* is the dream, and the other . . . that that's who I really am."

His eyes grew glassy with unshed tears, and he buried his face in his hands.

Rose had never seen Hugo cry. On the island he was always calm, happy, serious when the occasion called for it. But never had she seen him broken like this.

Her heart ached for him. His back shuddered like Adam's. A little boy.

"Oh, Hugo." Instinctively, she reached out and touched his shoulder.

He lifted his head, thumbed an errant tear from the corner of his eye. "That's the problem. To everyone else I'm someone else. I'm David. I'm only Hugo to *you*."

He leaned toward her, wrapping her in a hug. Rose felt the scratch of his whiskers against her neck. His hot face pressing against her hair and scalp. His arms over hers, so different from Josh's—their shorter length intensifying the angle. Making his grip on her stronger.

"Only you know how I really am. Who I really am." His chest vibrated against her.

Rose let herself lean into him. Her chin cupping over his shoulder.

Caramel. He smells of caramel.

He whispered, breath dancing in her hair, "And I'm the only person who knows who you really are."

Rose heard a small squeak come from somewhere inside her.

"I love you, Rose."

He turned his head, his nose sweeping an arc until it was only an inch from hers.

Rose held her breath. Her mind cleared of the images of

brains in jars, swept away by another familiar phrase. *Of what consequence are the dreams of housewives?* . . .

And then he was kissing her.

It was different from the dream. His lips were rougher, their texture different beneath that foreign shelf of whiskers under his nose. But Rose felt that blooming within herself nonetheless, that rising syrup of a feeling within.

Yes.

Rose parted her lips and began to kiss him back. Hugo pressed her into the couch, moving his torso up against hers. Rose could feel his heat on top of her. His hands were suddenly everywhere.

Yes.

Hugo clung to her, a lifeline, even as his mouth and hands struggled to possess her. "I need you. I need you."

And Rose wanted him to take whatever would make him feel better, whatever would make them both feel better. Their clutching became desperate, almost flailing.

"Do it."

Rose had said it, her voice a desperate whine.

Suddenly Hugo was seizing her hips, yanking them forward on the couch. He fell forward onto her, burying his face into the space between her breasts, leaving sweaty trails on her shirt. His hands left her body to fumble at his fly. Rose pulled up her skirt and yanked her panties to the side.

"I've thought . . . about this . . ." His breath was a mutter, his weight sinking into her. "You . . . you feel like home." Rose held him tightly as he trembled, sinking her hips into him, traces of his kisses drying on her skin.

Home. Yes, he was right. This was *home.*

Then Rose reached down. She touched him, brought him toward herself.

But he remained soft in spite of the urgency of the rest of his body.

"I'm sorry, I—I don't . . . I don't know why . . ."

She heard the frustration in his voice. The turmoil. And she knew.

"It's okay. It's okay, Hugo." But he shook his head, turning away. Ashamed. *He's a broken boy*, she thought. *My poor, sweet man.* Rose slid off to comfort him. "No. No." Kissing his face. "No. No. No."

She wrapped her hands around his head, pulling him into her chest. "No. It's not supposed to be . . . this isn't *how* we belong."

He had a bottle of expired sleeping pills in his medicine cabinet. They were fifteen months past the "use by" date printed on the label, and Hugo did not remember buying them.

They took them anyway.

The pills had been Rose's idea. Hugo had led her to his bedroom. She had pulled the coverlet up over his unmade bed and rumpled pillows. There they had tried to fall asleep, the backs of their hands touching, their eyes gazing across the expanse of inexpensive cotton.

But neither had been able to slip off consciousness unaided.

As they lay in the bed, Rose felt things bubble up through the sweet, syrupy feeling of Hugo's affection. Her obligations. Her responsibilities. Josh. The kids. *What was she doing, anyway? In bed with a man who was not her husband?*

Rose tried to put out these impurities. To drown them in the honey of her desire for Hugo. She *wanted* this, she wanted to *know what it would be like.*

And besides, *it was just sleep.*

She had stopped just shy of any *real* infidelity. What haunted her was the possibility that she would have to think of herself as an unfaithful wife. A few minutes more and she would have been denied that . . . but this . . .

Well really . . . this was just a nap.

But regardless of these mental acrobatics, thoughts of her husband continued to bubble up through the syrup of desire, keeping her from sleep.

Hugo, too, seemed to be struggling, his eyes bright.

When Rose asked if he had any sleep aids, she did so shyly . . . almost the way one would ask about a condom. Hugo nodded quietly and the two of them went to his bathroom.

There was a moment, before Hugo swung open the mirrored medicine cabinet, when Rose saw both herself and Hugo standing together at the sink.

A moving picture framed in stainless steel.

Hugo and Rose.

But they were the wrong versions of themselves. Both fat. Too old to be beautiful. Wrinkled. Hugo's shirt unfashionable and cheap. Rose's breasts and belly too saggy under the fabric of her shirt.

She felt herself pushing at the image, kicking away to swim toward the dream. To who they really *were.*

She was relieved when the mirror finished its arc, revealing its contents, hiding their images from them.

The bottle was directly in the center of the chest. A sun to the solar system of Hugo's deodorants and aftershaves.

"I think these were my wife's," he said, pulling them out. "I've never had a problem falling asleep."

Mention of Hugo's long absent wife brought Josh bubbling up through Rose's mind. Rose shook it off. She wanted to feel like *herself* . . . like her *real self.* She snatched the bottle out of his hand as he read the expiration date.

"It'll be fine," she said, squeezing off the childproof cap. She shook two pills into her palm. "Open your mouth," she commanded him.

Rose tried not to think about how similar she sounded to when she gave medicine to her sons.

But Hugo complied. A good little boy.

Rose placed the pill in the center of his tongue. A communion.

They each took sips of water from the mug he had washed for her and went back to his bed.

Despite their expiration date, the pills were potent.

sixteen

They were in the Blanket Pavilion. Rose could hear the snapping of its sheet walls against breezes of the island. She could feel the sand shifting under her body, yielding and warm.

She could also feel Hugo's hands.

Hugo's hands on her firm breasts. On her strong thighs. On her tucked waist.

Rose moaned as his kisses left warm traces on the skin of her chest. This is what it should be like. *This. This.*

She kissed his neck, wrapping her legs around his torso. She heard his breath shudder. *This.*

They were on Hugo's bed. An image of what they must look like popped into her mind. Two middle-aged bodies, prone on the covers of an old mattress, breathing deeply. In unison.

They were there. But they were also *here*. Together in both places.

This. This.

Here Hugo did not cry. Here there was no desperation in his hands. He was not clutching at her, seeking comfort. His grip was firm, not grasping.

Rose arched her back to press closer to him.

Oh, God, why had they never done this before? This was so nice, so right.

Hugo and Rose.

Hugo shifted his hips away from her, his knees making furrows in the sand. It was almost time. Rose closed her eyes.

Oh please. Yes. This. This.

She felt his arms snake up beneath her shoulders. His fingers wrapped themselves in her hair, twisting gently against the roots. His mouth pushed into hers, lips soft but insistent.

This.

There was a sudden shift in the light. A darkness falling over the diffuse walls of the Pavilion. The change registered through Rose's shuttered eyelids. Something was wrong.

She opened her eyes.

The Pavilion was gone. Hugo's face was still pressed up against hers in a kiss, but beyond it she could just make out the painted grid of a cinder-block wall. Where the hell were they?

"Hugo?"

He pulled away from her, alerted by the alarm in her voice. As he pulled back Rose caught a glimpse of her hair, still twisted in his hands. It was blond, straight. The tacky shade chosen by women who don't care about looking natural.

Hugo's eyes went wide when he saw her. "Summer Cameron."

"What?"

"Rose, is that you?"

"Of course it's me."

"You don't look like you."

He was right. Rose looked down at her body. It *was* different. More petite. Her blond hair trailed over a slouchy sweater
worn over a spandex miniskirt . . . and beneath that—

"Am I wearing anklets with heels?"

Hugo was looking around. "You're Summer Cameron. That's
how she dressed."

Rose looked at Hugo. He, too, had been transformed, though
he was still Hugo. Or rather a version of Hugo. He looked to
be about sixteen. His skin was raw with acne, his hair spiked
and short, a thin line of a rattail ran down the back of his neck.
Plastic-rim glasses. Pleat-front acid-washed jeans. A well-loved
"Rush" T-shirt.

"This isn't the island."

They were in a stairwell, the concrete landing between two
flights. Rose took in the institutional metal railings, the gray-
painted blocks.

"This is my high school." Hugo was taking it in.

He turned and looked at her again. "Oh God."

"What?"

"You're Summer Cameron."

"You said."

"You're the girl I had a crush on. You never talked to me,
but then one day you brought me down here to make out after
school."

Rose was frustrated. Between her legs the *want* that Hugo had
been building was still there, embers waiting to be blown into a
flame. "That's kind of hot."

She wrapped her hands around him and pulled him into the
wall. *Why were they here?* She didn't care. She wanted to feel

Hugo against her body . . . even if it looked to him like this high school bimbo's.

"No!" He pushed away from her violently, fear in his voice.

"Hey, asshole!" a young male voice echoed down at them.

Rose looked up. A crew of jocks in letter jackets leaned over the metal guardrail above them, their faces caught in cruel grins.

Hugo started shaking his head, his breath short. "No. No." He put his hands at his groin, attempting to cover the huge erection that strained at the pleat of his jeans.

"Dude!" Above, the jocks were pointing. "Loser!"

Their laughter bounced off the close walls, turning their trio into a chorus.

Hugo looked at Rose. "She did it on purpose. They put her up to it. To humiliate me."

Rose's heart ached at the look of pain in Hugo's eyes. The way he was trying to hunch over to hide evidence of his arousal. "This really happened?"

She took a step toward him and heard a soft splash. Rose looked down. The lace of her anklets bobbed, lifting in a pool of cold water.

"What the—"

Rose turned her head. The whole stairwell below them was submerged, flooding from below. Through the gray water Rose could make out the steps of the stairwell. It was rising fast from below . . . already the lace of her socks was underwater, the edge creeping closer to her knees.

"Oh, God." Hugo's face was stricken. White with panic. Staring at the water at their feet.

"What's going on, Hugo?"

Above them the jocks were still laughing. Their cackles were loud in Rose's ears. Hugo seized her hand and pulled them toward the upper stairwell, dragging Rose away from the flooding stairs. "Come on!"

"What's happening?"

They crested the stairs, water dripping from their legs, painting wet Rorschach blots onto the concrete steps.

Hugo blew past the still laughing and pointing jocks, his fingers digging into Rose's hand. "We have to get back to the island!"

Rose's ankle twisted, pink heel giving way under the slippery linoleum, but Hugo kept dragging her, yanking her down the tiled hallway of classrooms. Frantic, he began opening doors, revealing the fluorescent-lighted desks and chalkboards within. Portraits of the presidents, inspirational quotes.

"Hugo, I don't understand."

He dragged her to another door, twisting the lever and pushing it open. The door vibrated as it hit a wall of file cabinets. "This place isn't safe. We have to get back."

Rose looked back at the end of the hall. The jocks were still there, laughing and pointing, their grins monstrously huge. Gray water broke from the threshold of the stairwell and was spilling over their ankles, reaching its way down the corridor.

Hugo spotted something across the hall. Through the wire-laced safety-glass window of a classroom door, they spotted a curl of pink sand. A glimpse of a turquoise sea. The cloudy promise of the island.

"Come on!" He hauled Rose toward the door.

The thin line of clear water approached them. The leading edge of the spilled contents of a mop bucket. At the end of the hall, the jocks were waist-deep, laughing monsters, their eyes pinpricks beneath their rictus smiles.

"Hugo . . ."

Rose felt him yank her inside the classroom and shut the door. She turned.

This was definitely not what they had seen through the door. Pink sand blanketed the floor of what looked to be a boy's bedroom from the late 1970s. *Star Wars* sheets on the bed. Rock'em Sock'em Robots nestled in a hollow between dunes. A flip-board alarm clock at the bedside.

Rose was reminded of her best friend's older brother's room when she was a girl. That stale young-male smell. The scent of sweat socks and ringer tees.

"Where are we?" she asked, but Hugo was lost in thought. Taking in the details. His hand found a small Matchbox Camaro on the desk in the corner, his finger tracing the outline of the wheels.

"Hugo?"

A shadow passed by the window and Rose went to it. Looking outside.

Wherever they were, they were on the second floor. Rose looked down on a placid scene. A flat river in the distance. An expanse of scrubby grass. A dirt road leading to a gravel drive. And a car—the make flew into Rose's head—a Subaru wagon.

Instantly Rose knew that the car didn't belong. It was out of place. She was peering through the window into another time. In this room, it was the seventies . . . but out there, it was a more recent past.

There was someone in the car. Two someones. Rose squinted and leaned into the glass.

"That's me," she said, and it was.

But it wasn't her. Not the dream her. It was the "her" that lived in the waking world, glaring out at the house through the windshield. Her face was angry, ugly, her mouth a thin line as she turned the ignition.

Movement drew Rose's eye to the passenger seat. Two small hands pressed up against the dash. *Penny.* Unsecured, next to her in the front seat, her daughter smiled and waved up at her. *Hi, Momma. Bye, Momma.*

Rose's dormant mind suddenly regained its lost strength. *Penny not in a car seat? In the front of a car? She would never . . . not in a million years.*

Rose felt Hugo by her side at the windowsill. He wasn't looking at the car below them. He was looking at the river, panic spreading. He looked to Rose the way he had the day she showed herself to him in the Orange Tastee. Sweaty with fear.

"We can't be here! We can't be here!" he cried.

R ose awoke certain that Hugo had punched her. That he had flailed out in his attempt to wake himself and connected with the meat between her breast and shoulder. Pain radiated from that site, yanking Rose out of her slumber.

Hugo, for his part, was panting by the side of the bed. He had thrown himself off of it, distancing himself from Rose and the dream. His panic still following him.

"Hugo?"

He put his hand up. Blocking the sight of her from his eyes . . . blocking her from seeing his face. A small sound eked out of him.

Rose sat up. There was too much to think about. They had not been on the island. She had not been herself. There had been other people.

Rose started as a yellow *thing* jumped onto the bed. The cat.

It rubbed itself against Rose's elbow and made its way up to the nightstand. And then she noticed the time on the flip-board alarm clock. It was six P.M.

"Oh, my God."

_____

R ose's skin was salty with dried sweat by the time she pulled
into the garage. The ride home had been torturously long.
She had driven without the radio on, her car tomb quiet. The
better to hear her own thoughts, *Idiot.*

Rose sat quiet and stewed in the things that had occurred
while she had been having Hugo's nightmare. She knew that
the boys had gotten home from school and that no one had been
there to let them inside. She knew that Penny had been with the
Widow Delvecchio much longer than either her daughter or
the old woman could tolerate. She knew that there were certainly hundreds of missed calls on her cell phone and that Josh
had likely been called from work. She knew that she was at least
an hour's drive away from her home and that her husband would
be waiting for her on the other end of that drive . . . full of the
knowledge of where she had been.

Her husband, who had not replied to her text that she would
be home in an hour.

His silence frightened her the most.

The door to the garage squealed as she opened it. The house
was dark, though Rose could tell by the flickering blue light and
the nattering sound track of an animated movie that her family
was home. Of course the house was dark. She was the one who
turned on the lights, setting the mood for each time of the day.
She was the one who clicked on the lamps and turned off the
overheads after dinner was finished, signaling to everyone that
the time had come to slow down. She was the one who pulled the
shades in the morning and drew them at night.

Josh was more binary. Lights were on if he needed them, off
if he didn't. When they had first lived together, it had taken

Rose a while to adjust to the fact that she might come home from work to find Josh in a dark apartment, a single bulb lighting his textbooks.

Rose stepped into the family room. Addy and Zackie sat on the couch, blank faces, entranced by the television. Penny had fallen asleep on the floor, rump in the air, head to the side, rosebud mouth pressed against the carpet. They were all still in their day clothes, and Rose could make out ketchup stains on Addy's shirt. Fast food, the dinner of last resort.

"Hi, Mom." Isaac lifted his hand vaguely. He didn't even look away from the screen.

Rose walked into the kitchen, stopping at the threshold.

Josh was at the table, his shape little more than a silhouette against the windows. She could make out that he was still in his scrubs, a polar fleece jacket the only indication he wasn't prepping for surgery.

He did not look at her.

"The boys waited for two hours on the porch before a neighbor finally saw them." Rose could hear the sound of his lips meeting, the fleshy pause. "They pulled me out of the OR. Adam couldn't stop crying. They thought you were dead."

"I—"

Josh ignored her. "This life we have, this is all I've ever wanted . . . I thought it was what you wanted."

"I do want it." Rose's voice sounded whiny and small in the darkness.

"Then . . . why?"

"Hugo—"

Josh exploded: "Is not real! None of this is real, Rose!"

"Mr. David told us he's Hugo. This morning."

Rose turned. It was Adam, a few feet behind her, his face side-lit by the sputtering light from the television. Rose's mind was suddenly filled with the image of Hugo bending over her boys in the backyard. The way they had been whispering.

"He told us he and Mommy have been best friends since forever. That they live in each other's dreams."

At this Josh stood so quickly that the chair under him fell back, bouncing off the floor. He barreled toward Rose and Adam, and for a moment Rose thought he was going to hit the boy. But then he was ripping the car keys out of her hand and continuing. He launched himself up the stairs, taking them three at a time.

"Is Daddy okay?" Adam's little face tilted up toward her.

No, Little Boy, no. Daddy is not okay. And neither is Mommy. None of this is okay.

But she did not say it. And then Josh was back. Thundering down the stairs. In the darkness Rose could make out a rectangle of paper in his hand. The envelope from the comic, Hugo's address in neat script in the upper right corner.

He blew past her, on the way to the garage.

"Josh." He did not reply, footsteps loud and large in the house. "Josh!"

The door to the garage slammed. Rose did not have to guess where her husband was going.

She did not try to stop him.

seventeen

Josh had large fingers punctuated by a set of particularly knobby knuckles. His fingernails were short, well trimmed, their cuticles dry and callused, a casualty of the lengthy hand washing that preceded the practice of his profession.

When he had been in medical school, before he started his surgical residency, Josh used to stare at the large phalanges radiating out from his palm and wonder if in the end it would be his fingers that would betray him . . . if it would be his large hands that would keep him from being the surgeon he had always dreamed of being. He worried that his hands would fail him and he would end up in some lesser field in which dexterity wasn't quite as important: dermatology, perhaps, or pediatrics.

But as it turned out, Josh's hands, though large, were quite adept. He had "the touch." He was gentle and precise with the scalpel. His sutures were small and neat. He was inordinately proud of this last fact, often electing to "finish up" himself when he could have had one of the interns do it. He rather liked the meditative quality of moving that thin needle in and out in a clean, straight line—the symbolic restoration of order to the chaos of the injured human body.

Even the largeness of his hands had turned out to be an asset. In his residency, Josh was a favorite of the older surgeons, who preferred him, with his long reach and wide hand span, over his shorter-statured colleagues. A long reach meant he wasn't crowding them to maintain his angle. Large hands meant a less tenuous grip on the slippery innards.

Once he learned that his hands were not going to let him down, Josh came to love them. They were, after all, the way he earned his living.

Because of this, Josh, for all his schooling and pride, would occasionally think of himself as little different from an auto mechanic. His job was to fix a machine (albeit a human one) that was not working correctly by using a specific set of tools that he manipulated with his hands. The level of peril was different—obviously no one is likely to die immediately if a mechanic accidentally cuts an antifreeze line—but nonetheless, both professions are dependent upon the dexterity of one's hands.

Of course, Josh also knew that a surgeon is a surgeon not because of his hands, but because of the connection of his hands to his *brain*. A brain that was specifically trained to recognize the various maladies and traumas that can occur within the human machine and has the knowledge to fix them.

Nowadays, no longer a student and no longer insecure, Josh would occasionally stare at his hands and think about how they had shaped his brain. People who work with their hands, musicians, surgeons, needlepoint enthusiasts, do develop stronger neural pathways with regard to nuance and precision. Their hands are bigger in their brains than those of mere dilettantes. Their lacy network of hand-related neurons is larger, stronger, and brighter.

But a musician without hands is still unable to play, no matter how many tunes his brain may know.

A surgeon who cannot use his hands is not a surgeon. He is at best a former surgeon, a consultant.

Josh knew this and so was careful with his hands.

He hired a company to mow the lawn of their house. When a piece of furniture needed to be moved, he knew a "guy" who for a few twenties could be relied upon not to scratch up the walls. Josh knew where in the house Rose kept the tools, though he could not have told you when he had last wrapped his hand around a hammer. His wife had long ago learned that if she wanted something "manly" done around the house, she was going to have to either hire it in or do it herself.

He avoided all of these tasks in hopes of maintaining the health of his hands. His hands were their future: their home, their retirement, their children's education. They were the agents of all his knowledge. It seemed foolish to risk all that to save a few bucks on gardening or hanging a picture, when a single misaligned blow could threaten their entire livelihood.

Yet as he drove to Hugo's house, his hands wrapped dryly around the steering wheel, Josh knew he was going to have no hesitation about using his hands to inflict pain upon this stranger who had infected his family.

He landed his first blow before Hugo had even finished opening the door.

Josh's hand snaked through the opening threshold, punching

through the light bleeding onto the stairs. The flat table of his proximal phalanges shot out and met Hugo's mandible with a pleasing crunch.

David's mandible, Josh reminded himself. *Not Hugo. David.*

The smaller man tumbled backward, tripping over an end table. His body folded over it, caught on his legs, and they both, man and furniture, hit the floor.

"Josh!" he cried, his voice pleading.

Josh was still moving, his anger finally in the presence of a target. The first contact had been good, but not nearly enough to sate the need for hurt inside him. His footsteps carried him across the room, the final step transforming into a kick to the man's lower ribs. Josh imagined the organs just beneath the blow, a shock to the kidney, the connective tissue between the ribs straining, the bones' tensile strength flexing.

"Get up!" he bellowed down.

Hugo (*David!*) was cowering away from him. Covering his head with his hands. *Pathetic.*

Josh grabbed at his collar, trying to haul him up. *Had she touched this shirt, too? When they were together?* Suddenly he was driving punches down into the man's face. *Had she touched this face? Kissed it?* The flesh of David's cheek barely softened the edge of his maxillary jaw against Josh's fist. David was batting his hands up at him, trying to stop the blows. He was twisting away under Josh's grip, the shirt pulling red marks against his neck.

"Stop! Stop!" he was screaming.

His batting hands finally gained hold of Josh's wrist. Clawing at it. Digging into the soft skin of his inner arms.

Josh cried out and ceased punching, turning his attention toward unsticking his opponent's grip. He looked at the hands on his wrist. *Had these hands touched her?* He heard himself screaming, a feral cry. He wanted to break every one of those fingers.

Somewhere a very small part of his brain noted that the hand that clutched him was covered in paint. Blues and reds inked the fingertips, and a particular vibrant shade of pink lodged under the fingernails. But even as it marked this unusual detail, Josh's mind was still fixed on the goal of hurting the man who was trying to take his family, and he did not stop to think why there would be paint on his hands.

The fabric of his victim's shirt finally slipped from Josh's grip, and Hugo (*David!*) twisted away, righting himself against the wall. Josh swung out, connecting a body blow (*stomach, diaphragm, liver, lung*), and the man stumbled away from him, retreating down a short hallway.

"We couldn't do anything," he cried.

What the hell does that mean? Josh landed another blow to his back (*ribs, lung*), and Hugo fell to his knees. Then he was crawling away from him.

Hugo (*David, goddamn it!*) reached up to grasp the knob of one of the doors, his hand slippery with blood on the brass. Josh kicked him, the top side of his foot meeting with the soft hang of belly (*small intestine, stomach, gallbladder*), and Hugo fell toppling into this new room.

There he lay, fetal on the floor. Josh loomed over him. A hulk. "Get up!"

"Look," a thin voice begged from behind those cowering hands. "Just look."

Josh hauled back his foot to land another kick when he finally realized where he was.

The island.

The walls of the room were painted with exquisitely painstaking detail. It was clearly the work of years, thousands of man-hours devoted to re-creating a dreamworld. It was all there, everything he had heard Rose talk about. The Plank Orb. The Green Lagoon. The Blanket Pavilion. The mural continued up the walls onto a vaulted ceiling, where a watery sun peeked through a cover of clouds.

It was a masterpiece. The detail so fine that the effect was almost photographic.

Josh's anger fled as his eyes skipped from one detail to the next. Fireflies hovering in the green surrounds of the forest. The placid stare of a herd of Bucks. Rose once had described it to him—how unusual it was to see that many male deer together— but he had never *gotten* it.

This wasn't the work of a con man. This wasn't some comic book, jotted on paper to fool his sweet, gullible wife.

And then he saw her.

She was lying on a field of coral sand (*Oh, that's the pink she meant*), looking out from the wall. It was his Rose.

Not Rose now, but how she looked when he had first seen her. Rose in college. Rose in full bloom. Rose before she knew what her life was going to be.

She gazed back at him from the wall, a secret smile on her lips.

Josh touched her painted face, his fingertips sending signals to his brain, informing him of the topography of the painting. The blips and blops of dried paint that somehow together created a picture of his wife.

Josh's knees buckled under him. He fell. The reality of this room was overwhelming.

He had never for a moment considered that Rose might be telling the truth when she told him she had met the man from her dreams. Of course, he had believed that *she* believed it; that was easy. It was easier for Josh to believe that something had gone wrong with his wife's brain than that she was nightly dreaming the same dreams as a stranger.

Josh believed that human beings are closed biosystems. Blood and hormones circulating over and over along the same pathways, trailing their way through the same organs. Living meat. Consciousness reaching no further than the surface of our skin.

But somehow the surface of the wall beneath his fingers disproved everything that he had once believed.

"It can't . . ."

Hugo sat up, pulling himself away from the suddenly changed man. He leaned against the opposite wall.

Josh's fingers swept over the line that described Rose's collarbone. "I thought she was lying."

"She wasn't."

Josh could barely get a fix on what was happening to him. He felt like . . . like what? He didn't know. "How . . ."

Hugo (*Hugo*) drew his legs up into himself. "We need each other. We've always needed each other."

There was silence for a moment. Josh traced the line of Rose's lips.

Hugo's voice was small but confident. "We belong together."

"No." Josh shook his head.

"That has to be why."

"No."

"This doesn't happen without a reason."

"This *can't* happen."

Josh felt something wet and hot break a trail across his cheek.

Hugo glared at him, his face bloody. "But it did. It does."

———

R ose was awake when he got home. After Josh had left she clicked into automatic, activating that deep-seated belief of motherhood: *Restore order and everything will turn out fine.*

She had struggled a nighttime diaper onto Penny's sleeping body and deposited her into the crib. Penny cooed as her face touched the cool sheet, but she did not wake.

She had a tougher time with the boys, who were clingy, hopped up on soda and television. Isaac and Adam jumped on their beds while she pulled pajamas from their drawers. Their constant motion was grating, but Rose tolerated it without comment. She had let them down. Left them waiting, wondering.

Adam seized her legs in a hug after she pulled the shirt over his head.

"I'm so glad you're not dead." He smiled up at her and buried his face in her belly.

Isaac, uncharacteristic, slammed into their embrace, wrapping his arms around Rose and Adam both. He, too, laid his head against her belly.

"I love you, Mom."

"Me too. I love you, Mom."

Rose's chest hurt. "I love you guys, too."

She held her breath as she leaned in to kiss them good night. She felt dirty, her lips still tainted with evidence of Hugo's kisses. *She was disgusting. A disgusting person to kiss her children with the mouth that betrayed their father.*

She took a shower after that. Soaping her body once, twice, three times. She rubbed her lips raw with a washcloth—but each time she ran her hand over them, the texture there felt different. Permanently changed.

Disgusting, hateful, horrible woman.

Idiot. Idiot. Idiot.

She dried herself off and dressed herself in a pair of Josh's pajama pants. She climbed into bed . . . but she did not want to sleep.

Sleep would bring *him*.

Rose's mind tumbled over the events of her last dream with Hugo. Kissing in the Blanket Pavilion, escalating to *more* than kissing.

And then they were no longer on the island. And she was no longer herself . . . trapped in this cruel memory of Hugo's as it crumbled and transformed into a nightmare. Hugo's fear had been intense, overwhelming.

It reminded her of the dream she had had of Adam spewing pink sand from his mouth. A terror she was glad to have awoken from.

She did not hear Josh come in. The bed suddenly shifted as he sat on the corner. His back was to her, his body slumped. Something had taken the fight away. He started to talk, his voice low and quiet. Almost a whisper.

"Sometimes, when I'm at work, I'll be with a patient, and I'll catch myself thinking about how Adam is exactly what you would look like if you were a boy. And that Penny sounds like you, even when she babbles." He paused, swallowing. A soft breath. "I love you, Rose. I've loved you since the first day I met you."

"I love you." Rose's voice was thin, tense.

"I believe you now . . . about him."

Rose made a little sound, a release of pressure. He believed her. Josh *believed her. It would be okay. He understood now.*

"But—" Josh stopped suddenly, and Rose realized that he was crying. Choking on emotion. His voice quavered. "I won't believe that our life together wasn't supposed to happen. I can't believe that our babies weren't supposed to be born."

Rose shook her head. "I don't believe that."

"Then why have you been dreaming of him your whole life? Why has he been dreaming of you?"

"I don't know," she whispered.

The silence between them stretched. Rose wished desperately that Josh would touch her, put his hands on the places marred by her mistake, write new memories on her flesh. She didn't know why she dreamed of Hugo . . . but she knew now that she wasn't meant to be with him. Their attempt at being with each other had tossed them into a nightmare world painted by Hugo's insecurities.

She was meant for Josh. Josh, the good and faithful husband. Josh, the patronizing and the proud. Josh, who saw beauty in her, even when she could not see it in herself. Josh, whose gaze and affection frightened her when they were making love.

How could she have ever thought differently?

Josh was the man *of* her dreams. Hugo was just the man *in them*.

His voice cracked. A whisper. "I wish—"

Rose was vehement. Pleading. "I'll never see him again. I promise. Never."

"You can't make that promise."

"I can."

He sighed as a great sadness broke over him. The grief that came with the belief. "You'll break it the moment you go to sleep. Every night. You'll go to sleep with me, but you'll spend the night with him."

Rose let this wash over her. It was true. Hugo was inescapable.

"Then I'll stay awake." Even as she said this, she knew it was impossible. The promise of a child.

"Not forever."

Rose was distraught. She had thought that if he believed her, things would be better. That he would know she was not crazy.

That he would forgive her for the way she had failed him today and on all the other days.

But this was so much worse than when he believed she had lost her mind. Worse than when he threatened to remove her from her children. It was sadder. Deeper. Like a death. Like she was a ghost in their bed and he a new widower.

He still had not touched her. One cannot touch ghosts.

"I love you, Josh."

He was quiet for a moment. "That only makes it worse."

Josh watched Rose later that night as she fell asleep. He sat on the floor opposite their bed.

They had conceived Penny in that bed. Josh thought of that while he watched Rose's chest rise and fall in the dark. The mattress she slept on was witness to hundreds of hours of marital discussion: where they would retire, how much the cable bill was costing, whether or not they could afford private school, whether or not it was worth it if they could.

He loved her so much.

Josh could tell by the sound that she had finally slipped away. He wondered what it was like for her. *Was it like waking up in a new world, suddenly delivered on a new shore? Or was it more gradual than that?*

He went over the little he remembered about the dreaming brain from medical school. REM sleep. Theta waves. Josh could see the textbook in which he'd studied these phenomena in his mind. He remembered being exasperated that they even had to cover it. So many more important things to study.

Rose's breathing stopped for a moment. A pause in the rhythm. *Was she with him right now? On the island?*

He felt a pain in his chest. *Oh, Rose. My sweet Rose.*

Asleep, his wife looked younger. Like she had on the wall.

Rose's eyelids betrayed the movement of her corneas beneath them. She was definitely dreaming.

What about when they are not both asleep? What then? Surely, every time Rose takes a nap, Hugo cannot also be sleeping. And yet she says he is all she dreams about. He is always with her.

His hands hurt from the beating he had given Hugo. Somehow, he had cut his knuckle. It was scabbing over, but the small fan of dried blood was still there. He had probably left stamps of his blood all over Hugo's face and back.

He was lucky the man had not called the police. He was lucky he had not broken his fingers, given the force of the blows he had landed. He was lucky he was not in jail right now, facing the end of his career.

But he did not feel lucky.

eighteen

I f it had not been for her legs, Rose would have not known she
was dreaming. She was loading the dishwasher, moving plates
from sink side to the prongs of the trolley basket. It was something she did at least twice a day in her waking life, the never-
ending cycle. A volley of plates from the cabinet to the table, from
the table to the sink, from the sink to the dishwasher, from the
dishwasher to the cabinet. Repeat morning and night, ad infini-
tum, forever and ever, amen. She was finding a home for one of
Penny's sippy cups (*top rack only*) when she caught sight of her
legs.

They were bare, her skin honey silk stretched over shapely muscled calves. This could not have been more different from their
usual state, pale stubble, with a few bruises of mysterious origin.

She was dreaming.

She was dreaming of *loading her dishwasher.*

That's new, she thought. *A little mundane and weird . . . but new.*

"Mom?"

She looked up. Josh and the kids stared at her from the table.

"You're here!" she heard herself say. It was so strange to know that she was dreaming and yet to see her family. Apart from her nightmare about Isaac and the brief glimpse she'd had of Penny in Hugo's nightmare, the experience was completely new to her.

Josh grinned. "Of course we're here. This is our home."

It *was* home. Rose looked around. This was her kitchen and her kitchen table. Her family. Her life. *Her dream.*

She laughed. It was wonderful.

"Honey, can you bring over the waffles?" Josh nodded at a platter on the countertop.

Rose was giddy. She was dreaming about having waffles with her family. No monsters. No Castle City. No Hugo. "Of course."

Her hands were wet from the dishes and she wiped them on her apron.

Apron?

She was indeed wearing one. The fabric of it was busy with brown and yellow marigolds. Yellow piping outlined the edges and the pockets. It looked like something Mrs. Brady would have worn if Alice took the day off.

Rose grabbed the platter and walked to the table. She sat and forked a waffle onto each of the boys' plates. Penny gummed at hers, softening the bread.

Josh took her hand and smiled.

Rose grinned at the touch. Somewhere in her mind, she remembered something about wanting him to touch her. Needing him to touch her. His hand felt good over hers.

"I love you, Rose."

"I love you, too."

God, this is good. Rose was so happy. *This must be what it's like for other people. They dream about their families. About their lives.*

Adam's face was sticky with syrup. "Can I have another one, please?"

"Sure, honey." Rose leaned over to put another waffle on his plate.

When she sat back, Hugo was sitting in Josh's chair.

Rose was startled, but nobody else seemed to register the change. The children kept eating their waffles as if their father had not just been replaced by a stranger. Hugo looked broodily at her kids.

"I don't like this, Rosie."

His hand was in the same position as Josh's had been, cupped over hers. Rose slid her hand out from beneath it. Some strange cruel trick had been played. Hugo in Josh's chair. Hugo in her husband's place. A spark of anger flared inside of Rose. *He has no right to be there. No claim to it.* Rose felt suddenly as if Hugo had borrowed something without asking. Something deeply personal and beloved. Something she never would have loaned. To anyone.

"Where's Josh, Hugo?"

Hugo scratched his head. Looked away. His face was . . .

His face is grumpy, thought Rose, *like a child who isn't getting his way.*

Hugo sat back in Josh's chair. The chair the kids called Daddy's place. It was Josh's. Left empty if he wasn't home. A representative in his absence.

"I don't like it here, Rose. I think we should go back to the island."

Rose suddenly felt very sure that Hugo had *done* something
to Josh. Hidden him or hurt him in some way. He was dodging
her eyes.

"Hugo, where is he?"

He crossed his arms at his chest, frowning at the kids. "I
don't like them. I want it to be just us. It's better when it's
just us."

God, he was so frustrating. Like Isaac and his negotiations.
Intentionally slippery and dissembling.

Rose heard a thump on the ceiling. Movement upstairs. It
was heavy. A sudden, almost violent drop. She stood. "Did you
do something to him?"

Hugo looked up at her, his mouth closed, smug. Bratty.

But he said nothing.

Rose wanted to smack him. She hated it when the boys did
this. Lied. Treated her as if she were an idiot. Made her pry
information out of them. Made her find the evidence of their
wrongdoing.

She shook her head. This wasn't the boys. The boys were still
politely eating their waffles. This was Hugo. Hugo, dissembling.
Hugo, making her pry.

Another thump sounded upstairs. He glanced at her. Guilty.

"Josh!" Rose broke for the steps, taking them two at a time.

She heard the squeak of Hugo's feet behind her. Following
her up the stairs into the hallway.

Rose began opening doors. The bathroom. The boys' room.
Penny's. The guest. "Where is he?"

Hugo watched her from the top of the steps. "You're not
listening to me. It should only be the two of us."

Rose turned the knob for her room. "Honey?" The door
swung wide into a space that wasn't her own. Her bed, her nightstand, gone, replaced by the boy's bedroom from Hugo's

nightmare. The one into which they had fled from the rushing water and those laughing bullies. *Star Wars* sheets. Rock'em Sock'em Robots. Flip-board clock.

But no Josh.

Hugo stepped just behind Rose and she heard his breath stop at the sight of the room's contents. He was nervous. "He's not here, Rosie. Let's go."

Laughter came bubbling through the open window. Rose moved away from him, toward it. Looking down.

Below was her backyard, Isaac's birthday party in progress. The bouncy castle jerked and swayed. Little boys with water pistols chased one another, serpentine around the trees, screaming with delight. The smell of barbecued meat filled the air.

Josh was standing at the grill, a pair of tongs in his hand. A relief flooded Rose. Hugo hadn't hurt him. Hadn't made her husband disappear.

Rose turned and ran back toward the stairs, passing Hugo on the threshold of the room. She needed to get to Josh. Somehow it felt imperative.

"Rose, we need to find a way to get back to the island," Hugo said, urgent. His feet clattered on the steps behind her.

"I don't want to go to the island, Hugo. I want to stay here. I want to be with my family." Even as she said it, she realized it was true. She never wanted to go back to the island. She didn't care what was in Castle City.

"But it's not safe here for us, Rosie."

"What do you mean?"

Rose reached the bottom of the stairs. Through the window she could see the party in the backyard. Parents with their coffee cups. The balloons waving in the breeze.

There were still three children sitting at her table, eating waffles.

But they were not hers.

Rose stopped short, stunned by the wrongness of it.

Adam, Isaac, and Penny had been replaced by a boy.

Or rather three identical copies of the same boy sat before each of her children's place settings. Eating her children's waffles. Rose stared at them.

"Hugo?"

The boys at the table all looked up at her. "Yes," they said. In unison.

It was *him*. Or rather *they* were him.

Three Hugos as he had looked when she met him. Hugo as a little boy. Sandy hair. Crooked smile. Chocolate eyes. Three pretty little boys sitting at her kitchen table in place of her children.

The larger version of Hugo stopped just behind her, taking in the sight of the three changelings eating waffles. He wrapped his hand around Rose's arm. She looked at him. Hugo—big Hugo—was frightened, his face pale. The defiant brat from earlier was gone.

What the hell was going on? Hugo replacing Josh. Hugo replacing the children. There was something sinister about it. Wicked.

At the table, the three little Hugos suddenly chorused, "We love you, Rosie."

"Whatever you're doing you need to stop it." Rose yanked her arm away from him.

He was stricken. "I'm not doing anything, Rosie." Shaking his head. "I promise."

Rose's anger flared. "Where are Isaac and Adam, Hugo? Where is Penny?"

"I don't know. I really don't know. I'd tell you if I could. But I don't know." He was quivering. More a little boy than the other versions of himself at the table.

Movement behind him on the ceiling drew Rose's eye. A

ceiling fan had sprouted where there was none in the reality of her home. It was spinning on its axis. The strong light from outside cast a shadow double on the cottage cheese of the ceiling.

Grown Hugo followed her eyes. Suddenly he snatched her hand and began to haul her toward the back door. "We need to go, now!"

Rose pulled against him and squinted at the fan. Something about it. It was starting to slow in its ellipses. And the shadow . . .

It was beginning to . . . coagulate. To join with the actual fan. Shadow blades and wooden blades pulling into one another. Morphing into the motor, stretching out across the ceiling. A familiar shape somehow.

Then, one of the blades sprouted a *tarsal hook*.

Rose gasped. The fan suddenly sprang to life, bending upward, animating. The center popped off the ceiling, pull chains swinging, its exhaust screen forming an ad hoc abdomen.

One of the island's Spiders.

It was growing rapidly, its legs stretching. Its carapace creaking with the metamorphosis.

The little Hugos kept eating their waffles, watching the Spider transform. Their faces pleasant. Unworried.

Big Hugo, however, was trying to drag her out the front door. "Come on!"

Through the window Rose could see the party was still going on. All those people. And—

"Josh," Rose heard herself say.

And suddenly she was running out the back door. Leaving all the Hugos behind her.

She tripped over the threshold and fell face-first into a mound of pink sand. For a moment Rose was terrified that somehow Hugo had transported her back to the island.

But when she looked up, what she saw was somehow two places that had become one.

The pink sand of the island's beaches blanketed a place that was somehow both Rose's backyard *and* the parking lot of the Orange Tastee. Isaac's birthday party was still in progress. Parents were eating cake by parked cars. Someone had placed a party hat on the grinning fiberglass Orange drive-through speaker. The bouncy castle rocked and danced as inside a dozen young Hugos jumped and drank soda from wax paper cups. Rose looked around. All the children had been replaced by little Hugos. A party of one, multiplied.

Rose turned. Through the glass she could see that the Spider was still growing. A single leg bent down and made contact with the floor. She didn't have much time.

Josh was still barbecuing, the grill perched on a dune. His back was to her. Rose felt certain she needed to get him. To get them out of there. She stumbled upright, the sand spraying out from behind her struggling feet. "Josh!"

He turned.

It was Hugo. Again.

"Stop doing that!" Rose was infuriated.

Hugo's voice a whine: "I'm not doing it."

"Then why is it happening?"

"I don't know."

"You're not my husband, Hugo."

"No, I'm your Hugo. And you're my Rose."

He reached out to touch her face, but she slapped it away. "Don't."

In the far corner of the parking lot, Rose spied a gathering of the young Hugos. There were more than a dozen of them, standing placid-faced around her car.

Rose took a step toward it, her feet skidding down the dune. *What were they looking at?*

Her minivan was *filled with sand*. Like one of those jars you bring back from vacation. Filled to the brim with pink grit, pressed against the glass. It rocked slightly in its place. Small jolts.

A few more of the young Hugos joined the gathering.

There was a mouse of a movement inside. Small pink curl, pushed up against the glass of the window.

A hand.

"Oh, my God." Rose knew. Felt it. Was sure of it.

It was Isaac. Or Penny. Or Adam. Suffocating under all that sand. One of her children, drowning inside of her car.

Rose burst into a run. She had to get them out.

She weaved her way through the group of Hugos. Behind the glass, the small hand was limp, no longer moving. *Was it Isaac? Adam?* She wrapped her hand around the lever and pulled. The door jammed. "Please!" She yanked again, but the latch wouldn't give. "Oh God, please!"

A small hand landed over hers. One of the young Hugos. His eyes were calm. He brushed hair off of his forehead, the way she had seen him do it a million times before.

"They don't belong here, Rose. Leave them in there."

Rose screamed. Pitched his hand off. She gave a final pull to the handle and the door swung wide, spewing forth pink sand. Rose plunged her hands into it. Digging.

Her fingers brushed the softness of flesh, and suddenly they were wrapped around a small arm. She pulled, calling out as she did it.

Isaac.

Rose wrenched him free, dragging his torso from the weight

of the sand. On his head was his dark red bike helmet. Red like a blood clot. He was cold, his body lifeless. Rose cradled him in her arms. She was sobbing. The group of Hugos contracted around her as she fell to her knees, their faces blank horrors. "Why?" she cried. "Why?"

They all looked up suddenly. Movement on top of the car. Rose turned to see the Spider, grown to full size, perched on the roof of her minivan. Mandibles raised.

She didn't even have time to cry out before it launched itself at her and her son.

R ose sprang from their bed so quickly that Josh could barely believe she had a moment before been sleeping. In seconds she was out the door, her voice loud and panicked in the hallway.

"Isaac! Isaac!"

Josh twisted and rose to follow her, his body sore from his earlier ministrations and sitting these past hours against the wall. He reached the threshold of their room just in time to see Rose stumble over a toy that had been left in the darkened hallway. His wife fell to her knees, still moving, still yelling, "Isaac! Isaac!"

"Rose?" Josh hissed.

Still on her hands and knees, Rose pushed the door of the boys' room open and began crawling across the floor. "Isaac!"

"Rose, stop." Josh whispered as loudly as he dared. "You're going to scare them."

But her panicked hands were already roaming over the blankets of Isaac's bed, searching for his sleeping form. She cried out as her fingers found his mouth, felt his warm, moist breath across the palm of her hand. *Not dead. Not dead. Not dead.*

She collapsed onto Isaac's bedspread, crying hot tears into the fabric.

Not dead.

"Honey?" Josh knelt by her.

She turned, seeing her husband for the first time since waking. She put her hands on his face, confirming the reality of him. Confirming the *Joshness* of him.

Rose worried that if she let go, this world might start slipping the way the last one had. That the moment she took her hands from the flat planes of Josh's cheeks, they would change into someone else's cheeks. If she moved too far from Isaac's sleeping body, it would cease to breathe once more, and she would experience the loss all over again.

Suddenly everything in real life felt threatened. Tenuous.

She cried into Josh's neck. "It was so awful."

He cradled her on the floor. Folding her inside his long arms. Rocking her the way she rocked the children when they were upset. Rose sank into Josh's warmth.

His touch was a relief. She was not a ghost. He was not a widower.

She felt his hands stroke the back of her head. "You're okay. You're okay."

Rose shook her head. "He's . . . torturing me. Hiding you. Hurting the children. He says he's not doing it . . . but he is . . . he has to be."

"Why?"

Rose could think of a dozen answers. *Jealousy. Anger. Rejection. Hate. Love.*

"Mommy, are you okay?" Across the room, Adam had woken up to the sound of Rose's cries. His eyes had found the shape of his mother and father huddled together by the side of Isaac's bed.

No, not okay. Mommy is not okay. Rose buried her sobs in Josh's chest.

Josh answered for her. "Mommy just had a nightmare, sweetheart. Go back to sleep. Everything will be fine."

nineteen

Rose was not so sure that everything would be fine.

In fact, she was pretty sure that things would never be fine again. She wished that she could reverse the order of her life. That she could hit the rewind button and fly backward through these last few weeks, undoing the mistakes she had made, righting the wrongs.

She pictured herself and Hugo peeling themselves up from his bed, pulling the bedspread back into an unmade mess. The strange dance as Hugo's limbs pulled away from hers, picking imprints of kisses off her neck, her breast, her face. Then Josh handing the comic she had shown him back to her and watching her put it in her bedside drawer, his mind suddenly erased of the knowledge of it. The crumbs scattering themselves away from the line Josh had made of them on the kitchen table. Hugo stepping backward away from her home, holding that plastic clamshell of grocery store cupcakes. Isaac's birthday party in reverse, the children floating in the bouncy castle in an inside-out gravity. She would close the albums containing Hugo's artwork and unknow them. The meeting in the outlet mall would unhappen. She would pull herself up off the floor and put the comic book on which some stranger had written her dreams back into its envelope and walk it out to the mailbox. She would find herself back in Naomi's office. The Man Who Was Not Hugo's car would follow her backward on the highway, through a disparate series of bachelor chores. She would unfollow him to his home. She would unsee him putting trash into the Dumpsters behind his work.

And all of it would lead her back to the moment when it all happened.

I should have just taken them to fucking McDonald's.

Rose thought about that rainy day in Hemsford. The line of cars spilling from the drive-through out onto the street. The wail the boys made when the motions of the car made it clear that they would not be stopping there.

But before the *everything* that had happened . . . in that moment in the car . . . had Rose been *fine*?

Or had she been simply less confused about the *not fineness* of her life? More settled with it?

Rose longed for the way she used to be unhappy. The general gripes about the state of her marriage and the difficulties of child rearing. The repetitiveness of life. The disappointments of her body and the tyranny of other parents.

That old unhappiness was a haven to which she longed to return.

But she had destroyed it when she looked up into that drive-through window and saw *him*.

She could never unsee him. She couldn't unknow what she knew.

And the mysteries that she had pursued with such delight, that had seemed a respite from the old unhappiness, they were the new tyrannies of her life.

Why? How? To what end?

Her dreams had been entwined with Hugo's for decades, but now that their lives had intersected, the entanglement felt more like entrapment.

Hugo was inescapable.

She no longer cared about the mystery of their circumstance. The questions that had been so seductive before had all faded before a single practical quandary.

How do I make it stop?

R ose and Josh had returned to their room after her sobs woke Adam.

Josh held her while she cried quietly into his chest. When she had felt herself softening into sleep, Rose had pinched her arms and bitten the back of her hand. She did not want to return to the nightmare. She did not want to again experience that shifting hell of a dream.

Finally, she forced herself to her feet. Josh had showered and left for work, two tan Band-Aids on his busted knuckles. He kissed her forehead as Rose pressed the plunger on the French press.

"We will figure this out. . . . There has to be something."

"What if there isn't?"

But Josh was certain there must be. A pill for dreamless sleep.

Something to give Rose's body the rest it needed while cordoning off her mind to . . . well, to whatever it was it usually did.

"I'll do some research. Maybe among the side effects. . . ."

He told her strange dreams were reported with many pharmacological interventions. But the absence of dreams wasn't the sort of thing test subjects usually noted.

"I'll find something, Rose. Something that will knock you out so much you can't dream." He gripped her arms. "*We will* figure this out."

But until then, Rose wanted to stay awake. She drank coffee and waited for the children to wake up. She knew now was the time to lean on routine. Just do what you always do and don't think about what will happen when you fall asleep. Bodies dressed. Lunches packed. Cheeks kissed.

She had pulled Zackie into a hug as he and Adam came crashing down the stairs in their pajamas. His skin was so wonderfully pink and yielding and *alive*.

Not dead. Not dead.

"Jeesh, Mom. Let go," he finally complained.

Adam was bit more subdued than usual. He finished his breakfast and got dressed without being asked. He remembered seeing his mommy and daddy in his bedroom the night before. Mommy crying on the floor by Zackie's bed. So sad. Sadder than a mommy should ever be.

He decided it must have been a dream. He must have been dreaming. That made more sense.

After he cleared his plate, he pulled out his Lego bin. Started assembling the map of Hugo's island. *Why had what Mr. David told him made Daddy so angry?* He and Isaac pretended to be Hugo all the time and Daddy didn't get angry. If Mr. David was Mommy's friend from when they were kids, he would have pretended to be Hugo, too. Adam thought about the loud sound the chair had made when Daddy stood up. The smack of it hitting the floor. It had scared him.

Adam set up the Blanket Pavilion on the bumpy surface of the Lego mat.

"Hi, honey." Mom was sitting on the ground next to him. This was unusual, but then, she *looked* unusual. The skin on her forehead was shiny with grease, and there were gray bags under her eyes. "I was thinking we should get you a new Lego set."

Adam nodded and snapped together the brown domes that made the Plank Orb.

"Is there any one that you think you may like?"

Mom was looking at the map as he built it. Adam shrugged.

"I think we should put this back in the bin." Her fingers trailed on the edge of it. Poised to tug it away. "It's almost time to go to school."

Adam suddenly felt sure his mom was going to steal his toy. Or break it. It was that feeling he got about Isaac sometimes—that even though he said he would give something back, he wouldn't. That it would take telling Mom to get it back.

But here, he was getting this feeling *from* Mom. Who would he complain to if his mother stole his toy from him?

And somehow, this all tied up in his mind with the sound of the chair slamming against the floor last night and the dream about Mommy crying. Somehow, it all had something to do with Hugo.

He put his hand protectively on the map. "I want to play with this when I get home. . . . Okay, Mommy?"

Mom nodded slowly and her hand pulled away from the edge. Adam felt the *feeling* drain away. Mommy knew how much Hugo meant to him. She wouldn't take him away.

"But put it away for now, Addy." Her voice was sad. Tired. "Okay, honey?"

Adam nodded and snapped the pieces apart quickly, getting them into the box before she could change her mind. He carried the bin to its place on the shelf . . . for a moment he thought maybe he should hide it. Put it in his room somewhere or under his bed.

But there was no way he could do it without Mom seeing. Without her knowing that he wasn't quite sure he could trust her.

R ose found boxes of temporary solutions hanging in the drugstore. Brightly colored packages hanging like ornaments from the metal prongs of the shelf, their names themselves like promises.

NoDoz.

Boost.

Bolt.

Pep.

Rose got one of each, glancing at each "proprietary formula" and seeing the same usual suspects: ephedra, ginseng, caffeine. The ingredients of perpetual motion.

Rose's hands trembled as she dumped the last of them in her cart. Too much coffee this morning. Penny watched her from the seat in the basket. "Candy, Momma?"

"No, honey. Not candy."

The cashier was an old woman. Rose considered her while she put all the packages on the counter. Her mouth was a delta of lipstick wrinkles, a lifelong smoker. Her fingers cluttered with cheap rings. A red-and-blue vest strained over two large, saggy breasts.

What does she look like in her dreams? Probably not like that,

Rose mused. *Why have I been dreaming of Hugo and not her for all these years? What makes him so different from this lady?*

The woman laughed suddenly, her voice a jagged peal.

"Mine wouldn't let me sleep either," she said.

Rose felt jolted. *This woman had a Hugo, too? She had someone who kept her awake? Someone who gave her nightmares?*

The old woman reached out from behind the counter and made a game of snatching Penny's hand. Penny giggled, flirting with her. Her chubby little fingers reached toward the woman, then away again. Rose watched the dance of their hands.

Idiot, thought Rose. *She meant the baby.*

The woman finally caught one of Penny's fingers and Rose was reminded of Hansel and Gretel. Of the witch feeling Hansel's chubby digits through the bars of the cage. "Gotchyu!" cried the woman, and Penny squealed with delight.

The cashier flashed a nicotine-stained grin at Rose and went back to scanning the boxes. "You be careful with these. Too much can be bad for your ticker."

Rose nodded and scanned her credit card.

She opened the first box in the van and swallowed a pill dry.

How long could she go without sleep? Two days? Three?

Too long without sleep and everything begins to fray.

Already she had had almost one sleepless night. Her nightmare had taken less than an hour to play itself out. What could Hugo have done to her family if she had given him a full eight?

Her heart ached at the memory. Isaac dead in her arms. So real she had to fight the impulse to keep Zackie home from school. To spend the day reassuring herself that he was breathing.

In the dream, Hugo insisted he wasn't doing it.

But he was.

All those creepy boys had been *him*. He had made Josh disappear . . . and the children. Surely he had put Isaac in the van, drowned Isaac's beautiful body in the sand of the beach. Forced the Spider to attack her.

It had to be Hugo. It wouldn't be Rose's mind threatening her children. Killing them.

Could it?

Rose shook off the thought. It had to be Hugo.

Josh would find something soon, a few days at most. She could stay awake until he found a prescription and then she could sleep again. Sleep without dreams. Sleep without Hugo.

She hoped to find a distraction from her weariness in the activity of Penny's day. But as she sat on the carpet (*Seriously, why can't the big people have chairs?*), she had a hard time focusing.

The teacher (*Miss Annie!*) welcomed them back with enthusiasm.

"We're so glad you're back, Penny and Penny's mommy!"

Rose felt that old disappointment flare up. This woman didn't know her name. *Her* name was irrelevant. She wasn't Rose here. She was *Penny's mommy*.

Adam's mommy. Isaac's mommy.

Not a person outside of the role defined by her children.

Just another mommy in the circle, bouncing and clapping her way through the class. Sitting behind little versions of themselves. No one special . . . no one worth even remembering another name for.

She was special to Hugo.

The thought had bubbled up unbidden. His face when he saw her for the first time in line at the Orange Tastee. The way he'd clutched her in the parking lot of the outlet mall.

One of the other nameless mommies handed her a tambourine. The mommies would play while the children danced. *We're background*, thought Rose, *insignificant*.

Hugo had been a break from this. She had been special for a while. Part of the mysterious universe.

The other mothers were spreading their legs wide. Bouncing their knees and shaking their instruments. Miss Annie was standing in the circle of their legs, leading the children in a routine. Little hands balled up into little fists, little rumps making little figure eights.

Rose looked at the other mothers, big, wide smiles on their faces. *Surely some of them are faking it, too. Surely some of them are disappointed in their lives. Surely they have dreams themselves. They each have their own name . . . names they have partially given up for the little ones in front of them.*

Rose looked back at the children.

One of the little boys was lying on the floor in protest. The curve of his arm against the floor made Rose think of Isaac's limp body again.

She would lose herself rather than lose Isaac. Or Adam. Or Penny.

She knew that now. Just as she knew that her old unhappiness would always be there. But it was different—because now she understood that she preferred her reality to any other life. That she would never want to change it.

Her complaints were the disappointments of the good life. The small resentments and minor losses that are worth enduring for the sake of the greater whole. It was wrong of her to think that any life could be lived without them. They were pebbles in a well-fitted shoe. Inevitable and endurable.

The children broke up their line and headed back to their mothers' laps. Miss Annie held out a bin for the tambourines. Rose dropped hers in.

"Thank you, Penny's mommy."

She would be Penny's mommy. Adam's mommy. Isaac's mommy. She would be Josh's wife.

But she couldn't be Hugo's Rose.

That would cost her the waking world, and nothing was worth that much.

Rose popped a second pill in the afternoon. Something to help her get through the quiet hours of Penny's nap.

She was beginning to feel it. That stretched-thin feeling she used to get when the kids kept her up all night. She felt shaky. Nervous from the pills, but sleepiness had been banished from her body. Her knees bounced up and down when she tried to watch television.

Josh checked in. He'd found something they used for people with night terrors. He jabbered a couple of multisyllabic words at Rose, drug names that meant nothing to her. He couldn't prescribe them for her himself, that would push the boundaries of ethics, but he was going to talk to somebody. He might be able to bring home some samples tonight.

"Good." Rose's voice was clipped. Businesslike.

The drug Josh thought might work was an antiepileptic. It worked by lowering the electrical activity in the brain, like a dimmer on a switch, bringing the lights down from bright to dull.

Josh thought of what his wife's sleeping brain must look like on an MRI scan. The flushes of reds and blues and yellows, dancing across the walnut-shell stage of her brain, describing the activities of her sleeping mind.

When they dreamed, did Hugo's brain dance with hers? Did they synchronize across time and space? Or was it a call and response? Hugo's brain flashed blue and Rose's responded by blooming with red.

Entanglement.

The written word rushed into his mind.

An answer to a question on a physics test. Sophomore year of college.

His professor had been young and enthusiastic, the kind of teacher hated by the faculty but adored by students. The course was a general overview, not for majors, but Josh remembered a particular day when the teacher had caused the entire class to go silent.

The professor had told a quantum love story.

Physicists had found evidence that two particles created together through radioactive decay remain linked no matter how far apart they strayed. Changing the charge of one particle will immediately reverse the charge of its entangled mate, no matter the distance between them—be it inches or light-years. Entanglement meant a signal could travel *faster* than the speed of light. An entangled particle on one end of the universe could *turn on* its mate on the other end of space.

Josh remembered the look of rapture on his professor's face when he told them about this. The excitement the idea held for him. He remembered thinking what a geek the guy was. Even at nineteen, Josh was a materialist, a pragmatist. This particular lesson smacked of space dust and mysticism.

But he still took notes. Josh was nothing if not good at exams.

Until this moment, the professor's story had been nothing more than an answer on a test for Josh. Multiple choice. Pick A, B, C, or D.

But now . . . thinking of the electrical charges of his wife's brain, the nightly dance of her brain with Hugo's, hiking across the dreamworld of the island, and his own reversal, staring at the practical impossibility of Hugo's home-built Sistine Chapel . . .

Rose and Hugo. Binary particles. Bound together by some accident of the universe, their dreaming minds blinking positive/negative. The ions in their brains firing on/off/on/off, like fireflies in a dark country field. Their bodies lighting up with electric glow, signaling to each other, *I am here. I am here. I am here.*

This drug his colleague told him about would be a chemic fog . . . a pesticide to those blinking, winking lightning bugs dancing in his wife's brain.

She would be dulled, dimmed, cut off from this inconvenient miracle.

Hugo.

If she were not his wife, she should be studied. She and *he* should be brought in and scanned. Poked. Prodded. Blood drawn. Tested for hormonal imbalances. Put inside large thunking machines and sedated. Eventually, some hadron collider should be constructed to plumb the particle impossibility of their circumstances—two brains wink winking together in the dark.

But she *was* his wife.

His Rose. Mother of his children. Keeper of his home. Holder of his heart.

Josh's throat hurt. It felt as if it had been locked in an uncompleted yawn since he had seen the fullness of Hugo's mural, pulled and stretched into a moan of despair. His body ached. His hands throbbed, protesting against the blows he had landed on Hugo's face.

This thing between his wife and this man should be studied. It should be understood.

But Josh didn't want to understand. He just wanted to be assured that this was just some accident of fate. That it didn't *mean* anything.

Accidents happen. Cars crash. Trees fall. Bones break. Lungs collapse. Blood spills.

Patients search for meaning. Next of kin search for meaning. But Josh was a surgeon.

One did not get far in that line of work assigning meaning to the accidents of life . . . other than the binary of luck.

That car didn't hit you? Good luck.

The train that did? Bad.

But it did not *mean* anything. It was not part of some larger cosmic plan, pulling you toward a destiny on an operating table, your chest open wide, a dozen medical personnel struggling hard to keep you alive.

Josh needed to believe that this thing his wife had with Hugo . . . it was just bad luck. She wasn't being pulled toward some fate with this man, some destiny. Their *entanglement* was just an accident.

Josh was in the business of fixing what happened in the wake of accidents.

As long as it was just that, and nothing more, it could be repaired.

twenty

He came home with the wrong pills.

Josh did not feel right prescribing the antiepileptic for Rose and had tried to get a medical doctor he was friendly with to do it for him. His colleague had played coy, knowing that Josh was asking for a script without a patient consult, and suggested that he would be able to see Josh's wife in a few days.

Josh had felt his pride flare at this. He was certain his "friend" the doctor was acting on some latent inferiority he felt toward Josh and other surgeons. That he was lording the prescription over him.

But now that somebody knew that Josh was trying to bend the rules, Josh didn't feel comfortable asking anyone else to do it for him. He reluctantly agreed to get Rose to come in for an appointment. He would need to coach her on what to say to make sure she got exactly what she needed.

So it would be a few days before he was able to dim the lights in Rose's brain.

But he was able to secure a few sleep aids from some pharmaceutical reps. The single-blister trial packs of new formulas of old drugs were commonly passed around the hospital . . . though both parties knew there was little reason for the doctors there to prescribe common sleep medication. The availability of free and fast sleep drugs was a perk of the job.

But Rose refused to take them.

She was worried that instead of promising her deep, dreamless sleep, the sleeping aids would lock her in the dream . . . her body would be sedated, but her mind would be imprisoned in a nightmare with no escape.

"I'll just stay up."

"Rose . . ."

"It'll be fine."

Josh set the single-blister packs on the kitchen counter. Rose's eyes lingered on them for a moment—thinking of the medicine chest in Hugo's bathroom. Their faces framed in the mirror. The feel of the expired blue pill as she placed it on Hugo's tongue.

How long ago was that?

Yesterday.

It didn't seem possible. It had been only a day.

Yesterday she had embraced sleep . . . and Hugo.

Today she was running from him.

What a difference a day makes. Rose snorted at the thought. Almost a laugh.

"Rose, are you okay?" Josh put his hand on the small of her back.

God, she was so tired. Lack of sleep was making her feel light-headed, slightly giddy. A little punch-drunk.

"I'm fine," she heard herself say. *Everything will be fine. Or at least it will be the "not fine" it was before.*

Then Josh kissed her.

He pressed his face into hers, his lips soft and open on her mouth, his tongue a gentle presence between his teeth. Rose could sense him inhaling her, taking her in. His fingers caught the greasy hair of her ponytail, frizzy and loose above her ears.

His eyes were closed, but he was *seeing her*. Seeing her with his mouth and his nose and his hands. Claiming her.

His mouth pulled away as he locked her into an embrace, his chin against her forehead. Rose felt one of their pulses at the contact. His or hers, she wasn't sure.

"I'm sorry," she whispered. "I'm so sorry."

Even as she said it, she was tugging on his clothes.

They made love, first against the countertop and then, when logistics made that difficult, on the floor of Rose's kitchen, stray crumbs and pieces of lint embedding themselves in the flesh of Josh's bottom.

From the vantage of the floor, Josh stared up at his wife, filling himself with the sight of her, the feel of her, the *her* of her. His Rose.

And for the first time in years, Rose did not mind.

In fact, Rose had the odd sensation that she wasn't even really all there for Josh to see. While part of her was aware of her body grinding and enfolding itself against Josh's, another part became convinced that she had somehow slipped out of her skin.

She wasn't Rose at all.

She was a glowing ball of golden light set loose in a field of dark time. Rose felt herself expanding from a central core, her consciousness floating, hovering in space, as she grew larger and larger.

Josh's hands on her body, the building feeling of potential between her legs . . . it all seemed somehow related, but distant from the radiating light of herself. She was both on her kitchen floor and at play in the universe.

She cried out, and the orb that was her pulsed. It suddenly pulled away from an unseen force, unfettered at last.

She exploded, her edges straining away from the gravity at her center until they were no longer edges . . . until she was just bits and pieces, molecules of matter, spinning in a forced trajectory away from what she had once been. She was everywhere. She was everything.

To Josh, pinned on the floor beneath Rose's orgasming body, she looked not just like herself, but like every self she had ever been or ever would be. She was as she was now in this moment. But she was also as she was when he met her. And as she was when she was pregnant with Isaac. When she was nursing Adam. When she told him to expect the arrival of Penny. She was young Rose from the pictures her parents had shown him when they had gotten engaged. And she was also Rose as he imagined her to be in their future together, her hair streaked with white, her face an etch of elegant wrinkles.

His wife in all forms, in all places and times.

He reached the precipice of fullness . . . and tipped over.

He did not stay awake with her, though he had wanted to. But Josh's body was stretched even thinner from lack of sleep than Rose's at this point. He had not had an illicit nap on

Hugo's bed. He had not even had the hour of sleep that had granted Rose the nightmare of Isaac's death.

Josh's wife led him to their bedroom and tucked him under the covers, as she did with all of her babies. She kissed his mouth.

Assured him, "I'll be okay."

She even believed it for a moment.

The wash of oxytocin was still cresting through her body, those love hormones of orgasm and childbirth and breast-feeding.

She remembered a thousand sleepy nights with the children when they were new. Infants latched pink mouths to her nipple. Tug, tug, tug until she felt it. The let-down of milk accompanied by the "ah" of hormones, tingling outward, drifting from her shoulders to her toe tips and fingers. It made her sleepy and happy, drunk with hormonal love for the tiny people staring up at her, noses pressed to her breasts, filling themselves up with *her*. Tiny eyes in the dark, surfeiting themselves with the sight of their mother. Sustaining themselves. With her.

Isaac. Adam. Penny.

Each of them a part of Josh and Rose.

Two cells that had found each other in the dark tunnels of her body. One pushing its way past the fortress of the cellular wall, until it finally exploded itself inside. From the two there was suddenly one . . . that then divided again and again and again— half, half, half . . . somehow the division of itself making more instead of less.

Twisted strands, beads containing the instructions for growing humanity. Forming into miniature organs, pencil tips fluttering, dark buds of eyes and ears. Blobs of limbs. Each already with its own proclivities and propensities. A seed that could bloom into a tendency toward depression, or genius, or risk taking . . . All there in the fish-shaped sliver in the dark of the womb, burrowed down into its endometrial bed. Mother's first home-made meal.

Rose felt full of the miracle of what she had with Josh.

What they had built together.

People. Life.

The glow of the orgasm still felt warm inside her.

Josh fell asleep quickly in their bed, the length of his chest rising and falling under the blankets.

It will all be okay.

twenty-one

Rose held on to that feeling of okayness for most of the night. She stayed awake in the electric glow of the TV, keeping company with broadcast-ready doctors holding forth about vaginal odors and the benefits of green tea.

She didn't even feel tired . . . not really, not the way she should have after more than a day and a half without sleep. Her limbs felt jerky and sensitive—but not tired. Likely it was the caffeine. Or the ephedra. Or the ginseng . . . though Rose felt sure that particular ingredient in her energy pills was ancient Chinese bullshit.

But as dawn crept its fingers into the windows, Rose felt herself begin to fray again. There was now a constant ringing in her ears, a consistent pitch made louder by the quiet of her sleeping house. When her head pitched back from her neck one too many times, Rose decided she should no longer sit still.

There were things that could be done. If she needed to be awake, there might as well be some benefit to it. There was laundry to wash and fold, drawers to organize. Rose fixed her mind on a dried brown puddle of mysterious origin that had appeared on the top shelf of the fridge. It had bothered her for a week . . . but there had never been time to take care of it.

No time like the present. Rose headed to the kitchen.

Hugo was behind the door of the refrigerator.

Warm washcloth in her hand, Rose lifted the pitcher of filtered water off the shelf and knocked the topmost package off of a stack of yogurts. The container tumbled onto the tempered glass.

Blood orange.

As Rose's wrist twisted to put the container back onto the stack, her brain took the picture on the lid and lit up a twisty pathway from *orange* to *Orange Tastee* to *Hugo* in a paper cap in the drive-through, then to *Hugo* as she had last seen him.

I hope he's okay.

That word again. *Okay.* And as she thought about Hugo's *okayness,* she felt the last remnants of her own slip away.

Selfish. So selfish. He lost his job, remember? No more paper cap for him now.

The sight of Josh's hands filled her brain. Their swollen red knuckles. The bruises across them. The scatter of small cuts.

You didn't even ask what happened. Because you knew. *Your husband beat him and left him.*

Rose tried to shake off the thoughts. She didn't deserve this. She had made a bad decision, but it was over. She couldn't be concerned with him. She couldn't worry about what her decisions did to the feelings of a stranger—

Not a stranger. Hugo. Your *Hugo.*

So very selfish.

He NEEDS YOU.

"My children need me," Rose said aloud.

"What, Mom?"

Rose turned. Isaac stood in the kitchen in his pajamas. He yawned and scratched his thigh, oblivious to the storm in his mother's mind.

"Who were you talking to?"

Rose was suddenly aware of the washcloth in her hand. It had grown cold as she had stared into the recesses of the refrigerator. The dried spill was untouched.

How long had she been standing there?

"Mom?"

"I'm sorry, sweetie. . . . No one. I wasn't talking to anyone."

R ose's perception of time was askew, her patterns off. She spent the morning just responding to the children's needs rather than anticipating them as she usually did. The stretched feeling now encompassed the world . . . everything was liminal. Between states.

Somewhere Isaac and Adam were playing. Rose remembered supervising their dressing . . . but maybe what she remembered was yesterday. Or the day before that. Or one of the thousands of times before that.

Penny's potty seat was on the kitchen floor, a small turd sitting dry in its center. *Had she brought that out?* Rose didn't know. Maybe. She wasn't sure. She must have. *Right?* If not her, then who else?

"Honey?" Josh was trying to get her attention.

"Yes?"

"Are you sure you're okay?" Josh was crouching down to look her in the eye, his brows pressed together above his nose. Two commas of worry.

Rose felt her head tip forward in a nod. Her tongue felt bitter and wide. A fat flap of stale, coffee-flavored meat in her mouth. Rose forced the sluggish thing into service. "Yes. Of course."

Rose waited until she heard Josh's car pull out before she pushed two more pills out of the blister pack. She swallowed them dry, feeling their hard forms scrape down the sides of her esophagus, foreign bodies leaving a trail against the smooth muscle of her throat. The pills dropped through the sphincter at her stomach's north pole, before falling into the slosh of bile at the organ's center. The pill's cheap coating began to slough off, and the chemical promise of sleeplessness released itself into Rose's body.

At the playground mommies flanked the edges of the sand pit, their eyes flitting from their children and their cell phones. A few were sitting together, chatting politely. If any of them noticed Rose and Penny's arrival beneath their wide sunglasses, their faces did not betray it. Rose found an empty bench and directed Pen to go play. Penny had taken a direct route to another girl child digging in the sand on the other side of their play park. She picked up one of the shovels lying next to the girl and immediately began digging. The other child did not seem to notice, but Rose lifted her hand to signal to the woman she supposed was her mother. Playground sign language. *Is that okay?*

The woman lifted her hand back with a nod.

It's okay.

Rose ironed her eyes with the heels of her palms . . . pushing the sleepiness out of them. The tyranny of sleep pressed down upon her. How much longer could she go? Even with chemical help she didn't think she could continue to function much longer. Solution or no, sooner or later Rose would have to sleep.

And the nightmares and Hugo would be waiting.

The squeal of the swings was hypnotic. Rising and falling in a squeaky "ee-oo-ee-oo." Rose's eyes found Penny. She was playing well with the other girl, having co-opted her bucket now.

Next time, I'll have to remember to bring sand toys. I always forget.

Rose watched the children on the swings pumping their legs. *Ee-oo-ee-oo.*

ee-oo-ee-oo-ee-oo-ee-oo

In the distant corner of the playground, a smatter of sand tumbled from its perch atop a tower. Rose sensed the movement in her periphery, the subtle shift in the landscape of the park.

ee-oo-ee-oo

Next to the mound, two blond boys of about three were fighting. Twins. Dressed identically. They were arguing, bickering over taking turns on one of the spring-mounted bouncies. A grinning elephant. Both toddlers wanted to be astride it (*that one!*), even though there was another bouncy creature (a tiger) right next to it. The boys pulled at each other's shirts and ripped each other's hands off of the elephant. Their voices carried over the playground, the high-pitched tone children get before tipping into tears. *Where is their mother?* Rose wondered. *She* would have stepped in by now. She remembered Zackie and Addy at about that age . . . she would never have let a spat between them like the one she was witnessing go on for so long without intervening.

A sudden spray of sand shot up behind the twins. Loosed from the ground.

Rose squinted. *Was someone throwing sand?* But then there was another spray, followed by another. A volley of grit landed in one of the twins' faces and he began to cry, his eyes squeezed shut, face red. His brother looked around, guilty, though he had not thrown the sand. Rose followed his gaze . . . the patch of playground containing the eroding mounds was vibrating. Shifting oddly. Rose stood to get a better look. Something was moving about under the sand, digging itself up from beneath. Rose could see its dark green body wending its way toward the sunlight, sand catching on its scales.

The twin who was not crying took a step toward the creature moving under the sand. Curious.

It was then that Blindhead exploded from the ground, sending a blast of dirt and grit into the air.

The beast pulled its muscled bulk out of the ground, rearing back and up until it could support the heft of its three sightless heads. They loomed over the children, the topmost parallel to the play structures. The heads waved out over the playground, independent of one another, their wire-thin tongues flickering out behind jagged fangs. Rose could see the reflection of the playground on the too-taut skin of their eyeless skulls—children standing frozen on redwood bridges and platforms. Shocked into silence by the sudden appearance of a monster in their midst.

Suddenly, the lowest head shot out and seized the first crying twin, driving the boy into its mouth. A small morsel. A flash of blond hair was visible for a moment between the folds of its maw. And then the boy was gone.

The screaming finally began.

Mothers and children were suddenly everywhere, leaping off

the play structures, knocking one another off swings. Screams of "Mommy!" rang out from dozens of throats . . . the same name for so many different women.

The youngest among the children were frozen in place, screaming with tears but unable to command their legs to move. Women were running into the fray from all over the park, the sand shooting up from their scrabbling feet.

Blindhead angled from the ground and whipped itself onto the monkey bars.

Rose tore her eyes from the snake.

Penny was gone.

Through the legs of the women, Rose could make out the bucket and shovel Penny had co-opted lying abandoned on the sand on the other side of the playground.

On the other side of the monster.

Rose burst into a run, screaming Penny's name. She ducked under a structure—the small hideaway fort—then followed the path through.

"Penny! . . . Penny!"

The sun shining through the plastic tunnel above revealed the snake's still heads, tongues waving above the shape of a little girl. The shadows sat poised, waiting for movement.

Rose watched from below as the shadow of the child tried to pull herself out of its reach. The plastic resounded, betraying her with a dull thud.

There was a scream and the sound of denim sliding against plastic.

Rose pushed herself out into the open as the topmost head pulled the girl out—a snail from its shell. The force of the movement snapped the child's spine and suddenly her cries ceased. It held her flaccid body aloft a moment.

If possible, the pitch of the screaming crowd got even louder.

The creature dislocated its jaw, swallowing the girl whole, as Rose spotted Penny.

Her daughter was sitting on the sand by the swings, oblivious to the violence around her, pulling a moat around herself with her chubby hands. Her movements were broad and wide. An easy target.

Rose broke into a run as Blindhead's body turned toward Penny's movement. It was lightning quick, slithering from the structure behind Rose—

Alighting right above Pen.

Rose dove into the sand, her arms reaching out for Penny just as one of the creature's jaws closed around her small body and lifted her upward.

Rose screamed as a second head joined it, biting into the soft flesh of Penny's lower half.

Momma? Okay, Momma?

Rose looked down.

Penny was sitting across from her, a look of concern in her large eyes. "You okay, Momma?"

Rose was sprawled out across the hot sand, her arms outreached around Penny's spread knees.

All around the playground, mothers and children were staring at her. Watching. Stock-still. Alarmed by her strange behavior.

"I was awake, Josh. I was completely awake."

Rose paced on the phone. Her heart was thumping.

She must have looked like an idiot running through the playground. Screaming Penny's name. Rose imagined what the other mothers must have seen, no idea of the horror that was unspooling before her eyes.

It had been so real.

So, *so real.*

"Sometimes the brain . . ." Josh's voice on the phone sounded careful. As though he were picking his words. "Given enough sleep deprivation, the brain will give itself little naps. Micro-sleeps."

Rose winced as she remembered the sound of the little girl's spine as it snapped above her. The image of Penny's shoulders disappearing into Blindhead's mouth.

"I can't do this much longer. I feel like I'm breaking. But if I fall asleep . . ."

Josh was quiet on the phone. Rose could hear the change in his breath, his lips pursing. "I'll get the Klonopin."

Josh had that dark sound. Rose could tell he was going to do something he considered wrong. Bully someone into giving it to him. Steal it from somewhere. Lie.

She didn't care. She needed sleep.

Sleep without nightmares.

Sleep without Hugo.

"I love you, Rose."

"I love you, too."

The room tone on the other end went dead. Josh was setting about his task. It was almost over. Josh would do what he needed to do to get her the drugs. Tonight she would go to sleep with the buffer of the antiepileptics stifling her brain, no matter what—

The sound of the front door slamming against its frame echoed through the house. The familiar refrain of the boys getting home from school.

"Adam! Isaac! I told you! No slamming the door!"

Her head felt so heavy.

She could sense Zackie standing right next to her. The smell of him. "Sorry, Mom."

Rose's brain ran an auditory loop of the sounds it had just registered. *Door slam. Footsteps. Door slam. Footsteps. Door slam. Footsteps.*

Something was missing.

She looked up. Isaac stood in the kitchen, his backpack still on his shoulders.

There had been the sound of only one pair of small feet.

"Where is Adam?"

Isaac shrugged. "He wasn't on the bus."

twenty-two

A dribble of ice cream broke across Adam's knuckle.

He licked it off, his tongue catching paper, cone, and soft serve in the same sweep. He would have to eat it a little faster not to make a mess in Mr. David's car. He didn't want Mr. David to think that he was a baby who didn't know how to eat an ice-cream cone. Someone who didn't know how not to make a mess. He was a good boy. A big boy.

He was such a big boy that Mr. David even let him sit in the front seat, without a booster or anything.

It was awesome.

Adam was so lucky he had seen Mr. David waving across the street from where the buses all lined up. Mrs. H, the bus monitor, had been talking to a teacher and some new crying girl and had not seen Adam step out of the line and step behind the bus to shout hello to Mommy's friend.

Then Mr. David had curled his hand, telling him to cross the street.

Adam had hesitated. He wasn't supposed to do that on his own yet.

But Mr. David, who had told him he was actually Hugo, seemed to think it was fine. He looked both ways and then curled his hand again. Adam took that as permission and he had jogged across the street as fast as he could. He felt giddy when he reached the other side. A sense that he had done something big. Crossed the street by himself! Something big boys do.

Mr. David told him he'd asked his mommy for permission to take Addy on an adventure. Would Adam like that?

Oh yes, please, and thank you very, very much, please.

And now they were in Mr.-David-who-was-Hugo's car on their way to a movie. And Adam had gotten a Happy Meal and an ice-cream cone, but he got to eat the ice-cream cone first because otherwise it would melt, and it wouldn't be there when he was done with his hamburger.

It was awesome.

And it was even better because it was just him . . . no Isaac. If Isaac had been there, it would be *him* in the front seat. He would be telling Addy not to let the ice cream drip, even if Adam was already being careful about it.

Addy felt special. Big. Good.

Outside, the highway rolled by and Adam could make out the full sweep of it from where he sat. The dash of Mr. David's car was really cool, with lots of knobs instead of buttons. Adam's fingers itched to turn them, but he knew that was something grown-ups didn't like, so he held himself back. The car was shorter than Mom's car. Closer to the ground. He could feel the vibration of the tires under his feet.

Adam decided the car was also his favorite color, blue. Sometimes his favorite color changed . . . but today it was definitely blue.

And it smelled good. A sweet plastic smell, kinda melty and old. Adam liked it.

Mr. David was quiet as he drove. He told Adam that the radio didn't work so they would have to talk to keep themselves entertained, and would that be okay? Adam said that it was. He wanted to talk to Mr. David about what it was like to be Hugo . . . but instead Mr. David had gotten quiet and kinda drifty, like grown-ups do when they think about things.

Adam took another big lick of his ice cream and snuck a look at him. There were some purple and yellow marks on his face. His cheek and jaw looked sore and puffy. When Adam had asked, he had said he had got the black eye from falling down. Adam had kinda quirked up his mouth at that. Mr. David's eyes didn't look black at all.

Musta been quite a fall, though.

Maybe when Mr. David took him home after the movie he could get his mommy to kiss Mr. David's face. That sort of thing always made him feel better when he was hurt, even though Isaac said it made him a baby and it didn't *really* do anything. Adam wasn't quite sure about that. He always felt that the pain did go away a little bit whenever his mommy kissed his hurts. Maybe she could make Mr. David feel better.

He would like that.

As they drove, Adam thought about his Lego map . . . he would have to remember to check that Mommy hadn't gotten rid of it when he got home, too. After he asked her to kiss Mr. David's owies.

But, of course, it would still be there. Adam was silly to worry. Because Mommy had sent Mr. David to have an adventure with him—and Mr. David *was* Hugo. She wouldn't take away Adam's Hugo toys but then send Hugo to play with him. That would just be goofy.

Adam pushed the remains of the cone out of its paper holder. He popped it into his mouth, the liquid ice cream seeping from the gummy remnants in between his teeth. He wondered if Mr. David would let him get popcorn *and* candy *and* a soda with the movie.

Adam thought he probably would.

P lease, I just . . . I need someone to help."

"Ma'am, I'm still not clear. Is your son missing or do you know who has him?"

"He's . . ." There wasn't time to explain. "Both. He's both."

The 911 dispatcher sounded irritated, her voiced edged with efficiency. Rose imagined her in a dark room, in the cool lights of a monitor. A million miles from Rose and her missing son. A million miles from the chaos that was breaking out in her life. Josh had not picked up his cell. The hospital was paging him. The school bus monitor had marked Adam as getting on the bus—but someone in the main office would be speaking to her.

Rose's body was thrumming with adrenaline. Her skin was puckering and releasing in waves of gooseflesh. She wanted to run. She wanted to punch someone. But she could not do anything until she got through this godforsaken phone call.

"Have you tried calling your friend to see if he has him?"

"He's not . . ." Rose swallowed the words *my friend*. He *was* her friend. The man she had invited into their life. This was all her fault.

She thinks you're crazy. You probably sound crazy. Bipolar. Like one of those schizos who tears off her clothes and jumps into bushes. All those mothers saw you freak out at the playground. Screaming.

Maybe you are crazy.

Rose tried to modulate her voice, to make it sound sane. "Please, my son should be home by now. . . ."

The police would come. They would talk to her. They would see her . . . and how crazy she looked. And then they'd talk to the neighbors. By now everyone on the block would have heard about the playground. And then the police would think *she* had done something to her Addy. That she had hurt him. Hidden him.

Rose's throat ached with a stifled sob. *She* had *hurt him. She had brought Hugo here.*

Rose looked up.

In the rounded archway that marked the transition between the living room and kitchen stood a trio of Bucks. The animals placidly raised their heads and regarded her with their still, dark eyes. . . . As if she were the intruder.

"Ma'am, are you still there?"

No. Yes. Maybe. I am here. But I am also somewhere else. I am on an island I have been dreaming of for almost my entire life . . . and I am in my kitchen begging you to believe me that someone has stolen my son.

The Bucks lowered their heads back to the ground, browsing on invisible grass that sprouted from the wood floor of her kitchen.

Rose hung up the phone.

She would call Mrs. D to come over. Tell Isaac to let her in when she got here.

———

M r. David had driven them for a long time until they got to the movie theater. It was one of those big ones they built on the edge of town. Adam knew that the numbers next to the movie theater names meant how many screens they had. The one his mom and dad took him to was an eight. The place he went to when he visited his baba and papa was a twelve.

This one was a thirty-two, the number huge and red on the sign that stood by the highway. Behind it the sun was pink and orange on the mountains. Sunset. Adam had a funny tickly feeling . . . he was going to get to stay up late. On a school night.

Mr. David pressed through the parking lot without holding Adam's hand. Addy doubled his steps to keep up. Maybe Mr. David didn't know they were supposed to hold hands when they were around cars.

Or maybe he just thought Adam was a big boy who didn't *need* to hold hands. Maybe he thought he was big enough to do it by himself.

If that was the case, Addy wasn't going to make him think he was a baby by reaching out for his hand. Mr. David said he was *Hugo* . . . Hugo killed Spiders the size of cars and climbed mountains and had his own submarine. He wouldn't want someone like that to think he wasn't big enough to cross a parking lot on his own.

Adam followed him up over the clean curb of the complex. There was a huge wall of digital movie listings and times. Mr. David gave him a tight smile as he bought the tickets. Adam smiled back at him.

"Thank you, Mr. David," he said when the cashier handed

the tickets over. Adam was very good at remembering to say thank you.

R ose's palms were slippery against the steering wheel. Sweat collected in the creases of her fingers as she drove. She wiped them, alternately, against the legs of her pants, leaning forward in the seat.

She felt awake. Thunderously awake to the world.

If her hands were wet, her eyes were dry, lids skidding across them painfully whenever she felt she could afford to blink.

She didn't remember getting on the highway, but surely she had, because that was what lay before her, the dusty cars of commuting Colorado. People on their way back from work, home in time to have dinner with their families, to put the kids to bed and maybe zone out in front of the television. The setting sun flared off their side-view mirrors, piercing shards in Rose's eyes. She winced—always a second too late to keep the light trails from burning themselves into her eyes.

She needed to get to Adam.

She imagined herself getting to Hugo's house. Adam would be fine. Happy to see her. Hugo would apologize. She would take Addy home. Everything would be fine.

Blindhead, looming eagerly over Penny . . . Isaac's limp body under the crushing weight of the pink sand . . . and now Adam.

Could the nightmares—the *day*mares—have been mere reflections of some unconscious will or desire inside of Hugo?

He attacked them in your dreams. And now he's taken Adam in real life.

A strange sound burst from her lips. A choking sound. Dry despair.

Dear God, please no. Please no. Please no. No. No. No.

Rose saw it just as she drove over a bridged ravine. Movement in her rearview, different from the metallic, human-directed consciousness of the cars.

The tarsal fold, hairs flaring in the pink light as it curled around the beige concrete of the highway barrier. A second joined it . . . and then a third.

And then the monster launched itself over the barrier and onto the highway. Rose turned her head, quickly looking behind her . . . framed through the dust-speckled glass of her minivan was one of Hugo's Spiders. The thing was huge . . . larger than Rose could remember the creatures ever being in her dreams.

Of course she was dreaming now. Wasn't she?

Behind the Spider, a red sedan suddenly veered out of the way, swerving to avoid the monster that had just appeared before it. It was clipped by an SUV in the next lane, pushing its back end toward the cement barrier.

Rose whipped her eyes back toward the road as she heard the cars collide with the wall. The sound of metal meeting concrete wended its way past the minivan's windows, making its way to her ears.

It's not real, she told herself.

But in her rearview she could see the sedan suddenly launching into the air, thrown back by the force of the collision. The car landed on its roof and spun, catching the wheel rim of a compact, whipping it into the spin.

The beast leaped, bouncing off the exposed engine of the sedan, gaining ground on Rose and her fleeing minivan. It overtook a speeding pickup, its tarsal piercing the windshield, driving itself into the soft body of the driver.

There was a blare of horns as the Spider lifted the pickup

off the road and flung it off the highway. A pesky nuisance, keeping it from its intended target.

Her.

The creature dropped its thorax and its legs bowed out, ready to spring—

Rose's hands slipped from the steering wheel. Terror had all of her. Screaming through her veins, seizing the striations of her muscles, soaking into her bones. This could not be happening—

The Spider landed ten feet in front of the van. It lifted its metatarsals and pedipalps—those terrible ninth and tenth legs—ready to grab Rose's car and peel her out of it.

"It's *not real*!"

Rose drove *into* the spider . . .

. . . and straight through it.

Its monster thorax was replaced by the too-close tailgate of a freight truck. The van was inches from its bumper.

Rose's foot flew off the gas and hit the brake pedal before her mind had even cleared the monster's abdomen from her view. Her car dropped back . . . a near miss.

Rose sobbed, a dry husk of herself. Was she even flesh anymore? Or was she something else . . . a paste made of fear and fat and a single refrain? *Oh please, oh please, oh please.*

Hugo's car was in the drive.

Rose's heart leaped at the sight of that shitty blue beater. *He was here.* Which meant Adam was here. She need only extract him, lay her hands on his body, swing its warm weight onto her hip, and run with him.

As long as Hugo hasn't done anything to him.

She stopped the van and twisted to get out—she was only feet from her son and salvation. In the distant corner of her mind she heard a chime begin to sound, an insistent protest.

The ground rolled beneath her foot as she moved to set it on the pavement. Rose was disoriented. Confused for a moment. Was this another part of the dreamworld leaking in?

Her brain finally fitted together the puzzle of the sensation. The car was still moving. . . . She had not put it in park.

Rose wrenched her torso back into the cabin as the van jumped the curb and angled onto Hugo's lawn. The door bounced, no longer held open, and slammed its full weight against her still dangling leg. Rose cried out as her hand grasped the shift, depressed the button, and pushed it forward. The chiming ceased as the car lurched to a stop.

Her leg was a red scream of pain.

Rose looked down. A bead of crimson broke down her calf from behind the tasteful leather upholstery of the door. Something under her flesh was very definitely no longer intact.

The world began to fuzz at its corners . . . a yellow buzzing. She was going to pass out.

"No!"

She could hear her voice. She held on to it. Pushed into it. It kept her here, in this world. Here, where Adam needed her—where she was so close.

She twisted and wrenched herself up, pushing at the door. A fresh wave of pain hit her as the metal pulled away from where it had mated itself to her leg. Rose clutched at the door frame and looked down. There was blood, yes. Pain. But no bones had broken the surface.

Jesus Christ, it hurt.

Rose's stomach betrayed her suddenly, pushing its contents

up into her mouth. She lurched forward and wretched, a thick yellow goo of sputum, bile, and half-digested coffee.

Adam.

Rose looked up at Hugo's house. The steps were ten feet away. She could get there. She could get him. *Littler Boy. Addy. Adam. Child of my body.*

Rose moved. Somehow she moved. Three-legged creature pushing its way across the dry reaches of Hugo's lawn, banging on the door that she had knocked on before, standing where she had stood with Pen on her hip, nervous and excited.

The door opened.

"Where is he?"

She looked up from Hugo's belt into his gray face. He looked like a little boy who'd been caught doing something bad. An aged boy. "Rosie, you're hurt."

Rose pushed at his chest, her hand leaving a bloody smear on his shirt. "Where is he?" Her voice was stronger now, anger behind it. Her eyes swept the couch. *No Addy.* The kitchen. *No Addy.* She stumbled in, looking down the hall. *No Addy.*

"Did you hurt him?" She turned on Hugo.

He shook his head. "No, Rosie. I could never . . . I would never . . . I just took him to a movie . . . that's all."

"Then where is he?"

"Still there."

Almost right after the movie started, Mr. David had whispered to him that he was going to go to the bathroom. Addy wondered why he hadn't just gone during the commercials like his mom always said to . . . but in a way, Adam understood.

Sometimes the stuff that they played before the movies—the trailers, they were called—were better than the movie was.

Still, he didn't want to have to go with him. *He* didn't need to go.

But then Mr. David was handing him the tub of popcorn and telling him he'd be back. Would Adam be okay?

Adam nodded, barely taking his eyes off the movie. If Mr. David thought he was old enough to be alone in a movie theater for a few minutes, he wasn't going to tell him that his mommy didn't think so yet. His mommy wouldn't even let Isaac be alone in a movie theater.

But the movie was happening and it didn't seem like such a big deal. It was just for a little bit, anyway.

Right before he left, Mr. David had leaned over Adam's seat, pushing his shoulders forward. "Hold still, you got something back here," he'd said as Adam felt his hand smooth across the back of his shirt. Adam moved his head to the side to see the screen—but right after that Mr. David stepped out of the way and left the theater. In the corner of his vision, Adam could see him stop at the bottom of the stairs to look back up at him, before turning and disappearing into the tunnel that led to the way out.

Adam took a handful of popcorn and shoveled it into his mouth. He laughed. The movie was funny.

"You left him there!"

"I told him I was going to the bathroom so he wouldn't be scared."

"He's six!"

"I put something on his back. Your address. A sticker that

says who he is and that he's lost. Someone will find him. They will bring him home."

Rose imagined Adam in an empty theater. Adam as the lights came up, looking for Hugo. Adam wandering his way down the steps, looking for the man who had abducted and then abandoned him. Her little boy filling with fear as he realized that he was alone.

"How could you think I would hurt him, Rose? I only did it because I knew you would come . . . it was the only way."

"You're crazy." If she left now, maybe she could find him. Maybe she could be there before the movie was finished. Before Addy even knew enough about what had happened to him to get scared.

She broke for the door. Hugo's hand grabbed her wrist. Rose spun about to free his grip.

And what happened next?

Was it an accident? An accumulation of elements finally reaching the sum of their parts? Rose's exhaustion, her injury, the fuzzy edges of oblivion tickling at her vision, the slipperiness of the blood and sweat on her hand beneath Hugo's grip?

For a moment it is a dance, frozen. Dancers poised, centrifugal force pulling the weight of one's body from the other, pivoting from the fulcrum of their grasp.

Her body whipping around, balance unsteady, nerves jangling with fresh new alerts that too much weight had been put on that injured limb. And then a slip, mere millimeters the difference—

Her head meets the door.

A bouncing reverb, nasty thud.

The dancer crumples to the floor.

With the trauma, her consciousness is finally broken. Too much to bear, a literal final blow.

Was it an accident, this meeting—cranium to carved wood—or did her partner let her fall on purpose?

A small, petty strike. A seizing of opportunity. A little slip from his hand to keep her in his grasp . . . the object of his intent.

He did not know himself.

He knew he would not hurt her. Never intentionally . . . but unintentionally?

Was there a part of Hugo, buried deep within him, that had loosened his fingers, *just so,* enough to drive her temple into that door?

Because accident or no, he had what he wanted.

Mouth slack. Eye closed. Loose fists curled on limp wrists.

A sleeping Rose.

He cried when he saw her. Fell to the floor. Cradled her body.

Still crying, he brought her to his temple. His room of worship, the one he had painted so carefully. The place of Josh's conversion. He laid her down as gently as possible, her closed eyes facing up into a painted simulacrum of their dreamworld's clouds. Pearl seams bursting with light.

He left her only once and returned with the host they had shared only days before and a cup, unwashed but full to the brim. Next to her sleeping body, his beloved Rose, he set down a communion of blue pills.

More than enough for a congregation of worshippers.

More than enough.

He hoped.

He lay down next to her as the sleep took hold, whispering apologies.

twenty-three

There was a Tickle Crab in the Blanket Pavilion. It waved its pearly claws just inches from Rose's face, the feathery tines of its carapace fluttering.

It had never occurred to Rose how much the small creatures looked as though they were made of dandelion fluff. From where her face lay on the sand, she felt she could breathe hard, exhale in just the right way, and set the tiny thing aloft.

It skittered sideways, and then she felt him next to her. His warm presence, only inches from her prone body.

"Want a snack?"

Rose turned and there he was, beautiful Hugo, holding out a small cowrie shell just as he had when they had first met. Before everything had changed.

So like it had been in that moment. The peace of the seashore. The gentle battering of the sheet walls of the Pavilion in the wind. The warmth of the sand.

It was so nice.

Rose reached out to take the shell from him. Anticipating its maple crunch.

A little something tickled the back of her brain. A memory, fleeting images. *What was it?* Anger, desperation, the sensation of falling forward.

Her hand paused in midair.

"Hugo, what did you do?"

He looked away from her and suddenly it flooded back. Adam. *The hallucinations. Her mangled leg. And the hard surface of a door rising up to meet her.*

"I'm really glad you're here, Rosie. I've missed you so much."

Rose sat up.

Through the parted sheets of the Pavilion door she could just make out the spires of Castle City in the distance.

Something was wrong with it.

Rose stood to get a better view, making her way toward the door.

The city was decaying. Crumbling without its shield. Bits of buildings were breaking off even as she stood there. Rose could make out tiny bricks tumbling from their towers to the unseen streets below. Vulture shapes circled in the space between.

A wind blew in a carrion scent.

"What happened?" Rose asked.

"I'm glad you weren't with me when I went there. It's a horrible place, Rose. Someone like you doesn't belong there."

Rose looked at him, still on the sand, his eyes turned firmly away from the door . . . as if even a glance of the city would be too much.

"I didn't want to go without you, but I had to. You made me. Because you wouldn't go to sleep. Because you wouldn't meet me here."

"Hugo, what did you find in there?"

He didn't answer. Instead he said, "I'm not angry. It was better that I did it alone. . . . Even though I missed you."

Hugo seemed broken. Delicate. There was something about the way he was sitting, his knees curled up toward his chest, that made Rose think of Adam. The way he would put on a brave face after an injury. The way he soothed himself with words, pretending to be more courageous than he really was.

What had happened while she was away?

What had he faced alone?

"I think it's better this way," he continued. "Maybe sometimes people shouldn't get rescued. Maybe sometimes people should stay behind the walls. . . . Besides, it was always better when it was just the two of us anyway. Just the two of us alone . . . and nobody else."

"Hugo, I don't want it to be just the two of us."

"Hi, Mommy."

Rose turned at the sound of Adam's voice and found him sitting at her kitchen table, suddenly occupying a corner of the tent. Isaac and Penny flanked him, smiling, beatific. They waved at her.

"It would be okay for them to be here. If it was what you really wanted."

Rose thought of her nightmares of the island attacking her children. This was the last place she wanted them to be, even if—

"It's not real, Hugo. It's not really them. It's you, you're putting them here."

He sighed and the children flickered out, little depressions on the sand the only evidence of their appearance.

He lay down, a fetal curl. "I don't understand why I'm not enough for you, Rose. You were enough for me. You have *always* been enough for me. That's why she left. . . ."

"Your wife?" Rose moved closer to him. His voice was vague, listless.

"She said there wasn't enough room for three people in our relationship. . . . Because she knew that she could never be you. So she took my little Rose and she drove away."

"I don't understand."

"My daughter. We named her for you, before my wife started to hate you. Before the end. Our little Rosalie. My wife took her away because of you."

Rose flashed to the view from the nightmare, the bedroom that had come after they had escaped the flood in the high school. The Subaru below the window, pulling away, herself behind the wheel, Penny leaning against the dash, waving good-bye. The way Hugo had looked on in horror.

Like the high school, it had been a memory, the day his wife had abandoned him. But Rose and Penny had overlaid Hugo's wife and child, new refrains for distant echoes. New players for the old script. Wife scowls and turns the wheel, reverses out of his life. Little girl enthusiastically waves good-bye, innocent of the finality of the farewell.

"She said she couldn't compete with you. This woman I drew pictures of and told my daughter about. She left because she could never be you. She could never be my Rose. She couldn't be the woman of my dreams . . . so strong, so beautiful."

Rose's heart ached. Of course Hugo's wife couldn't compare with the Rose in her husband's dreams. A woman without flaws or fears who had no demands on Hugo other than that they continue to romp around the playground of the island.

Rose herself fell short of the fantasy.

She was nothing like she was in their dreams.

But neither was he.

Hugo closed his eyes, pushing his face into the pillow of the sand.

Something was terribly, terribly wrong.

She shook him. "Hugo . . ."

"I'm sorry, Rosie. It shouldn't be too long."

"Too long until what? Until what, Hugo?"

A crunching sound came from the corner of the tent. Rose pulled her eyes from Hugo, searching for the source.

There was a little boy popping seashells in his mouth. He grinned at her. Held out a small cowrie.

"Want a snack?"

Hugo, the boy . . . as she had first seen him. Rose's eyes dashed from the sleeping form of his grown self to the child he grew from. He looked precisely the same as he had when she met him, his legs splayed in the sand, quick brown hands bringing seashells to his sweet, crooked smile.

Rose remembered that he had seemed so grown-up to her then. A big boy. Eight years old. So much more mature than her.

But he was just a little boy, wasn't he? No older than Isaac.

The grown Hugo was still on the sand . . . asleep in the dream.

Rose stood up.

"You can't leave," little Hugo snapped. He was watching her closely.

"What?"

"You can't leave. I won't let you."

"What do you mean you won't let me?" Rose took a step toward him, her toes making trails in the sand.

"This is my island, you know. Mine. I can do whatever I want here and I don't want you to leave."

Rose would never have tolerated that tone from her own children. They would have found themselves in time-out or short a toy or a privilege. She didn't remember Hugo being this way when they were children.

"I could hurt you if I really wanted to . . . since he's not here anymore. I won't, but I could."

"Who's not here anymore?"

Little Hugo nodded his head in the direction of big Hugo, asleep on the sand. "Him. He never let me hurt you, even when you deserved it. Even when you tried to leave. Even when you forgot. . . ."

Rose tried to make sense out of what little Hugo was saying. "Forgot what?"

"That you belong to me."

Rose should have known better than to reason with a brat, but she responded instinctively, "No, I don't," her voice strident and high.

"Yes, you do."

"No, I don't." She sounded so childish.

Little Hugo stood, smug hands on his hips. "I made this place, Rosie. I *made* it. It's mine. I can make it do anything I want. And I don't want you to leave, so I'm not going to let you."

There was something so cruel about his face. Little psychopath in a pirate shirt. Rose turned back to the sleeping form of big Hugo.

He was made of sand.

A perfect sculpture of the grown Hugo lay where only moments before she had watched him lay his head. Sandy eyes closed in rest, his shoulders a solid mound of grit. Like those carved marble sleepers that lay on the tops of tombs . . . but created by some meticulous beachgoer.

Something was terribly, terribly wrong.

Rose did not decide to run, but suddenly she was doing it. She needed to get herself away from this monster that looked like a child and Hugo. Get as much distance between the two of them as possible.

She bounded toward the door of the Pavilion, toward the decaying city. She crested the threshold—

And stepped right back into the space she had been standing the moment she had started to run.

"See! I told you!" Little Hugo's pretty face was curled into an ugly smile.

Rose took off again. Faster this time. Her body leaning into the run. She felt the unfiltered light of the outside world hit her nose—

And she stepped onto her precise starting point.

Again.

Again.

Again.

Each time she landed, Rose felt a sickness rise, her stomach lurching at the impossibility of what was happening to her body.

"Stop it!" she screamed.

Little Hugo was calm. "You stop it. I don't want you to run away from me anymore."

Was it true? Was this mean little boy in charge of the island? Had he made it, as he said?

Rose realized that there had to be some truth to it, even in how she thought of this place. *Hugo's island.* That was what she called it. That's all she had ever called it . . . even in the recesses of her own mind . . . even when she thought she was dreaming of the place all on her own . . . it was always *Hugo's* place. A place she visited. Never *hers.*

Rose's eyes skimmed the sand form of the grown Hugo. She

could see that it was drying, losing its structural integrity. Soon the whole thing would crumble, abandon its shape and disappear into the ocean of sand. *What did he mean, "He never let me hurt you"?* This little boy *was* Hugo, wasn't he?

Or at the very least, he was some *part of him.*

The part of him that has been sending you nightmares.

Rose needed to get away from this boy. This monster with the face she had loved.

Rose took another step toward the door—

—then jerked her body to the side. Her hand touched the wall of the tent, the leading edge of her dive. Her fingers caught the bottom of the blanket and lifted it as she rolled under its hem. Rose held her breath, bracing herself to find that little Hugo had sent her rolling back into the same room again.

He had not.

She was in the Orange Tastee.

Or rather, the Orange Tastee was in the Blanket Pavilion, its cloth walls and ceiling hanging over the order counter and aluminum-faced kitchen of Hugo's former place of employment. A gentle tide lapped in among the supports of the bolted tables. Above the counter hung the illuminated menu, with its listing of orange whips and dogs—all the different joinings of the same five ingredients.

The price listed for every item was the same.

Tastee Dog.........................\$RO.SE
Super Tastee Dog.............\$RO.SE
Classic Orange Tastee.....\$RO.SE
Kid's Combo......................\$RO.SE

Rose heard the gentle *whoosh* of sand buffeting the tent wall. She turned. Little Hugo had stopped short of his pursuit, taking in the Formica tables and the cheap bentwood benches. His eyes were wide.

Rose flinched, ready to bolt, but the boy wasn't even looking at her.

Instead, his lips were pursing, pressing against each other as his eyes devoured the facts of the room. Rose could sense that something was rising within him. Something familiar.

Embarrassment?

"You didn't put this here, did you?"

Little Hugo's eyes whipped back to her. Pupils narrowing.

And then Rose knew. As surely as she knew who the instigator was in a fight between Isaac and Adam. As surely as she knew when Penny needed to poop and when Josh was going to put the moves on her. She knew.

"You said you made this place. But you don't completely control it."

The boy's fists tightened. "Yes. I. Do."

Rose sensed it before she saw it, the snaking twist of sheets reaching out from behind her. A venomous cotton tendril.

She yanked her wrist out of its reach and threw herself forward. The sheet reared up, foiled, a cobra ready to strike. Rose pulled herself across the sand. She ducked under the tent and tumbled outside.

A strong wind was setting the saw grass that flanked the beach to dance. The stalks waved their verdant bodies, kissing their neighbors before snapping back to the sky.

Rose gained her feet and aimed herself toward the tall blades. Maybe she could lose him in the saw grass, hide until she woke up.

Or maybe she could kill him.

Rose's bare feet reached the dry embankment that marked the boundary between beach and field. She bounded into the tall stalks, her mind racing.

She could kill Hugo.

Maybe. Possibly.

If he didn't control everything on the island, then it was possible that she could defend herself against him. She could fashion a sword from the saw grass . . . as he had taught her to do so long ago. She could wait for him to find her and surprise him. She could pierce his body as she had done to so many of the island's monsters. She could drive the blade into his heart.

No, she couldn't.

"Come back, Rose!" She heard his voice over the clatter of the blowing grass. A child's voice, still unchanged by puberty. "You're being a silly head!"

A silly head.

Only a child would threaten to hurt you, imprison you, and then call you a silly head as you flee.

The image of little Hugo threaded on her grass sword resounded through Rose's mind. She couldn't do it. She couldn't hurt him. Not a child. Not one that looked so much like the boy she loved.

Not one that once *was* the boy she loved.

Rose turned her head, still moving forward, but angling so that she could see if he was following her. Through the blades she could see little Hugo's legs as he moved through the grass, looking for her. "I told you, you're being silly. Anywhere you go I'll be there. I am everything and everywhere here."

Rose stumbled. Her hands splayed out, palms biting the grit of the earth.

Hovering a half inch from the cornea of her eye was a bone-gray prong . . . just short of blinding her.

Rose pulled back, taking in the full view of what she had nearly impaled herself upon.

It was an antler. It sprang from the skull of a mounted

Buck's head, the kind Rose was used to seeing in tacky restaurants or the rec rooms of her childhood friends whose fathers hunted. It was just the head, suspended from a wooden plaque. Its fur was piebald, patchy. Gray with dust. The taxidermist who had created it had clearly been trying to re-create some wild aspect of the living creature, as he had posed it with its neck turned, its teeth bared, a frozen gnash at some unseen foe.

The head was leaning against a pile of dusty furniture. An old easy chair, once a red that had faded to a mottled pink. A chipped highboy dresser. A few cane chairs, the woven seats of which were in various states of unravel.

It was as if someone had emptied an antiques shop or attic into the saw grass.

The rattling blades behind her quieted. Hugo had stopped moving.

"I can see you." His voice was playful, but still distant. Rose's eyes scanned the green stalks, looking for him.

The furniture began to *fuse*.

Rose watched in horror as the highboy and the chairs began to join together . . . their edges leaning toward one another and melting into an unnatural six-limbed *thing*. The mottled velvet of the chair spread a sick skin over the wooden struts and faces as they morphed and popped like muscles.

Rose pushed herself back from it, flailing against the stalks.

What had once been the back of the easy chair bent forward, reaching toward the Buck's head on the ground. It locked on.

The whole thing shook, a big cat getting out of the water, and then it lifted its head.

The Buck's head snarled and snorted.

And then it saw Rose. Glass eyes animate with life and hate.

It stamped the ground and *charged*.

Rose twisted and threw herself into a run. Headlong into the saw grass.

She could hear it behind her as she crashed into the green. The edges of the stalks caught her flailing arms and face, splitting cuts into her skin. Her heart was pounding.

He had sent this thing after her. Hugo had sent her this monster.

She would never get away.

Rose felt the despair push its way up into her mind.

A vicious, meaty snort sounded right behind her. Rose turned to look—

Suddenly she was *falling*.

Rose gasped, trying to make sense of the shift. The world was upside down and she was tumbling over the end of it.

The Spider Chasm.

Somehow she had tumbled off the edge of it. The cliff face was flying past her.

She screamed, reaching toward the rock wall.

Her fingers caught a slight crevice in the rock and her body swung downward, hitting the stone with a queasy thud.

Rose could feel that her fingernails had snapped somewhere inside the darkness of the crevice. Her body was in pain. Shoulder screaming, nearly wrenched out of its socket. Lungs bruised, the air torn out of them. Chin scraped against stone.

She willed her other hand to move. To find somewhere to take hold.

Her fingers scrabbled over the rock. *There has to be something here. Please. Please.*

Her breath reflected back off the stone, hot, panicked wind.

Her searching hand found a small outcropping in the cliff face. A tiny hold, barely there.

But it was something.

Rose glanced down, through the small window of space between her shoulder and the cliff wall.

The canyon floor was distant. Miles away, it seemed.

A small sound of despair bubbled its way out of her lips.

A smatter of pebbles bounced down the wall in front of her
face. She looked up.

She had not fallen far. Maybe twenty feet from the cliff top.
Her eyes strained against their sockets for a view; she didn't dare
shift her weight to angle her neck for a better look. But even so,
she knew.

The *thing* was there.

The outer prongs of its horns whipped over the edge of the
Chasm for a moment. Rose could hear its sniffing. Smelling out
her location.

She suppressed a whimper.

Above, the sniffing stopped.

Rose held her breath.

Then she felt it . . . the enclosure around her hand, the one
that had stopped her from falling . . .

It was closing.

The rock was sealing itself, growing over Rose's hand and
wrist.

Rose cried out and pulled her hand free, the sides of her fingers scraping against the narrowing gash of stone. Her body
swung down, held only by the little outcropping. Her fingers
were cramping, protesting against the weight of her.

She sensed movement above. A small face peering over the
edge of the cliff.

"Hugo?"

Beneath her hand, the outcropping began to shrink back
into the rock wall.

"Hugo, please!" she cried.

Her nails broke against the rock, losing their purchase.

And then she was tumbling backward toward the floor of the ravine, the air screaming in her ears, hair blowing a soft cradle around her face. In the growing distance she could see little Hugo's face watching her placidly from the cliff's edge, a ready witness to her destruction.

Rose braced herself for the pain that would come with the ground.

Maybe I'll wake up. Isn't that what they say? If you fall in a dream that you wake up before you hit the ground?

Her body slapped a surface . . .

And kept going.

Rose was enveloped in a cool green world.

Water.

Bubbles flew upward, ascribing a trail to her plummeting body. Rose took in her surroundings, confused.

Somehow she had fallen into water, instead of hitting the rock floor of the Chasm.

Rose's descent stopped and she righted herself. A white shape danced in the gloom. She swam toward it.

It was a woman's body, her eyes closed and peaceful. She looked young, maybe thirty, and *pregnant*. Over her belly was an apron decorated with a familiar brown and yellow marigold print.

Rose recoiled, turning away from the corpse—

Right into another body floating in the dim. This one male. Rose could just make out the mustache on his still and silent face.

A scream of bubbles escaped her lips. Rose pushed away from them. This dead couple. Ghosts in the water. Sediment swirled up from the lake floor, and they disappeared into the cloudy murk.

Rose couldn't see anything. Her lungs were burning. She needed air.

Something cold and hard brushed against the back of her hand.

A chain.

Rose clasped it and pulled. Hand over hand. Above her she could make out that the gloom was getting lighter . . . she was nearing the surface.

She broke it with a gasp.

The Green Lagoon.

Rose beached herself onto one of the enormous roots that bordered the edge of the pool. Her body spasmed, coughing up the insurgent water that had invaded her lungs.

"See! I could have let you hit the bottom of the ravine—but I didn't, Rose. I could have hurt you, but I didn't."

Little Hugo was standing on the other side of the pool. He looked proud of himself.

Just in front of him floated the Plank Orb. . . .

Or rather, the *remains* of the Plank Orb. An ax rested in the small part of the vessel that remained seaworthy. It had clearly been used to create an enormous gash in its upper hemisphere.

Orphaned bits of wood bobbed on the surface of the Lagoon.

Rose coughed again, her cheek pressing against the rough bark of the root. "Who are the people in the water, Hugo?" Her voice was strained, torn. She barely sounded like herself.

"Nobody. Come on, Rose. I want to go back to the beach. I think the sun is going to come out. We can jump on the rainbow trail. You always like that."

"I want to wake up, Hugo."

"We're never going to wake up, Rosie. You're going to stay with me here forever."

twenty-four

"What did you do to us, Hugo?"

Little Hugo was making his way toward her. Hopping from tree root to tree root. He looked pleased with himself. Like Isaac when he came home with a good score on a math test. *Look, Mom!*

"Let's go back to the beach."

"What did you do to us?"

"God, Rosie. Nothing bad."

"Why aren't we going to wake up?"

"Because I don't want us to."

His face was infuriating. Smiling Eddie Haskell shit-sated grin. Rose felt the desire to slap him grow in her palms. An itchy want.

"But what did you do?"

He rolled his eyes.

God, I hate it when they do that.

"He did it. But it was my idea. To take them. To give them to you."

Rose suddenly became aware of a faint, familiar bitterness spread across the width of her tongue. *The pills.*

Grown Hugo turned to sand, crumbling away into nothing.

"How many?" she asked, but she knew.

"All of them."

All of them. All of the pills. Divided in half. Swallowed whole by Hugo. Crushed and poured down Rosie's unconscious gullet.

To sleep, perchance to dream.

Suddenly she was running *toward* him. Driven forward by fury, propelled by hatred of this selfish child who had taken her from everything she loved. Her arms raised. She did not care anymore that he looked like a little boy. She did not care that he looked so much like Hugo . . . whatever part of Hugo she had once loved was crumbling into sand. . . . And this *thing* wearing his skin needed to be destroyed. Ripped apart.

Her hands reached his shoulders, palms poised to curl around flesh—

And then she was stumbling onto the dry earth of the meadow. She tumbled to her knees, bent grasses caught in her fists instead of the insipid little boy she had been looking to throttle.

"Goddamn it!" she screamed. Why was she being tossed from place to place like this? Battered and buffeted around the island like some grocery sack in the wind?

Because Hugo is dying.

Rose felt the rightness of the thought. Maybe he had just tried to put them to sleep. To knock them into comas like the one she had been in when they met. A permanent dreamworld.

But he had overshot.

"Oh God."

He had trapped her here. Trapped her here in his dying, collapsing mind. Lured her away and poisoned her so that she couldn't escape his nightmares, the nightmare of himself.

Rose looked up. Castle City loomed a short walk away, its green walls crumbling a hundred yards distant. Rose could see that portico that had thrilled her weeks ago, the gate to the city, the long-sought-for way in.

Through it, she could see the streets of the metropolis.

A dead place.

She stood. All around her the meadow was littered with discarded dusty furniture and storage boxes. The contents of a thousand emptied basements and attics, church rummages and garage sales.

She took a step.

"Rose, I told you. I went to the city. You don't belong there."

He was behind her. The darkest part of Hugo. The part he'd left her with.

Rose didn't turn to look at him. "What's in there?"

"Things you shouldn't see."

In her periphery, Rose sensed the rummage sale debris begin to shift . . . accreting into clumps on the field. She didn't need to look to know what was happening, what was forming. Hulks of tired cardboard and wood. Monsters of metal and old picture frames.

"What shouldn't I see, Hugo?"

Small showers of earth burst up from the ground all around her. Spiders making their way to the surface from below. In the distance she could hear Blindhead's distinctive slither.

She heard him right behind her. Was he still wearing the

little Hugo skin, or had he made himself look like something else?

"Bad things. Dark things. Nightmares."

All around her the piles of furniture were waking up. Shaking life into their wood-and-fabric muscles. The hard-packed earth was giving beneath the giant carapaces of the island's Spiders, bits of clay tumbling from their bodies as they pulled themselves out of the ground.

"Hugo, everything is a nightmare now."

If he didn't want her in the city, that was where she needed to go.

Rose ran.

And the beasts came after her.

Came after her on their stilted improvised legs, limping, hulking beasts. Half-things. Rose's toes bit into the dry earth, pushing her toward the dying city. She felt the wind press drily against her eyes. The creatures were sluggish, partly formed. The Spiders not yet free of the ground.

The portico grew closer.

She could make it.

Rose gasped, one huge long pull of air into her dormant lungs. *Had she been breathing before that?* She thought of her body—not the one here running from these makeshift monsters, but her *real body,* her sad overweight *poisoned* body on the floor of Hugo's house.

Rose regretted every ugly thought she'd ever had about her living *breathing* working body.

She willed another breath into her lungs.

She could not die on the floor of Hugo's house.

She could not die.

She would not.

Rose crested the threshold of the city, pushing her way past the portico gate. She turned, ready to fend off the beasts.

The meadow behind her was empty of monsters. Wild poppies and brush grass waved in their stead. Rose bent over, hands on knees, recovering from the exertion. Another breath. Another breath. Another breath.

He's still there. Even if you can't see him. Still there.

Something soft and light pressed itself against Rose's leg. A faint fluttering.

Rose looked down to find a piece of paper, pushed by the breeze against her calf. She peeled it away from her skin.

One of Hugo's drawings. A self-portrait. The artist as an almost man.

A few more drawings flew by. Tumbleweeding. End over end past the reaches of her toes. There was a pattering. Like a summer rain.

Rose pulled her eyes away from the pencil sketch of Hugo's dreamy, sad-boy face and toward the source of the sound.

A library's worth of paper tears cried from the towers of Castle City.

Rose saw snatches of each page's contents as they weaved and wended their way down. A watercolor foot. A pastel lock of hair. A limb in charcoal.

Hugo's drawings fluttered down to the pink drift sand floor of Castle City. Pooling at the bases of the towers like windblown trash.

And the towers?

Rose pushed into the streets, reaching out to touch the wall of the nearest building.

It was flat. Painted plywood and two-by-fours. Like a stage flat in a high school play, it wobbled under her touch.

Rose's heart hurt.

There was never anyone in this city. Never anyone for them to rescue. It was a prop. A painted backdrop, cheaply made. Empty.

Hugo's drawings made flup-flup sounds as they freed themselves from one pile and flew to the next. Shuffling and unshuffling themselves by some unknown system of categories.

Rose walked through the city's pretend streets, her feet sifting through that ubiquitous pink sand. It threaded hotly through her toes, breaking small rivers across the tops of her feet. The same sand that could send her bounding into the air. The sand that had spewed in a nightmare from the mouth of her son. The sand that had claimed Hugo . . . or a part of Hugo.

She stared up at the backs of the towers, making out the joins and the couplings of MDF. The supports and the struts on their unpainted sides, reaching impossibly high.

Hugo's drawings went flup-flup. Flup-flup.

What the hell had it all been for? All these years. A lifetime of slumber spent trying to get to this ugly, vacant place.

Then she saw it. A brief flash of orange in the shadow of a tower.

The Orange Tastee.

Its fiberglass arms frozen midwave, dumping out into four-fingered white gloves. Jaunty blossom hat. Friendly leering wink. Battered screen in place of its teeth.

The speaker from the drive-through. First contact. The place where Hugo had first spoken to Rose in their waking lives. *What had he said?*

"Are you okay?"

And she had thought, *No. I am not okay. Nothing about me is okay.*

Rose felt like crying.

The Orange spoke. Hugo's voice. It was fuzzy, distorted by

the speaker. She couldn't tell which Hugo was talking to her, young or old. But whoever it was, he was frightened. Pleading.

"Please, Rose. Please come out. I don't want to go in there."

"There's nothing here, Hugo. There's never been anything here."

"Please come out."

"What is it that you don't want me to see?"

It was then that Rose saw it. The flat towers and sand of Castle City replaced in an instant, like a slide show moving on to the next frame.

Before her stood a little yellow house with gray shutters like eyelashes on its second-story windows. White trim eaves and a round shutter vent like an eye in the temple of its roof.

It sat on the bend of a flat river, brown, fast, and cold. The kind of place her father would call a trout river. A place for throwing rocks and icing beer in the elbow crook of a narrow valley. Gray-and-pink granite crags and pine reaches on either side. Just enough of both to keep the eye from lumping it all in one as "trees" or "rock," but to keep it jumping, contrasting the softness of one with the hardness of the other. The air was rich with constellations of dandelion fluff. The seeds hovered, dancing above water, tumbling in the air before some unseen current swept them away.

The house was smartly distant from the banks of the river. Separated by an expanse of close-cut wild grass and a quartz rock drive. Everything covered in a dewy gloss of a summer rain, ceased momentarily. Though the sky above was still covered with a layer of tawny clouds, the sun was kneading its way through in spots . . . setting the white quartz pebbles and the scrub grass to sparkle for an instant whenever an insurgent beam touched the ground.

A pretty house. A pretty place. A pretty day.

This is what he didn't want me to see? Rose took a step closer.

A small boat sat by the side of the house. A sportsman's boat. Modest battered aluminum, small outboard on its rear. Too tiny to merit a name. Next to it a faded yellow station wagon. Fake wooden paneling on its sides.

And farther out . . . closer to the river, on a patch made muddy by the rain, sat a boy.

A circumference of action figures around his hunched form. Some small towers of mud and rocks in a ring in front of him. A playground for his toys. Somewhere not too far off, someone had made a tent of weathered sheets and chairs, pinning the faded hems under the chair legs so that they would not blow away.

Rose recognized the place, though her view now was different.

She had seen this river and this driveway from one of those second-story windows. Seen Hugo's wife spin her tires, grinding away from him on this flat of land.

But now she was standing on the grass below. Standing above a child folded into a position she knew well . . . the pose of deep, concentrated play.

In the boy's hand was a Han Solo action figure. Loose white shirt, black vest. The toy was clearly well loved. Battle-scarred and bitten. Han Solo, the rogue hero. Rose smiled and took a step closer.

The boy looked up at her through a pair of Coke-bottle glasses, widening his eyes, the color of chocolate. And her heart stopped.

A screen door slammed and the boy looked away from Rose to the house. A man and a woman stood on the poured-concrete steps, relaxed smiles in the direction of the boy.

Ghosts from the water.

She in her marigold apron, stretched and tied above a high,

pregnant belly. Brown hair swept into a shiny ponytail. Pretty and young.

And he with a mustache and easy smile. Sideburns and short shorts.

Hugo's parents.

And the boy . . . Hugo as a boy . . . as he really was. Not the version of him she knew in the dream. Not the one who had been chasing her across the landscape of the island, sending her nightmares. The real Hugo. As she had never seen him.

"Rose. Please. We need to leave."

Rose pulled her eyes from the family toward the sound of his voice, and there he was . . . the other *real Hugo*. Waking Hugo. "David" Hugo. Overweight, wrinkled, graying Hugo. He of the face that had stopped her heart in the drive-through.

"What happened here?" Rose's voice was small.

He didn't answer her. He seemed lost in watching his father lift the lid of the charcoal grill, checking the heat. Rose could see the resemblance. Father and son . . . though Hugo was older by a decade than the man blowing air onto the coals.

His eyes tripped to his mother as she brought a thick slice of watermelon to the boy on the ground. "Only one piece now, to hold you until the burgers are ready. Okay, sweetie?" The boy nodded. He held out his action figure in exchange for the treat. An everyday exchange. The woman slipped the toy into the pocket of her apron and gave him the fruit. Kissed him on the forehead.

"Hugo, tell me."

Hugo's eyes were fixed on the boy on the ground.

"It had been raining. For more than a week. It was summer. It finally stopped. I remember I was so happy. I was so tired of being stuck inside."

Hugo's mother, headed back toward the house, slowed suddenly in her motion. She stopped, turning toward the river. There was an alertness about her, a slight shift in her demeanor. Lips pursed. Eyes searching.

Rose followed her line of sight.

The river was *changing*. Its level was swiftly starting to rise. Brown bubbles rolling, picking up speed, swelling the banks.

"I don't want to be here, Rose." Grown Hugo watched as his mother walked out past the lawn, angling for a better view upriver.

And then they heard it.

A resounding crack echoing its way down the valley. An ugly snap.

On the ground, young Hugo jerked his head up. His father stepped away from the barbecue, his eyes on his wife.

"All the rain filled the reservoir too quickly." Rose could hear the fear in Hugo's voice.

There was another crack.

And then a boom.

Rose felt the sound in her bones. The sound of the world ending. The sound of a planet torn apart.

Upriver, a wall of brown, churning water was racing, rising, toward them.

"A dam break." Rose whispered it aloud even as she realized the truth of what was happening . . . what had happened.

Hugo's mother pivoted, falling back onto her heel and breaking into a run toward the house. Behind her the river was transforming into a rapid, suddenly loud, overboiling. She yanked the boy to his feet, roughly by the wrist, and the watermelon slice flew from his other hand and tumbled to the dirt.

The boy stumbled as she dragged him toward the steps of the house. Transfixed by the water.

Hugo was gone. Rose's eyes swept the ground for him, but

he had disappeared. Gone and abandoned her to this viper of a memory. What would happen if she simply stood here on the banks of the river while the water overtook them? Would she wake up? Be swept to the shore of the island?

Rose didn't think so.

She beat a path to the house.

Hugo's father was holding the screen door for his young family. Yelling over the onslaught. Rose could just make out his words.

"I'm going to get the boat."

She looked back at the tiny dinghy perched in a hauler at the side of the house.

No.

But then Hugo's mother was nodding and pushing her way into the house, her hand still wrapped around her son's wrist. Hugo's father turned, headed away from them. Away from the safety of the house.

Gray-brown water was fanning out from the banks of the river. An inch every three seconds. A rapid rise.

Rose tore herself away from the flood into the recesses of Hugo's childhood home. She saw Hugo and his young mother's feet at the top of a sensible wood staircase, thump, thump, thump- ing their way to the second floor. Rose threw herself up the steps, three at time, cresting the landing just behind them.

Through an open door, she saw where he had gone.

Waking Hugo. A grown man. More than grown, huddled on the *Star Wars* sheets of his childhood bed. Rocking himself for comfort. "We need to get out of here. We need to get out of here. We need to get out of here." A mumbled whisper.

But he was a ghost to his mother, the pregnant beauty in the ponytail, who in two quick steps was at the window looking down.

Rose looked over her shoulder.

"Oh, my God."

Below, Hugo's father was trying to lasso the dinghy's rope to the chimney of the house. The water already waist deep. He was bracing himself against the railing of their small porch. The cord fell short. Skittering off the bricks.

Hugo's mother turned from the window and ran into the hallway. Rose felt the boy step into her place at her side. Behind his glasses his eyes were angled upriver—

Where an impossible swell of water was cresting the bend. It looked unnatural. An ocean wave set loose in a little mountain valley.

"Hugo!"

The little boy turned away from the horror and ran toward his mother's voice in the dark hallway. Rose watched as the woman crouched so she could look at him eye to eye.

"Honey, I need you to reach it for me."

It? thought Rose. But then the woman was grabbing the little boy by the waist, bracing him against the baby in her belly. Lifting him. The boy reached toward the ceiling for—

The chain from the Plank Orb. The thought jumped into Rose's mind unbidden. *Is it?*

It was an attic access panel. A square door in the ceiling. A length of chain threading out of a small, circular bracket opening. The boy wrapped both hands around it ("Here we go!") and pulled.

The door swung up.

"Now pull down the ladder, Hugo, my love." Rose recognized the tone in the pregnant woman's voice. The mother tone. The "keep the child calm even though the world is coming apart" tone.

The ladder slid smoothly down past the boy's blank face.

"Up we go," said his mother, forced cheer.

The house shuddered suddenly. A moaning complaint.

But the boy was climbing and his mother after him. Rose moved from the doorway to the top of the stairwell.

Below, the first floor was submerged beneath four feet of torpid water. Rose could make out the woven rug at the base of the stairs, like a manta on the ocean floor.

The only way to go was up.

The bed in Hugo's bedroom was empty. Had Hugo disappeared again? Or followed his mother and his other self into the attic?

Rose pulled herself up into the small space. The ceiling was low, maybe six feet at its peak. Errant rusty nails from the roof poked through at odd angles. It smelled of hot dust and spiderwebs.

A shuffling from the other side of the space drew her eye. Hugo's mother leading the little boy by the hand across a fluffy bank of pink insulation batting. They crouched as they made their way past the dark shapes of boxes and stored furniture. Toward the fractured light of the round shutter vent at the far end of the space.

"Now you stay here."

Hugo's mother settled him against the wall. She pulled something from the pocket of her apron and handed it to him. His Han Solo.

"Now I'm going to go get Daddy and I'll be right back. Everything is going to be okay. You stay right here. Promise me?"

The little boy nodded. "I promise."

"No!" a broken scream came from behind Rose. Real-life Hugo suddenly at her side, his face a mask of terror. "No!"

Hugo's mother kissed the boy's forehead. One last time.

"I love you forever."

And then she was moving. Quickly, she covered the space

between the boy who was her son and the man he would become.

She twisted her awkward body onto the stairs and stepped down into the water that had gathered on the second-story landing. She gasped as its coldness claimed her ankles. For a brief moment, she turned, facing the window visible through the door to Hugo's room. Her eyes full of whatever horror the water had washed up there. A hollow banging resounded, sending shivers through the walls of their home.

She looked back up into the trapdoor . . .

And pushed it closed.

twenty-five

I t was dark.

The house moaned again. Wood straining against water.

Next to her, Rose heard Hugo collapse on the floor of the attic. She felt his warm shape there, pressed against her legs.

Who was he now? There on the dusty floorboards next to her? The man from the drive-through? The dreamy hero dissolved into sand? The beautiful, sneering boy? There were so many Hugos, weren't there?

But in the darkness she couldn't tell which one had taken refuge next to her. Muffled sobs under mortified hands.

The house groaned again.

Such a familiar sound. Water and wood.

Rose felt a faint wetness lick the bottom of her foot. In the dim light that reached them from the attic vent, she could make out the faint outline of the trapdoor in the floor. Water lapped up from the seams . . . but it didn't rise.

"She said she'd come back."

Rose looked instinctively toward the ground, but Hugo—whichever Hugo he was now—wasn't there anymore.

"She said."

The voice was coming from the far end of the room. Toward the light. Rose put a searching hand out toward the floor. The ceiling was too low. Better to crawl. Her hands sank into the pink batting of the insulation.

Fiberglass. If this weren't a dream, my skin would be burning.

Hands and knees, Rose made her way to the edge of the attic and there she found Hugo.

Or rather, both Hugos.

Or rather . . . all Hugos.

Because while the little boy was still situated by the round shuttered attic vent, the man who sat hunched across from him, leaning on some discarded furniture, was flickering from one version of himself to another. His features were hard to get a fix on as they kept melting from one instant to the next. His hair graying and then brown, belly round then taut.

Rose felt strangely intrusive. Like walking in on lovers in the act or reading someone's diary. But somehow, looking at Hugo as his body fluttered and shuffled through all forms of himself was even more invasive than that. As though she were witness to some private phenomenon, meant only for the workings of one's own mind, more personal than desire.

She turned her eyes from him and looked at the little boy.

His face was unreadable. Passive.

Rose thought about her boys. Isaac and Adam. What if it

had been them in this attic? What if they had seen the things this boy had witnessed?

Would they be as calm as he?

Maybe. If their mommy had told them everything was going to be all right.

But Rose could tell, by the whiteness of the hand that clutched his Han Solo doll, that he was scared. Frightened almost to death.

"How long were you up here, Hugo?"

The voice that answered her was neither young nor old. But it was Hugo's. "They told me . . . they told me six days."

"Your parents?"

"They never found them."

Rose felt a bubble of pain break from her heart to her throat.

Next to the shuttered vent window, the little boy pulled his legs up into his body. Behind the glasses, his chocolate eyes swept the contents of the attic.

"What did you do up here for six days?"

His eyes fixed on something in the darkness, and then he was crawling past her on the padding. Retrieving two objects from the floor, quickly so as to lessen the infraction against his mother's orders ("You stay right here").

One of the objects made a clinking, shuffling noise as he carried it back.

A jar of seashells, in a bank of white sand.

As he settled himself back into the hollow in the wall, Rose moved closer to get a better look at the rectangular shape he held.

A paint-by-numbers of the city of Oz. A flat corona of yellow surrounding its green-tinted towers.

Castle City.

"You made this place your dreamland."

Rose looked around and saw the attic the way this small, trau-matized boy had seen it. Everything was there. A mounted Buck's head leaning against the old bureau. A broken ceiling fan, its blades and motor ascribing the shape of the island's Spiders. A coil of broken Christmas lights, the broken bulbs the shape of Blindhead's mouth. The pink of the dusty insula-tion the exact shade of the beaches of their dreams. The flat, amateur rendition of Oz. Han Solo and his costume . . . the vest, the shirt . . .

"Everything from our dreams . . . it was from this place, wasn't it. The beach. The city. The water. You went to sleep."

The house moaned again. The wet, lapping sounds and dark close, as familiar to Rose as the confines of the Plank Orb.

The little boy gingerly took off his glasses. He folded the tines and laid them on the floor next to him . . . before curling up. His arm held his Han Solo action figure at a blurry dis-tance, twisting its plastic body in his fingertips.

Rose's eyes caught a small movement above him. A dande-lion seed. She squinted. No, there were two. They hovered in the half-light, blown in through the vent. Their gossamer skel-etons twirled as they fell, branches caught up in one another. They danced through the air over Hugo, the draft driving their waltz upward. Tumbling. Tumbling.

Rose felt a tugging somewhere within her. A slippery pull within herself, like wrinkly fingers held before an open drain at the end of a bath.

And then suddenly she was in two places.

Here in the attic of this drowned house with Hugo in the distant past.

And on the floor of another house with Hugo in a rapidly narrowing future.

Her mouth an open well of vomit . . . one breath away from her lungs.

· They were dying.

Hugo and Rose.

Dying the deaths they didn't that day when they first dreamed of each other. Little Rosie and her bike-battered brain and little Hugo, locked in a waterlogged attic, orphaned and insecure.

How did these two tendrils twist in such a way?

Of what consequence are dreams . . .

Two dreaming minds, lost in fear, foundered on the shore of a made-up land. The dreams of frightened children seeking solace.

The boy on the floor in the attic closed his eyes and sang to pass the time. Something he often did. And as he began, Rose remembered running through the high saw grass for the first time, following the same boy singing the same words at the top of his lungs:

"And you may find somebody kind to help and understand you . . ."

His voice was sweet and soft in the dusty stillness of the attic.

He was alone . . . but not while he slept. If he closed his eyes and slowed his heart, he was joined by a little long-haired girl whose heart-shaped face housed a hard mouth. For days they made the island their playground . . . longer than it ever should have been. Longer than they ever should have been allowed, and somehow they became locked there.

Their paradise a prison.

On the floor of a cheap house in the dry reaches of Colorado, the same hearts, older now, beat slower and slower. Sluggish.

The melting, morphing thing that was what was left of Hugo whispered: "When I'm asleep I'm not alone. Rosie is with me."

"Hugo." Rose pulled against the tug-tug-tug inside her. "Hugo, you left this place. You are not this little boy anymore. You left this attic."

"I don't remember leaving."

"But you did. You were rescued, and even though you lost your mother and father, you found a family. You had a wife and a daughter. But they're not in this place."

"You were with me. You rescued me."

"I didn't. I was a thousand miles away in a hospital. We did need each other, when this happened. I did help you. And you helped me. This was the reason. This is why."

Rose had the distinct sensation of being rolled . . . and felt the faint wash of warmth across her cheek. The draining sensation slowed.

A familiar warmth bloomed inside her chest. A presence that had a name and a scent and flesh.

Josh.

Somehow Josh was with her.

Rose cried.

Next to her the thing that was Hugo . . . all the Hugos . . . stutter-stopped and diminished into a small, flickering light . . . a single bright star that flashed and died.

The little boy on the floor was all that was left of him.

Her Hugo.

Rose caressed his face. He could have been Adam or Isaac. Awakened from a nightmare.

"Maybe . . . maybe that's what dreams are. Maybe the people we see in our dreams are real people who have something to teach us, some way to help us. . . . But we're supposed to wake up from our dreams. Our dreams are supposed to help us live our lives . . .

not keep us from living them." A tear broke from behind the closed lids of the little boy that was all that was left of Hugo. His eyes opened and locked on Rose's.

Rose wrapped him in her arms. This was something she knew how to do. She knew how to comfort little boys after they had nightmares. She smoothed his hair. Rocked their bodies back and forth.

"Hugo, we've been locked in this dream—because part of you never left this place. . . . You need to let us leave."

The house shook with a thundering crash. The sound of wood ripping. Nails screeching against their bonds. Protests of destruction.

In her arms, the boy that was all that was left of Hugo said with the last part of his soul, "I love you, Rosie."

And Rose felt herself dwindle. Her arms grew shorter around him, her body small. She felt a press of soft cotton on her fore-head. A bandage. Rose felt a hot wetness beneath it. A wound.

She was a little girl. The one who had awakened on the shore of the island.

Two children hugging each other for comfort.

She said, "I love you, Hugo," in a tiny child's voice.

Somewhere above them, a hole was rendered in the roof over the attic. The darkness peeled away, pouring sunshine on the dusty pink fluff of the attic floor. A pool of light, iridescent.

The last bit of Hugo stood and walked into that sparkling air. He angled his neck so he could look up into a hot, bare sky. Stepped upon it. And then he bounded into the heavens, ascending upward like they had all those times upon the beach.

He was gone.

She couldn't feel him anymore. As though someone had

closed a door in her mind, shuttering a draft. The very air was different.

Little Rose had a blink of a breath and then the attic was gone . . . banished from her view, replaced by something else.

The terrified face of her father. Looking down at her.

And then he was gone, too.

epilogue

Later, when she was home from the hospital and sometime after the police interviews had ceased, Rose found that she often forgot that anything had happened at all. The business of the children's lives seemed to subsume any other concern. Isaac needed new shoes. Adam was the lead in the first-grade play. Penny had figured out how to unlatch everything in the house that had been baby-proofed.

It was only when Rose would catch *that look* in a neighbor's eye or from a parent on the soccer field or at school drop-off that she would remember.

The look was always the same. A curiosity overlaid with pity, played off with a too-ready smile and a certain rising tone to their voice when they greeted her, "Hi, Ro-oooh-se."

She could see that they wanted to ask. That they knew about the hospital, had seen the flashing lights of the police cars in their driveway, heard gossip about another man, whispers of a child abduction.

But no one *did* ask.

And so Rose smiled back. And waved.

And let them wonder.

After her dream, she remembered only a fleeting image from that night. She had opened her eyes briefly onto the tableau of her husband on the floor, pushing rhythmically at Hugo's chest. The rib-breaking violence of true CPR, the kind that looks nothing like it does on TV.

It seemed to her that she was floating above them, away from them. Like an angel, she had thought, but in retrospect she knew it was just the motion of the gurney as the paramedics had wheeled her out.

She now knew that Josh had preceded the police and the ambulance's arrival to Hugo's house by a full five minutes. That it was Josh's hand that had scooped the vomit from her throat. Josh's hands that had turned her to her side and confirmed her breathing.

Afterward, in the blinking dim of her hospital room, Rose had rolled to her side to face him. She had looked at his hand in the cup of her own. So loose and large in her flimsy grasp.

"Why did you . . ."

Josh looked up at her, his face quiet.

"I saw you . . . trying to save . . . *him*."

Josh creaked out in a whisper, "I didn't want to. . . . I didn't want to touch him. I was so angry, but . . ."

Josh shrugged, his slumped shoulders and the defeated look on his face making him look more tired than she'd ever seen him. She squeezed his hand.

"Thank you, Josh."

"I just did what I was trained to do."

Rose shook her head. "Not for Hugo." She cast a look down at their entwined fingers. "For this."

He leaned down and kissed her forehead. "You're welcome, Rose."

There were twelve angry stitches where the car door had met Rose's leg. The flesh around them was pulled and puffy.

The doctor who had put them in had made it a point to tell her how lucky she was not to have broken her tibia.

As if Rose didn't know how lucky she was.

Though they had worried about Adam's response to the whole event, it was Isaac who began climbing into their bed in the middle of the night. He would snake in under the covers, hooking one long foot around Josh's shin and resting a hand on Rose's arm.

Neither Josh nor Rose complained about this new development. The one time Rose mentioned it, Isaac denied it was happening at all. *I'm not a baby, Mom.* And so Rose let it alone and looked away as Isaac slipped out of their bedroom every morning.

Adam had treated the whole thing as an adventure: quite proud of how he had gone to find an usher when he could not find Mr. David; excited to have ridden in the back of a police car, though disappointed they had not turned on the lights or sirens for him.

He continued to play with his Lego map of the island, though playing Hugo lost some of its luster when Isaac refused to go along with it. Rose knew Hugo was on his way out when she overheard the two of them conducting a very serious conversation in the car:

"Superheroes are either aliens or mutants."

"Or gods."

"Yeah, or gods. Like Thor."

"And Wonder Woman."

"What about Iron Man?"

There was silence a moment.

"Okay. Superheroes are either aliens or mutants or gods or . . . rich guys."

"Yeah. Or rich guys."

When they got home, Adam had asked for a Green Lantern costume for his birthday. Rose said she'd put it on his list.

The first of the new dreams was strange to Rose. In one, she carried a cat from room to room in an enormous house, ultimately giving it to her college roommate when it grew a pair of human hands. In another, she was stuck to a piano bench, playing music for party acquaintances and celebrities she neither admired nor liked.

But most of the dreams, Rose did not remember at all.

And since the dreams she did remember were either ephemeral or silly, this seemed to her to be a good thing.

The police seemed disappointed when Rose told them she did not want to press charges. Rose and Josh had painted for them a fuzzy picture of that night's events. Miscommunications and interactions lost in a drugged haze. The truth of the story felt like a fiction, so a fiction was preferable to lawsuits and criminal trials.

And after all, what was the point, with Hugo as he was?

Through the police, they found out that the doctors did not know if Hugo (*David*) would ever wake up. His brain was still active, but comas were mysterious things. He could wake up tomorrow or never.

Rose visited twice. She felt compelled when it became clear that there was no hint of the island in her dreams.

Both times before she left, she told Josh what she was doing. And both times Josh had nodded and said nothing.

On her first visit Rose did not go into his room, choosing instead to stand in the open doorway. Hugo lay on the bed, sheet and blanket tucked neatly under his arms, IVs and monitor leads radiating outward. Once in a while his eyes rolled beneath their lids. Dreaming.

Rose wondered if he had gone back to the island. She imagined him alone on their old playground, restored to his ideal self. Beautiful, brave Hugo. Wasn't this permanent sleep what he wanted? To be forever the dream of himself and never the reality? In the end, after he had rewitnessed the tragedy of the dam break, acknowledged the losses he had taken there, after he had coalesced into that lovely bright boy that flew into the sky . . . after all that, had he still returned to his island?

Maybe. She didn't (*couldn't*) know. Hugo's mind was a shut door to her now.

But she hoped not.

Instead, she hoped Hugo was having all the dreams he had not had because he had been on the island. The weird, slippery things she had just started to experience, with cameos from his dead parents and half memories from his past, new places with impossible architecture populated by strangers and composites of old friends.

Real dreams seemed less lonely to Rose than what the two of them had shared. And whatever she wished for Hugo, she did not want him to be lonely.

She did not get farther than the door on her second trip either. As she had crested the corner, she had seen a woman sitting

by Hugo's bed. About Rose's age. Thin, denim shorts and a
tank top.

In the corner of the room, a little girl of about seven lay on
the floor, lost in a game on her phone, a lock of hair between
her teeth.

Rose stopped short, just as the woman shouted her name.

"Rose!"

The little girl looked up.

"I said spit that out! I swear, you'll get hairballs."

The little girl spit out the damp strand as Rose turned and
hurried toward the exit.

On her way home, she allowed herself the bright fantasy of
Hugo awakening to his wife and daughter. Of the three of them
packing up his house and driving eastward, toward the green,
fertile promise of Florida with its real beaches and actual jungles.

Maybe someday she'd get another manila envelope in the mail
with another comic book. This one telling the story of man re-
claiming his life. A mundane adventure in the mundane paradise
of everyday life, where the only monsters are the ones trapped
inside ourselves.

Rose hoped that was how it would be. But she never went back.

L ife after.
      That was how she thought of it. *After.*

After Hugo. After the island. After everything.

Life after felt easier to Rose. As if she had been living her
life before with weights on her legs and shoulders. Like that
Vonnegut story she had read in middle school.

Things after mattered more and yet somehow less. If the

neighbors' faces were filled with curious pity, Rose did not begrudge them their right to curiosity. She only denied them answers.

The monitor in the boys' room had lost power during a thunderstorm. When the power came back, Rose had simply turned off the insistent, beeping receiver. *They didn't need it anymore anyway. They hadn't needed it for years.* The receiver eventually fell behind her nightstand, forgotten among the dust bunnies beneath her bed.

And finally, Rose began to notice her husband. Not Josh's absences while he was at work, but his absolute presence when he was with them at home. The way he was there with them, seeing them all, loving them all.

I've been the one who's been away, she thought. *Not him. I'm the one who has been missing it.*

She was sitting in the grass of their front lawn with Penny, the blades tickle-itching her legs, watching Josh teach Adam how to ride *his* new bike, Isaac rolling rings around them, when it visited her again. That canker of a thought, in the mouth of her mind.

Of what consequence are the dreams of housewives?

A bubble of laughter escaped her. Her dreams for her children, for her husband, for herself . . . these things mattered so much more than the odd plays that rehearsed themselves in the stage of her mind at night. It was these dreams and not the others that had the true consequences.

Rose stood up, brushing herself off.

"Isaac!" she called. "Give me your helmet. I want to learn to ride."

ACKNOWLEDGMENTS

Someone asked me, long before I started this book, what kind of "stuff" I wrote. Without hesitation, I answered, "Mommy nightmares."

At the time, I was living in Los Angeles and making a habit (rather than a living) of writing femalecentric screenplays. They were the sort of scripts film executives love to read but no one intends to make, since movies with unarmed female leads rarely do well at the box office.

And "nightmare" was the right word for these yarns I was spinning, since I was using them to channel my anxieties about raising my son, living in a city, and adjusting to the pace at which modern life is evolving.

Hugo & Rose began life as one of these tales. I had a dream in which I was talking with a man in what appeared to be the hull of a ship. He was vividly real to me, more like a dream about visiting with my mother than some sort of amorphous dream archetype. He had a name (it was not Hugo) and a history, and it was clear to me from the way we laughed together that we had known each other for a long time.

Over breakfast with my husband, I wondered about the man. He had been so real that it seemed completely plausible for me to someday meet "the man of my dreams." As my husband handed me my second cup of coffee, my first thought was "How inconvenient." I was in love with my husband, my son, and, quite frankly, my life, and the thought of some cosmic connection with a stranger messing with the order of my world seemed more of a threat than a blessing. The idea took hold, and this book of literal "mommy nightmares" is the result.

Shortly after I finished the first draft of *Hugo & Rose,* I became pregnant. When the ultrasounds revealed identical twins, my husband and I experienced the unique combination of joy and terror that accompanies every diagnosis of multiples. We felt fortunate and overwhelmed . . . but mostly just fortunate.

I spent the pregnancy revising the novel and hobbling after our five-year-old.

In September 2013, just as this book was going to market, I delivered my girls, Gideon Rose and Haven Emerson. They were ten weeks early, born by emergency C-section, due to an abruption of their shared placenta. Though they were small, they were perfect creatures, with their father's dark eyes, my ax-handle jaw, and dancers' toes of unknown provenance. Peering in at them in their million-dollar incubators, my husband and I held each other's hands, thankful for how lucky we had been and prepared to settle in for a long stay in the NICU.

On their third day of life, Giddy took a turn.

She died sixteen days later, on a dark Thursday, in my arms. We sang her one last song and kissed her sweet forehead. Then we spent the night holding her sister, our Haven, whose name now seemed prophetic.

Hugo & Rose found a home with St. Martin's Press three days later. It was a dream come true, amid my own personal nightmare, and one for which I will be forever grateful. The idea of this book finding its way to readers gave me something pleasant to think about in the midst of the grief, loss, and worry that had suddenly consumed my life.

The pace of publishing being what it is, as I write this, Haven is ten months old. She is crawling everywhere and holds forth during her diaper changes in a stream of happy babble and drool. She is our joy.

One of the cruelest blessings of losing an identical twin is that we will always know what Giddy would have looked like. . . . It is all too easy for us to imagine her among the toys cluttered in our family room, grinning a familiar smile, drool running down a similar chin. The edge of her loss is sharp, made more keen by the happiness Haven has brought us.

The process of editing this book after losing a child has been strange, since I now have firsthand experience of things I had previously only imagined. The playground scene in which a monster devours an identical twin was written well before the girls were conceived, but it now has new poignancy. Rose's father's vigil, and his helplessness in the face of her condition is now something I have experienced, rather than just written about.

And like Rose, I now know exactly what it is like to watch someone grow up in my dreams.

Despite my scripts, and this book, being about "mommy nightmares," I have never been so cruel to one of my characters as to actually take one of their children. I do not know if in the future

I will be so kind to them. Some stories do end in sorrow while others begin in them.

And even more stories have sorrow in their centers. But I know now that joy and possibility can branch out from the pain, made brighter by the darkness beneath.

I would like to thank to Arun Chopra, Helena Crowley, Yanick Vibert, Ogechukwu Menkiti, Brandon Poterjoy, Ara Moomjian, Ralph Schrager, Steven Snyder, and Katie Zeigler at St. Christopher's Hospital for Children and Abington Memorial. They had nothing to do with the creation of this book, but instead were Virgils through the ring of hell that is having a baby in the NICU.

Jillian Junod, your name is etched in my heart. Thank you.

There is a very real possibility that I never would have finished this book without the regular support of Kate Pickett. I swear I didn't know your middle name until the book was done.

Thanks to Paul Foley and Tim Lebbon, whose input at the inception and conclusion of this project (respectively) shaped the book you are holding today.

If heaven is a library, then the librarians at the Bucks County Public Library are angels.

No mother would ever write a book without someone to watch her children. For that I must thank Nancy Deputy, who loved my boy for who he is while I was working.

Constanza Flores, Jen Prince, and Ashley Christie, who constituted *Hugo & Rose*'s first book club, thank you for your input and encouragement. The depth of your friendship humbles me.

Chris Van Etten, I love you. That is all.

Brandy Rivers, thank you for constantly asking where Hugo was and for putting up with me. I was so happy when I was finally able to say "Here he is" to you.

Brandi Bowles, thank you for your patience, your kindness, and your insight. Were it not for you, they would both still be lying on the floor.

Rose Hilliard, a woman who understands this book in ways even I don't comprehend, you are the editor of my dreams. I look forward to sending you many poorly worded e-mails in the future.

A thank-you to Terry Foley for teaching me that synaptic jumps make for more interesting stories and that's why they shouldn't build Two Forks Dam. And to Patti Foley for being my first copy editor and fan of my work. When I grow up, I want to be just like my mom and dad.

To my boy, Harper Benjamin, there is so much of you on these pages and yet you are neither Isaac nor Adam. You are something else entirely, and I am so glad that it's my job to spend the rest of my life getting to know you better.

To my girl, Haha, I do hope that by the time you read this, you see nothing of your mother in Rose. I doubt that will be the case, but I can hope.

And finally to Stephen, you are both the man of my dreams and the man of my waking life. Thank you for saying yes.